Mary Ryan is the bestselling author of *Whispers in the Wind*, *Glenallen*, *Into the West*, *Mask of the Night*, *Shadows from the Fire*, *Summer's End*, *The Seduction of Mrs Caine* and *The Promise*. A solicitor for many years, she now devotes her time to writing. She is based in Dublin and is married with two children.

The Song of the Tide

Mary Ryan

HEADLINE

First published in 1998
by HEADLINE BOOK PUBLISHING

First published in paperback in 1999 by
HEADLINE BOOK PUBLISHING

10 9 8 7 6 5 4 3 2 1

ISBN 0 7472 5824 4

Typeset by CBS, Martlesham Heath, Ipswich, Suffolk

Printed and bound in Great Britain by
Clays Ltd, St Ives plc

HEADLINE BOOK PUBLISHING
A division of Hodder Headline PLC
338 Euston Road
London NW1 3BH

To Michael

ACKNOWLEDGEMENTS

Many thanks to my sister Anne for the psychological insights, Norma Sheehan, RADA student, who gave me invaluable help, my brother Michael for letting me tag along when he went to Virginia, Bernice O'Mahoney for sharing the trauma of a broken ankle!

This novel was inspired by Rosturk Castle, where I spent a wonderful holiday. My thanks to Mrs Miriam Healy who made that possible.

Mary Ryan,
Dublin, March 1998.

Listen! You hear the grating roar
Of pebbles which the waves draw back, and fling,
At their return, up the high strand,
Begin, and cease and then again begin

Matthew Arnold
Dover Beach

Part One

Chapter One

Rupert once said to me that reality has no fixed abode, but Rupert was a pilgrim. I was ten at our first meeting, an encounter that was to mark the cards of my existence. It was the summer of 1986 when he came with my Aunt Isabelle, his mother, to stay with us at Dunbeg.

Dún Beag is the Irish for Little Fort. The real fort was a few thousand years old, a conglomeration of old stones on the island of Inishdrum dating back to the Bronze Age. It faced the 'new' Dunbeg, the Victorian castellated house built above the rocky mainland shore where my family holidayed in summer. Like its ancient namesake on the island, part of this 'castle' was crumbling, but as my parents did not have the means to restore it, we simply ignored the tottering bits, locking doors to the portion which might fall about our ears.

This castellated house at Dunbeg was built by my great-great-grandfather, William O'Malley, for his bride, Sarah, on the occasion of their marriage in 1850, just after the Great Famine. It was a sombre time in which to build either a house or a new marriage – surrounded by a wild countryside filled with melancholy, emptied through starvation and emigration.

Sarah was reputedly a beauty, although apparently deficient in wits. She was the daughter of the local landlord, himself ruined by the Famine, who was glad enough to give her hand to the solid solicitor, William O'Malley. For her dowry he gave the beautiful stretch of headland called Dún Beag after the ruined prehistoric fort guarding the inlet, a parcel of newly forlorn countryside, about a hundred acres in all, dotted with abandoned stone cottages. William's practice had offices in Castlebar and Westport and monopolized most of the legal work in County Mayo. He had made his money before the

3

Famine, and could afford to indulge the caprice of his bride and build for her the house of her dreams.

When the 'castle' was built Sarah and William used it as a summer retreat, and Sarah lived there in isolated splendour during the summer months. She was petite and very fertile; but although she produced a child every year for the first nine years of her marriage she was not really cut out for childbirth. Nervous and highly strung, hearing sounds and seeing things no one else admitted to hearing or seeing, she became increasingly unbalanced as one horrific childbirth succeeded another. She had three live children from her nine confinements before she died by falling from the high window in the north turret during her tenth pregnancy. Some said she jumped; others rumoured that William had had a hand in it, albeit from a distance. The house contained several servants, any one of whom might have helped an increasingly erratic and embarrassing wife to a better world. And there was talk of an unpleasant incident, said to be her doing. It concerned the eviction of a tenant who lived in a cottage on the headland nearby, and it left a strange taste in the mouth, even after a hundred years.

William seems to have recovered quickly from his untimely loss. He buried Sarah in the small graveyard at Askreagh which was about five miles away from Dunbeg and situated beside a ruined Cistercian Abbey which had been suppressed in Henry VIII's time. But she wasn't long buried before he brought back another bride. This lady was the daughter of a doctor and quiet and obedient, as men in those days liked their women. She also turned out to be barren.

Dunbeg came down the generations to my own grandfather, who inherited it in 1930. There was a farm attached to the 'castle', the hundred acres that had comprised Sarah's dowry, and he ran it with the help of a manager, rearing store cattle for export, until this activity was blighted by the Economic War when Britain refused to take Irish produce because the De Valera Government refused to keep up paying annuities for the land of Ireland. This resulted in wholesale hardship: the market for the country's goods was gone at one fell swoop.

My grandfather sold most of the land, but he kept twenty acres that overlooked the sea and the 'castle' as a holiday retreat. The grazing of these acres was given to the O'Keefes who lived nearby, and who in exchange acted as caretakers for Dunbeg. They did a spot of horse breeding, more out of love than commerce, and exercised their two mares along the sandy inlet when the tide was out.

In this retreat our whole tribe, grandparents, parents, my four brothers and I, stayed during the long summers of my childhood. Sometimes my mother said how nice it would be if the Lyalls, the American branch of the family who lived in Virginia, were to come to Dunbeg too, and she wrote every year to my father's sister Aunt Isabelle pressing her to visit us with her American husband and to bring Rupert. But half the time Isabelle never even replied.

Rupert was the product of the unlikely marriage between my father's sister Isabelle and a young American student she had met one summer's day at a cricket match in Trinity College, Dublin. I heard the story from my mother – how the young Alexander Lyall had fallen for the eighteen-year-old Irish beauty, and how they had eloped to Gretna Green, returning to brazen it out in a Dublin flat. Alex had never graduated, and on his father's death had gone back to Mount Wexford, his home in Virginia, taking his bride with him. But there was always something in the recounting of this story that struck me as unsaid, some hesitancy when my mother spoke my uncle's name.

Once I had said to her, 'Is Uncle Alex a good man?' and she had started and told me not to be asking silly questions. And then I had said, 'What does Aunty Isabelle look like?' and she had shown me photographs of an outstandingly beautiful young woman, saying, 'You met her once. You were four years old . . . you had measles . . .' and I recalled a pretty young woman with dark hair halfway down her back looking down at me as I lay sick in bed. Isabelle, on that occasion, had returned to Ireland to attend my grandmother's funeral, and she never came again, not even when her father died. Her absence gave her an almost mythic aura; her scant letters gave accounts of an exotic and very foreign life in the former Virginian plantation, where her

5

husband bred trotters for the racetrack and black servants waited on her hand and foot. In the early days she sent snapshots – of the place, of herself and of her son Rupert who stared into the camera with quiet, observant eyes.

'Looks like she's holding up!' was my father's comment, and I wondered what he meant. 'And the little boy looks all there anyway . . .'

My siblings dubbed our American cousin 'Rupert Bear' before we had even met him, or sometimes 'Yogi Bear'. As far as we were concerned the name Rupert was stupid, fit only for the cartoon bear of the same name whose adventures we all read. My brothers had razor tongues, particularly Seán, fourteen years old when this story begins, protecting his quick with his ready wit, not easy to be around, although he possessed a brutally funny charisma. He was worshipped by Simon who was nine. Seán in turn called Simon 'the Pupa', from his habit of rolling himself up in his bedclothes leaving only the top of his dark head visible, so that he resembled a pupating maggot.

My other two siblings were the twins Martin and Jack now twelve, sandy haired, with brown eyes like my mother. They did everything together and were, for this reason, a force to be reckoned with, solid, secret and unflappable. Seán called them 'The Gruesome Twosome'.

Seán was precociously tall for his age. Perpetually hungry, he was nicknamed 'Sir Eat The Lot' because of his readiness to eat everything in sight, regardless of whether or not his siblings died of starvation. My mother bought large quantities of food, and expected it to feed her family. When it disappeared she saw this as a sign of how well-nourished we were, and remained blithely ignorant of how much the greediest bird in her nest could put away. As a result, when we were on holiday together, when the only family meal of the day was supper, we children hid our food – usually rapidly-cobbled-together sandwiches. Sometimes we forgot where we had hidden them, but the smell would announce them in due course.

'What's this?' my mother howled one summer's day in Dunbeg as she was rooting around in the kitchen trying to locate the source of the stench. 'Another mouldy sandwich!' And she marched into the drawing room where I was ensconced with a box of paints and a colouring book, and where my father sat reading the paper.

'Áine . . . is that antique sandwich at the back of the cupboard in the kitchen your doing?'

'No, Mummy. It's probably Simon's!'

'I've had as much as I can take with all these children of yours, Noel O'Malley!' my mother said.

My father thought this amusing. His lips quirked, and there was a sudden gleam in his eye. 'I seem to recall that you had something to do with them yourself, dearest,' he said mildly, without looking up from the paper.

'It's your bloody fault that you let them outnumber us!' she retorted. 'And I *am* outnumbered – two big crumbling houses – a crowd of kids, no one to help me. Am I expected to put up with that for the rest of my life?'

'You have Mrs Maloney . . .' my father suggested.

'What! Twice a week? With this lot it's like expecting someone to clean up Calcutta for a pound!'

On that particular occasion she went to search for the train timetable, presumably to plan her getaway, but this was a futile endeavour as this document could not be found.

'Blood comes from a woman every month!' my mother announced around this time on an evening when we were alone together. Her voice was husky with embarrassment. She had seen the first tentative changes taking place in my small body and wishing, perhaps, to warn me in case puberty arrived suddenly and took me unawares, she broke this fact of existence with all the subtlety of a freight train. I said little, hiding my stunned reaction as I had schooled myself to do in most things, but when I went to bed I wept. How could you be expected to put up with something like that? Did God really do that to women? The sense of outraged pride gripped me for days and I gritted my teeth and prepared myself for the worst. Would my brothers know about it? I inspected my knickers every day in dread. But nothing happened and I eventually began to think I had been hallucinating or mistaken or that my mother had a peculiar sense of humour.

My mother was fascinated by international affairs. She had taken a degree in History and Politics, and was absolutely subsumed in the events taking place in Mother Russia or China or anywhere else they ate their young. Her nose was perpetually in a book or current affairs magazines such as *Time*.

'I told you that would happen!' she often observed to my father, referring to some insurrection or bloody coup on the other side of the planet, and he would nod and make non-committal noises from behind the paper. She hated cooking, housework, rearing children. She was stuck with the latter, but the two former were the subject of continual evasion manoeuvres. Except for Mrs Maloney's attentions when we were on holiday she had no home help. My father was still waiting for his solicitor's practice in Dublin to take off; he had taken a professional risk in leaving one of the biggest firms in the capital a few years earlier to set up on his own, and his earnings were now barely adequate to the strain imposed on them by a large family and two old houses.

'You have a choice. You can either do something with your life, or you can do the housework,' my mother told a Dublin neighbour who looked around one day at our less than pristine kitchen, and at the dresser loaded down with books, at the full sink, with an expression bordering on awe. When I try to remember what she actually did with her life, other than read and engage in pitched intellectual debate with anyone interested, and look after five children, I recall how she groomed and looked after her body as though it were her ticket to an alternative universe. And she was certainly very handsome, possessing the kind of beauty that is taut and formidable, backed by a rigorous intellect and a mind in ferment. The only child of a Protestant rector, slim, dark, haughty, she had been the toast of her year in Trinity. She could have married anyone, but she had fallen for my charismatic father. Marriage to him required that she agree to bring their children up as Catholics, and she honoured this promise, not only because she had given her word but because she loved him to the verge of distraction. I knew this because I loved him too, but I knew her need for him was unassuaged. I knew he could not bend. He was immutable; in his lexicon of life, a wife had a certain place; she was not seen by him as a force, or someone whose love should be honoured and cherished above all things. No, she existed in relation to *him* and he would look after her and their children and do everything that duty demanded. Anything else was regarded by him as self-indulgent.

My father was tall and attractive, given to direct and dogmatic utterances, very fair-minded and straight, with his world well mapped. He did not see his wife as increasingly fragile, as lonely and unfulfilled. As I watched my mother exercise continually to retain her figure after four pregnancies, I knew she was doing it out of more than vanity. Only later did I realize that she was probably trying to provoke in my father the passion that would validate her own. She projected a certain strength, a tough carapace, hiding the vulnerability beneath. Perhaps if my father had given her enough love and recognition she could have explored her own reality in safety and we would all have been happier. As it was, maternal love was a pragmatic business, its full-scale expression withheld.

How did my mother feel about me, her only daughter? She seemed to regard me more as co-conspirator than child. Her angle on the world was that men determined the status quo because they thought they knew everything; but that women had a wider perspective although it was imperative they keep their knowledge to themselves. This communion of female understanding was a conspiracy to do with dignity and survival. And in a country ruled by clergy, whose misogyny coloured the nation's view of reality, the perception of women was not likely to change. Men comprised humanity; women were tolerated if they behaved themselves.

I hardly understood her perspective, although I was eager to be drawn into anything that would make me her comrade and partisan. As she detested weakness I hid from her the terrors of my child's life, the nightmares that tormented me in Dunbeg and made me afraid to sleep. I had read *Grimm's Fairy Tales* and, for some reason, the story of Peter and the Wolf lingered. 'He was a timber wolf,' my brother Simon said knowledgeably when I shared the story with him, and ever after I dreamt of him, the white timber wolf, 'my' wolf. He frightened me half to death, lying under my bed at night and stalking my dreams.

Once I dreamed I was standing on the island of Inishdrum beside the ruined fortress. It was night and I could see, across

9

the inlet, the lights of the 'castle', sense the life in it – the occasional silhouettes against the windows, my brothers and my parents. I realised suddenly that I was grown up, for I was much further from the ground, and my body felt strange, as though I had stepped inside a suit that was far too big for me.

Across the inlet an upstairs light came on. It was my room, and I stared at my own window and at the little girl who came to close it, realising with a curious sense of horror that it was myself.

I knew then that the present I understood was over, that I had lost it, been shunted into a dark future, shut out for ever. The castle suddenly became dark as though all life and light had been extinguished, and I was alone. I cried out, but the wind carried my voice away, and then, loping towards me across the wet, tidal sand, came the white wolf.

I woke at my own cry, sweating and afraid, glad to be in my bed, glad to have my parents nearby and my siblings asleep across the landing.

I longed to tell this strange dream, but I dreaded my brothers' derision, and my mother's exasperated sigh, 'Oh for Heaven's sake, Áine, you're letting a silly little fairy story bother you . . . You should take some hot milk before you go to bed.'

But the taste of the dream remained for a long time. For I knew that the years would pass and one day I *would* be grown.

What would life be like for me, then? What would have changed for ever?

I did not share any of this chagrin. I became known for my fibs. I hid what I felt and what I did. I wanted to please.

'Is that the truth, Áine?' my mother demanded on more than one occasion, when I had spun her some yarn in response to a complaint that I had disobeyed her.

'That's the trufe!' I lisped sometimes in those days, more for effect than anything else.

'Good!' she might intone. 'Now could I have the real *trufe* please!'

Sometimes she got it. And when she did she might say, 'You'll just have to stop telling lies, Áine! It's not right!' And then I would be sent to bed where I would promise the darkness that I would never tell the truth again.

Fibs made life easy and other people happier. All they demanded was a good memory.

One day in the spring of 1986 when I was ten years old my mother received a letter from Aunt Isabelle. She said she wanted to come home from Mount Wexford on a protracted summer visit; she would like to bring Rupert with her to Dunbeg. In this letter she hinted at some kind of domestic problem. My mother left this missive on the kitchen table and I read it surreptitiously while she was out, struggling with the writing and not understanding its import.

> Dear Joyce,
> I don't think I can go on much longer. I'm sorry I've been so out of touch, but there were reasons. I haven't been too well, and that man is intolerable although I have tried and tried.
> Would you mind if I came home ... descended on you in Dunbeg for the summer? It would look like a holiday.
> I'll take Rupert. He's dying to see the place. Anyway he should meet his cousins ... They shouldn't grow up as strangers.

My mother said later, 'Sounds like something's up with Isabelle, Noel ...'

They were in the sitting room of our Dublin home. My father was just home from his office and sitting in his favourite armchair with the paper. They did not know that I was in the dining room surreptitiously reading the *Beano* behind the curtain. The comic belonged to Simon and he would start World War Three if he found me with it, so I always hid when I was reading it. But at the mention of my exotic aunt's name I pricked up my ears and sneaked from behind my curtain to where I could hear and observe my parents through the dividing doors.

My father read the letter, shook his head and said there always had been something up with Isabelle.

'She's the proud possessor of the lunatic streak in the family ... Why do you think she ran off to get married in Gretna

11

Bloody Green, I ask you? Was there anything sane about that?'

My mother clicked her tongue and her face closed. 'She was young and romantic!' She glanced back at the letter. 'Poor thing says she hasn't been too well.'

'You know what that means . . .' my father replied with a knowing look.

'Neurotic or not, she's your sister,' my mother said. 'And she hints about Alex . . .'

'Of course she does. She shouldn't have married him. But she's made her bed . . .'

My mother regarded my father for a moment, but when he made no further comment she muttered, 'I'll write and tell her to come.'

At that time there was talk of sending me away to the Gaeltacht for the summer so that I could brush up on my Irish, which I had failed in my last exam. I had been looking forward to this sojourn in a native Irish-speaking area of the west. There would be plenty of other girls in the Irish college there, company I was starved of during the summer among my contending male siblings. But now that I knew Aunt Isabelle and my Cousin Rupert were also coming to Dunbeg I began to look for excuses. I said that I didn't want to go to the Gaeltacht, that I wanted to meet my one and only cousin. Eventually my parents conceded that it would be a pity for me to miss him, and said I could go to the Gaeltacht the following year.

It was two months later, in that far-off summer of upheaval, that Rupert and Aunt Isabelle came to Dunbeg. For her it was a return to the crumbling ancestral pile she had last seen as a teenager. For Rupert it was something else, an introduction to the Irish roots in which he had but scant interest. It was, he told me eventually, like hearing a strange music for the first time and realizing that you had always known it, had always feared it.

Chapter Two

'That little poof Rupert is downstairs feeding his face!' Seán announced.

It was the second week of July, and we had been in Dunbeg since the beginning of the month. I knew my Aunt Isabelle and her son had come, because we had heard the voices in the hall in the early morning, and had crept to the banisters to listen, looking down into the hallway between the antlers of the huge moose that some foolish forebear had nailed to the wall. My father had gone to meet the plane at Shannon and the returning car had woken us. But we had only caught a glimpse of the new arrivals. We were supposed to be still in bed and my father's roar for erring children was something we preferred to avoid.

'What's Rupert like?'

'A liddle Yaynk,' Seán said, pulling down his upper lip in mockery, evidently pleased with his 'American' intonation.

I ran down the stairs to the kitchen, eager to meet the 'liddle Yaynk', and was defeated by a wave of shyness just outside the door. So it was with more diffidence than usual that I pushed the door and found myself in the kitchen, looking straight into a grave, self-possessed face. It belonged to a thin, fourteen-year-old boy, smaller than Seán although the same age, dressed in cotton shirt and jeans, with brown hair and freckled skin.

'This is your cousin, Áine,' my mother said, addressing the newcomer. She was cooking bacon and eggs on the electric stove, and barely glanced in my direction. 'Áine, this is Rupert.'

'Hello.'

'Hi,' he said, standing up and holding out his hand. It took me a moment to register that he had got off his chair and stood up for no other reason than to greet me. I had four

13

brothers and had had to fight all my childhood to defend the small space that was my own, but now a boy I had never met before stood up because I had entered the room. The courtesy was obviously schooled, and cheerfully automatic, but it temporarily re-shuffled the cards of my identity. In that moment I did not have to scratch and claw and fight and be one of the boys. In that moment I was another entity altogether – a girl and free.

'Will you have bacon and eggs?' my mother asked me, oblivious to the significance of the moment.

She hated cooking and always felt that if you'd had a good breakfast you weren't 'too badly off'. Lunch during our holidays was a grab-what-you-could-find affair, and supper was usually a salad, unless it was one of Mrs Maloney's days. Mrs Maloney lived nearby and came in twice a week to clean the house and stayed to cook a hot meal. 'Them poor kids is running wild,' she used to complain to herself, 'half starved and runnin' wild!'

Now my mother turned to look at me. 'Áine, I asked you if you wanted bacon and eggs.'

I shook my head. 'No thanks, Mummy . . .' Then I sought the cornflakes, found them behind the big aluminium bread-bin where Seán had presumably stashed them, and looked around into a pair of polite, inquiring eyes.

'You look . . . very nice,' I whispered, off guard. I wanted to tell him he didn't look in the least like a little poof but thought better of it at the last moment.

But Rupert looked almost shocked at my outburst and blinked in a small, nervous spasm.

'Do you want some cornflakes?' I asked hurriedly. 'If you do you'd better take them before Seán gets down . . .'

'Sure . . .' he said and held out one of the willow-patterned bowls from which generations of the O'Malleys had eaten their porridge.

It occurred to me with a sudden sense of panic that if our guest were to be properly fed I had better make lunch arrangements before Seán appeared. I went into the pantry, took the one remaining pizza from the ice box and hid it underneath the salad in the fridge. I found a piece of cheddar, still wrapped, and put it into the empty egg container, a

14

porcelain hen which was never used, aware that if I were discovered Seán would say I was a greedy little weed.

I hated being called a little weed. It was unjust, because I was as fearless as the rest of them, foolhardy sometimes in order to prove myself, ready to attempt the cliff at the headland, ready to climb any tree although I skinned my hands, ready to swim where the water was deepest, although I was secretly afraid of deep water. For years I had tried not to be a girl, but at this point I knew the game was up. My nipples were expanding from pimples into small raspberries, the harbinger of my approaching womanhood which I dreaded in much the same way as a prisoner dreads a sentence of death.

But now I had before me a boy, not much bigger than myself, who was completely different to any boy I had ever met, who treated me with such automatic politeness that I wondered what I had done to deserve it. His American accent sounded exotic to my ten-year-old ears, curiously languid and musical, not at all like Seán's strident attempt at mimicry.

'I'll show you around if you like,' I volunteered from a mouth full of cornflakes, recovering my poise and wondering how he felt at finding himself in the midst of a family as weird as ours.

'That'd be real nice!'

He ate his bacon and eggs, thanked my mother, put his plate and cup into the sink, and turning to me and ascertaining that I was finished said, with a pragmatic ring to his voice, 'OK. Can we go?' Then he smiled into my eyes. Rupert in ten minutes of acquaintance had somehow stepped inside my private, personal space as though he knew the geography.

'Don't go up on the roof!' my mother warned as we left the kitchen.

'The turret stairs is just over here,' I announced to Rupert a few moments later, as we navigated the disarray of the boot room. 'It brings you to the roof.'

'But your mother said . . .'

'I know. She always does. But she won't find out . . . We're a very disobedient family.' I glanced at him and shrugged. 'And I'm probably the most disobedient one in it!'

'Why?'

15

He asked this conversationally, but I sensed immediately that he possessed scruples unknown to me, and that I was not going to impress him merely by virtue of my disobedience. So, for once, I told the truth.

'Because if I did everything I was told I would do nothing at all.'

The circular turret stairway was built into one of the castellated towers. Halfway up the stairs a door opened into the big first floor bedroom where the twins slept. This door was ajar – it was stiff and could not be closed – and through the open chink we could see my twin brothers still asleep, rolled up in their bedclothes, their feet sticking out at identical angles, their mouths open in identical snores. I thought, rather unkindly, that Simon was not the only pupating maggot in our family. I held my nose as I passed this door because from the other side of it came the whiff of the twins' famous smelly feet. Rupert glanced at me and I put my finger to my lips and preceded him up the stairs. At the top was another door, held shut by a piece of electrical cable, looped around a nail. This loop was removed, the door was opened and we stepped out onto the massive lead roof and the glory of a fine morning.

Even when I had been much younger I had often sneaked up here to think, to be alone, to avoid another game where I might be trussed to a tree for the 'Indians' to whoop over. Watching Rupert's reaction as he took in the sweep of the inlet, the vista of the bay and its islands, the majesty of our surroundings, I was suddenly proud. This incomparable place, after all, was my country and, standing there beside the castellations, I felt like a medieval chatelaine. Below us was the forecourt and beyond that the drop to the rocks, and the small stone steps to the beach. The tide was out, but beginning to turn, and the neighbouring island of Inishdrum with the old ruin was within easy walking distance across the wet sand. In the forecourt I saw my father cross the gravel to his car. The lawn was full of hydrangeas, pink and powder blue, and a hedge of crimson and violet fuchsia sunned itself by the old granite wall to the farmyard. You could see the beginnings of the avenue at the cattle grid, where it lost itself in darkness under a canopy of trees. There was a very lazy sea breeze. It spoke to me. It said what it always said when I happened to be alone with it: peace, peace, peace.

I waited for Rupert's reaction, but he was silent. He stood there, like me, part of the stone. Then he whispered, 'Some place!' And then he pointed to the headland where the remains of an old cottage could be glimpsed and said, 'What's up there?'

'That's just a ruined cottage . . . It's one of many around here.'

'Is there a path to the cliff?'

'Yes. But we're not allowed to take it.'

'Why not? Is it dangerous?'

I nodded and added, glancing over my shoulder and lowering my voice, 'I was up there the other day and parts of the path have fallen onto the rocks . . .' I said this in a whisper, confiding in him because I felt I could trust him, and because communicating with him was novel and exciting, and afforded a strange kind of release. He seemed impressed.

'I'll show you if you like . . .' I continued, 'after lunch, if the grown ups are out.'

For a moment I thought he would refuse, but his eyes betrayed an eagerness for adventure. 'OK . . .'

When we came down we bumped into Seán who was rooting around in the boot room.

'Ah the Squirrel Mistress in person!' he announced. 'I suppose you haven't . . .' And then he saw Rupert coming down behind me, gave him an embarrassed, curt nod, as though he were some esoteric species who didn't speak the language.

'Did you take my snorkel?' he continued, looking at me severely.

'I did not!'

He rummaged in a corner, scattering wellies, assorted old raincoats, buckets and spades from summers past.

'You'll probably find it in the cavern,' I said. 'At least it was there yesterday. And *I* wasn't using it!' The 'cavern' was a concrete boat shelter above a slipway constructed over the rocks. It was where the rubber dingy and the surf board were stashed.

'It was probably the twins,' he muttered. 'I'll break their sneaky little heads!'

He finally looked at Rupert, as though aware of his rudeness

17

and uncertain how to deal with it.

'You don't know how lucky you are to be an only child,' he announced, and he stamped out, his precociously tall figure disappearing into the hall and down the steps to the sunlit forecourt, en route for the stone stairway to the rocks and the cavern.

When I turned to look at Rupert his eyes had lost their erstwhile camaraderie and were full of silent laughter.

'Why did he call you "Squirrel Mistress"?' he asked.

'It's just a stupid name . . . He's always calling people stupid names. Come on, I'll show you the rest of the place.' I didn't want to tell him that two years earlier, in a flush of inventive loneliness, I had concocted a story about a squirrel. My story was that this little beast had become my friend because I had saved him from drowning. It was fantasy, based on the sight of a red squirrel among the trees, but when I tried to put it over on my family I learnt the power of derision. Simon, who was seven at the time, wanted to rush out to find the furry paragon, but everyone else was prostrate with mirth. 'Don't be such a little eejit,' Seán told him, and he called me 'the Squirrel Mistress' ever after.

Family is like nationhood; you don't choose the one you're born to, but you tend to be stuck with it.

I showed Rupert the drawing room. It was a large room with a bay window overlooking the sea, a blue carpet and a fine marble fireplace. It had two sofas, a cushioned window seat, a couple of armchairs, and an 'occasional' table which sported a few bottles of the grown ups' poison, sherry and whiskey and a bottle of gin. The western tower room was here, its entrance in the corner. This small circular room was the space where there might have been another turret staircase, similar to that of the eastern turret. But instead it was simply a kind of side room, with a small slit window to the outdoors, and separated from the drawing room by a tapestry curtain. It was used for storing a few old odds and ends, pictures with broken frames and a Singer sewing machine with a trestle. There was also an old armchair and a tartan rug.

'You can hide in here,' I told Rupert, 'if anyone is looking for you. It's also a good place if everyone thinks you're in bed

18

. . . You can listen to the grown ups talking. It's better than being scared in bed on your own . . .' I glanced at Rupert, suddenly afraid that I had divulged too much – he was fourteen after all, and almost grown up – but he nodded gravely, like someone who understood only too well the terrors of lying awake for hours with a timber wolf under your bed.

I brought him into the dining room. This room was next door to the drawing room, and had a gigantic fireplace. It also had a bay window and a long mahogany table, big enough to seat eighteen people. There was a sideboard, sporting an army of wine glasses, and an empty cut-glass decanter. A smaller table occupied the space in the bay window, and on it were a selection of potted plants – spindly, despairing geraniums, and a gasping aspidistra. There were a couple of prints on the walls; good paintings had long since been removed, either by my sensible forebears taking them to Dublin, or by enterprising robbers. It was said that the IRA had come to burn the castle in 1920, but as most of them were local men and their hearts were not in the work, they had contented themselves with removing whatever valuables they could lay their hands on, and had left the house itself to moulder in peace.

The dining room gave onto the library. This room was panelled in oak; its thick velvet curtains had once been cherry red, but were now a faded dusty pink. It sported some pieces of porcelain – a few Spode plates, which were arranged above the fireplace, a couch and an armchair. Bookshelves lined the walls, and a large window looked out on the bay. Glancing through it, I saw the racing of the tide up the inlet and knew the island would shortly be inaccessible on foot.

At the far end of the room was a French window that gave onto the small terrace and the sheltered garden at the rear of the house. It was on this patio, with its red and grey quarry tiles, that my great-great-grandmother, Sarah, had met her death, falling from a room far above. I knew she still walked in the garden at night, for once I had seen her move soundlessly across the grass. I had been in the library in the dark, to satisfy a private dare, and had stared in frightened disbelief at the white figure flitting across the garden. She had climbed the stone steps to what had once been the orchard and disappeared.

I told no one; I would have got into trouble for being up when everyone else was in bed, but had done so to challenge my own terror. I slept alone in a huge room, where my imagination peopled every corner, and where I sometimes lay almost petrified at the strange noises the house made at the dead of night. It seemed to me that everyone else had someone they could turn to: my parents slept together in a big double bed; the twins had their own room; Seán shared with Simon; sometimes I could hear them arguing before they fell asleep. But I was invisible, to my parents who were always so taken up with their world, to my brothers because I was a female and the member of a despised class. I wanted to be loved and there was no one to love me.

I had nightmares, vivid and highly coloured. The wolf lay under my bed at night and stalked my dreams. Sometimes the dream of watching my childhood world from across the inlet returned, and with it would come a sense of anguish for irretrievable loss, and also a sense that something perilous lay in wait for me.

As a result I was often afraid of going to sleep in Dunbeg, and, instead, I had become a lonely patroller of the night, slipping downstairs and checking the place room by room while the house slept, desperate to prove, to myself at any rate, that I was not a 'weed'. Dracula, a bat, who lived in some nook in the landing ceiling above the stairwell, used to swoop at me silently as I made my way down the landing. At first he frightened me and then we came to an understanding; I didn't rat on him and he accepted me as just another restless denizen of the darkness.

Now, in the sunlit library, all of these considerations seemed small and unimportant. I turned to Rupert and asked almost flippantly if he had heard the story about our great-great-grandmother and how she had died.

'Yes,' he said, lowering his voice. 'Mom told me the story.'

'She came back,' I whispered, pointing to the French window.

'What?' His eyes dilated, the pupils suddenly flooding the iris. His face paled beneath his freckles.

'Sarah . . . One night when I was here, I saw her through the

20

window . . . She was just over there, moving across the grass.' I regretted having divulged this as soon as it was out. I had told no one; I was afraid of derision; I did not want him to think me a nut case, or assume I was taking the mickey.

But my cousin just whispered, 'Weren't you scared?'

'Out of my wits. But she went away, up the steps to the orchard,' and I drew him to the window and showed him the ghost's itinerary across the lawn. 'There was something sad about her, as though she wanted to warn me . . .'

'About what?'

'I don't know. Look, don't tell anyone. I'd just get into trouble.'

I knew when I looked at him that he would not; that he was used to keeping his own silence; that he had secrets I could not guess at and terrors of his own. I felt it as surely as the fact that I was alive.

We stared at each other in silence and in that moment a peculiar bond formed between us, an understanding.

'I won't tell,' he said, frowning, anxious to reassure me. Then he leaned towards me and touched my hand. We looked at one another for a moment.

'Why are you called Rupert?' I whispered. 'It reminds me of Rupert Bear . . .'

Rupert growled gravely in mock bear fashion.

'You know,' I said, 'the little bear, the children's character!' I looked around the shelves, sure that some of our earlier Rupert Bear books were stacked somewhere, and when I saw them I ran to take one from the shelf.

'I know,' Rupert said gravely, examining the colourful pictures. 'I had these books when I was small. In fact I have stacks of them at home. Mom used to get them for me. But he's an English bear. American bears are different.'

'I know!'

After a moment he added, as he leafed through the pages, 'You're like *her*.'

He was pointing to Tigerlily, the inscrutable Chinese girl in the silk kimono.

'No I'm not.'

'Yes you are,' Rupert said. 'You don't have her dress, that's

21

true, or her funny eyes. But she's different,' he glanced at me, 'and so are you.'

'Rupert Bear and Tigerlily,' he intoned suddenly, 'are more than just a little silly!'

We looked at each other and doubled over in laughter.

We left the library by the narrow kitchen passage and I took Rupert to the billiard room. The baize was scratched on the table and a few of the balls were missing, but these deficiencies had never bothered my siblings and me; we had simply reinvented the rules. Rupert looked around at the oak benches built into the wall, and the slate fireplace. The window in this room was small and the light was green and dim because the virginia creeper outside was halfway across the panes.

'Do you play billiards, Áine?'

'Of course! Do you want a game?'

He shook his head, smiled. His teeth were even but his smile was lop-sided. 'What's through here?' he asked in a half-scared whisper, indicating the door from the billiard room to the old kitchens.

'It's locked. That is the part of the castle that is falling down.'

'Why don't your parents fix it?'

'Daddy says it would cost about half a million. He's probably joking, but he hasn't got enough money. When I grow up, when I'm rich, I'll get it fixed.'

Rupert rolled a ball across the baize. He didn't howl with laughter like my brothers and demand to know how I was going to be rich. He just said, 'Do you like this place so much . . . that you would spend half a million on it?'

'Dunbeg is everything!' I replied, surprised at myself. 'Mummy says it's a kind of matrix.'

'A matrix?'

I shrugged. 'She says that's a place in which things develop, or something. It's a bit weird, but you'll love it when you get to know it. Wait and see. It's in the blood. That's what Mum says; she says all the O'Malleys have this place in the blood, that it talks to them.'

'But I'm a Lyall! And I sure don't want any place "talking" to me!'

'You're an O'Malley on your mother's side!'

22

After a moment Rupert said, 'You have a funny name . . . Áine. Does it mean something?'

'It's supposed to be the Irish for Anne. But Áine was really a Celtic goddess . . . She was drowned in the Shannon.'

'She can't have been much of a goddess in that case,' he said, suddenly scornful. He looked out at the sunshine. 'I think I'll go for a swim.'

'Good idea.'

I was suddenly afraid he thought I was tagging onto him. As we left the room I pointed into the well of the stairs and the concave glass in the landing ceiling. 'A bat lives up there. His name is Dracula.'

I thought to increase my stature in his eyes, but he just laughed, and then he left me, running upstairs and saying he was going to look for his swimming trunks. I went out into the sunlight and sat on the front step to find my kitten, Tabbs, who was playing hide and seek with a sweet wrapper among the hydrangeas.

I smiled at Rupert when he reappeared with a towel and directed him to the path to the small beach. 'Don't go out too far and watch out for the currents,' I called after his departing back. 'There is a nice deep spot by the slipway that's safe . . .'

'I can swim like a fish!' he said, obviously annoyed at the inference. 'Not like your silly goddess . . .'

'She wasn't silly!' I shouted, but he had disappeared down the steps to the rocks.

I sat in the sunshine, stroking Tabbs who wriggled and attacked my hand with small sharp teeth and half-retracted claws. From the direction of the rocks I heard the exchange of voices, recognized Seán's voice and Rupert's.

Through the open hall door came the sound of footsteps descending the stairs, and turning towards the kitchen, I heard my mother's voice call out, 'I'm in the drawing room, Isabelle!' and then heard the second American accent that morning greet my mother. 'Joyce, I shouldn't have slept so late . . .'

There was silence for a moment and I peeped into the hall and saw the two women embracing.

'Sleep is the only thing for jet lag,' my mother said then. There was silence for a moment then I heard my aunt say, 'I had forgotten what an amazing old place the castle is. So many memories . . . Where's Rupert? I thought he would still be asleep after that journey, but his room is empty.'

'He had his breakfast about an hour ago. Áine took him off to show him around.'

'I haven't seen her since she was a baby. She must be . . . what? . . . ten years old.'

I drew back, out of sight behind the door.

'Yes,' my mother said. 'The years don't wait.' There was silence for a moment.

'Don't be hard on me, Joyce!' my aunt said. 'Things were difficult. Alex was never easy . . . he didn't want to come back.' Her voice became merry. 'He said the Irish should give the country back to Britain and apologize for its condition.'

I waited for the explosion from my politically sensitive mother. There was none, but I imagined her intake of breath and her contained anger. Her voice when she next spoke was brittle. 'What about your breakfast . . . Would you like a fry?'

'Good Lord no! A cup of tea and piece of toast would be all I could manage.'

The two women left the drawing room and I huddled down on the side of the lowest step so that they could not see me from the hall. But my mother walked to the porch, looked out and saw me playing with Tabbs.

'Come and meet your Aunty Isabelle, Áine,' she called. I put Tabbs down, walked obediently up the front steps and was embraced by a slender woman in a blue dress. She smelt of something lovely, had short fair hair and eyes like Rupert, grey and grave, but there burned in them something I had never seen. They possessed a strange penetrating quality, as though they reached inside and searched for a bit of your soul. I resisted this spiritual biopsy and the moment passed. Then I realized there was a nervousness in her body language that was absent in her son's, and I noted, when she took my hands, that the palms of her own were moist.

'Rupert is gone for a swim,' I told her. She looked immediately anxious. I added, 'I warned him about the currents!'

My mother gave me a look which silenced me, but my aunt

was already moving past me, down the front steps and across the forecourt to the parapet overlooking the rocks. I followed her. Rupert could be seen swimming vigorously near the slipway. The island was now cut off and the tide was racing up the inlet. I could feel its relentless momentum in my bones.

'Be careful, darling!' my aunt called, and with the clarity of sound peculiar to waterside locations Rupert's voice came back crystal clear, as he raised a hand from the water: 'I'm fine . . .'

Far out on the flat and sparkling sea we could see a rubber dinghy. This was Seán's, and it seemed simply to be floating on the rhythm of the tide, as though its captain was comatose. I knew he was just lying back, staring at the sky and letting the tide bring him where it would. I also knew he had a pair of paddles and was a very good swimmer.

'Don't you worry about your children . . . in this place?' I heard my aunt say to my mother.

'Of course . . . but they know it so well, and they know the rules. Áine is sensible and Seán looks after Simon . . . and the twins are twelve . . .'

They went indoors and I sat on the parapet of the gravelled forecourt and put my head on my knees, watching and listening. The water swished quietly on rocks below me; the air was warm; the blue panorama swept the eye out to Clare Island, and the coast of Achill. It was good to be alive in this blue world, with its relentless, rhythmic sounds. And then, with a certainty born out of stillness, I knew that there was a reason we were all here; that the place itself had a use for us; that we were not incidental to our surroundings, but an intricate part of its history. It was a moment of eternal present, when time stopped, when there was a great silence. I was locked in a kind of paralysis, which seemed normal while it lasted, frightening in retrospect. But it ended, perhaps in a matter of moments. And then my head turned, as though it had been pulled by a string, and I found myself staring at the drawing-room window where my aunt, in her blue dress, fixed unblinking eyes on me.

Chapter Three

At midday the grown ups announced that they were going out for lunch. 'The children can get their own,' my mother said to Aunt Isabelle. 'There's plenty of salad and cheese and pizza, and we won't be gone long. I want to show you the new restaurant that's been set up by Máire Kelly . . . if you remember her. She did catering in Cathal Brugha Street in Dublin . . . and then she worked in London for a bit.'

Isabelle asked Rupert, as he came up from the rocks, if he would go with them, but he said, keeping his voice low as though annoyed at being singled out: 'No, Mom. I'd like to stay with my cousins.' The grown ups left and I ran into the kitchen to check on supplies, wondering if Seán had found my pizza and if there would be anything left for Rupert to eat. Seán was already there, spooning tuna from a tin onto thick cuts of bread and butter. On top of this he heaped gobbets of horseradish sauce, flattened the lot down with a knife, stuck another cut of bread on top. I opened the fridge to find the pizza I had hidden beneath the salad, but it was nowhere to be seen.

'Have you taken my pizza?'

'Never laid eyes on it, Squirrel!'

I knew he was lying, that not only had he laid eyes on it, but all his teeth as well.

Simon came in, grabbed some bread, and began to make himself a peanut butter sandwich.

'Go easy on that!' Seán said.

'Why? So you can gobble it up?'

Seán gave one of his sheepish grins as though he knew it was only his sporadic charm that kept his siblings from murdering him.

The twins, up at last, came sleepily into the room, asking,

'Where's Mum and Dad?' They found an apple pie in the bread bin and proceeded to demolish it. And into this our guest, Rupert, with some diffidence, presented himself.

'Hello,' the twins said, eyeing him with curiosity.

'Hi,' Simon said.

'You have to grab what you can,' I whispered to Rupert. 'This is an awful family.'

Rupert cut a slice of bread. I found the piece of cheddar I had hidden that morning and presented it to him. 'I'll get you some salad,' I said, making for the fridge. My mother always made a green salad every morning, on the basis that it was good for us. None of us ate it, probably for the same reason.

'I didn't know there was any cheese left,' Seán announced, eyeing the piece of cheese Rupert had on his plate. 'Squirrel has been up to her tricks again.'

Rupert, with an expressionless face, made to hand him the cheese. 'You can have it.'

'It's all right,' Seán said gruffly, reddening at his own bad manners. 'I don't want it!'

'That's because you've just eaten my pizza,' I said, sotto voce. I turned to Rupert. 'There's salad if you want it . . .'

He shook his head, reached for a glass and poured himself some milk.

I was mortified by my awful brothers; by the fact that there was nothing for our guest to eat except bread and cheese. I was glad it was one of Mrs Maloney's days. She was due to arrive at three and with her would come a big box of groceries, and the prospect of a hot evening meal. I glanced at Rupert apologetically, but he seemed oblivious, sitting there at the end of the table, with his newly-made cheese sandwich and a glass of milk, looking from one of my siblings to the other. He was very quiet and they were unsure of him. So for the moment they were pretending that he didn't exist.

Rupert said eventually, as he watched the twins demolish the apple pie, 'Is that your lunch?'

'Yeah,' the twins said. 'Do you want some?'

Rupert eyed the bitten pie. 'No thanks.'

'Your American accent is very queer,' Simon informed him with his mouth full. 'Can't you talk properly?'

'He is talking properly,' I said. 'People talk differently in different countries.'

'What would you know about it, Squirrel Mistress?' Seán demanded.

'I know as much about it as you do,' I said hotly.

'Do you like it here?' one of the twins asked Rupert.

'Yeah!'

Everyone was pleased by this and seemed disposed to take Rupert to their bosoms.

'We're not such muck savages as we seem,' Jack said suddenly as though he would dissipate whatever bad impression had been created. 'We're just a weird family. We have a father who's seldom at home and a mother who prefers the newspapers to children. Not that you could blame her,' he added, glancing at Seán, 'when you think of what some of them are like.'

'We also have a brother who eats everything in sight,' Martin chipped in, 'so don't go too near him.'

'My mom says that people who are always eating are insecure,' Rupert said, and took another bite of his sandwich.

The twins and Simon laughed. Seán turned on Rupert and eyed him speculatively, his face registering a moment's uncertainty. 'Who did you say was insecure?' he demanded softly, but his eyes twinkled.

'No one . . .' Rupert said gravely. He looked around at them in wide-eyed innocence.

'Aren't you lucky you have no brothers,' Jack said to him, carefully dividing the last slice of apple pie in two, and handing the other piece to Martin.

'No. I would have liked one . . .'

'Or even a sister?' I interjected in an eager whisper, privately mourning the apple pie whose existence I had overlooked.

He nodded, smiled at me. 'Especially a sister.'

The boys looked at him suspiciously. Anyone who wanted a sister could not be one hundred per cent.

'Where do you go to school?' Simon demanded.

'I go to a boarding school,' Rupert said.

'Is it nice?'

'Yeah, it's all right.'

'Is it Eton?' Simon piped up.

'Don't be pathetic!' Seán said. 'Eton is in England.'

'I know,' his youngest sibling said hotly. 'There's a castle there where the King of England used to live.'

'The Queen, you little eejit,' Seán said. 'You may not have heard, but at the moment they have a queen. And you may not have heard, either, but America is not in England.' He placed a hand on Rupert's thin shoulder. 'And this is an American . . . Isn't that right, Rupert?'

Rupert looked momentarily intimidated, as though his sang froid did not extend to this – to finding himself unexpectedly in a country where the natives were all at war.

'Don't be so rude!' I shouted at Seán. 'Rupert's just got here . . .' adding, to introduce some semblance of normal conversation: 'Do you have lots of friends at home?'

'Yep, but mostly in school. The person I like most in our neighbourhood is a man called Gunther. He has a daughter called Brigitte. They live a few miles away.'

'What's so great about him?'

'He's into music and things, books . . . He came to the States after the war. He was a kid living in the rubble of Berlin, parents dead. A GI adopted him.'

'God!' Simon breathed. 'So he can tell you all about the war.'

'Yeah.'

There was utter, avid silence. The boys stared at Rupert as though he were in possession of all the riches of the earth.

All of my brothers were obsessed with World War Two, and watched as many war films as they could, and every television documentary on the subject. They often regretted aloud that they had been born too late to participate.

'What does he tell you? Did you ask him about the fall of Berlin?' Seán demanded. 'Does he remember?'

'Sure,' Rupert said casually. 'He was in the Volkssturm.'

'Jeepers!' the twins intoned.

'That's very interesting,' I said, delighted, not knowing anything about the Volkssturm but ready to sound initiated.

Seán pursed his mouth. 'Shut up, Squirrel!' He turned back to his cousin. 'Sorry for slagging you,' he said in mock apology. 'You should have been warned that this is a slagging country, where nothing is taken seriously except politics and horses, and not necessarily in that order.'

Rupert shrugged. 'We take them seriously back home too.'

We tidied up after a fashion; we didn't want Mrs Maloney complaining. Then we went outside. The afternoon was brilliant. The sea looked innocent; the tide had turned and stretches of sand had appeared at the upper end of the inlet. The twins went down to swim in one of the warm pools left by the retreating tide; Simon went over to the O'Keefes' to see their new foal. Rupert and I took bicycles out of the turf shed behind the ruined kitchens and were practising 'wheelies' in the forecourt when Seán appeared with his fishing rod.

'Where are you going?' I demanded, stopping my bicycle with a small crunch of gravel.

'I'm off to my creek, Squirrel,' he replied. He turned to Rupert: 'You can come if you like . . . We can get to it easily when the tide is out . . .'

I saw the light in Rupert's eyes, sensed that he was poised to leap up and follow. But he looked at me and his expression changed. 'Thanks, but Áine said she'd show me some stuff,' he said.

Seán gave a groan. 'What do you want to go with *her* for?' He made a face and stalked off across the gravel.

Rupert watched him disappear.

'Why don't you go with him?' I demanded, knowing how boring for him it must be, being stuck with me and Tabbs. 'You didn't have to stay with me.'

'But you have no one to play with.'

'That's because I'm a girl . . . You should go with Seán; you'll be slagged for staying with me.'

'Maybe I like girls.'

I knew he was just saying it to be kind. And the fact that he was kind was astonishing. Boys were kind to animals; but they were not kind to anything else. I glanced at his profile, his short brown hair, his freckles, the stubborn set of his chin. He was looking towards the path to the rocks where the tip of Seán's sea rod was disappearing. I sensed in him an innate strength, and a courtesy inborn. It came to me, that judged by all the experience I had had of life, Rupert was no ordinary boy.

31

He turned to me and said, 'Anyway you said you would show me that path up the cliff . . .'

Mrs Maloney's Ford Fiesta rattled over the cattle grid and came to rest a few yards away. She emerged from her vehicle with a 'Hello Áine . . . and who have you there?'

'This is my American cousin, Rupert.' I turned to Rupert. 'Rupert, this is Mrs Maloney.' He rested his bicycle against the steps and shook hands with her.

'Are you really an American? You have a very English name.'

'Yes ma'am.'

'Well you're very welcome and I hope you have a grand time. At least the weather is good . . . the best weather we've had for ages. So make the most of it.'

She opened the hatchback and began to haul out a big cardboard box. 'Here, give me a hand . . .' and she deposited the box into Rupert's outstretched arms.

'Put it on the kitchen table,' she told him, and as he disappeared into the house she said to me, 'That's a nice boy. Bit thin though. Is your mother at home?'

'No. They all went out for lunch?'

'And what did you lot eat?'

'Whatever we could find.'

Our home help shook her head. 'I suppose that scoundrel, Seán, left nothing for anyone else.'

'Something like that.'

'Well, you'll be having Irish stew for supper tonight. That'll fatten the lot of you.'

'Not with onions?' I protested.

'Well, you can't make it without them.'

Rupert reappeared from the kitchen, looked at me and then restlessly towards the sea.

'We can go on the cliff walk now,' I whispered. 'If you like . . . You can see the whole bay from it . . .'

His face brightened. 'OK.'

Mrs Maloney came into the hall, glanced through the open door of the boot room, stopped in her tracks and exclaimed as she surveyed the mess: 'Divine God! Was it a bomb?'

'It was Seán,' I called. 'He was looking for his snorkel.'

But before she could tell us to come in and tidy it up Rupert and I had escaped to the avenue and took the left fork which led through the old stableyard to the cliffs.

Rupert's legs were longer than mine, but he moderated his stride. Sometimes I ran ahead to warn him about parts of the path which I had already ascertained were slipping towards the beach, a drop of some hundred feet. Part of the path was lined with fuchsia, which grows wild everywhere in this part of Ireland, vivid hedges of cerise and purple. I broke some of the small flowers from their stems, pinched off the calyx and sucked the sweetness.

Rupert watched me in amazement. 'You'll poison yourself!'

'It's not poisonous. Here, taste.'

He obeyed, bending his head towards my hand, and tasted the nectar in the heart of the fuchsia. The breeze moved his shirt; sunlight touched his forearm and its short, blond hairs.

'Yeah, it's sweet . . . are you sure it's not poisonous?'

'It hasn't killed me yet.'

But sweetest of all was the camaraderie, my ability to show him things he had never seen, although he was a boy. Further along the path I found the spot I loved, a hollow surrounded by tall, tough grass. It had a flat stone where you could sit out of sight of everyone except the birds. I sat down at one corner and invited Rupert to join me. Down below us, and out as far as the horizon, the sea sparkled.

'I see your brothers,' Rupert announced. He was lying on his stomach and sticking his head over the cliff top.

'Seán?'

'Yeah. Down there.'

I ventured nearer the edge, was restrained by Rupert, who pulled me down beside him. 'Be careful . . .'

Below me I saw Seán, standing with his jeans rolled up, his bare feet on the sand, his runners tied around his neck. He was inspecting a lagoon, a deep wide pool left by the outgoing tide. Approaching him among the rocks was the figure of a man; I heard the greeting, heard Seán's reply and instinctively pulled back into the shelter of the long grass.

'Who's that?' Rupert said in my ear.

'It's old Aeneas Shaw. He's a bit weird!'

'How?'

33

I shrugged. 'He just is! But Seán likes him because he knows everything about fishing.

'Why didn't you come to see us before now?' I asked a few moments later. Rupert was lying on his back, staring into the sky and I was beside him. I was aware of his warmth. I was unused to human warmth or contact. I had never in my memory lain this close to another being, except Tabbs and our old spaniel Gracie who had died.

'I knew all about you and often heard how your mother and father met,' I pressed on. I leant on my elbow. 'Mummy says your father didn't like Ireland and that was the reason you never came.'

'My father is . . . set in his views,' Rupert conceded after a moment, squinting to look up at me. 'There's lots of things he doesn't like!' He laughed shortly. 'He doesn't like anything different – he doesn't like foreigners, or Civil Rights people, or feminists, or what he calls "nancy boys", by which he means professionals, or me becoming a doctor. He wants me to stay home and run Mount Wexford.'

'You should become a doctor if you want!'

He sighed and looked back at the sea.

'I'm glad you came, Rupert,' I said after a moment.

He smiled at me. 'So am I.'

A gull swooped and screeched overhead. Rupert turned to peer once more down on the beach. Seán was standing on the rocks by his creek, deploying his fishing rod and Aeneas Shaw was moving away out of sight.

'Do you think we should be getting back?' Rupert said.

'Why?'

'Well . . . what if my mother and your parents have come back? We're not supposed to be here . . . And what if your little brother has come back and there's no one around?'

'Simon? But the twins have to look after him. That's their job.'

'And who looks after you? I mean normally? This is not a very safe place.'

'I'm ten! I'm too big to be looked after. And I know this place, although I'm not supposed to be up here.'

He indicated the shoreline and the disappearing figure.

'What if you met that weird guy out here on your own?'

I shrugged. I was secretly afraid of Aeneas Shaw, afraid of things I saw in his red-rimmed eyes.

'Look!' I exclaimed, reaching for a hairy molly which was struggling in the grass. I wanted to prolong this moment. I did not want to leave Rupert's side, to lose his warmth, the mutuality between us, lying here like smugglers in the long grass. I pulled the hairy molly from the grass stems, put it on the back of Rupert's hand, where it weaved and bobbed. 'Do you like caterpillars?'

'Not much,' he said looking at me quizzically and then he laughed. I thought he was uneasy. I wondered if he wanted to be away from me, if he longed to be down there with Seán fishing in the 'creek'. He took the hairy molly from his hand, and set it back among the grass stems. Then he stood up. 'Come on . . .'

'I'll show you the rest of the headland if you like,' I said, and he replied after a moment's hesitancy, 'OK. Sure . . .'

We took the long way, because the cliff path dipped down towards Mulvey strand and then tucked itself around by the back of the headland. En route we passed the ruins of a few ancient cottages, their stout stone walls still standing despite the centuries.

'This place must have been well populated once,' Rupert said suddenly.

'Yes. Dad says there were loads of people living around here long ago. This was because a man called Cromwell grabbed the good land in the east and told the owners to go to Hell or to Connaught. So they came here because they had nowhere else to go. And then the Famine came and they got sick and died. Most of the ones who survived went to America on ships called Coffin Ships.'

We entered a ruin that stood at the most seaward point of the headland, stood in silence, listening to the wind playing through the remains of the chimney breast. There was a jam-jar full of wild flowers on the hearthstone. I can identify them in retrospect – pink thrift and sea holly – and I wondered who could have left them there. The ruin was miles from anywhere.

I remembered a school history lesson and imagined the fire

and the crane and the black kettle and the effort to live on fish and nettles, while the potatoes failed a second year and the typhus that was sweeping the country knocked on the door.

'These flowers are fresh,' Rupert said. 'Is someone living here?'

'No one could live here. There's no roof!'

But Rupert pointed to a bundle of rags in the corner by the chimney, a couple of dirty blankets and a milk carton. I shrugged.

'You can feel it,' Rupert whispered suddenly. 'The sadness.' His restlessness had gone. 'Where would the family have slept? There's not much room.'

'There would have been one bedroom and there was the kitchen; they would have had a kind of bed by the fire too . . . It was called the settle.'

We moved out of the cottage into the breeze and I turned and said to Rupert with some embarrassment, 'Will you wait out here for a moment . . .'

'Why?'

'Because I have to go for a pee.' I reddened at this confession. Looking back on it now I marvel that such a simple thing should have changed the course of my life.

'Sure,' Rupert said, 'I'll go down the path. You can follow when you're ready.'

I went back inside the ruin, peed in its shelter. But as I was pulling up my clothes I heard a furtive footstep and then a cracked voice whispered: 'What are ye doin' yer wee wee for in my house, ye dirty little trollop?'

My heart skittered. The person of Aeneas Shaw blocked the old doorway, his pale face a study in fury. There was spittle on his lips, and from him came a powerful smell, a combination of spirits, old body odours, wood smoke and something else – a sweetish smell of decay.

I stood back against the wall. 'It's not your house!' I retorted foolishly, although I was on the verge of tears from fright.

'It is my house, miss,' he replied in the same sibilant whisper, 'my people's house. But yeer people evicted them, drove the roof in upon them.' He paused. '*She* drove the roof in on them!'

And then, approaching me, he raised his hand. I saw his

36

matted hair and clothes, the cracked boots. I cowered back into the corner and screamed, 'Rupert!'

I heard the footsteps rushing outside and my cousin reappeared in the doorway. The tramp started back at the sight of him.

'Rupert!' I cried, my voice shrill. 'Run!' I darted through the door and down the path. But Rupert stood his ground.

'Ye pup!' I heard Aeneas Shaw hiss, and when I looked back I saw Rupert standing perfectly still and looking at this man as though hypnotized, as though the tramp had some kind of power over the boy which he could not break.

'Go away!' I screamed. 'Go away! I'm going to tell my Daddy!'

Rupert recovered quickly. 'Come on Áine,' he said urgently, suddenly behind me. 'Keep moving!'

We ran down the treacherous path and when I glanced back I saw our pursuer had not attempted to follow us, but that he stood looking after us, and then a sibilant threat of his came to me on the breeze: 'Never fear, but Aeneas Shaw'll get ye . . .'

When we reached the old farmyard I turned to Rupert. I was trembling.

'Thanks Rupert . . . If you hadn't come!'

'We'll tell your father,' he said, effecting as much grown-up coolness as he could now that the crisis was over.

'Did you hear what he said . . . after we had run away?'

'No.' Rupert turned his grave eyes on me. 'What did he say? I didn't hear anything.'

'He said he would get us yet.'

'That ol' guy should be in a lunatic asylum,' Rupert said after a moment.

'He used to be in one,' I told him with a nervous laugh. 'But they let him out a couple of years ago.'

'Are you serious?'

I nodded and we walked home. Rupert's face was set, a half scared, half furious expression.

'Why did Seán talk to him?' he demanded. 'He shouldn't talk to him!'

'Seán always says that his bark is worse than his bite.'

'Is it true that his people were evicted by our ancestors?' he asked a moment later as we crossed the stable yard. His voice was quiet and introspective.

'I don't know. There was an old story . . . But *our* family would never do a thing like that!'

Rupert was silent. Then he said suddenly, 'History isn't something that just happens and then is over. It leaves something behind it . . . You can feel it here – at least up there on the headland. You can feel it where I come from too . . .'

'What do you mean, Rupert? You mean in Virginia . . .? What do you feel there?'

He shrugged. Then he hurried on ahead of me, and I felt somehow that the bright day had dimmed. It was all my fault. I shouldn't have brought him to the cliff and I shouldn't have peed in the ruin. I hung my head and searched for wisdom. But I could not find enough to serve the moment. I was an old child, but I was not yet an adult.

'Wait for me . . .' I called after Rupert, but he just looked back at me almost in exasperation. 'I want to see if the grown ups are back. We have to tell them . . .'

'I don't want to tell them, Rupert,' I shouted after him in desperation, quickening my pace to catch up with him. 'I'll just get into trouble again. We're not allowed to go on the cliff path . . . I shouldn't have taken you! And I have this feeling,' I added, beset by a visceral panic, 'I have this feeling that if we say anything . . . there will be no end to it . . . it will never blow over. There's a chance now that he'll forget about us. But if we tell . . .'

Rupert picked up a stone and flung it dismissively into the sky. It came down some distance away among the copse of trees by the cattlegrid.

'I don't care,' he said. 'If you don't tell them, I will.' He turned and glared at me. 'How can you be so stupid, Áine? You *have* to tell them about something like this!'

This sudden cruelty, the released tension of a few minutes before, demanded tears; they came silently. I had tried so hard to impress, but all I had done was the opposite. He did not turn; he quickened his stride as though he were eager to shed me and I followed behind, the outsider once again, the mocked and derided one again, the weed, her face wet and her nose running.

I was sure he was gone from me. It was a bit like the time Gracie had died and I knew I would never have her love again. But it was much more; because with Rupert I had been vouchsafed a glimpse into another world, into the world of mutuality, into the shelter of a relationship, into a belonging I had secretly always hungered for. To lose it again so soon felt like death.

Chapter Four

When we got home the grown ups were back. The car was in the forecourt and my mother and Aunt Isabelle were sitting on cushions on the sunny front steps. Aunt Isabelle was frowning and as soon as she saw us jumped up and exclaimed: 'Where have you been?'

'Just for a walk . . .'

'A walk where?'

I looked at Rupert, terrified that he would rat on me. But he just shrugged and said, 'Oh just around, Mom . . .'

My mother interjected, 'Where's Seán?'

'He's at his creek,' Rupert said. 'We saw him talking to that old geezer, Aeneas Shaw.'

The cat was out of the bag. There was only one place that overlooked the creek.

My mother exclaimed sharply, 'I told you, Áine, not to go on the cliff path. You know perfectly well that it is out of bounds!'

She would have continued, but a glance at her sister-in-law made her pause. Aunt Isabelle had paled.

'Oh . . . but it's so dangerous . . . the cliff path,' she whispered. 'Rupert, you must promise me never, ever to go there again . . .'

Rupert shot me a sidelong glance. 'Yes Mom,' he said.

'And that Shaw fellow,' my mother said, 'I told Seán fifty times to avoid him. He gives me the pip.'

'Who is he?' Aunt Isabelle demanded, her voice tense and her eyes wide.

'Oh Isabelle, don't upset yourself. He's only a poor creature that wanders around. There's probably no harm in him. I just don't like him . . .'

'I don't remember him,' my aunt replied. 'Aeneas Shaw? I don't remember him at all. Where is he from?'

41

'He was in the lunatic asylum in Ballinaslie,' I said helpfully, 'for years and years.'

I caught my mother's eye and saw that she was ready to kill me. 'But they let him out because he was better,' I added reassuringly.

'Oh God!' Aunt Isabelle breathed. 'A lunatic!'

'Oh for Heaven's sake, Isabelle, he's all right,' my mother interjected. 'He doesn't bother anyone.'

Rupert looked at me and I looked at Rupert in sudden terror. I knew he was about to blurt out the truth, that we had met him on the headland and that he had tried to hit me, but I saw the determination leave him as he regarded the distraught face of his mother.

'Did you have a nice lunch, Mom?' he asked innocently, sitting down beside her on the step.

Aunt Isabelle relaxed. She ruffled his hair and he blinked in the same nervous way he had that morning when I had embarrassed him.

'We had a lovely lunch, darling, in such a sweet little restaurant.'

I knew she was referring to An Cuain Álainn, the local gastronomic pride and joy, a dicey enough venture that seemed to be working.

'Where's Dad?' I asked and my mother said he had gone over to talk to Teddy O'Keefe about the grazing. Teddy, at twenty-five, had recently inherited the adjoining farm, and maintained the quid pro quo with my father about the grazing of the twenty acres.

The twins appeared at the top of the stone steps to the beach. Simon came up behind them, his dark head bobbing with excitement. They were holding aloft a 'canoe' made of flattened tin cans. They had spent most of the afternoon making it in the cavern, floating it in the pools left behind by the ebbing tide. Behind them was the sweep of the inlet, wet sand and shining pools, dotted with sand spirals from the lug worms; oyster catchers were scurrying along the beach with long, businesslike beaks. The island, Inishdrum, was once again accessible on foot.

'Did you have a proper lunch?' Aunt Isabelle asked Rupert

sotto voce, when she thought none of us were listening.

'Sure, we all tucked in.' He met my eye, and his mouth curved into the ghost of a smile. 'It was a great feed . . .'

'Good,' Aunt Isabelle said. 'Nothing like nice fresh Irish food!'

I bit my lip. Then I said, mostly to reassure Rupert that there would in fact be a meal in the evening, 'Mrs Maloney is doing Irish stew for supper.'

Aunt Isabelle's voice was suddenly bemused. 'I haven't eaten Irish stew for years.'

'We're starving!' the twins said, almost in unison.

'Did you see the O'Keefes' new foal?' my mother asked. 'We met Teddy and he told us about him.'

'Yes. He's black, with white socks,' Simon said. 'Gráinne adores him. She's coming for supper.' Gráinne was Teddy's half-sister.

'Did you tell Mrs Maloney?'

'Yeah!'

We heard the clomping of wellingtons on the beach steps and Seán appeared. He was holding his fishing rod over his shoulder. He stopped and looked at the assembled company with laconic bonhomie.

'Hello chaps!'

My mother laughed despite herself. 'There are two ladies and one little girl present,' she said. 'And none of these persons are "chaps".'

Seán gave one of his reluctant grins.

'You can be chaps all the same, Mum. Special favour!'

Rupert seemed unaware of the badinage. He was looking expectantly at his cousin's canvas satchel. 'Did you catch anything?' he demanded.

'Some flounder, but they were too small so I put them back.' Seán regarded his American cousin's eager face. 'You can come tomorrow if you want . . . if you've had enough of the Squirrel Mistress.'

I saw the delight in Rupert's face and turned away to hide the pain.

'I thought I'd go to Mulvey pier tomorrow,' Seán went on. 'If Jack Leahy's boat is free he might bring us out for a bit of sea fishing. The bottom is very flat and sandy on the other side of Inishdrum, and there may be some ray. Have you ever done any sea fishing?'

'No,' Rupert exclaimed with alacrity, 'but I'd sure love to.'

There was a rattle on the cattle grid and a young girl emerged from the shadows of the overhanging trees. It was Gráinne O'Keefe with her pushbike.

'Hello Gráinne,' the twins called almost in unison.

'Hello,' she called.

Gráinne was fourteen, ash blonde and willowy, and as far as I was concerned, the most beautiful creature alive. She was dressed in blue jeans and a denim shirt. She had skin like a peach and was evidently wearing a thin shim of lipstick, for her lips were a lustrous pale pink.

I saw the sudden light in Seán's eyes. I saw Rupert straighten. I felt instinctively how the air, like an energy field, became charged around my brothers and around Rupert, realized that in Gráinne's presence I was invisible.

Gráinne propped her bicycle against the wall by the cattle grid and came towards us shyly across the stones of the forecourt.

My mother said to Aunt Isabelle: 'This is Gráinne O'Keefe.'

'I knew your parents,' Aunt Isabelle said.

Gráinne seemed uneasy under the scrutiny, but she extended her hand as my mother continued, 'Gráinne, this is my sister-in-law, Mrs Lyall, and this is my nephew Rupert.'

Gráinne shook hands with him too and blushed. I tasted defeat; in Gráinne's presence I was just 'a little girl' as my mother had just described me, and I suddenly knew that nothing in my repertoire, not my handstands, not my best cartwheels, not my impersonation of Mickey Mouse, could give me the power she possessed by simply being alive. It struck me for the first time that, far from being awful, femininity was mysterious beyond comprehension.

'Áine, go in and help Mrs Maloney with the supper,' my mother said, as though I was irritating her by standing there staring. 'And wash your hands. They're filthy.'

I went in, but did not go to the kitchen. I found my way upstairs and stared at myself in the full-length mirror on my mother's wardrobe. I wanted to see a lissome young beauty, but all I saw was a dark, skinny little creature, with grubby fingernails and mournful eyes.

My mother's cosmetics were kept in an elegant pigskin case which had been a present from my father in the early days of their marriage. It had a mirror and various fittings, and was lined with pink silk. It was virtually unused, although my mother, in some early surge of enthusiasm, had filled it with a variety of cosmetics. Nowadays she only bothered with make-up when she was going to some 'do' or other – when she could get her hair done and dress herself to the nines – and the case had the look of an expensive but neglected accessory. But I knew its contents thoroughly – every bottle of fluid make-up, every small palette of eye shadow, every shade from grey to subdued violet, the powder and the silken brushes, the interesting tubes of mascara with spiral applicator that could be pulled out with a sucking sound. The bottles of nail varnish were almost full. I selected a shade. The lid was stuck, but it moved at last and then I anointed my short, gnawed nails with 'Hollywood Rose'. The varnish dried quickly; I put on mascara and lipstick. My eyes in the mirror looked preternaturally bright, surrounded as they were by smudged eye make-up; my lips were glossy grape, imperfectly outlined in 'Burgundy Red'. The tissue box provided me with small balls of paper which I shoved under my T-shirt. Suddenly Gráinne had real competition – I had breasts. I stared with delight, until my mother's voice broke the spell. It came stridently from below. 'Áine, where have you got to?'

The reflected figure was abruptly absurd, a small girl with a thin body, a lumpy false chest and a face like something from a vampire movie.

'Áine!' came my mother's voice again. 'Do you hear me?' Her voice brooked no further dalliance. Reluctantly I came to the top of the stairs.

She was standing in the hall and wore her familiar 'what is that child up to now' expression. She frowned and came slowly up the stairs, staring at my handiwork.

'What on earth have you been doing? Were you at my make-up?'

'Just some lipstick, Mummy!'

'And eye make-up as well . . .'

She prodded my paper bosom. Her voice veered from censure to hysteria, teetered on the verge of laughter. 'And what on earth have you put in there?'

Aunt Isabelle came in, looked up at us and climbed the stairs to the landing. She surveyed me without mockery, my made-up face, my chest with its falsies. But I had an unexpected feeling of visibility, a feeling that she too had been in this place of powerlessness.

'You look very nice,' she said, 'but the thing about make-up, darling, is to wear only the teeniest bit . . . And you do have rather a lot of it on.' She glanced at my chest, lowered her voice conspiratorially. 'If I were you I'd wait for my own bosom. It will be ever so much nicer!'

My mother laughed at this, gently, even kindly, as though reproved by my aunt's sympathy. Shamed and crimson I scuttled to the bathroom where I locked the door and scrubbed at my face and removed my paper breasts. My eyes, rubbed and red, now looked as though I had been crying, and the lipstick had stained my lips to an unpleasant purple which no amount of scrubbing would erase. I crept downstairs, hearing the glad young voices outside the open front door in the evening sunlight and my parents and Aunt Isabelle talking together in the drawing room. But I tip-toed past the door and found the kitchen.

'Good wee girl,' Mrs Maloney said, only half glancing at me. 'Would you ever set the table?'

I obeyed. I set it for ten, wedging the last place at the end of the long, deal table. Mrs Maloney washed and dried her hands, said everything was ready, looked at me uncertainly as though something in my appearance was amiss. But she only said that she had to go home otherwise she would be late for the Bingo which Father McCarthy was organizing in the new parish hall. I heard her go into the sitting room and after a minute or two emerge and leave the house, closing the porch door behind her.

The supper table looked festive. Mrs Maloney had put out some candles in an old wrought-iron candelabrum, and had arranged some hydrangeas in the centre of the table. The meal began with grapefruit halves with one glacé cherry in the middle, and then there was the stew, with tender pieces of lamb, carrots, potatoes, a hint of mace and garlic, and plenty of the hated onions which I assiduously picked out and put on my side plate. The green salad had been rescued from the fridge and dressed up with wedges of tomato. Dessert waited on the side unit, apple pie and cream.

I sat at the end of the table watching the merriment, for it was a merry occasion, the boys being funny and almost civilized. I knew perfectly well that this was because of Gráinne's presence. Rupert glanced at her from time to time and spoke to her in short bursts, as though unsure of conversational currency. I hated the admiration for her I saw in his eyes. It made me feel invisible, relegated to the margins of existence, as though we had never lain together on a cliff top and watched the world.

The grown ups talked in low voices. My mother spoke of riots in a place called Soweto. 'There'll be terrible problems in South Africa yet . . .' I heard her say. 'They have their heads in the sand.' I listened to her voice, wondering why she was always interested in things far away, and never interested in what was going on under her nose. Aunt Isabelle sighed. She changed the subject to the weather. My father nodded. He was good at nodding. He frowned a lot, like a man preoccupied with weighty matters. He always gave the impression that anything mentioned by women could not possibly be of serious import, but must be listened to politely all the same. Sometimes I felt that this politeness was driving my mother crazy. Sometimes I felt the tense intake of her breath, and her fierce, silent longing for recognition.

The stew was polished off, Seán having second helpings. I helped my mother and Aunt Isabelle gather up the plates. The boys talked of the fishing, the new foal, Blackie, Gráinne suddenly waxing voluble about him. 'He's a gorgeous little fellow . . . isn't he?' She turned to the twins for confirmation and squealed at the hermit crabs Simon took out of his pocket and put on the table.

'Aren't they great little yokes!' he said admiringly.

'Did you know that hermit crabs have no shells of their own?' Seán said to Rupert. 'They steal the shells of other creatures.'

The fragile legs of the little creatures retracted into the purloined shells. Rupert said, 'No, I never knew that. Although there must be plenty of them in Chesapeake Bay.'

'Where's that?' Seán demanded.

'It's off the coast of Virginia,' my aunt said.

Rupert's eyes turned to where Gráinne sat beside me. 'I suppose you're well versed about these little guys, Gráinne?'

'Well . . . only because they try to nibble my toes when I'm paddling.'

Rupert raised his eyebrows and widened his eyes. 'Really! They nibble your toes?' And I knew at once that he wouldn't mind having a nibble himself.

'Yes,' she said, reddening. 'If you swim in any of the pools when the tide is going out you'll feel them . . .'

'Take those creatures off the table at once, Simon!' my mother said, abruptly emerging from her adult world.

Simon obeyed with bad grace and put the hermit crabs back into his pocket. Seán stood up suddenly, came to Simon's chair and put out his hand to his little brother.

'Right, Pupa, yield them up. They'll die in your smelly pocket.'

Simon took the hermit crabs out piecemeal and put them, one by one, into his big brother's hand. One of them fell. I caught it and handed it to Seán.

'What on earth have you got on your nails, Squirrel?' he demanded loudly as he put the tiny hermit crabs on the draining board. He resumed his seat, lowered his head and regarded me severely. 'Squirrel has been painting her nails!' he announced. 'And judging by the colour of her lips she's been painting them too!'

There was a titter of laughter from my brothers. Rupert looked at me interrogatively, blinked in his idiosyncratic way, as though in surprise. Gráinne looked at me sideways with an indulgent grown-up smile, examining my face for telltale signs of titivation. I felt about five years old. The power play in my family was suddenly intolerable; I could no longer endure the endless put downs, the jokes, the good-natured jibes, and I acted on an unconsidered surge of outrage, leaping up and thumping the table with my fist.

'From now on,' I shouted, 'I want some respect!'

My voice sounded reedy and uncertain in my ears, as though suddenly intimidated by itself. Seán gave a hoot of laughter that reverberated down the table. Simon trumpeted loud guffaws, as though he would choke. Rupert looked at me and then at his plate. My mother was smiling in adult bemusement, my father with the pained expression he reserved for his children's peccadillos. The twins were grinning. I felt suddenly foolish under the weight of the assembled mockery, caught my aunt's eyes and saw that she moved her head almost imperceptibly as though in warning. Suddenly deflated, I wished I had, like the hermit crabs, a shell into which I could creep. I pushed aside my chair and ran upstairs to my room, hearing my brother's voice: 'Oh, let her go and sulk!'

The thought of dessert, the demolition of the apple pie, to which I had looked forward, filled me with misery. There would be none left. But I was too proud to return to the kitchen and instead lay down on my bed, clutching Rastus, my ragged, once-fluffy elephant, a present on my third birthday, who always lived under my pillow. Rastus now had an eye missing, and his pale pink trunk was a grubby vestige of its former self.

After a while I heard the voices in the hall below, and the porch door opening and closing. I looked out of my window, saw Seán, Gráinne and Rupert approaching the steps to the beach. Gráinne's bright voice raised itself in laughter. I saw my brother looking at her with the concentrated gaze he brought to the few things he admired. Rupert was smiling, but when he raised his head, it was not on Gráinne that he rested his eyes. His gaze directed itself beyond her and focused on my window. He saw me, raised his hand in an almost imperceptible thumbs up salute and turned away.

I watched them as they took their shoes off, rolled up their jeans and walked off across the wet beach, Seán and Rupert, with Gráinne between them. I also saw, further out, on the shore of Inishdrum island, the figure of a man who stood perfectly still and watched the trio move across the sand. From his slightly hunched posture I knew that it could only be Aeneas Shaw. I heard the evening cry of the sandpiper, a lonely call to the approaching night. The sun was going down and great streaks of magenta coloured the horizon.

The room was darkening around me. I wanted to go downstairs, but felt foolish. Instead I let the loneliness envelop me. I sat on the edge of the bed and let my eyes pick out the contents of the room as the darkness swallowed them, the print on the wall, the mahogany table with the mirror, the marble fireplace, the lovely Japanese geisha doll on the mantelpiece which was one of my treasures, the old wardrobe in the corner. The scent of camphor, which I always associated with this house, wafted from some cranny and was carried on the breeze from the open window. I heard the light footstep on the landing, then the scratching at the door before it opened and my aunt appeared. In the gloaming she seemed exotic; she had thrown a shawl of some bright, silken material around her shoulders. Her eyes were very bright.

She glided across the room and put her hand on my arm. Her eyes looked into mine, pupils wide.

'You must never, ever let them see it . . . Áine darling,' she whispered. 'You must never show them!'

My mouth opened. 'Show them what?'

'You must never show men what you really feel,' she repeated. 'Men . . . eat feelings! They have none of their own and they live off other people's.'

Stunned by this confidence, I stared back into my aunt's face. But what I saw there was so vulnerable that it was unbearable. Although accustomed to taking adult utterances as gospel, I knew that what my aunt had said was driven by some private suffering of her own. There was a sudden shift in our relationship. It was as though I were the one with the resources, as though I had strength and the beginnings of wisdom, as though I were the grown up and she the child. I took her hand; it was warm and moist. But I knew I could not comfort her. I was ill at ease and said I must go downstairs and help my mother.

'Oh, everything is cleared up, darling. Your parents are reading; the twins and Simon are playing Monopoly in the drawing room. Rupert is gone off with your brother and that little Gráinne girl.' She dropped her voice. 'Do you think he liked her? Rupert, I mean?'

'Yes.'

She sighed. 'You invest your youth in them. And the first chance they get they desert you for other people's children! But he has someone at home you know . . . who thinks the world of him.'

'A girl?'

'Yes. She lives near us.'

Aunt Isabelle went to the window. I joined her and watched the young people on a beach that was quickly shrinking with the return of the tide.

'Look,' my aunt said, 'who is that man on the island? He'll be cut off!'

'He probably won't mind. It won't be cold tonight and he can sleep in the old fortress.'

The distant figure did not move, but remained staring with unnatural fixity at the young trio running back along the wet sand. His silhouette stood out, black and stark, against the sky. I shivered; I remembered how he had spat earlier, how he had tried to slap me. I saw his strange outline as though it were something threatening, immobile and simian, like the inhabitant of a nightmare.

'There's something wrong with that man,' Aunt Isabelle cried suddenly, her hand clutching mine. 'Look . . . who did you say he was?'

'He's just a bit strange in himself, Aunt Isabelle,' I said soothingly, although her horror communicated itself to me as though it were my own. 'He's just a bit odd, but he's harmless.'

In this I was repeating received wisdom. No one knew where this man came from, except that he was reputed to have spent a stint in the mental hospital. Father McCarthy had said one day when he had called on us, that the man was a harmless eccentric. But after today I knew differently. What stuck with me most was not so much his attempt to hit me, but the immobile menace of his stance as he stared down the cliff path after us.

I went to the door, looked back at my aunt and announced

I was going downstairs. Although I disliked crossing the dark back hall at night, I now made my way to the kitchen, turned on the kitchen light and looked for the remains of the apple pies. Mrs Maloney had made two, and I thought for a moment that maybe a piece might be left. The scent of cloves was still tantalizing the air, but of apple pies there was no sign. Then I saw the Pyrex plates newly washed and dried.

Resigned, I went into the drawing room, glad of the fire and the presence of my parents. The latter looked up; my father said, 'Hello Áine . . .' in a preoccupied fashion.

My mother said in a low voice, 'You should have controlled yourself at supper, although it was quite wrong of Seán to tease you like that. When are you going to learn that people cannot draw blood from you unless you let them?'

'Sorry, Mummy.'

The twins and Simon were finishing a game of Monopoly and asked if I wanted to join in a new one. So I sat on the floor and played with them. I was nonchalant now, and sported my smeared nails as though they were trophies. But inside I dreaded the loneliness of the approaching night.

Gráinne went home. Seán accompanied her. I knew the avenue was dark at night, with only the light from the stars and the shimmer of rock pools, and I half envied them the mutuality of night and adolescence, without consciously formulating it. At any rate I projected myself, in fantasy, into a long night-time walk with someone who loved me. In this fantasy I even saw a loving face bending towards me, Rupert's face.

Aunt Isabelle came in, her book in her hand, seated herself in the window seat, the table lamp on beside her. Behind her the moths clustered at the window. Through the glass I saw their fat, furry bodies and the spread of their grey wings.

Rupert entered the room as my mother was ordering Simon to bed. He had not had a chance as yet to speak to my father about the incident with Aeneas Shaw. I knew he would not mention it at the supper table. I was glad of this, because by now I just desperately wanted to forget about it, to let it go.

'Bedtime for you too, Áine,' my mother said.

'Just another five minutes, Mummy please!'

She sighed. 'Oh all right.'

My mother disappeared with Simon, who was overdue for a bath. 'Oh for God's sake, child, water won't burn you,' I heard her exasperated voice as she frog-marched him up the stairs. 'And your ears are black! Why can't you do anything for yourself?'

My father put his book down, stood up, gave a half-suppressed yawn.

'I think I'll hit the hay myself!' he announced. 'Goodnight Isabelle . . . Rupert!'

'Could I have a word with you, Uncle?' Rupert said quietly, following my father into the hall. Aunt Isabelle glanced at me, raising her eyebrows.

'What's all that about?' she demanded in a sibiliant whisper as the door shut. 'What does Rupert want to talk to your father about?'

I shrugged, but I felt something cold touch my heart, as though I knew that in spite of everything I might do, something evil had been unwittingly precipitated, unleashed upon the world. The door opened and my father's face appeared.

'Áine, come here please!'

When the door was shut behind me my father demanded, 'Rupert tells me you met that old Shaw fellow today and that he tried to strike you.'

'Yes . . . sort of. We were in the old cottage on the headland and he said it was his cottage and I said it wasn't and I think he was going to slap me for being rude to him, but Rupert came back . . . But there's no harm done . . .'

'How many times have you been told, Áine, not to walk on the cliff path?'

I hung my head.

'Rupert, did you see him trying to hit Áine?'

'No . . . but he was there and he looked kinda mad!'

Frightened by the grim expression on my father's face I said, 'Aeneas thinks he's back in the Famine or something. He says his ancestors lived in that cottage!'

In the silence I heard the bath run upstairs, the sound of the twins' laughter through the drawing-room door, Seán's returning step outside on the gravel. When my father spoke his voice was coldly angry.

'I don't give twopence what he thinks. This is my land and how dare he attempt to strike my daughter! I'm reporting this matter to the police. Thank you for being so courageous, Rupert. I apologize that you should have been troubled in this way.'

My father went to the phone. I looked at Rupert, who hunched his shoulders as though in acknowledgement that the die was cast, and wished I could jettison the misgiving.

'I wish . . . he wouldn't!' I whispered. 'I wish you hadn't told him.'

'But it's the right thing. That old geezer's dangerous!'

Seán came in, shut the front door behind him with a clap, then came through the porch door with a grin.

'Well, well . . . so Squirrel Mistress has got over her little tantrum?'

I ignored him. My father's voice came clearly from the phone alcove. '. . . an attempted assault on my daughter . . .' and then we heard the name 'Aeneas Shaw.'

Seán reacted as though he had been shot. 'Why is Dad talking about old Aeneas?'

'He's reporting him to the police,' Rupert said.

'For what?'

'He tried to hit Áine today . . .'

'What? But a good thumping would do Squirrel all the good in the world! Aeneas is a bit soft in the head . . . but absolutely harmless. He wouldn't have hurt you,' he hissed at me. 'Do you know what you have done, stupid Squirrel? He will be locked up again! And you don't know what it's like, do you, Squirrel? It's like Hell, especially for someone like Aeneas who needs to be near the sea.'

My father put down the phone, emerged from the alcove and said, 'The police will come to see us in the morning. I told them it was too late now.'

'Dad,' Seán burst out, 'Aeneas is all right . . . He wouldn't hurt anyone. And now they'll take away his freedom again!'

Rupert turned on him. 'That man would have hit Áine!'

Seán replied angrily, his voice tense with suppressed aggression, 'How do you know? Did you see him try to hit her? Do you think that she is famous for the truth?'

When Rupert was silent he continued, 'But you had to interfere. I suppose you'll be ratting on him to the guards tomorrow.'

Rupert seemed stricken, but before he could reply my father said: 'That'll do, Seán! Go to bed, Áine.'

At this point Aunt Isabelle came out of the drawing room.

'What is all this confabbing about?' she demanded, her eyes bright and anxious.

'Nothing, Mummy,' Rupert said hastily, touching her hand with strange reassurance. 'We were just discussing the day.'

'Goodnight,' I whispered, turning up the stairs. Behind me I heard my father alter his tone as he spoke to his sister. The two boys went out onto the porch. I heard their voices and felt they neither noticed nor cared that I had gone.

On the landing I heard Simon's protests from the bathroom as his ears were being investigated. I looked up at the ceiling and wondered whether Dracula would be flying tonight.

When I regained my room I did not turn on the light. I stood for a while in darkness, looking across the inlet at the island, where a man, cut off by the tide, would have to spend most of the night. For a while I saw nothing except the dark blob of the island, and its ruin, against the sea. Then I thought I saw something move. And it seemed to me that he was keeping to the part of the island where he could best watch the house.

He's harmless, Seán had said. I began to blame myself. I shouldn't have provoked him. I should have avoided any confrontation. He would be locked up far away from the sea. I imagined his despair in some padded cell, imagined him listening in vain for the voice of the Atlantic.

I undressed and got into bed, clutching Rastus tightly, rubbing my index finger along his tired trunk where the pink pile was long since eroded. I had left my door ajar, because I needed the landing light. But I was still wide awake when there was a soft knock and a shadow fell across my threshold. It was Rupert.

'Áine,' he whispered. 'Are you awake?'

'Yes.' I shoved Rastus under the bedclothes where he would not be seen.

55

'I have something for you, if you'd like it. You got none at supper.'

I sat up and took the proffered gift. It was a slice of apple pie wrapped in a paper napkin. I put my nose to it, inhaled fervently.

'Thanks Rupert.'

He hesitated. 'And Áine . . . don't worry about tomorrow. Just tell the police the truth.'

I burst into tears, tears for the day's tensions and tears for the terror of the night.

'They'll lock him away . . . and it'll be all my fault. I can't, Rupert. It would be terribly cruel! Please let's say it was a mistake or something. Please . . . and Seán will kill me.'

I could not see Rupert's face properly in the half light, but I could sense his chagrin.

'I know what he wants, Áine . . . but that man tried to hit you. And you're only a little girl! God knows what he's capable of.'

I sobbed even harder. I did not want to be a *little* girl. I wanted to be Gráinne O'Keefe with a bosom and have Rupert look at me for a moment the way he had at her.

Rupert sighed and put out his hand to my wet cheek.

'All right,' he said eventually. 'Don't cry. If you really don't want to tell them, we'll say it was a mistake. Now are you going to eat that apple pie or not?'

'I'll keep it for the morning,' I said.

He left. 'Thanks Rupert,' I called softly after him.

He turned in the doorway. 'Aw . . . it's nothing,' he said awkwardly.

Comforted, I drifted towards sleep. Even the noise from the twins' bedroom did not bother me until there were sounds of a scuffle, and one of the twins yelled, 'Fuck off, Seán!' and my father came out of his room and roared at them because of their language. But after that all was silent and the castle slept.

Chapter Five

I slept like the dead for a while, how long I don't know, but when I awoke the house was silent and no friendly chink of light gladdened the bottom of my bedroom door. There were no proper curtains in my room, just heavy lace nets, and the blue blur of night pressed against the windows. My heart was still thudding from the nightmare which had awoken me. In it I had been walking through dark city streets with a stranger, a man with a white face, with big hands and feet. I had been lost and this person had come out of the shadows to take me home, but although we walked and walked through an endless maze of silent streets, we could not find my parents' house nor the road in which I lived.

Instead the urban landscape became more and more sinister – closely packed houses without a vestige of life. Here and there the buildings seemed to bend forward, as though inspecting me. For a while I clung to the hand of my rescuer, but when I looked up I saw his eyes. They stared at me with an expression I had never seen; it was hunger of a kind, but it had within it a purpose I sensed without understanding. I felt the evil. It had a presence of its own like a taint in the air, as though some primeval part of me knew something I could not even recognize. I snatched my hand away and ran into a lane which suddenly opened invitingly between the terraces, and sped between high walls. The walls grew higher and narrower and curved overhead like a canopy; I met a dead end, a corner with ferns pushing through decaying brick, with a strange, rancid smell. I heard my pursuer's unhurried, approaching tread . . .

I woke with a start, paralyzed by a sense of horror such as the waking world never knew. I wanted to cry out, for my mother, for my father, but was frightened that I would summon the ghoul from the land of dreams. To get out of bed and run to my parents' room was also impossible; I knew not what horrors awaited me down the long landing and I also knew I would be told to grow up. I clutched Rastus and the feel of his grubby, matted coat, already well seasoned with my griefs, reassured me. 'It's only a dream, only a dream, only a dream . . .' I repeated over and over, and after a while the rhythm of my heart resumed a more regular beat. The room was filled with silver moonlight. I could make out the high corniced ceiling with the cracks, the magnificent fireplace, the dark niche by the door in which I suddenly imagined a pair of staring, hungry eyes. I dived beneath the bedclothes.

At last the grey dawn crept in the window; the first birds gave a few exploratory chirps, the freshness of morning permeated the room. Disempowered by sunrise, my gremlins vanished.

I got out of bed, went to the window and looked across the inlet to Inishdrum. The tide was going out. The morning mist lay over everything; the air was like gossamer. New light swept across the bay.

I studied the island for a while. I could detect no sign of life, no sign at all of Aeneas Shaw. But after a couple of minutes I saw a male figure coming around the side of the island, bending here and there among the rocks. He had a bag of some kind in his hand. I was sure it was Aeneas. He seemed to be searching for mussels and was so preoccupied by his quest, seemed so normal, engaged as he was at such a mundane task, that I began to be ashamed of my cold fear of the preceding evening. What was there to be afraid of? Not the poor man in the distance who was gathering his breakfast in the mist. My resolution not to tell the police the truth returned. I forgave Aeneas Shaw because I wanted to forget. I wanted to forget the incident of yesterday as much as I wanted to forget the night.

Although it was only sometime after five a.m. I could not go back to bed. I dressed quickly in the jeans and grubby T-shirt of the day before, and seized my wrapped up piece of apple pie. I opened the piece of paper, and the scent of cloves filled my nostrils with delight.

Then I noticed there was writing on the wrapping. I took it

to the window, saw a drawing of what vaguely resembled a
teddy bear and a girl in some kind of kimono, with a flower in
her hair. I read the short rhyming couplet:

> *Now Rupert Bear with much delight*
> *Helps Tigerlily in her plight.*

I laughed, restored somehow to a sense of the ridiculous, to a
sense of my own visibility. I tip-toed downstairs. The house
was silent. The tentative morning light was filling a drawing
room that smelled of turf and the sweet peas Aunt Isabelle had
arranged the day before. For a few moments I sat in the window
seat, eating apple pie and watching the panorama of the dawn,
the lightening of sea and sky. I remembered suddenly that, as
the tide was out, Teddy would probably be exercising Sapphire,
Blackie's mother, along the strand. I let myself out and walked
down the avenue to the gates, exultant, for some reason, in the
sense of the new day. Teddy was just arriving. He opened the
avenue gates, gave me a broad grin and a 'Howya Áine. 'Tis
yourself is the early bird.' He parked car and horse box in the
wide part of the avenue, just inside the gate, where a half-acre
of grass gave onto the sand, let down the trailer door and backed
Sapphire out onto the grass.

Sapphire was resplendent. She clattered her shoes on the
ramp, champed down on the bit, gave her eyes a few rolls to
show her eagerness. Teddy saddled her, gave her a thump in
the stomach to make her exhale, and tightened the girth. Then
he put his foot into the stirrup and leapt to the saddle.

'Could I have a ride, Teddy? When you come back?'

He grinned at me. 'Sure!'

The reins were shortened and he was off at a steady canter
across the sand. Sapphire's hooves left clefts along the beach
which quickly softened and filled. I watched horse and rider as
they galloped towards Inishdrum.

A white stone, big as a boulder and rounded from the sea,
provided a seat while I waited for Teddy's return. I saw him
slow Sapphire to a trot, walk for a minute or two near the
island shore, and then turn and gallop back, leaning over the
mare's withers. Sapphire sprang forward at every stride, tucking

up her legs and releasing them again with the steady motion of a piston. Horse and rider gradually loomed bigger and bigger and soon were beside me once more, Sapphire huffing and panting, Ted smiling.

'Do you still want a ride?'

'Yes!'

'Stand up on that stone, like a good girl.'

I obeyed, put up my arms and he lifted me into the saddle in front of him. Sapphire backed nervously.

'Easy girl, easy,' Teddy said. He glanced at me. 'She's still a bit fresh. What would your parents say if they saw you up on her?'

'Nothing. Sure don't I know how to ride!'

Ted grinned. 'Is that a fact?'

'It is. And I want to ride her on my own.'

He slipped to the ground, held the reins, handed them to me. I held them firmly, felt the quiver of the horse's mouth. Sapphire rattled the bit. Tom shortened the stirrups. 'Hold onto the mane,' he said, 'and you'll be grand!'

I tugged at the right rein, kicked, and suddenly Sapphire threw her head back and we were off. The wind seemed to come at great speed; my nose ran and my eyes watered. I had only ridden a few times before, and for a moment, I was mortally afraid. I saw the wet sand flying by underneath me and my body stiffened. The horse felt my fear, flattened her ears and thrust her nose into the wind. I gripped the coarse black mane as though it were a matter of life and death.

Away to the west, where sea merged into sky, pink and silver streaks brightened the horizon, thin clouds reflecting sunrise. The gulls were already up; they wheeled over a spot somewhere in the distance; probably a school of mackerel. My ears heard only the steady pounding of Sapphire's hooves, the contact of iron on wet sand. The fear evaporated, was replaced by elation. For the moment I was part of something elemental, part of Sapphire and the air, the pungent smell of horse and the salty smell of the sea. My performance had little to do with horsemanship; it was more a balancing act between spirit and sensuality, balancing into the mare's movements as though I were a spur newly grown out of her spine. I let Sapphire have her head; she galloped like a dervish towards the island. Oh God, after a night of horrors, how I felt powerful and free! As we approached the island I scanned what I could see of Inishdrum, but saw no sign of life.

Teddy shouted. His words were indecipherable but his voice followed me faintly, an echo on the breeze. I shortened the right rein and turned the mare's head. She turned, relaxed into a canter and we came back to the boulder.

Teddy looked relieved. He smiled broadly. 'Well done! You're a great little bit of stuff. You're well able to ride, although for a moment I had me doubts . . .'

He lifted me down. My legs wobbled as they contacted terra firma. Teddy leapt back into the saddle.

'Thanks very much, Ted. You're very kind,' I said in as grown up a voice as I could muster, hiding my sense of triumph.

He glanced down at me scornfully. 'Would you go away out of that! Sure if you can't go for a canter of a morning what's the point of bein' alive?'

I grinned up at him. 'That's true!'

'Well, I'll take her off for another trot so . . .'

'Ted . . .'

'Yes?'

'Did you see Aeneas Shaw on the island?'

'No. But he was walking up by the rocks near the castle, looking for mussels. Poor oul yoke gathers them for that new restaurant. The French tourists go mad for them.'

'They must be mental.'

'Why d'ya ask about him anyway?'

'Ah, no reason. He's a bit of a weirdo, isn't he?'

'Sure is! But you'd have to feel sorry for the poor oul creature all the same.' Ted turned Sapphire, called back, 'See ya, Áine!' and was gone.

I watched him for a moment or two. I thought of the day ahead of me, the police coming, and I was filled with dread. I made my way back to the house.

Rupert was alone in the kitchen munching cornflakes. He looked up, said, 'Hi Áine. You're up early!'

Why was it that the world changed, lost its pedestrian normalcy? Why, in this house, where I was never a real presence, did I feel visible when he was around, as though I had divested myself of a cloak of darkness?

'Thanks for the apple pie,' I said shyly, 'and the funny little poem.'

'Áine,' Rupert said, brushing this aside, lowering his voice and scanning my face, 'what do you want to do? What are you going to tell the police?' His expression was serious, his eyes wide.

Before I could answer we heard Seán's steps on the stairs. I knew it was him because no one else in the family thumped down like an approaching army. He entered the kitchen and his presence instantly filled the room. He had sleep in the corners of his eyes.

'Morning,' he muttered to Rupert, and he grimaced at me as he hunted among the boxes of cereals for the Weetabix.

'Everyone still in bed?' Rupert asked.

'Yes, although I heard stirrings in the parents' room. The Gruesome Twosome are sunk in swinish sleep and the Pupa is, no doubt, pupating.' He turned to me. 'Well Squirrel,' he said, filling a bowl and pouring in milk and sugar, 'have you decided on your story? Are you going to let your squirrelly whingeing destroy someone's life?'

Rupert made a sound, but before he could speak I said, 'If you mean about Aeneas Shaw, I *have* decided.' What I really wanted to say was, 'Leave me alone. What's wrong with telling the truth?' But the weight of the past twenty-four hours oppressed me. The private horror of the night, the thought of the 'poor oul yoke' as Ted had called him, the sight of him early in the morning gathering mussels, my brother's wrath, all inspired a wish to be done with the whole episode. But I knew I could not be done with it. I saw this in Rupert's eyes and in the subliminal warning that filled me with nausea.

'I'll just say I got a fright when he appeared suddenly, that I made a mistake.'

I heard Rupert's intake and expulsion of breath. 'It's not true,' he said matter of factly. 'If you had seen him yesterday, Seán, you would know what I'm talking about.'

'Crap!' Seán said.

★ ★ ★

The gardaí came at ten o'clock. A dark blue Toyota with 'Garda' written on the door came to a halt in the forecourt. I was on the steps. Rupert was in his room. Two gardaí in uniform got out of the Toyota and approached across the gravel.

'Hello. Is your father in?'

'He's in the drawing room.'

'Are you Áine?'

'Yes.'

'I hear you had a spot of bother yesterday,' he said as I brought him into the hall.

The drawing-room door opened and my father appeared.

'I'm Sergeant Touhy, Mr O'Malley,' the garda said. 'This is Garda Jim Sheehan.'

My father shook hands. 'Come in. Sit down! Áine here has something to tell you.' He turned to me. 'Where's Rupert?'

'Upstairs, but there's no need to get him.'

I turned to Sergeant Touhy who had taken a note pad and pen from his pocket and shook my head. 'You see . . . it was a mistake. I just got a fright . . . Aeneas Shaw didn't really do anything. He was talking to himself and waving his arms around. He didn't expect to see me.'

'Where and what time was this?'

'At the ruined cottage on the headland. It was about three o'clock.'

Garda Sheehan scribbled something. 'What were you doing there?'

'I was out for a walk with my cousin.'

'That's a dangerous enough oul place for two children to be wandering,' the garda said, glancing at my father. I sensed his start and his sudden hidden anger.

'Where is Rupert?' he demanded.

'I dunno Daddy. I think he's upstairs.'

My father went into the hall and called, 'Rupert!'

My cousin came downstairs, looked from my father to the policeman.

'Now Rupert,' my father said, 'this is Sergeant Touhy and Garda Sheehan. Tell them what you told me last night.' Rupert did not glance at me. He took a deep breath and said in a matter-of-fact voice that he had heard me call him and returned to find Mr Shaw in the ruined cottage and me very upset.

'Did you see him *do* anything?' Sergeant Touhy demanded.

'No.'

My father's brow darkened. The sergeant looked from one of us to the other.

'But you say, Áine, that the man didn't intend to hurt you,' he asked gently.

'No . . . I don't think so!'

'He didn't threaten you, then?' the sergeant said.

I gulped and lied. 'Not really.' I looked miserably at Rupert and my eyes filled with tears. Rupert opened his mouth and then shut it again.

'I'll have a word with Aeneas Shaw,' the sergeant said eventually. He turned apologetically to my father. 'That's all I can do.'

'What do you know of this man?' my father demanded after a moment. 'I gather he was in the mental hospital in Ballinaslie . . .'

'We don't know a great deal about him, actually. Some say he came from this area, but no one seems to know from exactly where. He was in the mental hospital; we've checked with them, but they just said he was from Mulvey and had no better address. He seems to have no relatives. Of course if he gives any more trouble . . .'

'What about trespass?' Rupert said, with the air of a boy who knew something about the law. 'He was trespassing. Can't you do something about that?'

The sergeant shook his head and looked at him with a half smile as though pitying him for his foreign officiousness.

'Sure no one in this part of the world would get worked up over a little thing like that.'

Rupert blinked. My father's cold, parental voice said: 'Áine, why are you telling a different story to the one I heard from you last night?'

'I'm sorry, Daddy,' I whispered. 'But now I think I really did just get a fright. It wouldn't be right to . . .'

'You're not saying this because you are afraid of anyone, are you Áine? Or because your brother has been pressurizing you?'

'No, Daddy!'

He saw the sergeant out. The window was open and I heard his voice. 'I'm sorry to have wasted your time.'

'Ah, kids!' the sergeant exclaimed. 'Sure you can't be up to them. Áine was probably in a daydream. And that young lad probably wanted to impress his little cousin.' He slammed the door and drove away.

'You *are* a silly girl,' Rupert said sotto voce. 'Now the police will think you're stupid.'

'But . . .'

He shook his head at me and left the room.

I met my father on the front steps, where he had remained standing, looking out to the island.

'Áine,' he said abruptly when I appeared. 'Kindness is often misconstrued as weakness. If that man has tried to hit you he may do so again and will you be believed next time? I do not want you wandering around on your own on the cliff path. It is completely out of bounds. And keep away from that man. Is that understood?'

'Yes, Daddy.'

Seán appeared, two fishing rods over his shoulders. He was wearing wellingtons and clumped noisily and purposefully down the front steps. My father drew him to one side, but I heard their exchange. I saw Seán's face brighten and he shot me a half triumphant look.

'Seán,' I heard my father say then, 'you should keep an eye on your sister and your cousin also. I don't like the sound of yesterday's encounter, however Áine tried to gloss it over. The child was frightened when she told me about it last night. And I don't want you having anything to do with that Shaw fellow either.'

Seán sighed loudly. He beetled his brow. 'Dad, it's not fair! Aeneas knows everything about fishing; he has wonderful stories about the Famine. Áine probably gave him cheek. And I don't see why such a fuss has to be made over such a little thing.'

But my father was unmoved. He did not raise his voice, but it was very cold. 'You will obey me in this!'

Seán made a sound which sounded vaguely like acquiescence.

Rupert came out of the house. He too was wearing wellingtons and did not as much as glance at me.

'Are we all set then?' Seán demanded.

'Yes,' he said, and I felt in that moment the shift in his allegiance, his citizenship of, and my exclusion from, the hostile, dismissive world of men.

The two boys disappeared down the steps to the rocks. My father remained looking after them for a while. Then, with barely a glance at me, he turned and went back indoors to his paper. I heard my mother's voice from the drawing-room window, and then Aunt Isabelle's.

I waited for a moment or two and then I sneaked through the farm yard and onto the cliff path. From the spot where Rupert and I had spied on Seán the day before I lay in the long grass and watched the beach below, my loneliness around me.

Chapter Six

The following evening my father said to me, 'I spoke to Sergeant Touhy again today. He has interviewed that creature, and *he* claims that he was only trying to keep you away from the chimney breast in that ruin, that it's ready to fall in. I went to see the cottage myself, and it's perfectly true that it's dangerous. The fellow's been sleeping there too . . . I'm going to have it knocked down . . .'

I stared at him, aghast. 'Don't do that, Daddy! He thinks it's his . . . that it belonged to his ancestor. He'll go really mad if you knock it down. He said that day that our people had evicted his, pushed the roof in on them . . . barred the door. Is it true, Daddy?'

He sighed irritably. 'Such nonsense!'

'How do you know it's nonsense?'

My father said acerbically, 'I'm not going to lose any sleep about it now. And neither am I going to accept it as an excuse for my daughter being threatened by a yobbo.'

I met Rupert's eyes as he said this and found no compassion there, just something bordering on contempt, something that said, 'It's your own fault, Áine . . .' It sat strangely on someone who was usually so grave and courteous.

He seemed to avoid me now and I mourned for our friendship as though it had been a real possession, and not just an unlikely camaraderie born out of his initial strangeness in alien company. He had found better things to do, taken up as he was by my forceful brother, but I missed the recognition he had given me as much as if he had made a present of me to myself and had then taken it back.

My recollection of the remainder of that holiday is fragmentary

67

– vivid vignettes of memory. I was mostly alone, playing with Tabbs, reading, making a private hideaway in the orchard where the small hard apples awaited the touch of autumn. The boys didn't bother me; they were busy with their own pursuits. Sometimes Seán and Rupert went riding of a morning along Mulvey strand where a stables, run by an English girl who had married locally, catered to the passing tourist trade. Seán, who rode well, thought he would teach his American cousin a thing or two, but he found out pretty quickly that Rupert belonged on the back of a horse and could ride like a dervish. Seán whistled when he came home, 'God, you should have seen Yogi Bear . . .'

My father brought me along when I pestered him, but I was unable to recapture the confident ecstasy I had experienced that morning I had ridden Sapphire, and fell off my lumbering mount when he stopped in mid canter on Mulvey strand. The slagging I took for this determined me not to ride with them again.

Rupert and Seán had become inseparable. The two of them disappeared together on daily adventures, important men's business as Seán would have had us believe, which took them with my father on boat fishing trips and trips to Achill – the wild and beautiful island connected to the Mayo mainland by a bridge. Sometimes the twins and Simon went on these expeditions too, leaving me behind with my mother and Aunt Isabelle. But these two women were company only for each other. They talked together in endless intimate conversations, either seated on the front steps in the sun, or in the drawing room or sometimes on the terrace by the library window. If I appeared talk would abruptly stop and my mother would find things for me to do. I began to regret that I had not gone to the Gaeltacht after all, but when I asked if this were still possible my mother snorted and said, 'It has to be booked months in advance. It's much too late. If you're bored why don't you read!'

I did read. I read *Robin Hood* and privately re-enacted his life, identifying with him and despising Maid Marion who sat around and had none of the real adventures. I built my hut in the orchard, pretending it was Sherwood Forest. I tried to read

Treasure Island, which my father put into my hands, but I didn't like it much.

Father McCarthy, the parish priest, came one day and had afternoon tea with us. He questioned Aunt Isabelle at length about America, and asked her about her husband and when he would be joining her. I saw the colour rise in her face: 'He won't be joining me,' she said. 'If I can help it he won't be joining me ever again!'

Now this was food for speculation and I registered it with silent avidity. Did this mean that she and Rupert would stay with us for ever?

The parish priest frowned and said something gently and reprovingly about marriages being made in Heaven whether we liked it or not.

'This one wasn't,' my aunt said, in a tone rapidly approaching hysteria. 'It was made in a registry office at Gretna Green when I was a girl of eighteen and he was twenty. I didn't know what I was getting into . . .' She turned her head, saw me and said irritably, 'Áine, go away and play.'

I obeyed reluctantly. I was fascinated by the world of grown ups. Who was this Gretna? I imaged Gretna Green as a sort of policewoman, in a venom green uniform, who made people get married whether they liked it or not. I already knew that married people were not necessarily happy, but for the first time I became aware that marriage did not necessarily last. This brought with it a sense of unease and insecurity, for I knew my mother was not often happy and I set to wondering if she would eventually run away to another country and leave us and my father. I tried very hard to please her until this particular terror melted.

'What's your father like?' I asked Rupert one day when I got him on his own.

'He's all right,' my cousin replied, but his face darkened and he looked at me suspiciously.

'Is your mother running away from him?'

He jerked as though I had struck him. 'What makes you say a stupid thing like that? Of course she isn't running away . . .'

But I had evidently hit a nerve, for he looked suddenly woebegone and uncertain.

69

'Rupert, don't mind me,' I said, adding, to justify my intrusiveness, using a grown-up voice for conviction, 'I'm just worried about things.'

Rupert recovered his poise and vented his annoyance. 'And what have you got to be worried about?' he demanded so scornfully that I knew he saw me for a nosy parker and a fraud. But I had not been completely disingenuous and his question elicited a truth I did not wish to consider, something that I constantly tried to put away from me.

'I don't know. I just have this feeling sometimes . . . that everything is going to change; that life will become like a nightmare . . . where nothing is normal!'

He stared at me. His expression changed. 'I have that feeling too,' he whispered. 'Ever since I came here . . . It's as though life is not real anyway . . . This place makes me feel like that . . .' He gave a short self-deprecatory laugh. 'But what is reality anyhow?'

I felt the small pricking at the back of my neck, like an electric shiver. 'Are you scared?'

Seán's voice could be heard in the distance demanding that Simon restore his snorkel. 'You can pay for it out of your pocket money, Pupa. I never said you could borrow it.'

Rupert looked at me and his thin face registered panic. He blinked and said on a note of pleading, 'Don't tell him what we were talking about.'

I registered triumph, at being once more within the pale of his confidence, and I shook my head reassuringly even as my eldest brother appeared and demanded loudly if I was bothering Rupert with my squirrelly talk.

Seán had obeyed my father and avoided Aeneas Shaw. He mentioned it to me as a penalty he had suffered because of me. 'Poor old Aeneas made a bee line for me today when I was out at the creek. But I had to make an excuse. He's a lonely poor sod and he's full of great stories. But I had to avoid him, thanks to you, Squirrel Mistress!'

'Have you spoken to him at all since . . .?' Rupert inquired, keeping his voice low in case my father were anywhere in the offing.

'Since Squirrel ratted on him? Yes. He told me the police

had called on him. He kept jabbering that he "didn't do nothin'". I told him he should have given her a good beating!'

'You didn't really say that, did you?' Rupert demanded, a look of disbelief and consternation on his face.

'Ah don't be stupid,' my brother intoned. 'I don't tell half eejits to beat up my sister.' He looked at me severely, adding, 'Even if she does deserve it!'

Three weeks into their holiday Aunt Isabelle and Rupert were summoned home by my Uncle Alex who phoned and demanded their return. Aunt Isabelle spoke with her husband on the phone and said she was staying on. I heard her stiff, nervous voice say, 'Well, no actually Alex, I *won't* be coming back for the time being . . .' Her voice had the quality of an automaton, as though the whole of her energy were being channelled into her will. But she was ordered to send Rupert home immediately. He was to fly to Washington where his father would meet him.

'I don't see why he can't stay with me,' I heard her say to my mother in one of their whispered confidences on which I routinely eavesdropped. 'After all, I'm his mother and he could go to school in Ireland.'

But my mother shook her head. 'Isabelle, he needs continuity of schooling . . . and Alex would never pay the fees for an Irish boarding school, would never agree. Everything would have to be settled; you'd have to be receiving alimony and support for Rupert . . . How would you live otherwise? And do you really know your own mind . . .? And what about Mount Wexford? Alex would never allow Rupert to grow up somewhere else . . .'

I didn't know what alimony was, except that it was obviously something to do with money. But I could see that there was trouble in my aunt's life.

Rupert became stonily quiet when told he had to go home. I expected disappointment, but I sensed in him a desperation that astonished me. He was needed in Mount Wexford, he explained, and I knew immediately that he was trying to excuse his father's peremptory summons.

'You're only a kid!' Seán exclaimed. 'How can you be needed?'

71

'I help with the horses . . .' He looked at us miserably. 'Anyway, I have to go back to school in a few weeks . . . when Mom comes home.'

He looked at his mother when he said this, a hopeful, doubting, vulnerable look, but she seemed far away in her own world.

On the last full day of Rupert's stay with us, my father chartered Jack Leahy's boat and he and the boys went out fishing in the bay. I would have liked to have gone, but when I suggested it the boys were dismissive and my father dubious. 'You can come if you really want, Áine, but think of what it will be like . . . Five boys, Jack Leahy and me . . . that little boat of his will be full to capacity . . .'

They were gone all day, a wonderful burning day. I tidied the boot room to please my mother, read in the shade, and towards evening kept a look out for Jack's boat, the *Kestrel* as she appeared from behind Inishdrum, heading for the small harbour of Rockfleet about three miles away. My mother drove down to the harbour to collect the returning seafarers and took me with her. She was pleased with me today, because the boot room was ordered as it had not been for years, with the wellingtons arranged in rows and the raincoats hung according to seniority, and all the bits and pieces of holiday junk, like punctured rafts and lilos, neatly stacked. For the first time in ages things in this room were get-attable. Mrs Maloney expressed pleasure at my handiwork, and willingly drove her car to the harbour behind my mother to help bring the family home.

The fishermen came ashore with sunburned arms and faces. Jack straddled his boat and the pier and handed the boys ashore, his face gleaming and red from the sun, and his grin showing a few blackened teeth sticking out of his gums like old tombstones. Simon chattered with excitement as the catch of mackerel and ray was handed up and put into the boot. My father and the twins got into our car. Mrs Maloney took the others. The smell of fish made me hold my nose all the way home.

'Jack took us first to where the mackerel were, and I caught fourteen!' Simon informed us in the kitchen when we got back to the house.

72

'You didn't catch as many as we did,' the twins said, almost in unison. 'They were simply leaping onto our hooks . . . Once, I caught four at the same time.'

'And then Jack hauled up the anchor,' Simon continued, 'and brought us to another spot in the bay, and he anchored the boat again and he baited our hooks with bits of mackerel and told us to put down our lines until we felt the bottom, and then I got a bite and it was heavy . . . and I hauled it in . . . and what do you think I had caught?'

'You didn't haul it in, you little faggot,' Seán said. 'Rupert had to help you . . .'

'It was a ray . . . this size,' Simon said.

Mrs Maloney good-humouredly seized on the fish and cleaned them. The ray wings were hung from the clothes line in the garden to rid them of ammonia and the mackerel were filleted and baked for supper. Gráinne had dropped over earlier and my mother had invited her to come back for the meal. Seán was obviously delighted when he saw her. His demeanour changed, became gentle.

'Guess what the best catch of the day was?' he asked his audience at supper.

I shook my head. My parents shook their heads.

'You mean there was something more?' Aunt Isabelle intoned. 'Something bigger . . .?'

'Rupert managed to catch a seagull!' Seán announced to general laughter.

Rupert nodded a little lugubriously, and looked around the table. 'The gulls were swooping over the boat and when I threw out my line one got hooked. He wasn't very friendly,' Rupert added, 'opening his big old beak and trying to bite Jack when he tried to get the hook out of his mouth.'

'Know why he was worried?' Simon demanded sententiously. 'He'd never seen an American before. Ha ha . . .'

'Oh God,' Seán intoned, 'the Pupa is as bad as the Squirrel when he tries to be funny.'

'I wish I had come too,' I ventured after a while, for it all seemed such fun, and to have missed it seemed suddenly like a tragedy.

'It's not for girls,' my little brother said with triumphant

73

male superiority, 'it's only for men!'

He was sitting across the table from me and I aimed a kick at his nine-year-old shins, getting him fair and square on the knee so that he yelped in pain and started to wail. 'She kicked me, Mummy!' he howled. 'She kicked me on the knee . . . Oh my poor knee.'

I tried to look innocent, but my father, who was tired after the day at sea and out of sorts for reasons of his own, said abruptly, 'Go to bed, Áine . . .'

It had happened again, the banishment that I dreaded. I knew remonstrance would be useless, so I obeyed and left the room, shutting the door behind me. But I did not intend to go to bed, where I would be prey to whatever horrors chose to haunt my dreams. Instead I crept into the drawing room for the purpose of hiding in the curtained 'sewing room', quite prepared to sleep there for the night. I could not bear my lonely room; I was scared of the timber wolf who once again had taken up nightly residence beneath my bed; I was terrified of the ghoul of my dream who now, in the dead of night, often lurked in the niche by the fireplace. I knew the old tapestry curtain of the 'sewing room' would conceal my presence, and I would be able to revel in parental companionship without the adults being aware of my presence.

The fire in the hearth had settled into a mixture of yellow ash and glowing incandescence. I threw a few more sods into the grate, and then I retreated to the curtained alcove, leaving myself a view of the room from the gap where the curtain did not fully meet the edge of the curtain rail.

My father came into the room alone, seated himself in his customary armchair by the fire and with a private sigh stared into the smoking fire. For a moment I toyed with the idea of revealing myself and perhaps getting a moment's attention and absolution, but I quickly thought better of it. Aunt Isabelle came in and seated herself on the couch. She was joined by my mother, who poured three brandies from the bottle on the small sofa table by the window, and handed them around. I was afraid she would look in my direction, but she did not. Once seated, her back was to me and I could breathe.

Rupert put his head in to say goodnight and then withdrew,

shutting the drawing-room door. The panels at the back of the door had been decorated many years before with a medley of painted roses, pink and faded crimson, and pansies which had once been violet, and were still very pretty.

I heard Rupert's laugh in the hall and the voices of my brothers. The aromatic warmth from the fire, which I could glimpse from my hiding place – it had put out new spears of flame – permeated the room. There was silence for a while, the rustle of my mother's magazine, Aunt Isabelle's occasional little cough, as though she was constantly on the point of saying something and then changing her mind, followed by the small sound of her brandy glass being replaced on the table.

'Will you have another brandy, Isabelle?' my mother asked.

My aunt replied, using an Irish idiom, that yes, she would have another one, 'For the night that was in it.'

Now as no particular night was 'in it' this was patently an excuse, but my mother poured her another brandy and my aunt sipped it greedily.

I saw my father's face in three-quarter profile. The firelight glowed on it, but he was not reading, just sipping his own brandy with a preoccupied mien as though troubled; his eyes dwelt on his sister from time to time, and he frowned privately and turned his gaze to the fire.

Suddenly Aunt Isabelle said in a slightly slurred voice, 'I hope Áine is all right.'

My father looked at her with irritation. 'Why shouldn't she be?'

'She's a very imaginative child . . .'

'So it seems . . . But she won't have any more trouble from that Shaw creature. I had the old cottage on the headland levelled today. That should keep him away from the place.' He glanced at my mother. 'You'll have to make sure she stays around the house.'

I put my hand across my mouth. I heard the growl of the sea outside, and felt the night pressing against the house like a predator. What have you done, Daddy? I asked in silence. What have you done? You should not have done that.

There was silence for a few moments and then my aunt spoke again. 'Noel, does this remind you of when we were children? Do you remember how Daddy used to read poetry around the fire of an evening?'

'Of course I remember it. He only stopped it after you ran off to Gretna Green!'

There was silence and then my aunt said in a voice full of attempted camaraderie, 'What was the name of that poem about the young girl who was sent to bring the cattle home and who was caught by the tide?'

My father sighed.

'Can you not remember?' my aunt pressed on with brittle gaiety and my father growled, '"The Sands of Dee", Isabelle. "The bloody Sands of Dee".'

'I used to imagine I was the little girl. But of course the name was wrong and *Isabelle* wouldn't really scan . . .' And then she drew a deep breath and said in a voice full of drama and nostalgia:

'Oh Mary go and call the cattle home
And call the cattle home
And call the cattle home
Across the Sands at Dee,
The western wave was wild and dank with foam,
And all alone went she.'

She looked at my mother. 'She drowned, poor thing,' she whispered. And then she continued in the same voice, louder and projected as though she were on stage, as though she were insisting on being heard in something:

'They rowed her in across the rolling foam
The cruel, crawling foam
The cruel, hungry foam
To her grave beside the sea . . .'

There was an expostulation from my father's chair. 'For the love of God, Isabelle! If you must quote poetry can't you think of something better than that old morbid drivel?'

My aunt fell silent. My mother looked at her with a concerned gaze and gave my father a reproachful look. In the

76

ensuing silence the air was full of something unspoken that longed to be said, something the two women might have said if the time had been ripe and the ear sympathetic.

Suddenly my father announced, 'I have to go back to Dublin the day after tomorrow.'

'But you have holidays for another week!' my mother exclaimed. 'Why do you never take your full holiday?'

'Something's come up in the office,' my father said. 'I phoned today. It seems Diskin Builders have had a bit of bad luck. A building they were shoring up in Lower Mount Street collapsed. They're blaming the sub-contractors, but I'd better get back to see what's happening.'

'But your office has five lawyers!' my mother said. 'That's what they're paid for – to cope with things that come up.'

'They're our biggest clients, Joyce.'

'Anyway, there's lawyers and there's lawyers,' Aunt Isabelle offered almost diffidently after a moment. 'I suppose I'll have to get one, won't I, Noel, if I'm going to divorce Alex.' She said this with a little-girl voice that may have been designed to awaken whatever gallantry lurked in the male breast. But she had mistaken her man.

My father sighed. 'For God's sake, Isabelle, wake up!' he said suddenly. 'You're forty. You can't just go gadding around the world as though you were a teenager with a rucksack. You'll have to make up your mind. If you want to make the break from Alex you have to tell him, get a lawyer, an American lawyer mind. It's no use looking at me,' he added severely, 'because I'm an Irish lawyer and this is a Catholic country and we do not have divorce here, and we do not pay maintenance to deserting wives. Then you must find yourself somewhere to live and prepare for battle. Because if I know your husband he won't give you a pennypiece without a fight.'

'I could always get a job, I suppose,' Aunt Isabelle said in softly articulated despair, like someone to whom male deliverance had always been one of the immutable axioms of existence and had found too late that it had not only betrayed her but left her helpless. 'But I've never worked in my life.'

My father clicked his tongue. 'Bella, Bella, cop yourself on! What sort of a job could you get? What qualifications do you

77

have, what experience of the work place?'

My mother was strangely silent during this exchange. I knew from the way she sat so still that her mind was churning; for a moment I even sensed the lines of comparison she was drawing, between her life and that of her sister-in-law, and the unease that had dogged me all this holiday filled me with a kind of queasiness. I knew her better than my father did. I sensed her hunger, her anger, and her perennial, crippling hope.

After a while the women said they were going to bed and left the room, leaving my father on his own by the fire. I made no move, being fearful of discovery, although I longed to go to him, sit on his lap and put my arms around his neck, bury my nose in the heathery, male scent of his tweed jacket, bask in his love. I had memories of this from several years before, when I was seven and had fallen down the stairs and he had picked me up, of being hugged by him and carried to the sitting-room settee. It was then, at close quarters, that I had sensed the great, privileged space men inhabited. My father's strength of body and mind, the scent of his skin and clothes, above all his certainty, were like a country of the blessed. He represented the safest place in my universe; only he could protect me from the timber wolf and the ghoul, but there could be no question of my being able to tell him about them. His mind was logical and intolerant of what he called nonsense, and I knew he would only tell me not to let my imagination run away with me. He would demand in a matter of fact voice, 'Now tell me this, Áine, do you really believe that any of these phantasms inhabit your room? Because if you do would you please show me where.'

I would have to say no. It's true that I *knew* they were not really there. But reality was always thin and powerless against the terrors of the night and an imagination which had not yet learned to dampen its vitality.

In due course my father put up the spark guard and left the fire. He turned off the lamp and I found myself alone in the dark. Leaving the curtained alcove, I tip-toed to the couch and settled down by the fire. It glowed comfortingly at me. The room was still full of grown-up power, the punch of adult command that they themselves either never noticed, or took for granted, although everything else in creation was aware of it, animals great and small, ghouls, timber wolves, children, everything. I had taken the old worn rug from the sewing room and nestled beneath it, and soon I felt myself drifting into sleep.

When I awoke the fire was dead, except for a few forlorn sparks among the ashes. The room was appreciably cooler, and the rug had fallen to the floor. I heard the murmur of the sea through the open window, and the verse my aunt had earlier recited returned to me, as though by way of warning about something that lay hidden in the folds of Time:

> They rowed her in across the rolling foam
> The cruel, crawling foam,
> The cruel, hungry foam . . .

I listened to the sea sounds of swish and retreat and swish again, as though I had never heard them. The sea was talking, but now I saw it as cruel and crawling and hungry. I retrieved the old rug, pulled it over my head and burrowed into the couch.

It was only a few minutes later that I heard the sound outside the window. I surfaced from my rug, but I dared not pull back the curtain to investigate. My blood froze. What was it? I waited, listening, and then, as I was about to dismiss it as a figment of my imagination, I heard it again.

Possibilities came crowding. It might be the ghost of my great-great-grandmother whom I had once seen flitting across the garden. It might be Teddy come to see my father, although why he should come at this hour was unclear. It might be my kitten Tabbs who was not allowed in the house at night, and had her private quarters in a box that had once held several dozen clementines, which I had kitted out with an old jumper for her comfort. It might even be, and here my imagination expanded into lurid possibility, some monster that had crawled out of the sea.

The sound came again, stealthily, but this time it was no longer outside the front window. Now it had moved to the side of the house, where the curtains had not been pulled on the bay window, a shuffling of gravel and stones as though they were disturbed by furtive feet. I forced myself off the couch and crept to the old window seat, and as I did so I saw Aeneas Shaw's white face suddenly press itself up against the glass.

For a moment he did not see me, for his gaze encompassed the room blindly, but I must have started, for I was very frightened. I knew my father had destroyed his ancestral home, the shrine where he put wild flowers, where he slept in the summer nights. I knew he had come for his revenge.

His gaze suddenly fixed itself on me and, even in the gloom of night, I could see that his expression changed from one of avid curiosity to a ferocious venom. He communicated all this without moving a muscle. It was in his immobile intensity, in the fixed, hungry expression in his eyes. He stood there and stared at me. Afterwards I remembered some kind of whiteness, as though I wanted to blank it all out. I could never recall his face.

I stood as though paralyzed. The scream which formed in my throat was not uttered; I stared back at him and our eyes locked. In that moment he knew me in some strange way, had my scent, like a bloodhound.

But the spell broke and I ran from the room, raced up the dark staircase with only the dim light from the glass in the roof to show the way, my heart thundering until I thought it would burst. My room was directly above the drawing room and I paused in the doorway and thought I still heard Aeneas shuffling around below, imagined the cunning with which he would push up the sash of the unlocked window and steal into the house. Or he might find a ladder in the stable yard and climb to my small, parapeted balcony while I slept. The timber wolf and the ghoul were relegated to second-class bogeymen in view of the presence of the real one down below. I stood at the door of my bedroom. I didn't even have the courage to cross the room and take Rastus from under my pillow. Of course I thought of waking my parents, of screaming. But Aeneas would simply disappear into the night and I would have to explain why, yet again, I was subjecting the family to my 'imaginings'.

I crept back to the landing and sat for a while on the top step of the great oak staircase, listening to the sleeping house. Down below me in the hall I could make out the poor dead

80

moose and his huge, dusty antlers. Like the houses of my recent nightmare the place seemed to snuffle around me, as though conspiring with my enemy to find me. There were creaks in the floorboards, small sounds behind me in the landing leading to my parents' room. And then came a sudden, abrupt rustle above my head; something dark winged its way along the gallery. The terror had almost knocked the breath from my body before I realized it was only Dracula, but for some reason, probably because my nerves were on edge, I was terrorized at the sight of his outstretched black wings. I looked around at the closed bedroom doors, stout mahogany portals all of them. How I longed to run into my parents' room and hide between them, wedge myself in their warmth and sleep till morning! But I dreaded the infamy. What a laughing stock I would be if the boys found out. My mother would probably send me back to my own bed anyway, on the basis that I was a big girl now. So, in desperation, as I felt I would rather die than trouble any of my brothers, I took the only other possible alternative, found the only other potential port in this storm; I went to Rupert's door and slowly opened it. In a moment I had closed it again and was standing in his room.

Rupert had been given the blue room, so named because the wallpaper was Victorian block paper of Wedgwood blue, although faded and damaged, and because it had a worn, blue Chinese carpet. This room had a solid mahogany bed, with a double mattress. He had not bothered to draw the faded old curtains and the window admitted the dim moonlight.

My cousin was fast asleep. I stood stock still and listened to his breathing, the deep, regular respiration of the healthily comatose. I could make out his shape in the gloom, and the furnishings – the marble-topped toilet table, the wardrobe, the brass candlesticks on the mantelpiece. I did not want to wake Rupert. I was just grateful to be in his room, to be safe. I felt like a hero I had seen in a film who was being chased by Indians and had just made it to the fort in the nick of time.

There was an armchair near the window with some clothes thrown on it and I thought perhaps I could sit there until the dawn and then creep away. But as I moved to accomplish this purpose Rupert stirred, moved sharply and was then still. His breathing was no longer audible and I knew he was awake. He sat up, demanded abruptly and sternly, 'Who's there?'

'Shssh . . .' I warbled. 'I'm very sorry, Rupert . . . I didn't mean to wake you up.'

'Áine . . .' he whispered crossly, 'what on earth are you doing here?'

'I was downstairs . . . and I heard a sound outside and saw a face at the window . . . it was Aeneas. He looked at me so terribly, Rupert. And I was afraid to go to bed, because he might get in the window.'

Rupert sighed, got out of bed in his striped pyjamas. He went to his window, pushed up the sash and looked out.

'I don't see anyone. You must have been imagining things. What time is it? You should be in bed!'

'I cannot go to bed,' I said in a voice so weary and resolute that he became silent, as though suddenly aware that my perspective was powerfully real at least to me and that it had almost overwhelmed me. 'Please let me sit in your armchair. I'll be very quiet and you can go back to sleep.'

'But . . . you can't stay in my room all night!'

'Why not?'

'The grown ups wouldn't like it.'

'But they won't even know. And I'm so frightened, Rupert! I cannot go back out there . . . And Dracula is flying and he gave me a fright.' I was now trembling, although my voice was very quiet.

Rupert touched me. His hand was warm and comforting beyond belief. 'That damn bat!' he said, clicking his tongue. 'I'll tell your father about him and he'll deal with him.'

'No! No! He'd kill him! Don't you understand, Rupert? You have to be careful about what you say in this family.'

In my mind's eye I saw Dracula's corpse, ridiculously small with his wings folded and still. Suddenly I wept, sobbed hopelessly in semi-silence.

Rupert, shocked by my tears, bent down to comfort me. 'You're cold,' he whispered. 'You're freezing. And you're trembling . . .' He knelt on the floor, and put his arms around me. 'Áine, please don't cry. I won't say a word about Dracula.' He drew me to the bed. 'Get in there. It's warm.'

82

I sat on the edge of the armchair and took off my shoes, then jumped fully clothed into the bed, burrowing beneath the bedclothes. The bed was soft and warm and had a faint Rupert scent. My cousin got back in beside me, held me in his arms. And after a while, cocooned, safe in this unexpected paradise of the blessed, I fell asleep.

When the dawn came I woke, but for a moment I did not know where I was. I put my hand out for Rastus. When I realized I was in bed with Rupert, I wanted to laugh, but I lay still, savouring the ecstasy. Rupert had his back to me now. I could make out the navy-blue stripe on his pyjamas and the short hair at the nape of his neck. And as I lay there, warm and safe against him, the first dim stirring of something new entered my life. I wanted to touch him, to reach out and stroke the fine hairs on his neck. He was not asleep, for he suddenly turned to look at me, as though subliminally alerted that I was awake.

'Are you all right now?' he whispered. 'It's nearly day.'

I sat up. 'Thanks . . . I'm sorry I ruined your sleep, Rupert . . . Sometimes I get really scared at night.'

'It's very lonely for you here,' he said after a moment. 'Why don't you tell your mother that you're scared to sleep on your own in that big room?'

'I have to be sensible. I have to do what's good for me.'

'But it's not good for you! You were shaking!'

'I'll go back to my own room now,' I said, 'it's the dawn and I'm all right now.'

'Áine,' he whispered as I reached the door.

I turned. 'Yes?'

'That Aeneas Shaw guy wasn't really at the drawing-room window last night, was he? You were just imagining it?'

'Oh no!' I said. 'He was there. He wants to get me. He hates me . . .'

'Why didn't you tell them the truth? He should be locked up.'

'Don't tell anyone, Rupert. Don't tell them I came to your room because I was scared. Don't say anything about Aeneas. I'd only get into more trouble. And Seán would say I was a

83

scaredy cat. And no one will believe me about Aeneas any more anyway!'

He sighed. 'I warned you. But if that's what you want, all right! You'd better go back to your room now.'

I hesitated, then returned with a rush and kissed his cheek.

He held my head against him for a moment. 'Tigerlily,' he whispered, 'you are braver than I am.'

It was then, glancing at his chest where his pyjama top was open, I saw the faint weals across his skin. 'Rupert!' I said, drawing back and staring at his chest. 'What are those marks? What happened to you?'

Rupert rapidly closed his pyjamas jacket and said, 'Nothing, nothing. Just an old accident.'

I went back to the door, opened it and tip-toed down the landing to my room. The bed was cold. I was still in my jeans and jumper, although I had forgotten my shoes which I had left behind in Rupert's room. I put my hand under the pillow for Rastus, clutched him and after a while, as the first fitful sunlight softly flooded into my room, I went back to sleep.

'Aren't you going to say goodbye to Rupert?' my mother's voice said what seemed a long time later. I woke and knew that the morning was well advanced. 'Your father is driving him to Shannon to catch his plane.'

I jumped out of bed.

'Did you go to bed in your clothes?' my mother demanded crossly. 'What kind of a little girl are you?'

'No . . . I was up earlier and then went back to bed.'

'Where are your shoes?'

I knew where they were – under Rupert's bed. 'I don't know,' I said. 'But I don't need them!'

I raced past her out the door and down the stairs. Rupert was in the hall. He looked up at me as I came running. I can still remember how pinched his face seemed, how different from its sleepy warmth of the early morning when I had awoken beside him. I saw strain in him, etched into his identity, that had not been apparent during the holiday, or perhaps had been shelved. He did not seem entirely collected, as though the effort of parting was suddenly too much. To the others, standing around in the hall, Seán and Simon ready to go in the car to Shannon, my parents and his silent mother, it might have seemed like the understandable upset at parting, but it struck me with fear. I wanted to kiss him, to jostle him back to exasperation, to the boy who had been ready with sternest censure and uncanny gentleness. But I dared not. Part of me wondered why he seemed to have no interest at all in a reunion with his father.

'Will you come to see me in America?' he whispered when I put out my hand awkwardly to say goodbye.

'Some day.'

'Promise.'

'I promise,' I whispered, surprised at his insistence. And then I added, because his answer mattered and I wanted to jolly him, 'I hoped you liked it here, Rupert Bear?'

'What do you think?' He kept his voice low. 'I feel I belong here now.' He gave me a small, confidential smile. 'You needn't think you're the only one, you know.' And then he added, with the flash of a grin, 'Tigerlily!'

Aunt Isabelle came hurrying. 'Come along Rupert; you'll miss the plane.'

When the car was rattling across the cattle grid my mother muttered to herself, 'That boy is carrying too much ... It's not right ...' She turned to look at me. 'Put something on your feet, Áine.'

I went upstairs, retrieved my runners from under Rupert's bed. I lingered in his room for a moment, running the palm of my hand along his pillow, and over the bottom sheet which still held the imprint of our bodies. I laid my cheek against his pillow. I had a secret now, and I hugged it to me with relish. When I was coming out of the room, runners in hand, I met my mother on the landing.

'Did you leave your shoes in Rupert's room?' she demanded, looking at the grubby footwear. 'Why did you do that?'

I shrugged. 'For luck,' I said airily. 'He's a lucky person.'

She seemed taken aback. 'Do you think so? What a strange child you are.'

I went downstairs, but my mother called after me, 'Áine ... what did Rupert call you when he was leaving? Something odd?'

I stood on the stairs and looked up at her. 'Oh it's just a joke, Mummy.'

I went to the kitchen, poured a glass of milk and took it with me into the library, sat by the French window. I wanted to be in this room again where I had shared my greatest secret with the only boy who had ever been nice to me. I mentally traced his journey to Shannon, wondered at his pinched face on his departure. I will go to Virginia to see you, Rupert Bear, I promised in silence. Someday I will.

That evening when my father returned from Shannon he took me aside.

'I saw that odd looking Shaw fellow in the village on the way back. At least he won't be able to use that ruined cottage as an excuse for any more of his shenanigans.' He regarded me closely as he asked, 'Have you seen him since that incident?'

I thought of the night before. But all I said, schooling my face to avoid giving myself away, was 'No Daddy.' What else could I say? I was talking to my father, someone capable of terrifyingly decisive action; someone who, to my mind, did not really know the ramifications of what he did. What else would he do if I were to tell him the truth?

I did see Aeneas Shaw once more. On the last day of our holiday, as we left Dunbeg behind and rolled down the avenue, I turned and looked out the back window. His pale face suddenly loomed out of the rhododendrons beside the gate, and stared after the departing car with unblinking fixity. I ducked down on the seat, to the annoyance of my siblings who were stacked in the back like sardines. But when I surfaced again and took a last look as the car turned the corner of the road, I saw him standing at the gate and looking after us with the same preternatural interest.

But the open road was ahead. For the first time in my life I was glad to be going back to Dublin.

Chapter Seven

On our return from Clew Bay Aunt Isabelle stayed in our house in Dublin. We lived in a redbrick Victorian terraced house on Upper Drumcondra Road, almost across the street from the Catholic Archbishop's palace. I went to school at Our Lady's College, St Stephen's Green, catching the number eleven bus every morning at the top of Clonliffe Road. My father's practice was on the Quays, but he generally left too early for me to get a lift with him.

My brothers were all at school in Belvedere College, and, as it was not far, they either walked or got the bus, depending on the weather. I hated getting the same bus with them, and was sometimes late for school as a result. My life was back to normal now, more or less. My nights were untroubled by nightmares; Dublin did not provoke them. If I woke I heard the desultory traffic in the road outside and the room was never completely dark because of the street lamps. Sometimes, when I could not sleep, I would creep downstairs to the sitting room and listen to tapes, sometimes eschewing pop music in favour of the majestic classical pieces that gave me a certain peace. I learned to love Handel and Mozart and would listen on headphones, wrapped in a rug on the couch, while the occasional car went by on Drumcondra Road and the house slept. Once or twice my mother surprised me at this in the dead of night and sent me back to bed. My mother no longer spent hours conversing with Aunt Isabelle. She had household duties to deal with now, whether she liked it or not, dinners to prepare, and a house to keep after her own fashion.

'You need something more than domesticity,' I heard my aunt tell her sotto voce. 'How can anyone be expected to live as a servant in her own home? Noel was always a selfish boy,

87

would always take everything you did for him completely for granted. Mummy spoiled him.'

My mother became oddly silent, no longer declaiming on the political story of the moment, and sometimes banged pots and pans when she was alone in the kitchen with a spirit that had nothing to do with culinary effort. When my father said to her one evening before going out again, in his matter of fact, preoccupied-with-important-matters voice, 'Joyce, I need a clean shirt . . . There are none in my drawer . . .' my mother erupted.

'I'm not a servant. I have enough to do with all these children of yours! Why don't you launder your own bloody shirts?'

Now this was identified by my father as a challenge and he reacted to it coldly. 'Very well,' he said. He dug all his dirty shirts out of the laundry basket and sent all of them to the local laundry.

Not long after this my mother, who had once been reasonably fluent in French, enrolled in a conversation class in the Alliance Française in Kildare Street. The classes did her good. She would sit in the dining room after supper, doing homework, reaching for the French dictionary, trying out phrases on me. '*Alors, comme tu es paresseuse*,' she informed me one evening when I cavilled at being put through my French paces just when a film I wanted to watch had started on telly.

'Who is your teacher, Mummy?' I demanded, startled by her fluency. 'She must be delighted with you.'

'My teacher is a young Frenchman.'

'Oh really . . . what age is he?'

'How do I know . . . about thirty-nine, I suppose.'

'That's not young. Is he very charming?' I added slyly.

'Yes . . . I suppose he is!' She glanced at me, laughed in spite of herself and pursed her lips.

As the term progressed my mother took to attending classes in the evening, instead of the morning. No one commented on this, nor did they comment when she began taking more than usual pains with her appearance, and always looked glamorous when she left the house. But I think everyone noticed the change in her; everyone, that is, except my father.

Aunt Isabelle's presence in the house became a strain. She

vacillated between finalizing the break with her husband and sporadic bursts of re-discovering him. Certain places in Dublin triggered memories. 'When I was in College Green today I saw the doorway Alex and I snogged in on the way home from a party,' I overheard her tell my mother breathlessly, like a little girl imparting some earth-shattering confidence. I listened to everything that passed between the grown ups, avid to understand their mystery.

Perhaps my poor aunt was hoping her husband would come for her, bear her back across the sea with the passion which had swept her off her feet at eighteen, convince her that her life was on course and not simply withering on the vine. I heard my parents discussing her one Saturday in mid-December. She had been on the phone to Mount Wexford to see if Rupert would be allowed to join her in Ireland for Christmas, but his father would not permit it. This led to a crying jag on her part. I heard her sobbing in her room, and crept downstairs to tell my mother, but my parents were already discussing her and I stayed at my old vantage point in the dining room and observed them through the chink in the dividing door.

'She's a liability,' my father said. 'She can't stay here indefinitely. Alex's written to me. He says if she does not come home soon he will divorce her.'

My mother said, 'You don't understand how difficult it's been for her, how unhappy she's been . . . Alex treats her as though she's part of the wallpaper. She had almost nothing to do and is surrounded by servants who spy on her.'

'So she's paranoid into the bargain,' my father exclaimed, with a snort of disgust. 'She is lucky enough to have servants and all she does is complain!'

'She doesn't *complain*. But I can read through the lines. Alex sees other women; she always knows when he has a new one because then he gives her presents. She's alone most of the time, in that big house. She's alone in a country where you can't go *anywhere* without travelling for hundreds, even thousands, of miles; she's in pain, for God's sake. And she's your sister!'

My father clicked his tongue. 'You're being absurdly partisan, Joyce.'

My mother bit her lip. Then she said, dropping her voice, and speaking with a brutal inflexion new to her, 'And there's something more, if the truth be told, although I don't expect *you* to believe it. That husband of hers knocks her around!'

It was clear from the ensuing silence that my father was rocked by this intelligence. But his voice had its usual rational tone when he replied: 'Has it ever entered your head that she might have concocted her stories? She was always one for alternative realities. And as for being alone, well, she has only herself to thank. She ran away with him, made her bed . . . When I think of how distraught our parents were . . .'

'Is she to be punished for ever for something she did when she was eighteen?' my mother cried. 'It's so easy to blame her when the whole damn system was designed to make her impotent. She feels plundered! She's trying to show that she has not lived in vain; she is trying to show that she has power of some kind.'

'*Power!*' my father snorted. 'What kind of power are you talking about? She's a married woman.'

My mother's face darkened, and her expression reflected a mélange of emotions too powerful for me to unscramble.

'You have a daughter!' she said shortly. 'What will she think if she ever hears you speak like this? Or is it the case that, knowing men as you must know them, you want her too to be powerless?'

My father did not reply. Not because he was struck dumb by her polemic, but because there was so little entente between them now. This absence of common ground, her longing on the one hand to find it and on the other her sense of outrage that he made no attempt to reach her, was the source of increasing domestic tension, like the current in the air before an electric storm. But it was the last disparaging remark I ever heard him make about women.

My mother muttered one day to my aunt that it was very hard on Rupert spending Christmas at Mount Wexford without her, but the latter said in her slightly breathless way, a voice laced with desperation, 'But I can't go back, Joyce. If I do I'll never get away again. This is my last chance!'

90

Rupert sent a long letter to his mother, apparently telling her he was fine and that she was to stay in Ireland for Christmas, and saying he was doing well at school. 'Look, Áine,' she said. 'He's enclosed an envelope for you as well.'

I took this away to open in private. It was a home-made card with pasted figures of Rupert Bear and Tigerlily in a winter wonderland, and a small rhyming couplet, whose tone gave the lie to the cheerful content of his letter to his mother. But I comforted myself with the knowledge that I would have the chance to speak to him when Aunt Isabelle phoned him on Christmas Day.

My father marched his entire household off to Midnight Mass on Christmas Eve, and we all sang the carols and *Adeste Fidelis* with good voice, returning home in festive mood. But the following afternoon, when my aunt phoned Mount Wexford and tried to speak to Rupert, her husband refused to let her talk to him, and her grief at this threw a pall over the day. I went to my room, fighting with my disappointment, taking down my cousin's little home-made card from my mantelpiece, and studying the two small figures in the snowscape. I read his words again:

> *But Rupert, feeling very low,*
> *Finds Tigerlily in the snow.*

In the New Year, Aunt Isabelle took a secretarial course, even got a succession of part-time jobs. But she was not a good secretary, being highly-strung, and prone to bursting into tears if she made a mistake.

When she was sacked for the third time my father said, 'Isabelle, for God's sake, you can't go on like this.'

She dressed herself up one evening, said she was going out on a date. My mother was at a soirée in the Alliance at the time and my father was working late, but I felt instinctively that neither of them would have approved of her escort. He arrived at eight in a dark blue BMW, a middle-aged man who looked at my aunt as though she were some succulent fruit on a branch just within reach.

I was awake when she came home around midnight. I heard the car pull up outside and got out of bed. Through a chink in my curtain I watched the balding, middle-aged man open the passenger door, saw my still girlish aunt get out and walk with him to the front door. He put his arm around her. I heard her voice, and his, then the door closed and he walked back to his car and drove away. From downstairs came the sound of raised voices. I went into the dimly-lit landing and peered through the banisters.

'Who is that man?' my father demanded of his sister. I saw Aunt Isabelle's face. She was glowing.

'That is none of your business, Noel!'

'It is my business. You're my sister and I'm not having you make a fool of yourself, traipsing around Dublin with married men.'

'How do you know he's married?'

'Well, is he or isn't he?'

My aunt was silent.

'You obviously don't even know, Isabelle,' my father said after a moment, 'whether he is or is not! And you obviously don't realize that you are giving out distress signals like a fish in extremis. Every shark in the ocean will be after you! And even you must know what sharks do with fish.'

The day after this contretemps Father D'Arcy, the parish priest and a good friend of my father, paid us one of his rare visits. He was a spare, middle-aged man, with dry patchy skin, sun-damaged from a stint in Africa. He spoke to Aunt Isabelle softly. 'I'm marrying two young couples on Saturday. Isn't the sacrament of marriage wonderful . . . giving people the grace to be together through thick and thin, to undertake a sacred life commitment.' He lowered his voice. 'Don't you agree, Mrs Lyall?'

Aunt Isabelle paled. 'Yes,' she murmured. 'Of course.'

And Father D'Arcy spoke some more about the dignity and indissolubility of marriage and the will of God. Not long after this Isabelle, her face stained with tears, wrote, at my father's behest, a letter to her husband. I saw a draft of it on her dressing table and read it without any compunction. Blissfully above all notions of honour, I investigated everything. I knew more about the grown ups than they dreamed – although it would be a long time before my knowledge became understanding.

Dear Alex,
I will be going home on the 16th, flying to New York and then to Norfolk. Please don't be angry with me. I needed these months in Dublin; it's so long since I was home. I know it was very silly of me to think of staying on, because, of course, my real home is with you. I promise I will never leave you again without your permission.
All my love,
Isabelle.

I was pushing eleven now, but my blood was up and I felt a kind of terror. *I will never leave you again without your permission.*

Aunt Isabelle finally went home in April. Some days before she left she brought me into her room, sat me down on the bed and gave me a present of a chain with a gold pendant in the shape of a heart.

'I have no daughter. I want you to have this and to think of me sometimes. I am going back to America. I would love you to visit me when you can. Would you like that, Áine?'

'Very much, Aunty Isabelle.'

'It is very pretty in Virginia this time of year,' she went on in a small voice, as though trying as much to enthrall herself as to educate me. 'The trees are in new leaf, standing up straight as masts, and the dogwood is in bloom . . . The dogwood is a wild rose,' she added, seeing my perplexed expression, 'like cherry blossom, only bigger. You can see it blooming through the forests . . . white and pink among the trees. The forest has not changed since the first white people created a settlement on the James River.' Her voice had a strange, spiritless monotone. 'There are wild geese and God knows what else in those forests. There is even a place called "The Great Dismal Swamp" with black bear, and bob cats and all sorts of wild things.

'You cannot imagine, Áine without going there, how vast America is, how limitless . . . It has a strange feel to it, older than Europe and as foreign as Mars! They call it the New World;

93

but it is not. It has a dimension before which overcrowded, overcivilized Europe is the real latecomer. You can still hear the echo of all those lost Indian tribes and the thunder of the buffalo that used to darken the plains.' She paused, added, 'It's just that *I* am lost there too . . .' She dropped her voice, added as though speaking to herself, 'But perhaps I would be lost anywhere.'

'But Aunty Isabelle . . .'

She smiled then as though suddenly recollecting my presence. 'I'm sure Rupert would be glad to see you,' she went on, changing her tone to one of ordinary conversational urbanity, 'introduce you to his friends and so on. Come and see me when they will let you go. All you have to do is phone me collect . . . Here, I'll give you my number,' and she wrote it down on a piece of paper.

I found this conversation strange and disturbing; but I found the prospect of visiting America exciting beyond belief.

'I'll ask Mummy and Daddy.'

'Don't say anything for the moment. I've overstayed my welcome here. But in a few years – when you are a bit older – you must come. You see,' she added, 'I think you and I were cut from the same cloth. We are both alone. We both feel things the others do not . . . Isn't that so, Áine? When we were in Dunbeg, for instance, you were greatly troubled, but I dared not try to help you. My help would have been worse than anything. I am not a lucky person.'

A shiver climbed my spine. Recollection came in a rush, of my great solitary room at Dunbeg, of the house at night when I dared myself to wander around it, of the sounds I had heard there, of what I had seen in the library and the face of Aeneas Shaw pressed up against the window of the drawing room in the dead of night. And although I just wanted to forget about him, the hairs rose at the back of my neck.

My aunt was observing me. 'Áine, you can tell me . . . did you ever see anything . . . strange at Dunbeg?'

'Strange, Aunt? Well, there was that queer man . . .'

'Oh I don't mean him, although he would give anyone the creeps. I mean anything *really* strange?'

When I was silent she added in a whisper, 'When I was a

94

little girl, we often stayed in Dunbeg for the summer. One night I decided to sleep in a little tent – one of those army surplus things your grandfather had bought to amuse us. It had been set up in the garden and I could not resist the prospect of a night under canvas, so I crept downstairs and out through the kitchen while everyone was asleep. It was a warm, moonlit night, and I lay down on the groundsheet with only a few old cushions and after a while I went to sleep. I don't know what woke me. I heard nothing, but I was suddenly aware that I was not alone in the garden.'

She glanced at me, but I was listening so intently that my face was immobile. 'I had left the tent flap open,' she continued, 'because it was so warm. I heard nothing except the sea; I could see nothing except moonlit shadows on the grass, and was about to call out, assuming that one of the family was also up, but just then I had the most powerful sensation that this presence was . . . not human!'

'An animal?'

'No. Neither human nor animal.'

'Did you see it?'

'I was too frightened to move; but after a little while something crossed my line of vision, a shadow, moving slowly . . .'

'Wearing white?' I whispered.

'Christ!' she exclaimed eagerly, looking into my face and gripping my shoulders. 'Did you see her too?'

For a moment I was tempted; but I feared the sequel. 'No . . .'

'The spirit – or whatever she was – turned as though she knew I saw her and then she raised her hand and beckoned. Her face was pale and she had such a cold little smile.'

Aunt Isabelle's eyes were staring and her breathing had quickened. 'Afterwards they told me it was a nightmare, but I don't think it was! And then your father told me I was crazy . . .' She put a hand to her hair, gave a short laugh. 'You don't think I'm crazy, do you Áine?'

'No . . . But Aunty Isabelle,' I added in a whisper, 'you said she beckoned. Did you follow her?'

Aunt Isabelle gave me a small secret smile and didn't answer. But the conversation put me in mind of standing in the library and telling Rupert of my own experience, while he touched my hand. And instantly a warmth filled me, a sense of belonging, a place in the universe. Rupert had found fault with me, had been angry with me; but he had neither ignored nor dismissed me.

'If I write a letter to Rupert will you give it to him?' I asked my aunt suddenly.

She nodded. 'He's in boarding school.' Her voice assumed a normal register, disappointed, perhaps, that I had not pursued with her the sequel to her spectral visitation, 'but I'll send it on.'

My aunt left Ireland for America a few days later with a letter from me to Rupert.

Dear Rupert,
Thanks for your card at Christmas. I hope your well. I'm well too. Tabbs is a cat now and is going to have kittnes. Do you remember Dunbeg? I was sorry youd to go home but you can come again if you want. Why dont you come to Dublin? It's not as much fun as Dunbeg, but their are queer things to see in the National Musmeum and some good picktures in the cinmeas.

Seán is still eating everything. The twins and Simon are well.
Love,
Áine.

During the days after my aunt's departure I often rehashed our conversation in my mind, but being aware of her excitability I wondered how much her story had gained in the telling. I was eleven years old now and reaching for judgement. And I did not want any confirmation of what I had seen at Dunbeg. What excited me now was the thought of America and Virginia with its primeval forests and flowering shrubs. But, secretly, I was aware that these thoughts only served as background to the memory of Rupert and the yearning that sometimes rose unbidden from the recesses of my heart.

This yearning was somewhat assuaged when he replied to my letter. His was very short:

Dear Áine

Thanks for your letter. Mom says you will come to see us sometime. I think about Dunbeg a lot and hope you've got over the scare you had there because of that crazy guy. People like him should be locked up. As you can see I'm writing this from school, a big redbricked 'academy' where they make us work. Here is a picture of you and me!

Love,
Rupert.

Gummed to the page was a cutting of Rupert Bear leaping over a gate, and the silken Tigerlily, her hands in her sleeves, looking on inscrutably.

The verse said:

> *But Rupert's brightened up no end*
> *For Tigerlily is his friend!*

My days at Our Lady's in the Green were numbered; I had moved into first year in the secondary school and was failing my exams. I was frequently admonished for day-dreaming in class – my maths teacher almost foamed at the mouth one day as she hissed: 'Áine O'Malley, if you're so interested in what's going on in the street . . . go out and stay there, for the love of God!'

'Áine dwells in cloudland,' was a comment on one of my reports. 'She's present in body only,' was another remark. 'I don't know where she goes, but it's not with us.' The final straw was the school report at the end of my first year advising my parents that, unless I pulled my socks up, I would 'not survive the school system'. When this arrived I was summoned to a parental council of war. My mother had already decided, in any case, that I would be better off in an all-female environment. She made this decision after Seán had invaded my room and written on my dressing-table mirror with the cheap, crimson lipstick I had acquired for experimentation purposes: 'Squirrels should be neither seen nor heard!'

I scrubbed at this daub and went downstairs to complain to

97

my mother. Seán was in the kitchen and I told him to stay out of my room.

'I can't stand it!' I said, turning to my mother. 'It's not fair. He's been writing on my mirror. He comes into my room whenever he wants. He thinks he can do what he likes!'

Seán smirked. 'Mum, what you have here is a squirrel that's just been blown out of her tree! Got that ruffled look. Landed in a pile of dusty leaves.'

I took up a spoon and flung it at him. It missed and hit the wall.

'Your sister is not a squirrel,' my mother said, rounding on him. 'And it's time you grew up and stopped teasing her!'

It was one of the few times I remember my mother standing up for me. I took up the sweeping brush and chased my brother into the garden.

That evening my mother returned to the burning question of my academic performance.

'You have to pass your exams,' she said. 'You can't just rely on getting married!' She added a little bitterly, 'Everywhere around me I see the folly of that.' My father, who had just come home from the office, made no answer to this comment, but he listened when my mother said she had found just the school for me – St Anne's in Kildruid, about twenty-five miles north of Dublin. It was recommended by one of her friends.

'Would you like to go away to school, Áine?' he demanded.

I had been reading a book called *The School in the Valley* where the girls had midnight feasts and other esoteric adventures.

'Yes,' I said with alacrity.

'Will you work,' my father said, 'and stop day-dreaming, or whatever it is you're doing when you should be studying?'

'Yes, Daddy!'

'What do you day-dream about anyway,' he asked, his voice tinged with curiosity and a parental frown in his eyes, 'seeing that you do so much of it?'

'Oh this and that,' I said airily. And then I said, to test him, keeping my voice light, 'Mostly I think about a white wolf and a ghoul I used to have nightmares about.'

My father shook his head and gave a small, dismissive laugh.

A few minutes later, when he thought I was out of earshot, I heard him say to my mother, 'I hope this place you're talking about knocks spots off them?'

'It's a bit old-fashioned,' she said, 'run along sixties' lines. But it certainly gets great results!'

'Sounds like just the place for our Áine,' my father said.

It sounded a bit dubious to me, but it still didn't quash the romantic notions I had about boarding school. That would come later.

One day while packing my trunk under my mother's supervision I said to her, 'Mummy, I suppose getting married is like going away to school? In a way?'

She laughed, her face lighting up with humour. 'Oh Áine, what a comparison!'

'Well, it's going to a strange place to be with someone you don't really know.'

The humour died in her eyes. 'No one ever really knows anyone,' she said. 'And marriage is a bit like a lottery . . . you draw a ticket and you never know your luck.'

I regarded her in silence. I wanted to ask if she thought she had been lucky to have found my father, but I feared the response. To me he was a king; I could not imagine a more wonderful man. I did not realize that the divide between my parents had happened almost by accident, but that, by now, neither of them knew how to bridge it. My father seemed perfectly happy to work until all hours and my mother was now taken up with the new project she had set herself of really brushing up her French.

'But sometimes, Mummy, one *does* know people,' I said, thinking of Rupert and the strange sympathy I had felt between us. 'Sometimes you know someone you have met for the first time.'

My mother gave me a careful look, and a small private smile played around her mouth. 'That's true, I suppose. But it's rare.'

'Do you think anyone will ever want to marry me, Mummy?' I asked then.

'Of course they will, you silly girl.'

'Well, if I don't like being married I'll run away . . . I can always go to Dunbeg.'

'It's a good place in which to get lost, at any rate,' she said in a speculative voice. 'A place of the spirit, I suppose.' She gave a short laugh, dragging herself back to pragmatism. 'What an imagination you have, Áine! The thing to remember about life is that it is a battle and must be fought. You only run away if you are certain of destruction.'

Chapter Eight

St Anne's Convent, Kildruid, had a no nonsense reputation. It stood on a site by the sea some twenty miles north of Dublin. The convent had once been a Georgian hunting lodge, but now had several additions: classrooms, a concert hall, dormitories. A railway ran between the playing fields and the sea, and I used to stare at it sometimes, longing to go wherever it was bound, wondering about its passengers as they regarded the schoolgirls in the navy gaberdine uniform through their flying windows. Sometimes I fantasized that a wonderful boy would see me from the train and would move heaven and earth to find me. '*When I saw you hit the ball with such passion I knew that I wanted you and only you, for my bride . . .*' and down he would go on one knee, like all good fairytale princes. This fantasizing arose because my friend Sharon O'Kelly, a new girl like myself, had given me the loan of several Mills and Boon romances, which I had devoured in secret. I particularly liked the word 'passion' as I did the fantasy of getting married to someone rich and powerful who would adore me and be my slave. I was looking for certainty and boundaries and a place which I ruled and was mine. I had no objection to any short cut which might get me there. And then I thought of Aunt Isabelle and was sobered.

The convent smelled of polish, prayers, and ordered minds where there was a place for everything, and everything had better be in it. There was lots of parquet flooring and it shone like the day. When you entered the square front hall of the former Georgian hunting lodge, the first thing you saw was a statue of St Michael the Archangel spearing Satan, and beside it a white wrought-iron spiral staircase that connected with Mother Superior's quarters and was strictly out of bounds.

Mother Superior, whom her young charges called 'The Rev', was a small, soft spoken little woman, with yellowing skin and teeth to match. Possessed of extraordinary dignity, she glided as though she were on castors. Her long upper lip impressed my mother, who was always of the opinion that long upper lips betokened leadership. The Rev wore her black habit as though she had been born in it. Rosary beads dangled from her waist. On the marriage finger of her left hand she wore a silver ring. This was her wedding band; she was a bride of Christ, one of a myriad. Sharon used to say that if the late JC ever had to come back for his brides it would cure him permanently of heterosexuality and Catholicism in one fell swoop. Sharon had become the class expert on matters sexual.

The headmistress, Sister Theresa, possessed nothing of the ethereal, and was a different kettle of fish to the Rev. She was a sturdy woman in her fifties, with rimless glasses and a pair of steely eyes. She always looked at you as though she suspected that you had either committed a crime or were on the point of doing so. Everyone was afraid of her.

The school had two playing fields, two hard tennis courts, and cinder walks around the fields that were overhung by chestnut trees. There was also an old garden with a high wall to the rear of the old house. This was used exclusively by the nuns, although we used to cross it on our travels to and from the shoeroom. It was full of flowers, and a few espaliers were trained against the sunny, south-facing wall. A gothic archway with balustraded stone steps separated it from the playing fields and tennis courts. A grotto, with the statue of Our Lady of Lourdes directing her pious gaze at Heaven and a kneeling Saint Bernadette, ornamented the east-facing wall.

Behind the nuns' garden was the convent cemetery, a mournful place with a few yew trees and perpetual shade. Here there were small plots, iron crosses, painted black, with the names of the deceased in white lettering. One of the old nuns died while I was at Kildruid and I found her funeral macabre and upsetting in the extreme, being of an age when I still did not really believe in death.

Kildruid had ninety boarders. The day began at six-twenty when the bell, an old fashioned clanger, was swung by Sister

Lucy in St Catherine's dormitory. Then she would come to each curtained cubicle in turn, intone '*Bendicamus Domino*' as she held out to each one of us in turn a small glass font of holy water. I found all of this very exciting for a while, but after a week or two I became used to the small morning drama and, instead of jumping out of bed immediately as I was supposed to do, would linger on for another precious few minutes.

Sister Lucy, guided presumably by divine inspiration, sometimes returned to my cubicle, put her head around the curtain and hissed, 'Get up you lazy, lazy girl!'

We would go silently down to the chapel at a quarter to seven, don our white net veils which were kept folded with our prayer books in a special cupboard outside the chapel, and file like novices into our pews. The nuns were already there, like crows on telegraph wires. The curate, Father Sheehan, came from the town to say Mass. Everyone took Communion. If you didn't the whole school would notice and wonder if you were in a state of mortal sin.

It was easy enough to be in a state of mortal sin. Although Church teaching required that to commit a mortal sin you had to have grave matter, full knowledge and full consent, what constituted grave matter was a matter of conjecture. At thirteen, grave matter was thinking about boys, allowing thoughts to intrude which had never until recently blighted the serenity of your days.

For most of the school year we saw only black night outside the chapel windows, but during the summer term the morning threw wonderful magenta, gold and sapphire light through the stained glass onto the white altar. It was easy then to imagine oneself in Heaven. We trooped down to breakfast at eight, and after this meal we were supposed to take some exercise by jogging around the hockey fields.

Lessons started at nine. I was particularly targeted in class because the nuns knew I had been sent away to school to improve my academic performance and they gave me no quarter. Stuck up at the front of the class, constantly asked questions, I caused the class to convulse on more than one occasion. This made me realize I had a decision to make. I could either improve or continue to be the class laughing stock. I chose the former. Long-term gain, I told myself, echoing something I had read in the *Reader's Digest*, was worth a bit of short-term pain. Anyway the day was so structured, and I was so bemused by my new surroundings, where people were never slagged to their faces, that I was happy enough to attempt conformity. In fact I even thought I was finding a new me.

'This essay is very good indeed,' Sister Aidan intoned one morning at English class. 'Áine, you've improved beyond recognition. You've got quite an imagination.'

All our correspondence was opened, and when my mother wrote – which was seldom – her note was always short and cryptic, enclosing some money, perhaps, or confirming she would be down to see me the following weekend. I had no hope of a letter from Rupert. Even if he wrote the letter would surely be confiscated, being from a boy. But one morning after breakfast, Sister Theresa stopped me as I filed out of the refectory, and drew me aside.

'There's a curious piece of correspondence for you from America,' she said, watching my reaction. I kept a poker face and she drew an envelope from her pocket. 'It contains only a cutting from a children's book.' Why did my heart miss a beat; why was the day brighter, and the rain that blinded the window no longer of account?

'It's from my cousin,' I said.

'Oh . . .' She seemed almost disappointed. 'Well, he's a very childish cousin. What age is he?'

'Oh, he's about nine,' I said hurriedly.

She handed me the envelope and I took it with me and opened it in the shoeroom, and removed the contents – a cutting pasted to a sheet of black paper. Rupert Bear, in a study of some kind, held an opened book in his hands. I read the verse:

> *The little bear cries 'Take a look!*
> *'There's Tigerlily in that book!'*

I turned the page over. There was nothing else. But a sudden idea formed. *Take a look*, I said to myself. I wouldn't put it past him! I held the page to the light, but it was opaque, so I left it on the hot radiator while I changed my shoes. When this was done I managed to tease off the pasted cutting. Underneath it, in tiny writing, was a note:

Dear Tigerlily,
I hate it that I can't write to you properly. I keep trying to imagine you, now that you're thirteen and almost grown up.
    I dreamed of Dunbeg last night. The place was in darkness, the shutters closed. We'll go back there sometimes and you'll laugh at being scared.
    Love, R.

Love! I thought. *Love*, R.

We had not been back to Dunbeg since that summer when I was ten. In fact I had felt no great urge to go back. Much as I loved the place for itself, it now had memories which conflicted and made me unhappy. I hated the thought of Aeneas Shaw and my pride was offended that I had ever been frightened of him. I was into my teens now and clutching at adulthood. My reflection in the mirror had become fascinating. I saw my new feminine form, and felt like the ugly duckling transmogrified. I had breasts, a very small waist; I was acquiring hips of a kind and the starved, gamine appearance of my childhood was gone for ever. I no longer dreamed of the white wolf and thought that being at the very edge of my adult life, I had left the nightmares behind me. My first period arrived one night while I slept. The event I had been dreading had come upon me after all, unheralded, without pain or fanfare, and I was still the same person.

'You are now capable of becoming a mother,' my mother said to me very matter of factly, in order to forestall anything of an emotive nature. It was also, perhaps, a covert warning. I would have kept the knowledge from her, fiercely private as I was, only it happened during mid-term break and she saw the sheets.

'I don't want to be a mother!'

She smiled. 'At your age, Áine, I should hope not.'

'Would you like to have another baby, Mummy?' I don't know why I asked this question. I think it was to deflect attention away from me and the embarrassing transition in my life. When she didn't reply immediately I looked at her and saw a strangely speculative expression on her face.

'Oh I don't think so,' she said then with a half laugh and would have added something but the phone rang.

'I'll get it!' she said, but I was already in the hall and picking up the receiver.

'Hello?'

'Chérie,' a male voice said, '*comme tu me manques!*'

'Sorry?' I said. 'You must have the wrong number.' The line went dead.

My mother was standing beside me when I explained that the caller had hung up.

'I told you *I'd* get it, Áine! Why are you always so headstrong and disobedient?'

'I'm sorry, Mummy. But it was a wrong number. Someone talking French . . .'

She went upstairs. I felt the weight of her silent disappointment. I had annoyed her again. I loved her and longed for her recognition, but I did not realize until it was too late how great a stabilizing influence in my life was the mere fact of her existence.

Before the end of the Christmas term the junior school put on a play, *The Miracle of Lourdes* in which I got the part of St Bernadette's aunt and Sharon O'Kelly played St Bernadette. It was also a turning point; I discovered a vast sense of relief in acting. It demanded no conformity to petty rules; it gave scope for daring; it allowed you to escape yourself. Above all, the buzz it delivered, as the curtain rose, was unlike anything I had ever experienced: electric, thrilling, almost a drug. I was so taken up with the excitement of this that I felt as though I had a new life.

The only shadow in my life was the unspoken tension between my parents, and I wanted to jolly them out of it when they came to visit, but I was in despair that nothing I

106

could say or do would restore the harmony that had been lost.

'You're becoming quite grown up now Áine,' my mother said approvingly. 'The nuns are very pleased with you; they say you're hard working and are sensible.'

All you had to do to be deemed sensible was to be quiet. No one knew what went on inside your head.

But at night, when the dormitory was quiet, I heard the sea. It never had quite the same voice as in Clew Bay, but it growled with rhythmic hypnotism to my half-conscious brain, swishing and retreating along the nearby strand. Perhaps it was the sea, or perhaps it was the small communication from Rupert which precipitated the return of my dreams. The white wolf came to me one night in a dream of which I only remember bed and dormitory and all the sleeping lives, rolled together like lottery tickets in a drum, falling, falling. In this dreamtime I emerged from freefall to find myself in the nuns' garden. Beside me the gardener was working, digging in a flowerbed. He had his back to me, was wearing an old coat and a peaked cap and when I tried to stand up I knew at once that he was digging a grave, and I got the strange, sweetish smell I had first encountered in the ruined cottage on the headland. He turned and I saw his face.

I woke myself when I cried out. I was sweating, and my heart thumped so loudly I thought the whole world must hear it. Sister Lucy, who slept nearby in a cubicle with a wooden partition and a door, came hurrying to see what the matter was. 'Are you all right, Áine?' she whispered. But I feigned sleep and she padded back to bed, muttering to herself.

But this dream did not repeat itself, nor did I dream of Aeneas Shaw again.

As time went by I found I had better things to think of in bed. I often thought of the night I had slept with Rupert. As adolescence got under way the memory of this became fantastical; I was the only girl in my class who had actually slept with a boy! And the fact that I had admired and loved the boy gave me a privileged secret that I hugged to myself. That I owed this experience purely to an act of kindness did nothing to dilute the importance of the memory. I often traced in my

107

mind the feel of the awakening on the following morning, the sight of his head on the pillow next my own. I had learnt that morning, in a half-formed way, the transcendence of waking beside the man one loves.

If I had been older, I wondered, would he have kissed me? The thought of such intimacy was breathtaking; alone, in bed with Rupert, warm and safe, while a magic I did not begin to understand star-studded the air.

And remembering this I recalled, with a start, the marks I had seen across his chest and which he had attributed to some accident. Had it been machinery of some kind? But the marks had been more like weals than anything else. Could someone have hit him? I thought about this for a while, but eventually dismissed it as nonsense. He would tell me someday. Someday I would marry him, sleep with him, know every bit of him. He would tell me everything then!

It was Sharon who imparted the facts of life to me. She was the least inhibited girl in our year. In inverse pattern to my parents, her mother was Catholic but her father was not. 'Actually he's an atheist,' she informed Sister Imelda one day in Religious Knowledge.

'My poor child,' Sister Imelda said with a frown, 'we must all pray for him.'

Sharon laughed about this later. 'Pray for him! He thinks they're a joke!'

In the course of rehearsals for *The Miracle of Lourdes* Sharon was overheard by our headmistress opining that the Lourdes thing was all eyewash; that there were no miracles; the cures were the result of powerful suggestion. 'That's what my dad says! And he's a psychiatrist.'

Sister Theresa told her she was a wicked girl, and after that watched her like a hawk.

Sharon did not know it, but her days in Kildruid were numbered. She brought back a pair of skimpy pyjamas after the Easter break, and was found by Sister Lucy wearing these in bed. They were made of black lace. Sister Lucy, who found her lying on her bed in this offending garment one warm May night, made out that she was lying in an 'immodest position'. And when a note Sharon had passed across the study fell into the hands of Sister Theresa her doom was sealed. The note contained a drawing of male genitalia and bore the legend, 'An enlarged detail.'

Her trunk was packed for her and her parents sent for. She was made to wait in the parlour. I saw her through the window and, desperate to talk to her, I sneaked back indoors.

'Stupid, stupid,' she kept whispering, her face tear-streaked and her voice unsteady. 'The Church tells them everything is a sin unless you're a straw-stuffed, sexless hypocrite. I did nothing wrong! The Church just hates normal women.'

She left at four that afternoon and I did not see her again. Her departure made me feel the ice was thin under my own feet and the injustice of the thing ended my honeymoon with Kildruid. I just wanted to go home.

One day, when I was sent by Sister Aidan on an errand into the town of Kildruid, some men who were digging the street whistled at me. I found this unwelcome, even threatening, because it said that I was no longer invisible in the great world of men. What on earth did they see in me now? I was the same, after all; only the exterior was a little different, and the last thing I wanted was for that difference to be noticed at all. Then I thought of Gráinne O'Keefe and how I had seen her through my brothers' eyes and had envied her, and for a while a sense of new power possessed me. Whatever this power was I had not created it, and I marvelled at it like a child into whose lap someone had poured a fortune in foreign currency, which she can neither understand nor use.

Some days later I learnt more of this currency. Father John Bryan, a young curate recently come to the Kildruid parish, had been seconded to hear our confessions. When I told him I sometimes had bad thoughts, I saw him eyeing me through the grille. These bad thoughts were very small potatoes and centred on Rupert, and on the possibility of kissing him in bed. At Mass the following day I found the curate's eyes on me as he gave out Communion, and later that morning he cornered me into the sacristy where I had been sent on some errand by the portress. I saw how the pupils of his eyes dilated and how anxious he was to detain me in conversation and how his glance strayed over my gymslip. He wanted to know more about my bad thoughts, and when I said I imagined myself kissing a certain cousin he gave a low, unhealthy laugh.

I felt soiled without knowing why. It was not so much the priest's hunger that upset me, as his hatred of it, the shuffling of me into some minimal space of his own creation where I was not a person at all but only an occasion of sin.

But, ostensibly, I was getting on well in school, co-opted to the debating team, well behaved and well approved of. It was not until I had a vivid dream concerning Rupert that I refused point blank to go to confession. I was not going to share that dream with anyone.

'Áine O'Malley, have you been to confession yet?'

'No, Sister.'

'Well, Father Bryan is still in the confessional. Off you go!'

'No thank you, Sister.'

'Oh come along now, child. Everyone has to go to confession.'

'No thank you, Sister.'

I was in the Junior Study and I looked at her across the room. The other girls, already shriven, had their heads down, pretending to work, but their application deceived no one. This was a kind of mutiny and understood by them as such. Our headmistress was powerless. She could not force me to go to confession, nor could she punish me for my refusal. It was a private spiritual matter over which she had no jurisdiction, and she knew this perfectly well. But, smarting from her loss of face before the other girls, she shot me a furious look and said, 'It's not lucky to deny God. You should be more careful of your soul, child!'

After that the headmistress treated me coldly.

'Why don't you apologize to her?' Geraldine Ryder who sat beside me in study, demanded. 'You offended her.'

But the thought of creeping along with apologies I did not feel made me want to throw up. I was learning the law of one's own integrity and the impossibility of pleasing the world.

And then, as though the headmistress's dire warning had borne fruit, a bombshell fell which seemed to threaten my whole life. My father came to see me on his own one Sunday, drove me to a quiet place in a spot overlooking the sea, parked the

110

car and in a few moments I learned something that shattered my understanding of the cosmos.

My mother was gone.

Chapter Nine

'Why didn't Mummy come?' I asked innocently enough, but the hesitancy of his reply, the way his face closed, convinced me suddenly that something was amiss and that he was keeping it from me.

'She's gone away for a while . . .'

'Where has she gone?'

He didn't answer.

Against my ribs my heart started a hammering. My breath caught. My unease where my mother was concerned, the foreboding I always tried to side-step, presented itself now as reality, something I should have heeded, should have forced the rest of the family to heed.

'I'm sure she'll be back soon, Áine . . .'

I realized that he was hoping I knew something of her whereabouts, and this compounded my panic.

'Where is she, Daddy? Don't you know?'

'Don't interrogate me!' He glanced at me sternly, the look that used to make me quail, but then his face softened and he said in a gentler voice: 'She left a message . . . to say she was all right.'

'Can I see it?'

'You don't need to see it.'

'But Mummy would never leave us like that . . . without saying where she was going and when she would be back!' Why did I notice the cow parsley in the ditch and the late afternoon light on the hedgerows? The world assumed a sudden sharp focus, sprang out of its half sleep. Or was it I who had been asleep? The pain was almost physical in its intensity and I did not know how I could survive it.

'Was that all she said? That she was all right?'

'Nothing else that concerns you.'

The tears poured down my face. 'I want to see her letter!'

My father regarded me with sorrow. 'I don't believe you,' I cried, sobbing wildly, beyond circumspection now and licensed by his paternal gentleness. 'Mummy would never, ever, leave us like that!'

He put his hand into his pocket for his handkerchief, but as he withdrew it a folded sheet of paper fell to the floor of the car and half opened at my feet. I grabbed it. I knew my mother's writing; the mere sight of it caught me around the heart. I jumped out of the car and ran down the country road, clutching her missive and ignoring my father's command behind me to come back. I found the shelter of a gateway into a field and, leaning against the rusty bars I read the letter.

Dear Noel,

This is to advise you (isn't that a very legal-sounding term) that I've gone away and will not be coming back. Try to explain it to the children as best you can. I cannot face them and tell them I am leaving (in fact if I did try to tell them I would not be able to go) but they are old enough to do without me now. Áine is safe at boarding school and the boys are taken up in their own lives. I cannot live as just a domestic prop any longer and must find some life for myself or I will die. I am all right and no one need worry about me.

Joyce.

I held the letter in my hand and read it again, phrase by phrase. *'I must find some life for myself or I will die.'*

I heard my father's steps coming towards me down the road, a calm, unhurried tread as though the world was on course and not shifting on its axis. But his face as he retrieved the letter from my fingers expressed a vulnerability I had never known in him. I walked back with him to the car, sat in beside him in silence.

'I don't want to go back to school,' I said eventually. 'I want to go home.'

114

'You are using this as an excuse, Áine. You will stay at Kildruid.'

'But Daddy, what are we going to do? What are the boys going to do?'

'We will carry on. I have engaged a woman – Mrs Flynn – to cook and clean. No doubt your mother will return in due course.'

My father was now tight-lipped; the vulnerability of a few moments before was gone. He sat staring out through the windscreen. He was very handsome in his weekend garb, the old houndstooth tweed suit, a bit shapeless now, but dear and familiar. He was close shaven as always, and he emanated a certain kind of urbane male power, but for a moment I detected in him a brooding questioning; he was a man suddenly widowed in all but name, with a large family and a question mark over not just his marriage but the meaning of his life. His pride had taken a terrible blow, and I can still sense the ire at his betrayal simmering beneath his unruffled exterior like Hell fire.

'Áine, I am very sorry indeed that you should have something like this visited on you. I don't know what has got into your mother. But perhaps it is as well that you know the truth; it cannot be hidden indefinitely and it would not do if you were to hear it from someone else. For the moment we will say that your mother has gone on a holiday. But unless she comes to her senses and comes home soon that excuse will soon be transparent.'

'But . . . I want to talk to her. Maybe she would come home if we all asked her.'

'We cannot contact her until we know where she is. No doubt her whereabouts will become evident in the next few days.'

I stared at him, longing with a child's longing to be held by him. But my father was incapable of overt acts of affection.

'How are the boys taking it?'

'I told them she's gone away for a rest . . .' For a moment his voice faltered. 'Such a carry-on!' he said in a low voice.

'Do you love her, Daddy?' I asked him suddenly.

'Love your mother?' he repeated, starting the engine. 'Of

course I love your mother! She's my wife, the mother of my children.'

'Well then . . . find her, Daddy. Please don't let her just disappear.'

'My dear child,' he intoned in his pedantic lawyer's voice, 'she is not just "disappearing". And it is not my place to interfere with any of her decisions. She is an adult, and she presumably knows what she is doing.'

'I hate lawyers!' I cried. 'You all think black is black and white is white, but you never think of the elements which made up those colours in the first place! Do you think white is really white? No, it is a combination of all the colours in the spectrum! It only exists in the eye, because the eye cannot separate out the colours. And black is also black because it absorbs every colour and reflects nothing back, so we cannot see its reality. And everything, Daddy, everything around us is terribly mysterious, and nothing is really black or white at all.'

He gave a small dry laugh. 'And where have you come by all this extraordinary information?' His eyes dwelt on me with a gleam of sudden amusement.

'Sister Julia, our science teacher,' I said sulkily.

'What an admirable Sister Julia! It's good to see you taking things in, Áine. You seem to have acquired an interest in science, at any rate. Now,' he added, lowering his voice, and putting his hand on my shoulder, 'You are not to worry. Mummy is fine. She'll be back all the quicker if we do not make a fuss. Now, do you want afternoon tea or will I just drive you back?'

Normally I would not pass up a treat of afternoon tea with cakes, but my stomach felt as though it had shrivelled and I said he could drive me back to the convent.

Soon he turned into the main street of Kildruid and the high convent wall came into view. He stopped the car, and his hand sought mine, squeezed it between both of his in one of his rare moments of empathy and love.

'Courage,' he said. 'Sometimes people . . . grown ups . . . particularly women . . . need to sort themselves out and need to do it alone. But they always come back . . .'

'But Daddy, what will I tell the nuns?'

116

'The nuns?' He regarded me with sudden horrified hauteur. 'What has it to do with them? I see no earthly reason why you should tell them anything.'

It was a lovely evening. The peonies were blazing in the nuns' garden and the white candles were out on the chestnut trees surrounding the hockey pitches, which were now carefully mown and laid out as grass tennis courts. I was acutely aware of the world's beauty, and was subsumed in the premonition that I would not see much more of it. My soul was full of death.

In chapel before supper I knelt and prayed as I had never prayed, my head in my hands. Dear God, please send Mummy back. I'll never do anything bad again if You do. I'll work really hard. I'll get first in the class. I'll do anything You want!

And then I begged: Make sure she's safe.

Sister Theresa stopped me coming out of the refectory. 'Áine, have you been crying?'

It was easy to lie. The truth was too humiliating. How could I tell this little waspish nun, with her curious, gimlet eyes and her dislike of me – she had never forgiven me for the confession incident – that my mother had run away?

'Your eyes are red. You must be coming down with something. It might be a good idea for you to have an early night.'

This was a command and meant I would miss the film scheduled for that evening. But although this would, normally, be a dire punishment, I was happy to obey. I needed to be alone.

I went to bed and did not sleep. The other girls came to bed at nine-thirty. Rhiana, who had the next cubicle, put her head around my curtain. 'Áine,' she whispered, 'the film was great . . . it was *Sink the Bismarck*.'

I feigned sleep. Secluded in my little fastness I heard the girls stand in silence outside their cubicles and then kneel for the night prayers, the Litany of Our Lady of Loreto . . .

Sister Lucy intoned the invocations and the girls, after each invocation, answered in unison: 'Pray for us.' Mentally I joined in the cadence of the litany; the hope inherent in prayer comforted me.

Virgin most merciful,
Virgin most faithful,
Mirror of Justice,
Seat of Wisdom,
Cause of our Joy,
Tower of David,
Tower of Ivory,
House of Gold,
Ark of the Covenant,
Gate of Heaven,
Morning Star.

The strange names given to Our Lady conjured an alternative reality, mystical and invulnerable. It was still daylight outside, and in between the responses to the prayers, the eternal sound of the sea filled the dormitory through the open windows. When the prayer was over Sister Lucy said, 'Goodnight girls, God bless you,' and the girls answered, 'Goodnight Sister.' Then came the sigh of bed springs, the whisper as someone got out of bed and illicitly visited a friend, the sudden rattle as Rhiana opened her bedside locker, presumably to find her cache of sweets. She always had sweets; sometimes she shared them with me, tip-toeing into my cubicle and climbing into bed beside me, something that was strictly forbidden. In the smallest of whispers we would discuss our families, ducking beneath the bedclothes to laugh as we described our siblings. But tonight the last thing I wanted was to discuss my family. Rhiana, however, did not make any attempt to contact me and I was glad to be left in peace.

But the night brought no surcease. Was my mother's disappearance my fault? On self examination I saw I had always been a difficult child, impulsive, disobedient, inquisitive, secretive. The more I thought about it the more certain I became that I was the cause of this new family debacle. I should have helped her more when I was at home. Oh Mummy . . . What is to become of us if you are gone?

All night I tossed over in my head the possible places to which my mother could have taken herself. Did she have much money? I knew she could draw on my father's bank account, but how long would that be available to her? Did she have money of her own? Could she possibly have gone to live with Aunt Isabelle?

As the new day dawned I sat up in bed and wrote a letter to the only friend I knew who could help me.

Dear Rupert,
I don't know what to do, which is why I am writing. Mummy has left us. Maybe she has gone to be with your mother.

I'm at my wits' end worrying. Will you write to me and let me know if she's in Mount Wexford? You can put your note under a Rupert Bear cutting, like last time. I'm sneaking this letter out with a day pupil.
Love,
Áine.

The following day I despatched this missive by a first-year day pupil whom I bribed with a pound, impressing upon her that the letter was to go by airmail; she swore faithfully that she would send it. When more than a week passed without any response I began to doubt her, and muttered in my heart that she was nothing but a con-artist who took good money and failed to deliver.

By now I was half mad with my impotence, and performing poorly at everything so that the nuns noticed it and told me to pull up my socks. But I had more important matters on my mind than English poetry or algebra, which I hated anyway. I cudgelled my brains. Where had my mother gone? She had no job; she had no private means that would enable her to simply vanish. When my father phoned the convent one evening, and insisted on speaking to me personally, I was called from study by the portress, Sister Johanna, and went down to take the call with my heart in my mouth. Scanning the horizon of possibilities I envisaged that my mother was back at home; and then again I thought perhaps my father was phoning to tell me she was dead. But neither my hope nor my fear was well founded. My father just asked me if I were all right.

'Daddy . . . isn't there any news?'

The phone was in the front hall and Sister Johanna, who was hovering nearby, gave me a strange look.

'No,' my father's voice came down the line. 'Not yet. But I'm sure we'll hear from her soon. So keep your spirits up.'

For a moment I was back at home and my mother was referring to Dunbeg as a place of the spirit, the 'matrix' of the O'Malley soul.

'Have you tried Dunbeg?' was on the tip of my tongue, but I reconsidered it. What if she were there and Daddy descended on her and caused her to disappear again? What if, and this was a sobering thought, she couldn't bear him any more!

'Meanwhile,' my father went on, 'there is no need to tell your teachers about this. It doesn't concern them. But I want you to be sure that everything will be all right.'

'How do you know?'

I knew nothing was all right; I knew he was angry and I knew he was too rigid to seek her out.

'Because it will be, child. And you need not concern yourself about it.'

I put the receiver down, but I could not contain the welling grief.

The kindly portress came out of her little office and put her arm around me. 'What is it, Áine?' she asked gently. 'Have you bad news?'

I shook my head, mindful of my father's bidding, blinking back the tears.

'What is it, dear?'

But I shook my head and brushed past her, afraid that I would blurt out the truth. I wondered if I should have asked my father if he had checked Dunbeg. Even if he had checked, I reasoned, she might be there without his knowing it. There was always the gate lodge; it was dilapidated but would offer shelter. I imagined her on her own, regretting having left us, the awful loss of face in just coming home.

That night I dreamt of my mother. In the dream I saw her in Dunbeg, standing on the Victorian battlements, barely visible against the night sky. I called to her and ran up the avenue to the forecourt and then raced up the turret stairs to the roof. But she wasn't there. There was only the sea and a wind that was blowing so hard it knocked the breath from my body. And then I heard the heavy tread on the stairs behind me and turned to see approaching me the shadowy figure that haunted my dreams.

When I woke it seemed to me that I been given some kind of message: my mother had returned to Dunbeg and run foul of Aeneas Shaw, or would do so if I did not prevent it. She was alone and did not know her danger. Thanks to me, and my shut-mouth policy, she could not know how he waited for his revenge.

I thought about it all day and the idea gripped me harder with every passing hour until it became a fixation. The more I thought about it the more my instinct told me to find her. I was certain that there was no use leaving things to the men in my family, none of whom could see any further than their own reflection in the nearest mirror. But there was a cold premonition in my bones when I remembered the tramp's white face and the venom in his eyes, at that night-time window years before.

I counted my money – ten pounds – and put it in my pocket. At breakfast I secreted away a few slices of bread and butter. Afterwards I made my bed quickly, then hurried to the shoeroom where I put on my outdoor shoes and my navy gaberdine coat and went outside.

'Áine O'Malley, what are you wearing a coat for on such a lovely May morning?' It was Sister Theresa, who always appeared out of the stonework when you least expected her.

I started. 'I'm feeling cold, Sister!'

She regarded me doubtfully, approached and put a hand on my forehead. 'You're not feverish, so what is making you cold? You've been behaving peculiarly lately. Are you all right?'

'I'm fine thank you, Sister . . .'

She went away and when I was sure she was gone I made my way across the nuns' garden and then slipped into the little convent cemetery. Here I removed my coat and hid it and the bread, bundled together, among the lower branches of a yew. Looking back from the cemetery gate I was satisfied my bundle was invisible among the shadows. I knew that my determined course was going to get me into terrible trouble. But my mother came first.

When lunch was over I was first out of the shoeroom. I retrieved the coat, and then slipped away through the side gate used only by the day pupils and soon found myself in the main street of Kildruid. I hurried through the town without looking over my shoulder, hoping to give the impression of someone sent out on an errand; the last thing I wanted was some busybody shopkeeper phoning the convent. I could almost hear his do-goody voice: 'Sister, are you missing a girl? . . . No Sister, it wasn't one of the day pupils. Sure don't I know the lot of *them* . . .'

Once outside the town I put up my thumb at passing cars. Suddenly I was awash with nerves, fear of the unknown, fear of discovery. I thought of the roads I would have to travel: Kildruid to Dublin and then the road to Longford. After that the road to Castlebar and from there to Newport and Dunbeg. A journey of some hundred and eighty miles lay ahead of me.

The dark blue Mercedes pulled up with a sudden screech of brakes. 'Where are you going?'

'Dublin.'

'Hop in.'

The driver was in his forties. He asked me my name, where I lived. I told him the minimum. I said I lived in Dublin and had missed the Dublin bus.

He glanced at my school uniform. 'You're at school in Dublin so?'

'Yes.'

'So what are you doing in this neck of the woods at this time of the day?'

'I was sent on a message . . . for one of the nuns. I just missed the bus back.'

He gave me a queer little smile and shifted a little in his seat. I did not like the smile, or the shift of his seat.

'An errand?' he echoed. 'All this way? What age are you?'

'I'm fifteen.'

'You don't look fifteen. If you were my daughter I'd be worried about you . . . It's not safe for a young girl to be thumbing lifts . . .'

I shrugged. 'I'm grown up!'

'Where do you go to school in Dublin?'

I gave him the first name that entered my head. 'Muckross Park.'

He glanced at me, his eyes taking in my navy gymslip and I suddenly realized I had made a foolish error. 'Is that so? I always thought they had a green uniform.'

When I was silent he added softly: 'You're not up to some escapade or other, are you? Meeting a boyfriend or anything?'

'Certainly not!' I said crisply.

His voice, the sudden soft, insinuating timbre, impertinent and familiar, sent small shivers up my spine. I felt like someone who had trusted to the bonafides of what seemed an ordinary domestic pet and had glimpsed, while cornered with the creature, a gleam of feral teeth. I stared through the window, desperately calculating my next move.

'You can let me off here.' We were approaching the airport, from where I could get a bus to the city centre.

He gave an amused, impertinent laugh. 'Let you off here? Why do you want to get off here?'

'I have a plane to meet.' I knew this sounded lame, and he evidently thought so too, for he roared with laughter. His left hand suddenly touched my knee and moved rapidly to my thigh. 'Will you give me a kiss first?'

I shoved away the trespassing hand and a tide of murderous rage flooded me. 'My father is a lawyer,' I said in my coldest voice, apeing for the moment the crisp tones of my father. 'I am meeting him at the airport and you are committing an assault! Drop me off here at once!'

He turned to look at me and I looked him back in the eye. I already knew something about the power of the human voice, and even though I was acting a part and was privately terrified it was clear that the man was taken aback. His face registered doubt. He glanced at me again and then pulled over to the verge. 'Off you go then . . .'

The car sped away with a contemptuous screech, leaving me on the roadside. There was a bus stop a little further on and I waited there, leaning my shoulder against the stop and trying to contain the adrenalin. The bus duly arrived, brought me to Bus Áras in Abbey Street, in the city centre, and half an hour later I boarded the single-decker bus to Longford. From

123

there I intended to thumb another lift to the west. I wore the gaberdine coat, which hid my uniform and in which I sweltered. But I knew I would be glad of it that evening, when it became cold. I wondered about school and if they had missed me yet, glanced at my watch, knew that afternoon classes were about to start. They would search the school, assume I had broken bounds, even make inquiries in the town, before they phoned my father.

The journey before me now seemed interminable. I tried to calculate how late it would be before I came back to Dunbeg.

Chapter Ten

The Castlebar road on the outskirts of Longford was warm and dusty, drenched in the sunlight of late May. The traffic was desultory. I took off my school tie, stuck it in my pocket and now stood, my gaberdine coat slung over one shoulder, consuming the bread and butter I had taken from the school refectory, washing it down with a bottle of lemonade purchased in a sweet shop when I got off the bus. I was too nervous to be really hungry, but the thirst was another matter. The day was humid, wringing the moisture out of everything and hanging it in atoms in the air. There was a scent of new-mown hay and flakes of desiccated grass lay scattered like confetti on the roadside; the beeches sighed, capturing the occasional warm breeze.

A dirty lorry wheezed up the road, heralded by the smell of burning oil. When I saw it I dropped my upraised thumb and waited for it to pass. But it ground to a halt and the driver, wearing a filthy cap and missing a few teeth, shouted down at me from his perch in the cab:

'Where would ye be headin' for, girl?'

I assessed him rapidly. He looked all right, greasy from honest toil, full of the camaraderie of the provinces where the world consists of the immediate parish and the next one, and Dublin was only a poor pitiable place where everyone lived in a redbrick box.

'Castlebar?'

'Ye're in luck so, girl. Get in!'

I knew I need not fear this man. He belonged to the soil of Ireland, where mothers existed but women did not. Except to ask me if I came from Castlebar, to which I was dishonest enough to reply in the affirmative, and to deliver himself of a

125

comment on the weather – 'Heavy oul class of a day!' – he was taciturn. I was glad of this; relieved to be en route, to be safe after a fashion. I hardly noticed the fumes which came into the cab through some aperture near the gear lever, or the strains of Abba which emanated from the squawking radio.

After a while he demanded: 'Who d'ye think will win the cup on Sunday?'

'What cup?'

'The All Ireland Hurling Final!' he said in a tone of surprised reproach.

I neither knew about it, nor cared, but I said, taking a chance on his allegiance: 'Longford will walk it!'

He grinned and thumped the steering wheel with the flat of his hand, exclaiming, 'By Jaysus so they would – if they were in it!' He glanced at me and shook his head. 'It's between Tipperary and Antrim!'

'Tipp will win it! They're the best!'

This met with an interrogative glance. 'An' you a Mayo girl? Which part of Castlebar did yeh say ye were from?'

I thought of Castlebar, where my parents often fed us on our journeys to the west, an old garrison town, with its green at the town centre known as the Mall, and steep, narrow Castle Street dipping down from the convent.

'We live on the Mall.'

'Isn't that the grand place to live!' And when he drew breath I thought for an instant it was to question me some more, and I imagined him jumping out of the cab at the next village and heading for a phone box, but instead he said, 'So ye think Tipp will do it this time?'

'No bother to them!' I said.

There was a St Christopher medal hanging from the rearview mirror, beside a similarly suspended photograph of a little boy.

'Is that your son?'

'That's my boy,' he said. 'Michael Joseph, and he'll make a mighty hurler. I never saw in me life a young lad could handle a ball the way he does.'

The conversation now centred on Michael Joseph and how well he acquitted himself on the hurley pitch, and absolved me from the necessity of making conversation and from the

126

likelihood of being further questioned as to my provenance. In due course we got to Castlebar and I was set down in the Mall and looked around at the chestnut trees, the lengthening shadows on the grass and the ornamental chains fencing the green between short stone pillars. The birds had gone to bed and night was not far off. I was desperately hungry, and looked longingly at the Imperial Hotel where I had often lunched with my parents. But I was very poor; my small monetary store had been depleted by purchases of the bus ticket and my little snack in Longford. I went into the newsagents at the school corner and bought some chocolate bars, and when I realized I had only fifty pence left the enormity of what I had done overtook me. It was late evening now. I still had miles to go and I had run away from school. This was a crime punishable by expulsion. Worse, my father would have been notified of my defection by now and would be very worried.

But I kept telling myself I would find my mother at Dunbeg. Where else could she be? I would be in time to prevent anything happening to her, change her mind and she would come back and everything would be all right.

It was night when I came to Dunbeg. The gate was closed and the long dark avenue behind it seemed uninviting. I was very tired. After leaving Castlebar I had had two unremarkable lifts, one as far as Newport and one from there to my destination.

'What are you doing at all to be out thumbin' lifts at this hour?' one of the drivers said, and I lied with my usual glibness.

'You don't know what you might meet on the lonely road at night . . .' the woman said, glancing at me dubiously. 'Do your parents know you're doing this?'

'Of course. Sure aren't they waiting for me!'

Now I stood at the gate, peered into the avenue through the heavy iron bars and searched for a sign of a light in the gate lodge, but all was in darkness.

I had arrived at my destination to find myself beset with sudden certainty that my journey had been a foolish exercise. I was also beset by fear, but I had come too far to funk at this juncture so I pulled the bolt on the gates and pushed. The right-hand gate opened with a screech, terrible in the silent darkness. Why does Teddy never grease the bloody hinges? I thought, echoing my father. He's supposed to look after the place.

The avenue stretched ahead of me, very dark, tunnel-like, with the trees meeting overhead and the rhododendrons making a dense barrier on either side. I stepped across the small fence which bordered the overgrown gate-lodge garden, pushed aside the branches of the young sycamores that had rooted themselves there in recent years and soon, for the first time in many years, found myself at the front door of the lodge. As small children we had often played here, until my father, worried at the creeping decrepitude of the little house, had put in a new front door with a stout lock and forbade us the place. Although we passed it every time we went in and out the gateway at Dunbeg we never bothered to inspect it any more and the ivy had grown so dense over the front that the door was almost hidden. My father sometimes said, 'Must get something done about the damn lodge before it falls in,' but he never did. His principle concern was for the big house, where bits and pieces of repairs were systematically carried out over the years.

Pushing aside the ivy at the front door of the gate lodge I discovered how much the place had deteriorated; the stench met me, the powerful odour of unmolested mouldering, of damp, rank vegetation. It was clear that no one could live there, my mother, who detested damp, least of all. But I called 'Mummy, are you here?' just in case, and my voice sounded reedy and absurd as it broke the silence. I looked up at the dim upper storey with its still-intact windows. Nothing answered me. 'Mummy!' I called again, but all was still.

I retraced my steps to the avenue, and when I looked into the blackness ahead of me my courage momentarily forsook me and I stepped back towards the gates.

'You have to go up to the house, scaredy-cat . . .' I told myself, 'scaredy-cat, scaredy-cat . . .' And then I began an old rhyme of childhood as a kind of mantra to give me courage,

'Cowardy cowardy custard, Stick your nose in mustard,' daring myself as of old, when I had crept at night through the dark rooms of Dunbeg.

Although it was a clear night the avenue was Stygian in its darkness, thanks to the overhanging foliage. Every sound seemed magnified: the small scuffles suddenly among the trees, the sighing of leaves. I could smell the sea and when I emerged from the cover of the trees and saw on my left the inlet silvered by the moon I was surprised by the sense of homecoming embracing me with almost sensual recognition. The tide was coming in, dark and racing, its ripples visible under the pale night sky. This was my place. I was rooted here in ways beyond my comprehension and I felt it as though I were kin to every stone on the moonlit shore and every bush, as though they knew me from aeons ago. Out in the bay the island of Inishdrum lay like a hump-backed whale, the ruins of its ancient fortress stark against the night sky.

I was not afraid any more. I was exultant in a strange intoxication of the soul, as though I were one with the night and its forces, as though my spirit knew its roots in this ancient Celtic place and it, in turn, knew me for its own.

But I kept to the edge of the avenue. Once, yielding to impulse, I stepped down to the shore and dipped my fingers in the ice-cold tide. The sea slapped itself against the shingle, with small reassuring sounds. This made for impeded progress, strange for someone who had come on so urgent an errand. It was as though my errand was a subconscious blind, and that I had been called back to this place for reasons which had nothing to do with my mother or with family problems, but for another purpose altogether that had not yet been disclosed to me.

The castellated house towered above me as I emerged from the trees and climbed the small rise at the end of the avenue to the 'castle' forecourt. The shutters were closed. I searched the customary hiding place beneath the terra cotta planter for the key, but it was not there, and then I walked around the house, peered in the scullery window, crossed the garden where I had once seen a white shadow flit across the grass. But all was still and there was no sound except the murmur of the sea. I smelled the damp grass, came back through the gothic archway to the forecourt, felt under my feet the round loose stones that had once been taken from the foreshore. Sitting on the parapet overlooking the rocks and scrutinizing every inch of the castle

I had to admit that there was no sign of life at Dunbeg, no light showed in any window and everything was shuttered. Nor was there any sign of the lunatic Aeneas Shaw.

My options now were whether I should walk the three miles to the O'Keefes and seek the key, or find some nook outdoors. Neither alternative appealed to me, and as my mind scanned the possibilities I realized there was shelter at least to be found; I could stay in the old coach house in the stable yard; it was in better nick than the gate lodge. It would offer a roof if it rained and some sacking to sit on. And if the night continued fine I could spend it out of doors in one or other of my old haunts.

It was three years since I had been to Dunbeg, an age at thirteen, and I looked back on it with the indulgent nostalgia of someone newly grown. *There* was the place where I had sat with Rupert; *there* I had played tag with my kitten Tabbs. My feet crunched the loose stones as I moved to examine the house, looked up at the window of the room where Rupert had slept and where I had shared his bed that last, fearful night.

The castle was dark and forbidding, and the certainty that it was empty brought home to me the knowledge that nothing would ever be the same; that life had changed, that my mother was not here and that I had erred again in undertaking a foolish and pointless expedition that would almost certainly result in my expulsion from school. Tears of disappointment and apprehension trickled down my face.

I wandered miserably onto the cliff path and thought of my old nightmares. Had they been trying to prepare me for something, to steel me to horror, to let me know that life was an endurance test and pain inescapable? As I heard the sea sing below and the cool night breeze began to search beneath my open coat I realized I was vulnerable and alone. Suddenly it seemed that thirteen was not, after all, so much older than ten; the extent of my information on the world was not so much greater; and a great yearning rose in me for the shelter of my parents.

I smelled the fire before I saw it, woodsmoke, aromatic on the air. I was near the levelled remains of the ruined cottage on

130

the headland now and I stumbled among the pile of stones, hoping that perhaps my mother had decided to spend the night out of doors and that she was here among the residue of the past. But even as I saw the figure huddled over the fire I realized my mistake. I had dreamt of him, thought of him, tried to forget him, but he was here now, real enough in the firelight, his arm raised in alarm and then his exultant grin of calculation and recognition. But I could not run this time; there was no Rupert sleeping nearby; no one into whose arms I could creep. All I saw was firelight on the wild, white face. I backed away, but I was only too aware that behind me there was only the cliff path and the drop to the rocks.

'Ah,' he whispered, 'the devil's whelp,' and he turned his head as though addressing some unseen presence in the night. 'It's *her* . . . come back!'

He took a flaming brand, a small branch, from the fire, stood up and approached me slowly and deliberately. 'It's not lucky what ye've done,' he said in the sibilant whisper of three years ago. 'It's not lucky . . .' His face was grotesque in the shadows cast by the flames; then they died on the faggot in his hand and he was left with a smoking torch. My ears filled with a roaring; I knew he intended my death and my body reacted, turning me precipitously away from the cottage and further along the headland path.

He was behind me now and his furtive voice came on an eerie note of triumph. 'The path is gone . . .'

I stopped just in time. The path *was* gone. Down below me was the growling sea. I turned, saw against the sky the approaching madman with his glowing brand, but away behind him, down where the path began, my eyes were distracted by a white vulpine form that caught the moonlight and was loping behind us up the track.

Stretching out my arm I pointed and screamed, 'It's my wolf!'

Aeneas Shaw turned, whimpered and dropped his weapon, but it was too late. The ground, overhanging the now-fallen pathway, suddenly went from beneath me. The moment of falling seemed absurdly long, as though I had all the time in the world to right myself and could not. I flailed at the air, even at the crazed man, but nothing could save me and all I remember is the indifferent swishing of the sea and then the darkness.

Chapter Eleven

When next I surfaced it was to a dim world where hushed voices conferred against a background of music. I did not know where I was; I had no memory. I was in the dark. The voices were far away, indistinguishable murmurs from a distance.

'Áine!' a clear voice said then, puncturing the immeasurable distance. 'Áine . . .'

It was Rupert's voice and it seemed perfectly normal, after the shock of its immediacy, that he should speak to me. But I wanted to stay in the sleepy jumble of dreams, where I was comfortable and at peace. I waited, thinking he would speak again. But he did not and all I heard was the echo of whatever melody filled the far-off world.

The music was known to me; its stately cadence conjured gossamer images, teasing me to abandon for the moment the happy surfing of its dream world and attempt to identify the sounds. This concentration proved painful. Then, with a sudden sense of triumph, the name of the piece surged into consciousness: Handel's 'Largo'. It conjured up the sparse night-time Drumcondra traffic, the warmth of a rug and a sleeping house.

I realized that someone was stroking the fingers of my left hand. I became aware then that my both my arms were secured, and this conundrum demanded a moment's focus, preventing me slipping back into sleep, and the squeezing of my fingers suddenly hurt, and pain welled and crescendoed.

'Make it stop!'

The stroking of my hand ceased abruptly, and my fingers were seized. 'What did you say, Áine?'

The voice was a whisper half strangled by hope, and the pressure on my hand increased, dragging me away from my blissful voyage down the tide of forgetfulness.

'Stop it!' I said . . . and I heard my own words, sounding strange, like echoes, and the effort of speaking seemed to reopen a succession of doors that had closed behind me.

'Áine, you had a fall . . . at Dunbeg,' my father's voice came from the darkness, calm and rational as ever, as though he were discussing the weather prospects for the weekend. 'Teddy found you. You're in Castlebar hospital. Your mother is here.' And then I knew it was my mother who had whispered to me; her voice came stronger now, although a little hoarse: 'Everything will be fine, my darling.'

But everything was not fine. I knew that something was profoundly wrong, and the lure of the dream world from which I had emerged was still there, dragging me back to kindly depths of oblivion.

'Fight!' my mother's voice said into my ear. 'Don't let go, Áine! Remember what I told you? You must never give up in this life! Fight!'

'Mummy,' I whispered.

The effort of speaking was painful. My mouth felt dry and cracked, as though it had been baked in sand.

'I'm here, darling. I'm holding your hand!'

I think it was a few moments later that the light returned, tentatively, like the operation of one of those fader switches; I saw the faces around my bed, gradually illuminated, looking down on me, my haggard, anxious parents.

A nurse bent over me. She shone a light into my eyes, and when she saw my eyes track it she said drily, 'Welcome back, young lady. You've given everyone a grand fright.' Then she turned to my parents and I couldn't catch her whisper, but I saw them brighten.

But pain ambushed me again, as though it had been awaiting my return to the waking world. I cried out.

'We'll see if we can give you something for that. I have to ask Doctor . . .'

I wondered why my parents' eyes were full of tears.

'What happened?' I whispered.

'Everything will be all right now,' my father said, and then I asked, moving my eyes to take in as much as I could see of the

134

room, 'Where's Rupert?' gritting my teeth against the pain.

They glanced at one another. 'Rupert is in America,' my mother said gently. 'Where else would he be?'

'No he isn't. He was here a minute ago. I heard him.'

'Was he?' my father asked, frowning, but he did not contradict me.

Later they told me it had been Teddy's new dog, Gelert, that had found me. Teddy, alerted by my father that I had run away from school, and checking the house in case I had turned up there, heard him barking and followed him to the headland. Gelert was going berserk, sniffing down the cliff at the point where the path had fallen in. There was nobody in sight. Teddy had come armed with a torch and had shone the beam onto the rocks where he saw a body sprawled in the incoming tide.

'Teddy risked his life in getting you back on terra firma,' my father said briskly. 'He had to go around by the sand. Luckily he got to you before the tide did.'

After a moment I asked, 'But how could I have been in Dunbeg?'

My parents exchanged glances. 'We thought you could tell us that,' my father said in a low voice. 'You left school, Áine – don't you remember? – without permission and turned up on the rocks in Dunbeg.'

There was something terrifying about this information. I was as bewildered as they were. It was as if the earth was not a solid place, but a fantastical location where space and time played tricks.

'What have I broken?'

I was afraid of the question. My right leg was in plaster; my left arm had a splint which secured it to the bed and into it a drip fed.

'You have broken your right ankle and left arm. You'll be in plaster for a while . . .'

I asked no more questions, but lay, flat on my back, and stared at the white hospital ceiling, filled with the relief you have when you surface from a nightmare. I took what I was told on trust. But I was frightened at the hole in my memory and what this portended. I felt like a sleepwalker who has woken up in the wrong house and has no recollection of making the transition.

That night, fully alert in my strait-jacket of a body, I tried to coax movement from my limbs, but my attempts were fruitless. My legs lay there, one of them in plaster, the other useless and disobedient, like fallen warriors.

In the morning when the day nurses came to wash me, turning me over and giving me a bed bath I asked them, 'Will I be like this for ever?'

One of them, a sturdy redhead, with freckles and kind eyes, exclaimed a little too heartily, 'Go on outta that! Sure they'll fix you up in no time. And you have to help by being positive, and thinking positive . . . and we'll all say a little prayer for you.'

This confirmed my worst fears. In desperate need of comfort I told the nurse I wanted to write a letter, and she brought a pad and a biro. With immense difficulty I wrote:

Dear Rupert,
I've had an accident. I think my spine is broken. I might even die! But if I do I'll think of you in Heaven (if I get there).
    Love,
    Áine.

The nurse brought an envelope, sealed it with my missive inside, addressed it, and promised to post it.

My siblings came all the way to Castlebar to see me. 'Where were you, all that time,' Simon asked with scant sympathy, 'while you were out for the count? Were you in Heaven? Did you see God?'

I shook my head.

'Didn't you even see a tunnel with light at the end?' he asked hopefully. Later he told me about some programme he had heard on the radio about people who had died and been resuscitated.

'No. Go away!'

The twins were admiring. 'Can you remember falling? What did it feel like?'

'I can't remember anything.'

'Teddy shouldn't have moved you,' Jack said. 'You're not supposed to move people who've been in an accident.'

'Of course if he had left you you'd have drowned,' Martin said helpfully.

I listened in silence, trying to find in my mind some recollection that would explain why my body had been lifted out of the tide.

Seán said little, which was unusual for him. He stared at me as though it had been suddenly brought home to him that life was full of situations that were not answerable by flippancy, and that death was not just something that happened to other people, but a permanent opportunist waiting at the gates of life.

My parents waited until my siblings were gone to make another attempt to jog my memory.

'Áine, what were you doing on the headland?' my mother asked softly. She was stroking my forehead with anxious fingers, and pushing back my hair. 'Why did you walk up there, of all places? Try to remember.' She was sitting on one side of the bed and my father sat on the other. She never glanced at him and I hated the defeat I sensed in her.

'Oh Mummy,' I said, stumped for a moment and then borne up on a sudden surge of certainty. 'I think I was trying to find you!'

I did not see her face, for she turned away, but my father's eyes followed her and in them I saw a tiny, sober glint of victory. It was not the victory of conquest or successful attrition; it was the quiet satisfaction of having one's wife come to her senses and one's reasonable viewpoint prevail.

'But why did you walk on the cliff path? You knew it was dangerous,' she said then in a small voice.

But I could not remember being on any cliff path. The last thing I remembered was Kildruid and morning prayers.

'I don't know, Mummy. I wish I could!'

'Well,' my father said, 'Teddy is coming to see you tomorrow. Remember to thank him. You owe him your life.'

'He might help jog your memory,' Mummy said, and again she looked at me with haunted eyes and glanced not at all at my father.

Teddy came to see me next day.

'Well young Áine, you gave me a grand job . . . Are you all right in the head to be wandering the cliff path alone in the middle of the night when you're supposed to be safe in your grand boarding school?'

'Thanks for saving me, Ted. I'm very sorry for all the trouble.' My eyes filled with tears, pity for Teddy, self-pity, sorrow for whatever had taken away my grip on reality.

'Sure I've nothin' else to do of an evenin' except to be fishing you out of the sea! What were you doin' up there anyway? Weren't you supposed to be at school?'

'I don't know, Teddy. I can't remember!'

He shook his head. 'You're a cool one, I'll say that for you. Lighting a fire for yourself up in the old cottage and playing Batman off the cliff.' He laughed, but his eyes were devoid of humour, and he regarded me sharply as though mentally vetting a lunatic for the extent of her malady.

'Did I light a fire?'

'Well, I found warm embers in the rubble of that oul cottage that your father pulled down a few years ago . . .'

What was it about the word 'fire' that suddenly twanged the strings of memory? Why did it precipitate the mental picture of a man rushing towards me with a smoking faggot?

I gripped Teddy's arm. 'I know who lit the fire. He drove me off the path.' The picture in my head came into focus and my voice rose. 'It was Aeneas Shaw!'

Teddy's forehead creased into parallel grooves. He eased my grip from his arm and regarded me dubiously. 'My God, Áine,' he said, giving a small, sharp whistle. 'You'd want to watch the things you say. You have a terrible imagination. Don't you realize you could get that poor oul divil into an awful lot of trouble?'

I felt like Alice in Wonderland. Aeneas Shaw was only a poor oul divil? Perhaps in a moment Teddy himself would shrink or change into the Mad Hatter!

'How's Gráinne?' I said to change the subject and force normality on myself. At least Gráinne had not been a figment of my imagination.

'She's grand. She's here to see you. She'll be doing the

138

Leaving soon, God help her. It must be the worst exam in the world!'

'Why don't you bring her in?'

Gráinne, sensible, lovely Gráinne, came in a moment later and looked down at me with an expression of disbelief.

'Howya, Áine? I'm terrible sorry about your accident.'

'So am I.'

'But why did you . . .'

'I don't know!'

Gráinne knit her brow and half shook her head. When her brother indicated that they should let me rest, she said goodbye and Teddy said, 'You'll be out riding again to meet the dawn one of these days,' and they left. I heard him say to her at the door, in a low voice that was not supposed to carry, 'Sure don't be upsettin' yourself. They were never right. There's a lunatic in every generation of that family . . .'

After Teddy was gone I pondered what I had overheard and its implications. I thought for a long time about the man who had come for me with the burning brand from the fire. Had it really happened? What was reality – some kind of conspiracy, perhaps, that people entered into when it suited them? What value could I put on my recollections when they floated like wisps of nothingness, forming and dissipating according to rules of their own?

Are you sure? I kept asking myself. Could you have dreamed it? Are you mad?

But Teddy *had* found the remains of a fire. Could I have lit that myself? And then, as I thought about it, sharp and clear came the recollection of Aeneas's grin as he told me the path was gone, and I remembered how he had edged forward, clutching his smouldering faggot, and I had heard the sea murmuring below.

But it was not until the middle of that night that I woke, convulsed with the memory of leaving school, getting that first lift and finding my way to Dunbeg. The pieces were now forming and the jigsaw complete. I had gone to find my mother, a fool's errand, a childish expedition. But not entirely useless, I told myself. She had come back to us.

★ ★ ★

My father came to see me on his own early next day, to tell me arrangements had been made to transfer me to St Vincent's Hospital in Dublin, and that he would be returning to the city immediately himself. 'I can't take any more time out of the office.'

Before he left I blurted out, 'Daddy, there is something I should have told you!'

'What is that, Áine?'

Now that it came to telling him what I remembered I felt like a fool. It had all the banality of repetition, all the seeming nonsense of déjà-vu.

'The night I fell from the cliff . . . Aeneas Shaw was there . . .'

My father did not reply, but he looked at me intently and expressionlessly. In fact I had never before sensed in him the alternating doubt and savagery that I did at that moment.

'What did he do?'

'He threatened me.'

'Are you quite sure about this, Áine?' he asked, his voice conversational.

'I *am* sure. I backed away from him because he had a faggot he took out of the fire . . .'

'Did he touch you?'

All I could recall was my tormentor's precipitous movement towards me with his lighted weapon, and his strange, quiet grin. I glanced at my father and in his face I saw reluctant disbelief.

'No . . . He just threatened me . . . He said what we had done wasn't lucky.'

Then I remembered that the path was gone and that I had seen far down below the loping vulpine figure, the white wolf of my dreams. 'And then I saw . . .'

'What did you see?' my father pressed sternly when I did not continue.

'Well, I was distracted by something . . . and I fell . . .' I turned my head and looked up at him, aware of his silence and his unblinking regard. 'You don't believe me, Daddy?'

'I'm just trying to understand. How were you distracted? What do you mean?'

But I shook my head. I can't tell you about my wolf, Daddy, I thought in silence. What would you think of me then?

When I didn't reply my father sat for a while in silence and then he sighed and said in a low, patient voice: 'We've been through some of this stuff already, haven't we? Three years ago I got the police. If I get them again what will you tell them? Will you tell them you made a mistake?'

'No. This time I'll tell them everything that I can remember!' I glanced at him and dropped my voice. 'Everything that is except the real reason I went to Dunbeg . . .'

He stood up.

'And Daddy,' I whispered.

'Yes, Áine?'

'Is Mummy home for good?'

'Of course she is,' he said. 'That incident is closed.' He gave a small smile as he said this. He was so matter of fact about it, so certain, that I felt the old unease creeping through me. Oh no it isn't, Daddy, I thought. How can you be so blind?

'Love her,' I wanted to whisper. 'Show her . . . Don't you understand . . .' But his back was already turned and he was heading for the door.

When he was gone I reviewed our conversation. But I could not have told him that what had distracted me that night on the cliff was the sight of a white wolf loping silently up the path. I knew there were no wolves in Ireland. And dreams did not become reality.

It must have been Teddy's dog, I told myself.

Seán came back to see me. When I was alone with him, I tried to find the courage to ask him the question I couldn't ask my parents.

'Just what's wrong with me?'

'You were heavily concussed, Squirrel.' His voice was subdued. 'You were in a coma for five days, which is no joking matter . . .'

'But my back? Why can't I move my legs? Am I really paralyzed?'

Seán did not reply, and his eyes did not meet mine.

'But it's nearly a week now . . .'

141

He stayed silent.

'I can't move, Seán!' I repeated in panic.

My brother put his head down. The sight of his sudden tears, of his head suddenly bent against his knuckles, was surreal. For the first time since early childhood I had a glimpse of the intense individual behind the flippant exterior. His grief terrified me; neither he nor anyone else had mentioned the word paralysis; I had surmised it for myself without really believing it. And now it loomed in my mind like the prospect of a death sentence for life. I whispered, trying to catch his eye, brave for the moment: 'What is the matter with me? What are the doctors saying?'

He took out a handkerchief and blew his nose. 'They're not saying anything about paralysis, Áine . . .' He took a present from his pocket. It was a small squirrel he had carved himself, pretty and gentle, and entirely incongruous as a gift from him.

'It's lovely. Did you make it?'

'I thought you might be lonely!'

This made me laugh. As he was leaving I said, 'Seán . . . there's something I want to ask you.'

'What?'

'Do you know what kind of a dog Teddy has now?'

'It's an Alsatian,' he said. 'Why do you ask?'

'What colour is it?'

'What colour is it? Normal Alsatian colour, brown and black as far as I know . . .'

Sergeant Touhy came with Garda Sheehan and questioned me about the accident. They came shortly after lunchtime one day, while my mother was shopping in the town for a new nightdress for me, because I had complained of my inelegance when I heard I was to be transferred to Dublin.

The sergeant listened to my truncated story. I had run away from school and gone to Dunbeg, I said, and then I had taken a walk along the cliff path and met Aeneas Shaw who had tried to attack me.

The two policemen listened without comment until I had finished. Then the sergeant asked in a tone of bewildered

142

exasperation, 'But why in the name of God, girl, did you run away from school?'

'I dunno.' The truth was none of his business. 'I didn't like it very much.'

'Isn't it well for some!'

'You made a complaint like this before, Áine,' Garda Sheehan said softly. 'Didn't you? Three years ago?' He was writing in his notebook and when he repeated the question as to why I had left school and gone to Dunbeg I feigned weariness and shut my eyes. They waited for a moment, then Sergeant Touhy said, 'Would you believe it! She's dropped off.' He lowered his voice, 'What do you make of this?' he asked the garda sotto voce. 'It's a very serious complaint.'

'It's not her first complaint,' the garda said wearily. 'Last time she retracted it. She's got some kind of fixation on that fellow. And for the love of Jaysus, what was she doin' in that oul place on her own at that hour, having run away from a school that half the girls in the country would be only too glad to get into? She's a strange one!' And then he lowered his voice even further and muttered, 'Sure where would the craythur leave it with that family!'

'She always struck me as fully compos mentis,' the sergeant murmured. 'And in my experience children do not lie.' After a moment's silence they stood up and the sergeant said, 'But all the same, it doesn't add up.'

Later that day an ambulance took me to St Vincent's Hospital in Dublin. My mother accompanied me. She was pale, but smiled at me with tenderness and tried to amuse me on the journey, reading aloud and telling stories. But, glancing at her sideways when she thought I was asleep, I saw that she was slumped in the seat and that her head hung in an attitude of defeat.

'Where did you go, Mummy?' I asked in a whisper. 'When you went away?'

'Not far . . . You wouldn't understand, Áine. You're a child. I didn't leave you, you know. You could have come to me when I was settled . . .'

'Did I ruin everything for you, Mummy?'

She gave a shaky laugh. 'Just get better. Is there anything we can do to help you get better?'

'I would like to see Rupert,' I said, 'but I know that's impossible.'

When we got to Dublin she made a phone call from the hospital and even as she came back to me across the small ward I saw that she had something of moment to impart.

'I've just rung home,' she said, pushing back my hair and kissing my forehead. 'And it seems that Aunty Isabelle phoned earlier to say that Rupert is coming to see you, all the way from the States! We'll collect him at the airport on Friday morning.'

On Friday I said to the nurses, 'Please make my hair nice.' I whispered as I did not want Mrs O'Neill in the next bed to hear me. She had already been grilling me about the accident.

'Is someone special coming to see you?' one of the nurses asked in a low voice.

'Just my cousin, from America!'

I caught the smiles they exchanged. 'What kind of cousin would that be?' one of them demanded quietly.

'A kissing cousin, of course!' the other replied.

They laughed almost in unison and then one said, 'When was the last time you saw him?'

'Three years ago.'

'Sure you were only a kid then. And now you're such a stunning little bird you'll knock him for six.'

When they were finished I asked them in a confiding whisper if they would give me a mirror and I saw my reflected face with consternation. It had got thin and white; there were blue smudges around eyes that seemed too big for my face; my lips were pale.

'I look awful!' I whispered.

One of them took a red ribbon out of her pocket, put it in my hair. '*Now* you're grand! Do you see how it gives you a bit of colour?'

Ah, Rupert, do you remember when you came in that morning, how the sun filled the room, a sudden burst of light as though orchestrating your entrance? Do you remember how you came towards me so very softly across the ward and I pretended to

144

be asleep, but I saw you through my lashes. You stood by me quietly, and I saw that you were no longer the thin American urchin, but that you had changed and grown, splendid with the burgeoning manhood of seventeen, that you wore a jacket and a tie, as though you were presenting yourself for an interview and I wanted to laugh out loud with joy.

You waited, staring down at me, and you looked tired after that long journey, and very anxious, as though dreading what you would find. I opened my eyes and said in as dry a voice as I could muster, 'Sit down, for God's sake!'

You laughed. Somehow, in spite of everything, we always had fun together. I loved you then as I love you now, as I will always love you. I have no more choice in this than I have in breathing, although sometimes, after all that has happened, I wish I had been spared this passion and all that it has meant for my life.

Chapter Twelve

'And what brings Rupert Bear back to Nutwood?' I whispered.

'A wonderful little character called Tigerlily!' His eyes betrayed surprise, amusement, pity as he regarded me from his new height and his new persona. It was a young man, and not a boy, who leaned towards me with a teasing expression. 'Except that she's a bigger little character than she was.'

'So is he!'

He kissed me on the cheek, a formal and somehow strained salute, in which the frisson of a new perception hovered uncertainly. I experienced the scent of him, the rasp of his face, saw the red and blue in his tie. Subliminal recognition that we were no longer children coloured the air between us.

'So what have you been up to this time, Áine?' he asked in a voice that tried to be casual.

'I don't know what you mean by "this time"! I had a disagreement with a cliff.'

'So I heard. But why did you go to Dunbeg?'

'I was looking for Mummy.'

He was silent. Then he said, 'I did get your letter. But before I could reply Mom phoned me to say that you had had an accident. Oh Áine, why did you go back? Why did you go back to that weird place on your own?'

'Don't talk about Dunbeg like that!'

He sat down and his hands took mine.

'I was so sure Mummy would be there . . .' I confided, 'and I was afraid she would meet that man . . .' I paused, looked into his eyes, 'But one good thing has come out of it, Rupert. She came back! Even if I'm paralyzed she came back.'

'Of course she came back. You're her child! A mother will always come back to her child. That is the power of children.'

147

'You're saying I forced her hand?'

'Didn't you?'

And then I saw for the first time that I had acted out of an invulnerable instinct; that one way or the other I could not lose. Only something dramatic would have brought my mother home. I had known this, without realizing that I knew it. I had known that by acting wildly I would win.

For a moment I hated Rupert. Nobody had spoken to me like this since the accident. Everyone had walked around me on tip-toe.

'You'll just have to learn how to control that penchant of yours for the dramatic,' he said, 'before it lands you in a lot of trouble.'

I was filled with self-pity at his words. I hated being seen by him in this state, white as a sheet and ugly as sin. I was thirteen. I had fantasized about looking good, of reading in his eyes some instant of surprised delight similar to the one I had read there when he first clapped eyes on Gráinne O'Keefe, even of generating some soupçon of passion that I could have played with.

'Do I look awful?' My voice seemed small even to my own ears.

He regarded me seriously. 'Stop fishing! You look a bit fragile. There's a touch of the waif about you, but then there always was. But you're not that fragile, Áine. And you're not that paralyzed either. Your mother tells me that there's nothing wrong with your spine. You're stiff and bruised and I came all this way because you said you were paralyzed.'

'There must be something wrong with it! I can hardly bloody move.'

'You *can* bloody move!' He slipped his hand under the sheet and grasped my toes, ran his nails along the sole of my 'good' foot in a sudden movement.

'Stop it! You're tickling!' I cried.

Ah Rupert, you couldn't hide your reaction. The satisfaction lit up your eyes. 'If you can feel,' he hissed into my ear, 'you can sure as hell move, or will be able to when they dig you out from all this stuff.' Then he dropped his voice and said, 'I hope that Shaw guy had nothing to do with your fall, Áine?'

148

I shook my head. Fear squeezed my heart. Pride forbade the truth. I could not bear to hear him say, 'I told you so.'

'Rupert I don't want to talk about it any more!'

Through the open door I could hear the pompous phalanx approaching in the corridor, the consultant's footsteps and those of his acolytes. I knew them well by now, knew the nurses' reverential demeanour.

'Mr O'Byrne – the consultant – is coming now,' I said. 'Will you be back later?'

'Yes.'

'But what about jet lag?'

'What about it?' He made to move towards the door.

I whispered, 'Rupert!'

He turned back.

'When I woke up . . . I had the strongest feeling . . .'

'What was that, Áine?'

'That you were calling me . . .'

He looked at me. 'Weird,' he muttered.

'Did you, Rupert? Did you call me?'

'No.' He lowered his voice. 'But if you want to know the truth, when I was alone, thinking of you and wondering if you were dead or alive, I spoke your name.'

'I heard you!'

In the ensuing silence he added, 'Look, I think you should forget about Dunbeg and everything to do with it. When I remember the state you were in there . . . on my last night . . . I don't like the feeling I get. Forget it, Áine, and keep away from it. The world is full of wonderful places for you to go instead.'

It was May. The chestnut trees were resplendent around Elm Park Golf Club which I could see through the window of the hospital. The golfers strolled, lifting their clubs with unhurried calculation. In my mind they did not know how lucky they were, how miraculous it was to be able to move without pain. Sometimes I longed to call out to them, tell them their lives were wonderful, because I saw them as another species, blessed, like angels, with powers of locomotion denied to lesser beings, powers I had once possessed and taken for granted. The sunlight poured into the hospital. Along the

Merrion Road, which I could but glimpse, someone had a lilac tree in their garden, and immediately I was reminded of the mauve rhododendrons at Dunbeg.

Rupert stayed in Ireland for only three days, and spent most of every day with me.

'When you are better Mom wants you to come for a visit to Virginia,' he said the evening before he left, when my parents and Seán were around my bed. 'So look forward to that and come as soon as you can.'

'I will gladly buy you a ticket to the moon if you hurry up and get better,' my father said, with a wry smile and a wink at Rupert, and then said that he didn't mean that he wanted to get rid of me and we all had a laugh. It was good to hear the laughter, good to see that my parents had lost the haggard look of the damned. Seán was his old provocative self on that visit, and when my father made some further lame joke about children and the grey hairs inflicted by them on their parents his eldest son groaned aloud, 'Oh God Almighty, the Oldness of it . . .'

My father smiled at my mother and she smiled into the middle distance and never met his eyes. But they seemed to be mellower people and I could see my brother thought it was a tribute to his humour.

'Can I go to America too?' Seán demanded. 'If Squirrel can go, why can't I?'

'You might wait to be asked,' my father replied, 'though why anyone would want you with a tongue like yours I can only surmise . . .'

'Mom would love you to come too,' Rupert said. He turned to my mother. 'What about August? Áine should be better by then.'

She smiled, said she'd see.

'Please Mummy . . .'

'Get better first,' she said, 'and then we'll see.'

I was discharged from hospital and my mother took over my care. I was in bed, waiting for the time to pass, attending the fracture clinic, crossing out the days on my calendar. The plaster was heavy from knee from ankle, and the plaster on my arm put a strain on my shoulders. My back ached; I could not

150

turn in bed. As the swelling subsided under the plaster the stitches began to rub against the cast, causing localized inflammation. I had a crutch, but every time I tried to stand up the rush of blood to my leg made me gasp with pain, and I felt as though the cast were going to burst.

Everything had to be done for me. My mother washed and tended me, washed my hair. I was irritable. She bore it with a meekness I hate to think of now, bringing me my meals, drinks, books, reading to me, arranging for my old friends to visit. They signed their names on the plaster with occasional cryptic comments such as 'Stay off cliffs' and 'Hopalong O'Malley.'

Then, seven weeks after my accident, came the day when they removed the plaster casts for the last time, cutting them with the small circular saw I had initially feared. The sense of relief was matched by dismay at the appearance of my skin. 'It's a bit necrotized,' the doctor said. 'Wash twice a day. It'll soon be back to normal.'

Then came the physiotherapy. The medical people put my limbs through their paces, kick-started them into new life. The pain was dreadful. 'It's for your own good,' they said, when I inhaled sharply and tears started in my eyes. 'You have to make friends with your ankle-joint again.'

I felt as though bits of me had emigrated to the moon and were now making a troublesome re-entry into earth orbit. For the physiotherapist it was a challenge, a work of love, of art. For me it was a slow and painful return to a world where I could move, where the sweat broke out on me and the pain met me half way. I was given exercises to do at home. My ankle was still swollen, and to exercise it I used a towel, pulley fashion, until I got it to obey commands again.

The little card that came in the midst of this was encouraging. It was a drawing of Rupert Bear and a bedridden Tigerlily, looking disconsolately at her leg in plaster: The legend in small block letters said:

> But Rupert tells her, 'Please don't worry,
> Have courage, little Tigerlily.'

I gritted my teeth and got on with the business of returning to the world I knew. I wished Rupert were with me, but the mere fact of his existence delighted me, his insistence on my recovery forced me to pit myself against pain. I often stared in the mirror, willing back the beauty I had so carelessly flung away in undertaking my ill-considered journey, sure that without it I would never be visible to Rupert in the way I wanted to be.

I knew now that life was not predictable, nor was it safe, nor could anything in it ever be taken for granted. Perhaps I was also persuading myself that action or inaction should always be vetted for its consequences.

'That creature says he never saw you,' my father informed me one day. 'Sergeant Touhy phoned me today. He evidently thinks the fellow is harmless and wonders as to the extent you imagined the whole thing.'

'Well he isn't, and I didn't.'

My father said, 'I believe you, Áine. But there is a problem in that you acted so strangely in running away from school and so on. Coupled with the fact that you made a complaint before about this man and retracted it.' He turned to me angrily. 'I wish you hadn't been so foolish as to run away from school like that.'

'I wanted to find Mummy!'

'I know. But Áine, I would have known if she had been in Dunbeg. And you hardly expected to find her there, Áine, no matter what you say. Or were you just trying to control her, putting yourself in harm's way deliberately?'

This sounded like a re-hash of Rupert's accusation. 'No, Daddy. I was afraid for her! All of you think I was acting out of caprice and none of you understand. In fact, all of my life, you never understood.'

'What did we fail to understand?'

'Fear, Daddy. I was always afraid! And I had good reason to be . . .'

He sighed. 'I've spoken to your headmistress, and she said there was no reason for you to run from school. You were getting on well . . . you had made friends . . .'

'Yes – and she expelled one of them. She is an awful cow!'

'That is a common enough complaint about headmistresses,'

my father observed drily, 'but I don't think they will be taking you back in Kildruid. I have been invited to seek another school for you.'

I shrugged, hiding my delight, feigning chagrin. I didn't want to go back. The thought of Sister Theresa and her gimlet eyes and her covert pleasure in my disgrace was more than I could bear.

He shook his head, straightened his glasses. 'You can shrug, Áine, but this gives us a problem. I don't suppose the Green would have you back after the Kildruid business . . . ?'

'They might!'

'And as for the Shaw fellow – the problem is that he denies being near the headland that night; there are no witnesses except yourself and your evidence cannot be corroborated . . .'

'And would not be enough on its own,' I finished. 'Isn't that what you mean?'

'Yes . . . for a court case. But to put him back in the asylum is another matter. If two doctors can certify him . . .'

'Will they?'

'I need something to go on. If someone else complained . . . But he's cunning enough, seems to behave himself and not bother anyone in the locality . . .'

'He's as mad as a March hare, Daddy! You don't understand because you have never seen him as I have. He hates me, because I did something he cannot forgive.'

'What was that, Áine?' my father asked, his voice very quiet and his eyes penetrating. 'What did you do?'

'You know that ruined cottage on the headland, near the spot where I fell? The place you levelled?'

'Yes, of course.'

'Well, he thought that ruin was his ancestors' home and that they nearly all died in the Great Famine . . . I told you about this before. It was some kind of shrine for him . . . he put wild flowers there in old jampots and things . . .'

'So what did you do to provoke him?'

I took a deep breath. 'A simple stupid thing. The day I went on the path with Rupert I went in there to have a pee.'

His laughter filled the air.

'You needn't laugh,' I said sulkily. 'It's true! He caught me in the act, and he went berserk. He thought I had desecrated the place or something. If Rupert hadn't come back he would have hit me.'

My father's face became red. He said after a moment in a tight voice, 'He'll never lay a finger on my daughter or frighten her again!'

'What are you going to do, Daddy?'

His eyes narrowed. 'We'll have to see!'

The exercises were paying off; the muscles were doing their work; the slow pain in my back abated. Now that my recovery was no longer in doubt I noticed how my father relaxed, how his demeanour towards my mother held a covert smugness and as covert a relief. He had his wife secured to him again; she had learnt her lesson and was unlikely to stray from the nest a second time. At least I felt this to be his perspective, sensing him as I did. He was often lively, as though he had won some small triumph. And my mother was newly subdued. It was an unnatural submission for someone with so keen a spirit, and for a while I waited for her resentment. But it never came.

'Did you love me so much then, Áine, that you ran away from school to find me? Or was there some other reason driving your action; did you, perhaps, use it as an excuse?'

This question was posed out of the blue one sunny afternoon when we were together in the garden, me weeding to please her, she pruning roses. Stricken by what her question might intimate, remembering both my father's and Rupert's accusation, I turned to look at her, but neither her voice nor her expression bore any trace of resentment. The question was a question; quiet, a little wistful.

'Of course I love you, Mummy,' I said, putting down the hoe and struggling with the sudden lump in my throat. 'I thought you had gone because of me. And I was afraid you would meet that man!'

She nodded as though this intelligence was only part of what she wanted to ascertain, because she looked at me for an instant with something of her old sharpness and penetration. But it was gone in a moment and she went back to her work.

154

Why is it that silence can be so powerful? My mother's silence had a punch to it that her erstwhile sharp commentary on the world and its ills had never possessed. As I waited for her to volunteer some further comment I felt that silence to be unbearable, and even more unbearable was her gentle, defeated pose, back and head bent over a succession of rose bushes, a strand of greying hair falling from an ill-secured clip. There was no sign now of the glamour that she had assumed before her precipitous departure, when the grey in her dark hair had been carefully tinted and her body honed to its maximum elegance. And for her to devote time to gardening was out of character. Formerly she had hated gardening, would exclaim, 'They'd all live in a jungle if you let them . . . so why not let them . . .' and I longed for this acerbity to reassert itself.

I knelt beside her and helped her in silence. Then I said, 'Mummy, why did you go away that time? Daddy was terribly cut up; so were the boys . . .'

'I am owned,' she said, 'corralled by love. Oh, not by other people's, by my own. I went away because I was hoping to find something I needed; but I was tormented by the needs of those I had left behind. So I had a choice to make. You made the process easy. You are what is ultimately important; each of you . . . my children.' She smiled ruefully. 'Although not, perhaps, what is best for me . . .'

'What did you expect to find?'

She smiled, pushed back the long strand of hair, and suddenly muttered with a half laugh, 'My hair is getting long again.' She seemed lost in reverie as she added in a whisper, 'Like Samson's.'

I remembered the Biblical story, how Samson got his strength back with his hair. I glanced at her, but she seemed far away.

'What about Dad?' I asked, alarmed by her distance. She turned glazed eyes on me and then asked sharply, as though pulling herself back from whatever private vista she had been surveying:

'What about him, darling? He is happy.'

It was then I understood for the first time that domestic stability may come at a high price; that one family member

155

may provide the emotional gold for everyone, like a lode that is mined inexorably until it is spent. And it was not that my father consciously rolled out a desert of the spirit before his wife. He was simply blind, belonging to a mind-set which saw a woman's role as servicing husband and family and which knew nothing of the need for the dynamism of challenge, for nourishing, for reciprocity. He was the product of an Irish Catholic education which saw women as commodities, as props, as helpmeets.

I adored both my parents, but to neither of them could I talk about the other. Children know their parents, but when are they ever asked for their advice?

Everything had changed. Not outwardly; everyone thought my mother had simply been away on a holiday; the world saw the family as ever, but each member of it knew that nothing would ever be the same. What had been destroyed was our absolute certainty about the nature of life. Seán, for the moment at least, was gentler; his scoffing had lost its edge and he seemed to indulge in it now to prove to himself that life was going on as before. The twins were less mutually absorbed, and seemed to be looking at their parents and siblings with troubled eyes. Simon, glad that his mother was back, was the only one prepared to pretend that things were just the same. But I saw the sideways glance he sometimes directed around him, as though wondering if the parameters of his universe would shift again while he was not looking.

My mother contacted my former day school, Our Lady's College, St Stephen's Green, and announced to me one morning that we were going to see the headmistress. 'Get dressed, Áine. You need a school to go back to.'

'They won't have me back . . . not after running away from Kildruid.'

She murmured, 'We'll see . . .'

I went back to the Green and sat in the parlour while my mother had a confidential pow-wow with the headmistress in the latter's office. Then the good nun returned to the parlour with my mother, and asked me very kindly how I was now and whether I would be able to return to school in September.

I said with a gulp that I would.

'And will you work and stop idling your time away?'

'Yes, Sister.'

'You're a big girl now, Áine. Time to pull up your socks and think about what you want to do with your life.'

But I already knew what I wanted to do with my life. I had one talent; even Rupert in the midst of his exasperation had acknowledged it. I had, as he had put it, a penchant for the dramatic. The resolution was already forming in me to be an actress and put the only thing I was any good at to work for me, and in doing so to take control of my life.

My mother was silent as we drove home. It was raining; I heard the rhythm of the windscreen wipers, the swish of the wet tyres, saw the umbrellas sprouting along O'Connell Street.

After a few minutes I found the courage to ask diffidently, 'How did you work that particular miracle, Mummy?'

'You mean your readmittance to the Green? The truth, Áine. I told your headmistress the truth. You'd be amazed how powerful it is! And it made her happy, gave her the opportunity to work her Christian charity on a Protestant . . .'

I was still nursing the bitterness of this comment when the car turned in the laneway at the rear of our house. I got out to open the garage doors and my mother put the car away. Then I went, my jacket over my head, to close and bolt the doors behind her.

But something moved at the far end of the laneway. Hunched in the shadows a raincoated figure, his face half covered by a filthy scarf, was watching me. Although I only saw his eyes I knew who he was and felt my heart begin a tattoo, as though it, and not my brain, commanded my body.

'Mummy!' I whispered, hobbling into the garage where my mother was getting her handbag out of the car.

'What is it?'

I could not speak. My throat felt as though it had closed, but I pointed. She ran into the laneway and I followed her. But all we saw was a figure in an old raincoat hurrying around the corner to the street.

'Who was that?' my mother asked.

'It's him,' I whispered. 'I knew he would come for me!'

My mother shot me a concerned look. 'Oh Áine, you don't

mean the Shaw fellow. It can't be him. He was taken back to the mental hospital recently. Someone complained about him to the Western Health Board and when he fortuitously bothered some tourist or other in Mulvey who was trying to take a walk along the cliff they dumped him back where he belongs . . . the sergeant phoned the other day to inform your father.'

I knew better. I would know those eyes anywhere, watching, burning. But when I tried to tell my mother this she looked at me with compressed lips and said patiently, 'Really, darling, it's not healthy to overindulge your imagination like this.'

There was only one place left where I dared to be myself, and that was inside my head. I retreated into a silence where I talked to Rupert.

Everyone in the wider family commented on the change in me. I was keeping to my regime of exercises, and attending physiotherapy, driven to the sessions by my mother, and was gradually becoming, physically, almost as good as new, able to hobble, able to walk. But mentally I was haunted; by the figure in the raincoat, by the migration of the troubles of Dunbeg to my fastness in Dublin where I had imagined myself safe. I kept an eye out for Aeneas Shaw, and could not bear to leave the house on my own. When my father taxed me on this I said that I had seen the man again, and he repeated what my mother had told me, that he had been put back in the mental hospital and was out of harm's way. I had read about Cassandra and I felt like her now, doomed to tell the truth and never be believed.

'I saw him, Daddy. I'm telling you I saw him!'

My father looked at me in quasi-exasperation. 'Well, there's one way to establish whether that was even possible,' he said tersely, and he went into his study. A few minutes later I heard him using the phone, and I slipped upstairs and lifted the receiver of the landing extension.

'St Fintan's Hospital,' the voice at the other end announced.

'I'm trying to ascertain if you have a patient called Mr Aeneas Shaw,' my father said. 'He's from Mulvey in County Mayo.'

'Who's speaking please?'

My father assumed his 'legal' voice: 'My name is Noel O'Malley, solicitor.'

'Oh . . . Hold on a moment and I'll put you through to Dr Murphy.'

I listened, hardly daring to breathe. Dr Murphy came on the line, demanded the identity of the caller and seemed hesitant when my father repeated his name and occupation.

'We don't give out information about our patients to anyone except relatives.'

'My daughter was the victim of an attempted assault by this man,' my father said. 'I understand from the police that he was committed and all I'm looking for is your confirmation.'

'Yes. He was committed.' Then he added in a half apologetic voice, 'But I'm afraid Mr Shaw isn't with us at the moment.'

'What do you mean?'

'He . . . managed to get out recently and has not come back. But don't worry . . . the police will find him'

I put the receiver down softly. Even on the landing I could hear my father's raised and angry voice. When he came to find me a few minutes later and assured me with troubled eyes that I had nothing to worry about I did not tell him I already knew the truth.

Silence was a place. In it I was sovereign; in it I could attempt to unravel the enigma that was my life. I spent a good deal of time staring out of the window at Drumcondra Road, wondering if I would see the tramp whose face leapt into my consciousness night and day. I kept hearing the words he had thrown after Rupert and myself that long-ago day on the headland. 'Never fear but Aeneas Shaw'll get ye.'

'You'll have to stop this silent treatment, Áine,' my mother said one morning. 'What is the matter with you? You are a very lucky girl to be whole and alive after what happened to you.'

'I know, Mummy. I'm sorry.'

'Just what is bothering you?'

I longed to tell her, but dared not, shook my head.

'You need a break,' she muttered. 'You need a complete break before you go back to school. I suppose you'd still like that trip to America?'

'Oh yes . . .'

'But you couldn't go all that journey on your own,' she

mused then, looking at me sharply, as though trying to see me through the eyes of the world's predators.

'Why not? I'm not a baby.'

'Don't argue, Áine. You're a young girl and you're not going alone. We'd have to send your brother with you.'

'You could come, Mummy . . .'

She turned away. 'No,' she said in a low voice. 'I couldn't. I promised your father I would never go away without him again.'

I thought of my aunt and her letter to Uncle Alex. 'Oh Mummy,' I cried, 'that's just another form of slavery!'

She turned and gave me an odd look. 'Do you really think so, Áine?'

That evening in the kitchen my mother discussed the proposed trip with my father.

'I think it's a good idea, darling,' he said. And then he turned to me. 'I did promise you, Áine.'

I loved the word darling in his mouth, and glanced at my mother to see if it struck any tender chord with her, but her face was impassive.

I heard no more of this hoped-for trip for a few days. I thought of Aeneas Shaw every night and scrutinized every shadow on the pavement before going to bed, closing and locking my window. I sometimes woke, terrified that he was in the house, and would listen, my heart thumping at every tiny sound; the wind in the roof valley, the creaking in the house next door.

'Your room is airless, Áine,' my mother might exclaim when she called me in the morning. 'Here, I'll open the window for you.'

But when she was gone I closed and locked it again. I longed for someone to whom I could talk, someone who would believe me. I wrote to Rupert, thanking him for his card, but dared not update my news to him because I had not told him the truth about my fall.

And then came the reprieve. The body of a man was found in a ditch near Westport, on a lonely stretch of road south of Louisburg. The ditch was full of water and the body was badly decomposed and could not be positively identified. But as it fitted no description of any missing person and as it was obviously a tramp, the police told my father that they believed the body to be that of Aeneas Shaw.

He came to tell me this. 'Well, it seems to be the end of the business, at any rate, doesn't it, Áine?'

'Yes, Daddy. If they're sure it's him.'

'You've been fixated on that fellow,' my father said. 'Now it's time to let him go. Don't think of him any more.'

The letter from Aunt Isabelle was addressed to my mother and she showed it to me when she brought me breakfast in bed.

> Dearest Joyce,
> Thanks for your letter. If Áine is nearly better why not send her to us as soon as possible – otherwise the summer will be gone. I'm thrilled she's out of plaster and recovering well. Seán is very welcome to come with her. Let them stay for as long as possible. There is much to see and I am so looking forward to their visit.
> It's hot and humid here so light clothes are the thing.
> Your devoted sister-in-law,
> Isabelle.

'Well, Áine,' my mother said, handing me the letter with a smile, 'do you still want to go?'

'Oh Mummy, do you need to ask?'

Seán voiced excited enthusiasm. He had a badly-paid holiday job stacking shelves in Dunne's Stores and was only too happy to dump it.

'I'll ask Jennifer in the travel agency to see what she can do about fares,' my father said expansively when he came home that evening. He was in a very good mood these days; he had recently pulled off some major contracts with very substantial fees. It was as though life had decided to see things his way in everything. And so it was settled. There was an excited phone call to the States. I heard Rupert and Aunt Isabelle tell me how they were looking forward to seeing Seán and me in Virginia.

'If you fly to Washington we'll meet you there,' Rupert said.

161

'And then we can drive to Mount Wexford . . .'

My mother's birthday, her forty-fifth, took place the week before we left. My father took his family out to dinner and afterwards he led us to the garage.

'What have you got up your sleeve, Daddy?' I whispered, sure that this was some sort of treasure hunt.

He winked at me, put a finger to his lips. Inside the garage was a new BMW, parked in the place where my mother's little Renault usually sat. My mother's eyes widened and my father behaved like a boy who had bought the *Beano* annual for his mum.

'What do you think of this little number?' he asked casually.

'It's quite something,' my mother replied doubtfully. My father fished a set of keys out of his pocket and threw them to her. 'It's yours. Happy Birthday!'

She said nothing for a moment and then murmured, 'Thank you, Noel. It's very beautiful . . . but it's too much . . .'

'No buts! Will you take it for a test drive now?' he asked eagerly, like someone trying to jostle her back to the jaunty spirit of yesteryear.

'Later,' she said. 'It's a beautiful car.'

I realized that she was delighted with her gift. There was in her eyes an enthusiasm that I had not seen for a long time, a bright and fervid joy.

The plane took off from Shannon at noon. It flew westwards above an endless sea while we lunched and talked and I stared out the window. Seán, highly excited, craned his head from time to time, exclaiming at the sight of icebergs, tracing on the map in the in-flight magazine the trajectory of our flight.

'We are going north first,' he said knowledgeably, 'keeping to the curvature of the earth . . .'

Hours later we saw the white coast of Labrador, then Newfoundland, brown and cold, and soon we were high over Boston. The eastern coast of America looked like one uninterrupted, sandy beach. So it exists, after all, I thought. America really exists! And then I laughed at myself for being so silly. I watched in awe as New York and a glimpse of Manhattan eventually came and went.

'Does it never end?' I whispered. We were so high that I

could see over many hundreds of miles and still the land stretched away into limitless horizons.

'End?' Seán intoned, leaning across me to the window. 'It's a continent, difficult for leprechauns to comprehend . . .'

He was awed too. But the plane was dipping landwards and suddenly we were swooping over Washington, which came up to us out of the great, green land like a city from a fable. I saw the late afternoon sun shine on Capitol Hill.

'There's the Monument and the Lincoln Memorial,' my sibling whispered with bated breath and soon we were roaring down the runway. Even before I set foot on American soil I knew Aunt Isabelle had been right. This was an utterly different place. And I knew that Rupert would be there to meet us, take us in charge in this his vast homeland. And because of this, in an odd sort of way, it was a homecoming.

Chapter Thirteen

I saw Rupert almost at once. He was craning his head, scanning the arriving passengers. He was dressed in T-shirt and jeans, quite a different Rupert to the rather formal version who had visited me in hospital. I noticed again how adult he had become, how fit looking, muscled and brown. But it wasn't just Rupert that was different. The atmosphere was one I had never encountered; it spoke of an environment where comfort was taken for granted, and where abundance was the natural order.

I was wearing a short skirt which I had bought myself in Dunne's Stores.

'That skirt is far too short,' my mother had said.

'No, Mummy, it isn't. Everyone is wearing them that length.'

Rupert smiled, waved. He relaxed visibly as we came towards him and gave us his slow, private smile.

'How y'all?'

His southern drawl was deliberately exaggerated. He clapped Seán on the back. But the hug he gave me, while cousinly and proper, had in it an unspoken intensity that seemed natural as the light.

'How was the flight?'

'Fantastic!' Seán replied, and launched into a eulogy of transatlantic travel. But Rupert was looking at me, and in his eyes there was a half-speculative assessment, a humour and a warmth. His gaze lingered on the arm that had been broken, glanced down at my plasterless leg. 'It's good to see you up and about,' he said quietly. 'Are you completely better?'

'Still a bit wobbly; ankle feels like jelly, but I'm otherwise OK.'

We left the terminal building. I tried to conceal the residual

165

limp, but he said, 'But you're *not* completely better yet. Take your time!'

Outside Seán said, taking off his jacket, 'God, how do you breathe?'

It was heat such as I had never known. It came out of everything, the ground, the buildings, even the vegetation. The humidity was smothering.

'You'll get used to it,' Rupert said with a laugh. 'Anyway, the car is air conditioned.'

The tights I was wearing were unendurable; my legs felt as though they were liquefying. My skirt was also shorter than any skirt I saw around me and I wished I had listened to my mother. I hated the sudden feeling of being the Jezebel imported all the way from the Island of Saints and Scholars.

Our cousin led us to a Cadillac in the car park. A black man jumped from the driver's seat and came to take our luggage. I stared at him. I had seen few black people in the flesh and none at close quarters.

'This is Matthew,' Rupert said. He turned to the black man. 'These are my cousins, Áine and Seán O'Malley.'

'Howy'all?' Matthew said, shaking hands and smiling. He took our luggage, stowing it away in the boot.

Rupert opened the passenger door for me. 'Do you want to sit in front, Áine?'

'No. I'll sit in the back.'

'I'll sit in front,' my brother volunteered with alacrity.

I climbed into the back and Rupert got in beside me. I sat back in the leather seat and looked at my cousin, aware again of what passed between us in silence, a recognition, a blind understanding, only remarkable in retrospect.

'How long is the journey to Mount Wexford?' Seán demanded as we moved out of the airport and Matthew dodged around bends on the 'wrong' side of the road, making me gasp.

'About five hours.'

'Five hours!'

'No worse than going to Cork, but about twice the distance,' Rupert said with a laugh. 'Now what do you guys want to do,' he added, 'go straight home or have a quick detour around Washington?' He glanced at Seán as the latter turned to him. 'I suppose I shouldn't ask.'

The city was beautiful: architecturally European, atmospherically open, as though a piece of Europe had dropped out of the sky into a primeval landscape. The combination of New World innocence and wealth was powerful. Rupert's detour took us around the Capitol, down Pennsylvania Avenue. We saw the Mall, the Washington Monument and glimpsed the White House. He pointed out the Smithsonian: 'We can come up and spend a day there before you go home . . . if you like museums . . .'

Many of the Victorian houses had air conditioners sticking out of open windows, telling their own climatic story. The old part of the city reminded me of Dublin, but the air was free from received Irish wisdom, and the presence of so many black people on the street gave it a flavour of the exotic.

We left the city by a bridge across the Potomac River, Rupert pointing out the great five-sided building of the Pentagon, and then he took route 1 to the south. This was a seemingly endless motorway, flanked on both sides by forests and interspersed with occasional shopping precincts. I was reminded of what my aunt had once told me about America.

'You've plenty of trees here anyway,' Seán observed. 'We've been planting them in Ireland, trying to replace some of what we lost. But they're all spruce and pines; we'll never have great deciduous forests again.'

'What you're seeing here is the forest primeval,' Rupert said. 'It was here in the days when the first European set foot on American soil.'

Seán whistled. 'How many miles of this is there?'

'How many miles, Matthew?' Rupert demanded with a laugh.

'Oh 'bout a thousand maybe . . .' our chauffeur said with a grin.

Rupert glanced at me, as though waiting for me to comment. But I was silent. I felt his arm and shoulder touch mine for a moment.

'We'll stay tonight in Fredericksburg,' he said. 'No point in tiring you guys out.'

Seán said, 'Where's Fredericksburg?' He was studying a map

he had found in front of him. After a moment he said triumphantly, 'I see it. It's about fifty miles – just off this highway.'

'It was the scene of one of the early battles in the Civil War in 1862,' Rupert said. 'A victory for the Confederates. The town goes back a long way, to the early seventeen hundreds.'

'I didn't think anything went back that far in the States,' my brother said, and he turned to us with his annoying smirk.

Rupert looked back at him stonily. 'You sure have a lot to learn.'

I was suddenly aware how the relationship between these two people had shifted. Rupert was no longer the small foreign cousin who could be slagged to extinction. He was now the master in an unfamiliar environment, already possessed of precocious adulthood.

Fredericksburg was a quaint old town on the banks of the Rappahannock River: neat Georgian clapboard houses, a church with a spire like a witch's hat. We stayed at a bed and breakfast in the middle of the town. Rupert shared with Seán and I was shown to a room overlooking the street with a double bed.

The windows had louvred shutters and curtains with tie-backs, the wallpaper was striped, the beeswaxed furniture bore the hallmarks of generations of care. Although the furniture and the decor was classical European there permeated the atmosphere something spare, simplistic and almost Puritan. This was not the America that television had prepared me for. There was no brashness here, nor any kind of licence. Instead the place was redolent of an old and stringent discipline.

It reminded me that I was now three thousand miles from Ireland, remote from turmoil. Here everything that had haunted me seemed a nonsense. Anyway, I was exhausted, by excitement, by the journey, by the fact that it was ten o'clock before I got to bed – about three in the morning Irish time.

But that night, I was jolted out of my new complacency by a dream and I woke sweating and distraught. For a moment I thought I was back in my room at Dunbeg and that the sea was whispering outside. I got out of bed, drew back the striped curtains and looked out the window, but there was only the deserted street, with its shuttered shops and houses. The dream was fading like a will-of-the-wisp, but the certainty remained that, in it, something terrible had occurred involving Rupert, and I had seen it but been unable to shout a warning. Then it came to me – a sudden vignette from the nightmare. It was water that had filled my mouth and lungs and stopped me from screaming, and I saw again the rush of the tide in the dreamscape and racing towards me, down the headland, the lupine form. The wolf stopped and seemed to stare at me; I saw his form against the sky and his red eyes.

I put out my hand and touched the satinwood of the tallboy by the windowsill, oddly comforted to be here in Fredericksburg, a world away from Ireland and Dunbeg. I went back to bed and eventually slept until morning.

Next day Rupert announced that he would drive as far as Richmond, and Matthew said, 'You know as well as I do your mom's instructions 'bout that.'

'Mom worries too much, Matthew.'

After an hour or so on the highway we came to Richmond, the capital of Virginia, a port at the head of the James River. Here the air was full of something more than humidity, a secret sultriness. At least two thirds of the people I saw on the streets were black.

'This was the centre of the slave trade,' Rupert said, reminding me of Aunt Isabelle's cry, 'All those African faces and their historic wrongs!'

We did not stay long in Richmond, and were soon on the highway again, going west now.

'Not much longer,' Rupert said at one point.

We passed ornate gates and behind them I saw an avenue and a glimpse of a big white house that looked like something from *Gone With the Wind*.

'Is your house like that?' I asked Rupert.

'Nothing so grand! That place belongs to the Penroses . . . They drop by sometimes. Mr Penrose was at school with my father.'

'Do they have children?'

'A daughter. Gloria is her name.'

Mount Wexford was a white-pillared plantation house with

fluted Ionic columns. The front of the house had verandahs running the length of both the ground and upper floors. It was surrounded by trees: magnolia, tulip trees, white and pink dogwood, oak, trailing arbutus. A lawn, sprayed by a sprinkler, bordered the house and the whole place was beautiful and exotic, an ante-bellum house sheltered from the battering of time. I got out of the Cadillac, and was startled again by the stifling humidity waiting to overpower us, like some mythical beast that defies belief until it rears up in front of you and breathes in your face.

Aunt Isabelle came hurrying from somewhere and fell on my neck. She was wearing blue, her favourite colour, as she had once told me, and was much thinner than I remembered, as though the sap had been somehow squeezed out of her. Two wings of white hair now inhabited her temples.

She exclaimed in her nervous, dramatic way, 'Well, darlings, here's a sight for sore eyes!' She held me at arm's length. 'But you've grown . . . you're almost a young woman.' For a moment I felt in her a tinge of dismay, as though this was a development she hadn't considered and for which she was not prepared. 'Are you completely recovered from that nasty accident?' she demanded then, standing back a little to examine me.

'Yes . . . I'm grand now. I can't run yet, but I'm otherwise OK.'

She turned to Seán and surveyed him for a moment in silence. 'You bad, bad boy, you're taller than ever,' she said, with an almost coquettish movement of her face and body. I saw my brother squirm. 'What a bashful fellow he has become,' she said, turning to me, as though discussing the family pet. 'I had a different memory of him. He was much more voluble in Dunbeg!'

'That's one way of putting it,' I said unkindly, and caught the glint of humour in Rupert's eye.

My brother hung his head in mock subjection before this onslaught. I was surprised by my aunt's hungry delight in the sight of us, and I felt in Rupert, who stood by in silence, a careful assessment of her and her reaction to our arrival. She put an arm around each of us and drew us towards the house. Matthew took our luggage from the boot.

170

'Show these children their rooms,' my aunt said to her son at the front door. 'Áine is to have the pink room, and Seán the Governor's room,' and she laughed a little unsteadily. 'Come down when you're ready and we'll have some lemonade on the porch.'

Seán and I followed Rupert into the house. It was cool indoors, a different climate. Upstairs, we were introduced to a black woman who came towards us on the landing. She had burnished ebony skin. Her hair was tied into a hairnet, and topped off by a thin, scarlet ribbon.

'This is Milly,' Rupert said, 'Matthew's wife. She looks after the house.'

'How y'all?' she said, giving her hand. 'Your mamma was sure worried 'bout that journey,' she confided to Rupert. 'But I kept remindin' her that my Matthew was drivin'.' She looked at Rupert severely. 'But she said she couldn't be at all sure 'bout that.'

Rupert raised his eyebrows at his own foibles. 'But I wouldn't drive the Cadillac, Milly . . . you know that.'

Milly laughed. 'Wouldn't you, sweetheart chile?' she said archly, and went down the curved staircase.

I stood and looked around at the polished wooden floors, the rugs and antiques, the portraits, the landscapes, the vases full of flowers, and I heard the hum of something electrical that sounded like central heating, until I realized it was the air conditioner.

'This is your room, Áine.'

He guided me to the open door of a bright chamber. It possessed a French window that opened onto the upper verandah, which he called the gallery, and overlooked the lawn.

I walked across this room, feeling the delicious draught from a white electric fan that turned in the centre of the ceiling with leisurely sussuration, looked around at the pink Chinese carpet, the white walls, the Victorian dressing-table. The bed was a fourposter, with the hangings removed, and for a moment I thought of Dunbeg, the only other place I had ever slept in a bed like that. Through the French window was the shady gallery, with cane chairs and the potted azaleas. I went into this gallery and stood beside the pillars of the portico to look out at the lawn and the trees. From the verandah below I heard the clink of ice in a glass and wondered at my aunt's reluctance while she was in Dublin to return to this paradise.

'Look,' Seán whispered beside me, indicating a sudden movement in one of the trees and I turned and saw a grey squirrel flapping his tail just five yards from me. He was halfway up an oak and was displaying his elegance, showing his tail's white underside; then he straightened, and leapt with weightless ease to another branch, so that the tail stuck out behind him like a ruler.

'Now you can have a real heart to heart,' my brother continued, 'one squirrel to another . . .'

'Terribly funny,' I said with a sigh. 'Why don't you just grow up?'

Rupert laughed. From somewhere a bird called hoarsely, 'Tee hee, tee hee . . .'

'You are so lucky to own a fantastic gaff like this,' Seán told Rupert in a low voice after a moment. 'It's the most exotic place I've ever seen!'

'I don't own it,' Rupert murmured. He glanced around as though seeing the place through our eyes, and then added, 'But, if my father has his way, someday it will own me.'

For a moment there was something in the reflective carriage of his head as he looked away from me that reminded me of the vulnerability I had first sensed in him three years earlier in the library at Dunbeg.

I wondered with sudden dread how much of my mother's recent history was known to my aunt and uncle and whether we could expect to be questioned on it.

'Rupert,' Seán asked, as though he were telepathic, keeping his voice low, 'does your mother know about Mummy . . . about her going away?'

'No. And please don't tell her! She's very excitable and God knows what she'd read into it.'

'Áine and I will keep our mouths shut,' Seán said, glancing at me. 'The last thing either of us want to do is answer questions.' He looked down the length of the gallery and at the other French windows and asked, 'Who sleeps in the other rooms along here?'

172

'Oh that's my mother's room,' Rupert said, indicating the room next my own. 'And the one on the other side of it is mine. Your room, Seán, overlooks the back of the house. Come on and I'll show you.'

I did not remember my Uncle Alex. He breezed onto the porch just before dinner with the confidence of a man who owns the world. He was tall and overweight, with shrewd eyes and a wide mouth full of yellow teeth. He had the charisma generated by superabundant energy and a certainty that his perspective on any subject was definitive.

'Give your old uncle a kiss,' he said when I shyly extended my hand, and I was caught in a hug that squeezed me flat; I felt the rasp of his chin against my brow. I was uneasily aware that he held me for a fraction more than was necessary, releasing me to shake hands with Seán, exclaiming all the while on the passage of time and how extraordinary it was that we had grown up.

'Last time I saw you was when Bella and I went through Ireland back in '79.' He turned to his wife. 'Ain't that right, Bella?'

My aunt nodded.

'You were a little tyke who had lost a piece of his fire engine and was really kicking up about it,' he told Seán. Then his eyes reverted to me. 'And you, little lady, were in diapers, as cute as could be.' His eyes, as he said this, were steady and smiling, but I was uncomfortably aware that they saw every inch of me, that they were comparing me to my former diapered state. I was glad, for some reason, that I was in jeans and not in the short skirt of yesterday. Aunt Isabelle, who had been observing him in silence, poured him a drink, and sipped her own. In fact, she had been sipping since I came downstairs, in a slow deliberate fashion, as though drinking were like breathing, necessary and involuntary. Milly came out to tell us dinner was ready. We had the meal in the dining room, a room with two tall windows and Regency style furniture, where another electric fan created a small caressing breeze. The meal was a stir fry of shrimp with vegetables and rice and a side salad. For dessert there was pecan pie.

The conversation was mostly about Ireland – inquiries after

our parents, our siblings, the Irish political and economic scene, and suggestions as to what we should see during our visit.

'Colonial Williamsburg,' my aunt said.

'Sure! See the former capital of Virginia,' my uncle intoned, 'preserved as was . . . Pass the salt Bella, like a good girl.' The tone of this request, the first he had addressed to her in my hearing, had the ring of an old exasperation.

'I'll take them to see it,' Rupert said.

'Well, you needn't think you're driving,' Aunt Isabelle exclaimed.

'Why shouldn't he drive?' my uncle said. 'He's old enough. Do you want to make a complete pansy of him, Bella? Is that it?'

My aunt seemed to shrink in her chair.

Rupert hardly glanced at his father. 'I'll be careful, Mom,' he said gently. 'I'm a good driver.'

After dinner my uncle brought us around to the stables to see his trotters, and delivered a monologue on harness racing, and showed us the sulkies, the lightweight racing bikes drawn by the horses in competition.

'Are these horses thoroughbred?' Seán asked.

'No,' my uncle replied. 'They're Standard breds. That means they're thoroughbreds who have been interbred with sturdy farm stock. Which makes them smaller and quieter than their aristocratic cousins.'

We were conducted around the back of the stables towards the track, passing the garage where the Cadillac now rested after its journey, alongside a Buick. I exclaimed on the size of the garage, for it could hold three cars or more, as well as providing room for a workbench which held an impressive array of tools – saws, an axe, a Stilson and a row of smaller wrenches, hammers and do-it-yourself paraphernalia.

Leaving the garage we passed the old smokehouse and a row of clapboard houses, on which the paint was peeling.

'The old kitchen and former slave quarters,' Rupert said in my ear. 'The outdoor servants live here now.'

Some black children were kicking a ball; a woman was putting sheets on a clothesline; she looked at us curiously. On the porch of the last house in the row two black women sat in

174

conversation. One was middle aged; the other was young, and wore a red dress and bright lipstick. She was smoking a cigarette, and I could see her long, gold-painted nails. She examined us curiously, leaning forward a bit, and as we passed I saw the smile she gave my uncle and the way she thrust out her breasts.

The track, an oval of sand, was set back against the trees. A horse was being put through its paces, drawing a chariot with high-stepping panache, driven by a black man with a shining bald pate.

'Would you like to drive a sulky, Áine, hey?' my uncle asked, grinning. He raised his hand to the driver as the vehicle came around the curve of the track.

'No she wouldn't,' Rupert intervened, and I saw a faint flush mottle his neck.

His father turned to him abruptly. 'Can't she speak for herself, sir?' he demanded. He glanced at me. 'Lord above,' he continued in a gentler tone, 'did you think I meant the child to drive it herself?'

The driver pulled over to the side of the track and my uncle turned to me. 'Would you like me to take you around the track, Áine?'

'Thanks very much,' I said politely, although I had no great desire to accompany my uncle on a sulky or anything else.

I saw the glaze on my uncle's eyes as he looked at me, there for a moment like the shimmer from hot coals, and as quickly gone. The black driver got down from the sulky. He was a well-built man in his thirties. I saw the look he gave my uncle, nothing overt, just a sly movement in his eyes as though they were windows on a snake-pit. But his body language was obsequious and he handed the reins to his employer with alacrity.

'This is Turner,' my uncle said to us. 'Turner, these young folk are Miz Bella's kin from Ireland. They're staying for the week.'

Turner smiled, and delivered himself of some pleasantry. Next thing I knew my uncle had swung himself into the sulky and Turner was lifting me onto his knee. In a moment I found myself being driven around the oval track. The racing bike swayed and seemed to my uninitiated sensibility to be unstable, perhaps because of the unusual movement of the horse, which used a diagonal gait, front left foreleg with right hind leg, and vice versa. My uncle held the reins with one hand and secured me against him with the other. It was like being held by a bear. I smelled the alcohol on his breath and the musk of his sweat. I knew when his arm tightened around me that he was enjoying himself and I felt as I had on the day I thumbed a lift – possessed of an unpleasant power that I had not invented, but had chanced on by some malevolent quirk of fate.

My brother's smile was strained as we returned and he moved forward quickly to help me dismount. But Rupert was not smiling.

'For God's sake, man,' his father said to him in an undertone. 'You don't have to perpetually take after your mother! Your little cousin was perfectly safe.' He turned to me. 'Weren't you, Áine? Eh?'

'Thank you very much, Uncle,' I said. I was flushed, glad to be away from him. I was now aware that in the life of this family, one member was possessed of enough personal force to paint the air around him. I looked at Rupert, but he turned and walked away, as though containing anger or some other violent emotion. His father looked after him with a frown, and Seán, after a moment's hesitancy, in which he directed a half-anxious look at me, and a quick gesture of command to follow him, walked away also.

'Bad-tempered boy,' his father said, gesturing towards his son with ill-concealed irritation. 'I don't know why he wants to cross me in everything. He has no interest in the business; nothing will do him but this medicine nonsense . . . I sometimes wonder if it's anything to do with that absurd name his mother foisted on him . . . *Rupert!* What do you think of it, eh Áine?' He looked down at me, his mouth curving, his eyebrows almost meeting in a tangled canopy. 'A name like that? Bit pansy, ain't it?' His face darkened. 'But of course he wants to go to Harvard . . .' He gave a short laugh that invited conspiracy. 'I guess he's thinking of all the lovely . . .'

He gave me a squeeze in which his hand strayed for a millisecond to my buttocks, as though by the merest accident.

The flood of nausea caught me unawares. I moved back

176

from him sharply, but I was anxious not to validate the trespass by taking any notice of it, although my heart was beating faster and a taste coated my mouth.

'I think it's a nice name,' I muttered lamely, and I quickly left my uncle and followed my cousin and brother. When I glanced back I saw that Uncle Alex had surrendered the horse and sulky to the bald driver and that he was walking across the yard and into the trees. Turner, about to take off the harness, stared after my uncle's retreating back, with unhappy, narrowed eyes.

As I returned to the house I saw a movement at an upstairs window. There was a glimpse of a blue dress and I realized that my aunt had been watching us. I put up my hand to wave, but she had disappeared. When we returned to the house we found her swaying in the porch swing, a drink in her hand, one sandalled foot touching the floor.

'You two boys go away and play,' she said with brittle gaiety. Rupert said something to Seán about a game of snooker, but he turned and looked back at me as he and Seán crossed the threshold. I saw my aunt register his glance.

'Sit down, Áine; keep me company for a while. Have some lemonade if you like.'

I helped myself to some iced lemonade from a jug on a glass-topped table and then sat near her in a white wicker chair. It came to me that she was lonely; I could feel it draining out of her through the pores of her skin.

'Do you go out much, Aunty Isabelle?' I asked.

'Your uncle likes me to stay around the house,' she replied after a moment. 'And I myself don't drive . . . although I did try to learn once, but Alex said I'd never be any use . . .'

'Do you entertain much?'

She nodded. 'Sometimes we have visitors.' She paused. 'The Penroses, for example. They live just down the road.'

'We passed their place on the way here.'

'Yes. They're very rich,' she said, looking at me for a moment as though this would impress me. Then she added with a sniff, 'New money pretending to be old. But money is money. Their daughter Gloria is sweet on Rupert.'

Perhaps I looked crestfallen at this intelligence, for my aunt raised her eyebrows and smiled into her glass.

The darkening evening was full of scents and the air was heavy and warm. After a moment she said to me softly, 'I have to be blunt about this . . . But I think it is best, Áine, for you not to be alone with your uncle.'

I was unprepared for the private surge of humiliation. My cheeks flamed, and I was glad of the semi-darkness.

'Oh it's not your fault,' she said, as though she sensed the malaise that burned me from head to foot. 'But the fact is – he is not to be trusted around young women.'

'But I am not a woman, Aunty Isabelle . . . yet . . .'

'You're woman enough. He's not too particular.'

I looked at her in silence and her burning eyes met mine.

'There's a key in your bedroom door. Make sure you use it.'

The days passed in Mount Wexford. I was free from nightmares for this time, subsumed in the new ambience of this strange and exotic land. I avoided my uncle. I disliked the way he smelled of drink, and the way he would smile at me, while his eyes dwelt on my body. I kept myself always in the company of my brother or my aunt, like a proper young lady from a Jane Austen novel. When I exclaimed on the variety of southern dishes, Aunt Isabelle took me to the kitchen, and I spent a happy afternoon with Milly as she showed me how to make a few dishes, like hominy grits and southern fried chicken, hoppin' John and corn bread.

'The white folks was eatin' African before they knew what they was doin',' she confided to me with a laugh. Milly swayed as she moved, reaching to shelves and bins and the refrigerator with the grace of a dancer.

'How's your poor little leg now, honey?' she asked. 'And your arm. Miz Bella told me 'bout your accident.'

'I'm better. I just have to be careful.'

'That was one bad accident . . . how d'you come to fall from that cliff?'

'I got a fright,' I said, 'and the path had fallen in.'

'There'd be haints in an ol' place like that, chile. You shouldn't walk there in the night.'

I stared at Milly, wondering how much she knew about Dunbeg.

'Did Rupert tell you about Ireland, Milly?'

'Sure. When he came back that time he was all cut up, honey, missin' his mom and y'all.' She glanced at me, lowered her voice and added, 'He wanted to go right back, but his daddy wouldn't let him.'

There was silence for a moment while Milly sifted flour, but the substance of something unsaid hovered in the air.

'What's my Uncle Alex like, Milly?' I asked in a whisper. 'I don't know him very well.'

She gave me a glance in which her eyes were suddenly wider. Then she moved back and shut the kitchen door. 'You should watch out for that man, honey chile,' she said in a low voice. 'And don't you be alone with him. You hear me now?'

After a moment I ventured, longing to have my curiosity on something satisfied: 'Milly, did he ever beat Rupert?'

Milly stopped what she was doing and regarded me. Then she said grimly, 'Did he ever beat him? He beat that poor lil chile till he was all black 'n' blue. He beat him with his strap. When his mamma tried to save him he beat her too . . .' She shook her head, adding with grim satisfaction, oblivious to my horror, 'But he don't dare do it no more. That boy's gone in for body buildin' now. He's strong as a horse!'

My aunt, who had gone upstairs for her nap, came into the kitchen. We heard her step on the flagged floor and Milly reverted to culinary topics. 'You add three eggs, honey, and beat them in . . .'

My aunt stood and watched and then said, 'If you've learnt enough, Áine, you can help me pick out the new drapes for the breakfast-room. I'm having it done over.'

We went to this shady room, redolent with the scent of flowers in two great vases, and looked at books of samples, but she could not make up her mind.

'I always wanted a daughter, you know,' she said at one point. 'Sons only leave you for other women's daughters . . .' Then she added, with a sly glance at me, 'Isn't it a pity you and he are cousins . . . Otherwise you and Rupert might get to like each other.' She directed a bright penetrating glance at me. 'You might even get married . . .'

This prospect took my breath away. For a moment I wanted

to say that being a cousin didn't matter to me; that in the old days lots of cousins married, but I suddenly knew she was waiting for my response and had only mentioned the subject to draw me out.

'But of course, marriage between cousins,' she said, 'is prohibited by the Church . . . It's a form of incest.'

This made me feel cold, even though the day was humid and the air conditioner ineffective in a room with an open window.

'Only to the Catholic Church,' I blurted foolishly, remembering all the Victorian novels I had read where cousins were always getting hitched.

My aunt fixed bright, speculative eyes on me. 'Oh no, many states here prohibit it by law. Anyway,' she went on, 'you'll want to marry a rich man. Rupert needs to marry a rich girl too . . . this place needs money. Despite appearances, we haven't been making much of a profit here for a long time. Rupert wants to be a doctor and it'll be years before . . .' She glanced at me. 'And of course there's something more . . . there's the thing in our family . . .'

I waited. The ensuing silence was broken when she added, 'Tell me, are you completely better from your fall?'

'What thing in the family?' I whispered, outraged that she could raise such a topic and then return to banalities.

'Oh, nothing!' she said with a laugh. 'It's just that you're a bit like me . . . The doctor says I should avoid all upsets of an emotional nature . . . and maybe you should too.'

Her eyes watched me relentlessly, but I did not respond. 'But what on earth drew you back to Dunbeg . . . ?' she added after a moment when it was clear I would not be drawn further on the topic. She dropped her voice. 'Such a strange place, Dunbeg! I've been longing to ask you the whole story about that unfortunate accident. Áine, it was a very strange thing to do. Something must have drawn you back. Do you love that place?'

'Yes.'

I did not elaborate. I loved Dunbeg. I had always loved it; everything there spoke to me, the sea, the house, the stones along the shore, the great panorama of the sky. But I would not discuss this with my aunt, not if everything I said was going to be squeezed to extract esoteric meanings for her to play with.

I shrugged, avoiding her penetrating gaze. I would not tell her the real reason; I would not speak about my mother. *Her* life was her business and my foolishness was something for which I had already paid.

'And was that why you went there . . . because you *knew* something was waiting for you?'

I thought of my recent dream and the white wolf waiting in the headland. A shiver iced its way along my spine.

'No Aunty Isabelle. I hated school. So I ran away.'

'You've changed,' my aunt said suddenly, observing me with sudden coldness. 'You used to be an ingenuous child, but already you have lost your openness. When I was in Ireland I felt that we understood each other. I even told you something I had never, to that point, divulged to a soul . . .'

'If I've changed, Aunty Isabelle,' I said, unwilling to be drawn again into this recollection, 'I'm not aware of it.' I added quietly, 'I hope I haven't disappointed you?'

She gave a low and bitter laugh. 'But I am used to disappointment. It is the common human lot . . . Always for women and, eventually too, for men.'

She led the way into the porch and poured some lemonade, raising her eyes to watch a clapped-out car come half way down the driveway and turn off towards the trees and the servants' quarters. Turner was driving, and with him in the car was a black woman whose face I could not see, but she was smoking and for a moment I saw the glitter of gold nail varnish.

'There's Turner,' I said. 'Who is the woman with him?'

'His wife,' my aunt said, 'Emma Lou.' Her eyes darkened and her face closed. 'But Turner should have taken the back entrance,' she said. 'He's getting above himself.'

Chapter Fourteen

Rupert, as promised, brought us to Colonial Williamsburg, a town that had once been Virginia's capital, now preserved as a living museum, with its civic buildings intact. The old Georgian clapboard houses were freshly painted, and behind each of them was the half-acre garden and the kitchen and the outhouses that had once been the slave quarters. The shops were open, as was the courthouse, as though two hundred years had not flown away with the hopes and fears that had once flourished here. If you wanted to take yourself backwards in time you had come to the right place.

In the former jailhouse we saw the wretched cells where runaway slaves had been coralled like horses, with straw for a bed, and chained to the wall. And suddenly I thought of my aunt and wondered what happened to runaway wives in the days when Williamsburg was the capital of Virginia? What were their options back in the days when life was not open to women except as satellites of men? Or perhaps men were different then. Being colonists, perhaps they were appreciative of their womenfolk, the supply being presumably limited? And the women would have been close; I imagined their sewing circles and how they would have swopped recipes, and spoken in low voices about childbirth, and shared all the secret feminine scriptures.

But such considerations were easily banished in the face of the bright day. We were three young people on the oyster-shell paths of Colonial Williamsburg on a humid southern afternoon. I thought of Huckleberry Finn and of Tom Sawyer painting the fence. Rupert and I walked together. Seán was trailing along somewhere behind us, and I looked up at Rupert and said, 'This place, even though it's a museum, seems far more real and human than a modern city.'

Rupert smiled as though touched by my enthusiasm and for an instant his hand took mine as though in sympathy.

'Would you have liked to have lived here then?' he inquired, grinning down at me. 'Ride in buggies, wear long dresses, be married to an American?'

'Yes.'

'Even though they had slaves?'

'Yes. I would be kind to them. But all of this,' I added, 'is on one condition.'

'What condition?'

'That you were also here.'

Rupert didn't reply. He released my hand, but he said after a moment, lowering his voice, 'Áine . . . why were you so afraid that night in Dunbeg, my last night, when you came to my room?'

I reddened; the sharing of his bed had long since assumed a different and embarrassing perspective. 'I told you. I was a kid. I was afraid . . . I'm sorry I bothered you.'

'Did that crazy guy really come to the drawing-room window?'

'Yes . . . and you were right about him, Rupert. When I ran away from school and went back to the headland he was there. Oh, he didn't touch me . . . but he threatened me. I should have listened to you,' I added. 'I wish I had!'

'Was anything done about it?' Rupert demanded, glancing over his shoulder and keeping his voice low.

'I told Dad . . .'

'I can hardly believe that a weirdo like that is allowed to roam free after he has twice tried to injure you, and the last time succeeded. Next time he may kill you!'

I felt queasy and cold. This topic was like a great dark landscape, where my worst fears festered. I wondered why Rupert was so interested, why he assumed that Aeneas Shaw was all the things I feared he was. After all, it had happened three years before. And I suddenly remembered how he had stood there on the headland, as though transfixed, while Aeneas had stared at him, and how only my call had broken the spell between them.

'Were you afraid of him too, Rupert?' I whispered.

My cousin did not reply immediately. 'I don't know. There was something weird about him . . . something about his eyes . . . But, of course, I was a kid,' he added hastily, 'and probably impressionable.'

'He's dead now, Rupert. They found his body in a ditch. At least they think it was him.'

'Good!' He glanced at me and frowned. 'But you don't seem convinced?'

'I don't know.'

But I didn't want to think of Aeneas Shaw any more. Even talking about him exacerbated the unease in the pit of my stomach, as though a part of me sensed something I could not name.

'Shall we talk about something else now?' I said after a moment. I glanced at Rupert who was still frowning.

'I should have insisted . . . I should have made more of a fuss. Then you might never have had that fall. You mightn't still be obsessed with that man.'

'I'm not obsessed with him, Rupert. And I'm all right now.'

'Why didn't you tell me before, Áine, that you saw him again?'

'Because I didn't want to fill you with what I see in you now.'

Our eyes met. He gave a short laugh. 'Am I so transparent?'

I smiled up at him and as I met his eyes I knew again that I was not alone, that the world contained one other alien like myself, to whom I was visible. This thought brought with it an intense pleasure, almost a validation of the fact that I lived.

'You must realize then that you are important to me, Áine?'

'Am I?'

'I do not think I could bear it if anything were to happen to you.'

'Why?'

'Because . . .' He shrugged, smiled at me and looked away. 'Because I know who you are.'

'Is that so unusual?'

'I think it is.' He glanced at me. 'I hope you are never frightened at night here?' he added after a moment.

This made me think of his room just down the gallery. It also made me think of one night recently, when the handle of my door had turned very softly shortly after midnight. I had been lying awake, listening to the whisper of the white fan on the ceiling, when I heard the deft turn of the doorhandle. In obedience to Aunt Isabelle, the door had been locked, a stricture that seemed absurd, but one that I had observed. I turned on the bedside light and there it came again, the gentle turn of the handle. For a moment I had wondered if my would-be visitor could be Rupert, and dismissed this possibility. *He* could always come along the gallery to the French window if he wanted to talk to me. Then I had decided it was either my insomniac brother needing a chat or – and this possibility made me feel ill – my host and uncle, Rupert's father. This idea had driven me out of bed and into the gallery, thinking that if he gained access to my room I would run to my aunt.

The night outside was very warm, and, as I stood there against the balusters of the verandah I saw, after a couple of minutes, my uncle come out from the house, cross the lawn and head for the trees. I already knew that he did not share my aunt's bedroom, and that he came and went at strange hours, for I had seen him on another occasion coming back to the house when I had got up towards dawn and looked out on the dewy lawn and the first glimmer of the day.

'Was it you?' I asked, wondering if Rupert had come to me and found the door locked. 'Was it you . . . the night before last, at the door of my room?' Even before I finished the sentence I felt the tension in Rupert.

'Certainly not!' He turned and gripped my arm. 'Keep your door locked. And stay with my mother when Seán and I are not around. You should not have come to Mount Wexford, Áine. It was a mistake!'

On the way home Rupert said, 'We're dropping in at a friend's house for a beer . . .'

'Who?'

'Gunther Huchte.'

'Not the German you told us about in Dunbeg?' Seán said eagerly. 'The bloke who came from Berlin? Who was in the war?'

'The same.'

'What does he do?'

'He teaches high school, composes music, reads philosophy and develops friendships with strange characters . . .'

'Like you?' I asked slyly.

'Like me. Like his Indian friends . . . Like anyone who interests him.'

A little later Rupert turned the car into the driveway of a large bungalow, half brick, half white clapboard, with a stone chimneybreast and what looked like a few acres of garden hidden among the trees. Rupert drove beneath the magnolia and gave a short beep on the horn as he pulled up, spewing gravel.

Two men were seated in the porch. One of them was old, but the other, a big middle-aged man, waved and rose from his seat.

'Hi, Gunther!' Rupert called.

The big man came down the porch steps, grinned, held out his hand. 'Good to see you,' he said. He had a brown beard tinged with grey, and china-blue eyes.

'These are the Irish cousins I told you about,' Rupert said. 'This is Áine, and this is Seán.' He turned to us. 'This is Gunther Huchte, of whom you have heard much in dispatches.'

Gunther took my hand, bent over it with formal address. 'Fräulein,' he said, 'I am honoured.' His eyes twinkled as he looked at me. I thought of those war movies where the Germans always clicked their heels, and kissed women's hands. No one had ever bent over my hand, and I knew perfectly well that, where I came from, the chances of it ever happening again were slim.

He shook hands with Seán. 'Come and meet my guest.'

He conducted us to the porch, where a thin man with skin like a walnut rose from his seat. As soon as I saw him I mentally slotted him into a Western, the Indian guide.

'This is my friend Johnny Eagles,' Gunther said. I had never seen an Indian in the flesh, and took in the man's weathered face, his high cheekbones and slanting eyes. He shook hands cordially, but did not enter into the spirit of the badinage now being swapped between Gunther and Rupert. I looked around

187

me and when I turned back to the Indian I saw that his black eyes dwelt on me with a narrowed intensity, as though he were trying to read something in me. I looked away, but tentatively turned my eyes on him again because I was troubled by the sense of recognition, not of him, but something between us that hovered in the air.

He stood up abruptly to leave.

'Don't go, Johnny,' Gunther said, bringing cans of beer and glasses from the kitchen. 'Tell them their fortunes, or something.'

Johnny did not smile.

'Johnny can tell you everything you want to know. He has his ancestors' gifts,' Gunther's voice continued, as he handed Seán a can of beer.

The Indian made a small dismissive grunt.

Then Gunther said, 'Seán, give him your hand.'

Seán, swallowing beer as though it would soon be out of fashion, thrust out his right hand. Johnny scrutinized the palm politely; he looked abruptly at Seán's face and then back at the palm.

'What do you see?' My brother was watching the old man with sardonic impertinence.

'You will be successful in whatever you do,' Johnny said, in a bland and disappointing voice which might have done credit to Madame Lilly who reeled fortunes off in O'Connell Street.

Seán raised his eyebrows. 'Crap,' he said under his breath.

The Indian seemed not to have heard. He reached out for my hand with an imperious gesture, as though his aroused interest extended to me too by virtue of my kinship with his last subject. I did not want my palm read; I had always avoided such things, hands, tarot cards, Ouija boards, the lot, fearful of them for reasons I had never bothered to unravel, but courtesy now insisted that I obey. I put my right hand in his. He turned it over very slowly and carefully. Then he stared at it and reached for the other hand, comparing them for such a long time without any comment that I became uneasy.

'What is it?' Seán demanded sententiously. 'Will she meet her fate . . . a tall dark stranger . . . Ha ha?'

Johnny Eagles looked as though his patience had been

stretched. But his eyes met mine again and, leaning towards me, he said in a voice so low that I had to strain to catch it, 'Ah, but it's old trouble, isn't it? From long ago? But even if *you* could understand, who would listen?'

'Pardon?' I whispered.

He glanced around as he said this, and then back at my hands, and muttered to himself.

'I am never believed,' I blurted to Johnny Eagles, as though he were some sort of confessor, finding myself surprised at my own words. 'I feel things, but I am never believed.' I looked at my brother as I said this, startled by a resentment I had not known I nurtured.

'You have dreams,' the Indian said. It was a statement more than a question.

'Sometimes I dream of a wolf . . .'

'He is in a special place?'

I nodded. 'A place in Ireland.'

Johnny regarded me in silence for a moment. 'But don't you see,' he said very softly, 'the white wolf is your courage? You should not fear him. You have need of him.'

Although they could not have heard us, the conversation between Rupert, Gunther and Seán died away. Seán had another beer, and I felt his elation in being able to have it, in being free of the parental strictures which would never have permitted him beer or other alcoholic beverage. Johnny Eagles closed my hand, held it within his own and then let it go.

Privately I felt an unreasoning elation, like someone who has been vindicated. But I did not understand why this stranger knew more about what went on in my head than all the people I lived with put together.

'We will meet again,' Johnny Eagles said, looking from me to Seán to Rupert. Then, with a brief signal at Gunther his spare form disappeared down the steps and into the darkening trees. Behind him there was silence; the festive mood of the small party had dissipated.

'Was that really an Indian?' I asked Gunther.

'Yes. A Cherokee.'

Seán's eyes widened. He drank some more.

'They had their finger on things that we have lost,' Gunther

189

went on. 'Respect for nature, an ability to see the mystical in the commonplace . . . the reality behind the apparent . . .'

'Do you miss Germany?' I asked Gunther, desperately needing to change the subject, and aware of Seán's longing to interrogate him about the war.

'No. I go back there from time to time, of course. But this is my home.'

'Is it true that you were in the Volkssturm?' Seán blurted, his voice a little slurred and barely containing his almost indecent interest in everything to do with World War Two.

Gunther did not smile. 'That was a long time ago.'

'What was it like?'

Gunther's face was grave and for a moment I thought he would not answer the question. Then he said curtly, 'Children and old men fighting for everything they believed in . . . and they lost.' He turned to Seán. 'You see . . . you should be careful what you believe in.'

'I wish *I'd* been in the war!' Seán blurted suddenly.

'That is the comment of a boy,' Gunther replied, and his voice had a ring to it which made it clear the subject was closed.

His eyes refocused on the trees where the birds were sounding their vespers. There was silence for a few moments, everyone gazing at the woods where Johnny Eagles had disappeared. The night was falling softly, another scented, warm night, and all of us were, I think, affected by Gunther's sombre words and also by the sense of being on the fringes of another world.

'Where's Brigitte?' Rupert asked after a moment.

'In Richmond, visiting a friend. She's coming home tomorrow.'

'How's her music?' Rupert asked. 'I saw in the paper that she won that competition . . .'

Gunther's face creased into tenderness. 'You know Brigitte . . .'

'Does she still want to study in London?'

Gunther laughed. 'She does. She has dreams. Her grandfather – my wife's father – was English, and she is hungry for her English roots!'

'Well, it's time I took these guys home,' Rupert said, turning to us in the half-dark.

Gunther protested, but he rose, shook hands. I noted that his hands were very big and that mine was lost in them, like a small boat in a harbour.

'It's been a pleasure meeting you,' he said. 'Brigitte will be sorry to have missed you.'

He turned to Rupert. 'Bring your cousins back to visit before they go . . .'

'I'll phone,' Rupert said. 'Thanks, Gunther.'

It was very quiet in the car. No one spoke; Seán was silent in the back. I watched the headlights probe the highway, heard the swish of oncoming traffic, felt both languorous and stimulated as I retraced the evening in my mind, knowing at the same time that everything had acquired a powerful dimension of its own merely because it had occurred in Rupert's company.

'Are you asleep, Áine?' Rupert ventured after a moment, sotto voce.

'No.' I glanced at the back where Seán seemed to be snoozing, for his head was to one side and his eyes were closed. 'But I think someone else has nodded off,' I added in a whisper, trying not to laugh, 'someone who's had more than enough beer.' And then, subsumed by a sense of communion, I laid my hand on Rupert's in the darkness.

'I love you,' I said.

'And I you too, little cousin,' he answered after a moment in a tired, mellow voice. 'But you are still a child . . . even if you do not think so.' He gave a low caustic laugh and added, 'But they would burn us first.'

'They can't do that, at any rate.'

'Can't they? So you believe that the future is ours?'

'Of course! Don't you?'

'I know that it is not!' he said. 'It is already mortgaged.'

I withdrew my hand, offended in some way without knowing why. 'Will you bring me back to see Gunther again?'

He nodded and I added, 'And Johnny Eagles too?'

'If Johnny wants to see you you will not be able to avoid him and, if he does not wish to see you, you will not be able to find him,' he said. 'He does not socialize with white people. They despise him and they bore him. But he has some kind of rapport with Gunther.'

I pondered this. 'But he said I would see him before I left . . .'

'Then you most certainly will.'

As we approached Mount Wexford a white Mercedes sped out of the neighbouring, ornate gates that I had noticed on the day of my arrival and cut in front of us, headlights slicing the night.

Rupert braked.

'Who is that?' I said. 'He drives like a maniac!'

'Mr Theodore Penrose,' Rupert said. 'Our neighbour. He reckons he owns the world.'

The following afternoon, while Rupert was playing snooker with Seán, and Aunty Isabelle was taking a nap, and I was supposed to be doing likewise but found myself bored and wide awake, I slipped downstairs and went out. The lure of the woods was tantalizing. I wanted to explore them. I had asked Rupert on more than one occasion to show me the whole plantation, but he had not done so, although he had brought us back through the stable yard on our second day and shown us the mares and Magister, a black stallion with white socks. He had also brought us down to the creek, where the trees had left a clearing, and where sandy mud flats bordered the river. Here he had told us stories of how the Indians had once lived nearby and spied on the new settlers.

'The first white people here died like flies.'

'Because of the Indians?' I asked.

'No. Malaria.'

Now I found the heat outside stifling and wondered for the hundredth time how the people of long ago had endured life without air conditioning. The shade of the trees was very welcome and I moved in its green world, skirting the house and the stables.

After a short walk I came to a clearing in the woods. In this clearing there was a small, wooden shack. I thought of investigating it, but hesitated before leaving the shelter of the trees. Just as I was about to step into the clearing a black woman emerged from the shack and ran towards the man who came from the trees on my left. It was my uncle. I shrank back. For

192

a moment I was afraid he had seen me, but apparently not, for his attention was focused on the woman. I saw her face; it was Emma Lou, Turner's wife.

He caught her up, embraced her passionately, threw her across his shoulder as though she were a sack of potatoes, and strode towards the shack. I heard her laugh as I moved back into the shelter of the trees. I thought of my aunt and the shadow that had darkened her eyes when Turner had appeared in the driveway with Emma Lou in his car.

Above my head the trees reached up as straight as masts, touching a cloudless sky; families of squirrels ran up and down the branches, or jumped to another tree. The ground was littered with large pine cones and acorns. A bird high above me screeched, 'Chee, chee . . .'

After a while, disempowered by the languor of the day, I sat down, leaning my back against a bole, and absorbed the life of the woodland, mesmerized and at peace. I must have dozed for the next thing I remember is the sudden sound behind me of breaking twigs and the pair of arms that encircled me. I gasped and would have screamed but I heard my uncle's subdued laugh in my ear: 'Now ain't we the pretty little lady!'

Rupert brought us back to visit Gunther that evening. This time Gunther had prepared a 'cook-in'. There was enough food for an army; steaks, hamburgers, a variety of salads and for dessert a giant cheesecake, dotted with segments of mandarin orange, which Gunther said he had made himself.

A plump, spotty girl of about my own age came to greet us. 'This is my daughter, Brigitte,' Gunther said. She greeted Rupert with a hug, said Hi to Seán and me and asked what we wanted to drink.

Seán asked for beer with disguised eagerness, and I had lemonade. Neighbours arrived and we all sat around the pool at the rear of the house to enjoy the barbecue. There was no sign of the Cherokee.

'Is Johnny Eagles coming?' Seán asked Gunther at one point. He shook his head, munching on a forkful of salad. 'He doesn't bother with parties.'

Brigitte sat beside me on a recliner, eyed me for a moment

and said with a directness that amazed me, 'Are you a very quiet person?'

'Don't be fooled, Brigitte,' Seán said behind me. 'She's scheming and plotting! She misses nothing. Still waters run deep, you know.'

Brigitte smiled, pulled her seat closer and looked at me with something like sympathy. 'I don't have any brothers. Tell me about your family.'

I told her. 'It must be nice to have your mom,' she said wistfully. 'Mine died.'

'I know. I'm sorry.'

She lowered her voice. 'I still miss her something awful. She died three years ago . . . and it's never been the same since.'

Gunther glanced at the two of us.

'Áine, you're not done eating already,' he said when he saw me put down my plate. 'You've only had a bite of salad.'

I shook my head, and indicated that I wasn't hungry. When Brigitte excused herself and went indoors, Rupert came behind me and leaning over whispered, 'What's the matter, Áine? You've hardly spoken to me since we set out. Is your ankle hurting? You were limping as we came in.'

'It's all right . . .'

'Where did you get to after lunch?' he persisted. 'When Seán and I went looking for you you were not in the house.'

'I went out for a walk.'

I was still shaken by the shock of waking to find myself the object of my uncle's attentions, still sick at the memory of his hands. The forest had chattered around us with life, but I had been suddenly aware that I was facing a kind of private death, something to do with men and sweat and a feral lust I could not understand.

'Let me go, Uncle!'

'Tsk . . .' he had soothed, as though I were a filly to be broken to the bit, 'just give your old uncle a nice kiss . . . Don't you like your old uncle?'

He bent over me. His face came close, but I brought my knee up and got him where it hurt.

He roared and I stood up and ran for the house. Or tried to run. My ankle cried out and I hobbled out from the trees, half-running, half-falling, gasping with pain. But as I came out of the forest my aunt came hurrying across the lawn.

'I was wondering where you were,' she called. She came nearer, looked at me aghast.

'What has happened? Áine . . . did you fall?'

Before I could reply she stood still abruptly and stared over my shoulder, and I never saw such hatred in the eyes of any living thing as I saw in hers. I did not look back, but heard the heavy footsteps walk away towards the stable. My aunt's eyes were dilated as she turned back to me. 'Did he . . . ?'

I shook my head, limped indoors.

What had frightened me more than my uncle's attentions was his assumption, in my mind, of the persona of Aeneas Shaw, as though the latter's face had become his face, and his trespassing hands the dirty paws of my erstwhile tormentor.

It was my mind playing tricks on me, I acknowledged to myself. It was as though everything I experienced came back to the madman of Dunbeg. Rupert had said I was obsessed with him. But I did not want obsession.

'Please tell me what's wrong,' Rupert repeated now. I looked around at the wholesome gathering by the pool, at the laughter and the jokes.

'I'm just tired,' I said.

Brigitte reappeared and someone said, 'Hey Brigitte, how's the piano-playing going? Congratulations about the last competition . . . saw your picture in the paper . . .'

She made some modest reply and then someone else asked, 'Will you play something?'

Brigitte hesitated. Then she looked directly at me and said gently, 'Would you like me to play something, Áine?'

I thought, for some reason, of what I had heard as I had surfaced from the coma, Rupert's voice against the background strains of Handel.

'Do you know Handel's "Largo"?' I asked.

In a moment the stately music came through the open doors of the lounge and it filled the patio and stilled the listeners and drifted into the primeval forest. Brigitte played with passion, as though the music were an outpouring of her own being, and had little to do with printed hieroglyphs on sheets of paper.

Later, when the other guests had moved away and Rupert was talking of going home, saying, 'Seán and Áine have an early start tomorrow – they're leaving,' the Indian, Johnny Eagles, arrived as silently as though airborne. Suddenly he was there, greeted by Gunther with just a movement of his hand. He sat beside the darkening swimming pool, chewed some nuts, and regarded me from time to time with shrewd, considering eyes. He did not speak until Rupert, Seán and I were actually taking our leave of Gunther and Brigitte, and then he stood up and approached us.

'It is best that you do not go again to that place,' he said in a quiet monotone.

'What place is that?' Rupert demanded.

Seán made no comment, but kept his eyes on the Indian's face. Rupert's face was closed, but he was listening, for he frowned.

Johnny's weathered countenance maintained its immobility. 'That place far away,' he said with a slow, patient enunciation as though he were addressing a suspect intelligence, 'where you play at being children of the tide.'

Rupert turned and looked at me. I stilled the impulse to take his hand.

That night, my last night in Mount Wexford, Rupert came to my room, entering through the French window from the gallery. I was in bed and waiting for him, sure, without knowing why, that he would come. I was already aware that Aunt Isabelle was sitting on the landing with a book. I had passed her en route to the bathroom and she had stared at me half vacantly and said nothing.

'Your mother is sitting in the armchair on the landing,' I whispered.

'She is mounting guard,' Rupert said.

'Over what?'

'Over you, Áine . . .'

I moved over and he got into bed beside me, held me in his arms. Then he whispered, 'I have spoken to her. He didn't harm you, did he? My father?'

'No. I ran away.'

'I hate him,' he said in a low voice. 'He has destroyed her!

196

And he would have destroyed you.' He turned on the pillow and looked at me. 'Come here.' He pulled me against him and my head lay under his chin.

'I wish you weren't going home. I wish you weren't a child.'

'I'm not a child, Rupert. But I do have to go home . . .' And then I added, 'Why did that Indian say what he did? Did you ever talk to him about Dunbeg?'

'No. He's probably a bit intuitive . . . Maybe you should heed him.'

'Rupert, don't be ridiculous! How can I forget about Dunbeg? And there's nothing there to fear any more now that Aeneas Shaw is dead. But,' I added after a moment, 'it *is* a strange place. I sometimes wish I knew more about poor Sarah and why she died.'

Rupert didn't reply. I thought he was asleep. I lay, warm in his arms in the darkness, while his mother sat guardian outside my door like some sort of crazed duenna. What would she have done if she had seen us on the other side of it, in bed together, peaceful and still, whispering in the dark like children?

'Are you worried about your mother, Rupert?' I ventured after a moment.

'Of course. But she has done things like this before and is fine the next day, or the day after. Then she gets worried and thinks my father will try to put her away somewhere.' He breathed deeply. 'But I will never, ever, let that happen to her.'

'You love her very much, Rupert, don't you?'

'Very much,' he said, his voice low and intense. 'I owe her everything.'

We became quiet then, like sleepy children, snug in the haven of each other. But a thought suddenly intruded, sending shivers up my spine, and I shattered the bliss by sitting up and whispering in sudden panic, *'But, Rupert, Johnny Eagles wasn't talking to me when he said not to go back to Dunbeg. He was talking to you!'*

Rupert did not seem at all fazed by this comment. 'Well, any such injunction would be wasted on me. When will I ever have the chance to go back? If I'm lucky I'll be in Harvard next year; I'll be in college anyway. I don't know when, if ever, I'll get another holiday in Ireland.' He laughed softly. 'So the ancestral shrine will have to do without me.'

After a moment he added, 'But I do know something about poor old Sarah I didn't tell you.'

'What?'

'It was something I found in the library in Dunbeg. I didn't want to tell you at the time, because you seemed so uptight about her . . . and because of what you told me you had seen.'

'What did you find?'

'I found something that she probably wrote. It's at the back of the old Bible, folded up and hidden inside the back cover. There's other writing too, in Irish.'

'But I don't know where the Bible is.'

'It's on the bottom shelf, right up near the window.' He sounded quite pleased with this prowess of his memory. Suddenly I longed to be as near Rupert and as deeply into him as life allowed, as though we were old and need not expect many tomorrows. But when I lay down again and moved closer, nuzzling against him, he held me for only a moment. Then he laughed softly in my ear and slipped out of bed.

'Goodnight, my Tigerlily. Sleep now. No dreams, remember.'

My aunt called me in the morning. She looked haggard, and I dared not ask at what hour she had finally got to bed. But she seemed deliberately calm and sent her love to my parents. Uncle Alex made a brief appearance and took his leave of us with much aplomb, telling us to come for a return visit soon, while my aunt watched him in silence.

Milly prepared a breakfast of bacon and grits and 'Governor's Toast', dripping with maple syrup. As we left the house she called after us, 'Y'all come back now, ya hear?'

Matthew drove us away to the Interstate and Washington. I was in a dream, looking at Rupert who had accompanied us, imagining the future, the future he said was mortgaged, whatever that meant. How could you mortgage the future?

On the plane Seán sat back and said, 'That was one brilliant holiday. I was only sorry I couldn't get Gunther to talk about the war.'

'What did you think of Brigitte?' I asked, impatient with his perennial readiness to discuss the strutting and destruction that had left Europe in ruins.

'A lethal little sausage,' he replied. 'She'll kill anyone she sits on.'

'She's a brilliant musician.'

'She's good, all right.'

Late into the flight he woke me up, nudged me, and indicated the window where the dawn was silver. 'What do you see?'

I put up the blind and looked down. Through the cloud I caught a glimpse of coastline, green and sea-battered, and felt the catch in my throat. We were dipping down to Shannon and home.

Chapter Fifteen

We made a connecting fight from Shannon and were met by my father at Dublin Airport. He delayed going to the office to hear about our trip, and we sat at the kitchen table while my mother made tea and toast. Our siblings were still in bed.

Seán described Mount Wexford, the house and lawn, the flowers, birds and squirrels, the stallion and the mares, and the forest. We told about Rupert and Gunther and Brigitte and meeting the Cherokee.

My father said, 'But what about Isabelle and Alex? You've hardly mentioned them.'

'They're grand,' Seán said. 'Alex took a real shine to Áine and gave her a ride on a sulky.' He laughed. 'Isn't that a good name for any vehicle involved in transporting Squirrel?'

'Very amusing,' I said. I aimed a dig at my sibling under the table, which he had expected and expertly dodged.

'But what did *you* think of your uncle, Áine?' my mother demanded. 'You couldn't have remembered him.'

'I thought he was awful,' I said truthfully.

'He used to be a fine-looking man,' my father murmured. 'Just why is he so awful?' He looked at me with sudden, sharp interrogation, as though suspecting something hidden in what I had said.

I glanced at my mother. I could not tell him. 'Oh he's *big*,' I replied, 'if that's what you mean.'

'He's all right!' Seán interjected. 'Squirrel's criticizing everything again.'

'*Stop* calling me that!' For a moment I longed to spill the beans and say what my uncle was really like, how he was having it off with Emma Lou and how he had tried feeling me up in the forest on that torpid afternoon. But some audiences cannot be told the truth. Seán began to talk about what he had seen of Washington and the tension left my father.

'So Isabelle is OK?' my mother asked softly, during a lull in my brother's enthusiastic monologue. This question was directed at me, but Seán answered it.

'Of course she's OK. She has the life of Riley, a cook, a gardener, a chauffeur. Her lifestyle is amazing, and she lives in a paradise.'

'What about friends?'

Seán shrugged. 'You'll have to ask her about her friends.'

'Do you see any of them?' she persisted, turning to me.

'Nobody came calling,' I said. 'And she never went out. She says Alex likes her to stay around the house.' There was silence for a second or two and it struck me suddenly that during the entire conversation my mother's eyes had never once turned to my father.

He glanced at his watch, stood up and said he had to get to the office.

'Dad,' I said, looking up at him. 'Can a person mortgage the future?'

He looked down at me with amusement. 'But that is what a mortgage is all about. You receive a loan and you pay it back with future earnings.' He reached for his briefcase, said a cheery goodbye and left for the office.

As soon as he was gone Seán went upstairs to waken his brothers and my mother looked at me quizzically across the table.

'Why did you ask your father that question . . . about mortgaging the future?'

'I didn't mean money, Mum. I mean life. How can you mortgage your life?'

'People do it every day,' my mother said softly. 'It's called marriage. And now I think you should go to bed and get some sleep after that journey.'

By the following day we felt as though we had never left Ireland. I had a fight with Simon. He pushed me and I gave him a good thump. The household was gearing up for the autumn and the new school year, and I could not but be aware that it was a newly ordered household, neat and polished, and that my mother had a quiet about her we had never known.

My father, for his part, was ostensibly content. He and my mother were sleeping in the same room again, he had his meals prepared for him, and my mother had a submission about her that evidently pleased him. Sometimes he brought her flowers. He emanated victory, in the manner of someone whose sensible and rational viewpoint – the only possible viewpoint – has finally prevailed.

My mother had returned to laundering his shirts; the house shone as it never had; the boys were pandered to like so many little pashas. They seemed to take the sea-change in their mother for granted. They were too immersed in their own lives, and too certain of their centrality in the scheme of things, to remark on the vagaries of the fixture known as Mummy. Now that she was home, relief at her return had given way to an embarrassment that big fellows like them had ever been anguished over her disappearance. She had only been fooling around, their attitude seemed to say, only indulging in female vagary. The fact that she had left and then returned became, for them, an amusing glitch in family history, something that occasionally warranted a sly remark about feminine frailty. The unspoken comment was that women were rudderless without men.

When the phone rang my mother would sometimes answer it with a too-ready alacrity, and I could sense her deflation when the caller proved to be one of our friends. I wondered about this; who was she hoping to hear from? And when the answer suggested itself I did not want to know it.

I said to Seán, 'It's all very well making a joke about Mummy going away but *I'm* worried about her. Something is wrong.'

'Oh for God's sake, Áine, tell me when you're *not* worried about something! Mummy's fine.'

My mother took to driving her new car. She would take it out of an evening and disappear, and then return without volunteering where she had gone.

'Where did you go, dear?' my father might ask.

'Oh, just for a spin . . .' She would smile as she said this, but not at him, more at some private cogitation. I was uneasy, but there was no use trying to involve my father in this malaise. He was the pater familias, the head of the family with his world nailed down; he was doing all the paternal and husbandly things, earning the crust, giving birthday presents, sitting behind his paper, secure in the knowledge that the interruption in his domestic life had been successfully resolved and that his wife had come to her senses. His practice was now thriving. I had never known him so satisfied, so secure in his private fastness where no one would bother him again with anything that smacked of emotional need.

After our return from America I had gone back to Our Lady's College in the Green and was quietly fussed over by several of my former teachers who knew I had been very ill. They were, if anything, quietly vindicated by the fact that my boarding school career had been abruptly terminated. 'I never thought you were a girl for confines,' Miss Walsh said to me. 'But you'll have to impose some kind of discipline upon yourself, Áine, if you're not to let that active brain go to waste. What do you want to do with your life?'

I thought of Brigitte and her spellbound audience. I hoped and prayed I had a talent too. I knew, at least, that I had a passion for its possibility.

'I want to be an actress.'

Miss Walsh had friendly, irregular teeth and she showed them now in an involuntary smile. 'That shouldn't present *you* with any problems, Áine dear. You've been acting all your life!'

I looked at her with the old sinking feeling. 'But I haven't, Miss Walsh,' I said. 'Honestly!'

There was an optional study period after school, and I sometimes stayed behind for it, working now in good earnest, curiously glad to stretch my mind. I had seen nothing to alarm me since my return to Dublin and had accepted that the body of the tramp found in the ditch near Louisburg had been that of Aeneas Shaw. I forced myself to say, 'Poor man,' when I thought about him. I reminded myself that I could afford compassion now; I listened to the nuns when they talked about forgiveness. In retrospect Aeneas did not seem so fearful a villain. I blamed myself for my accident and absolved him as a poor bewildered man.

We put on a school play coming up to Christmas – an

adaptation of Jane Austen's *Pride and Prejudice*. I had the role of Mr Collins and I simpered and oiled my way around the stage and went down on one knee in the absurd proposal to Lizzie so that the house laughed.

My parents came to see the play, and afterwards my mother said to me, 'I hardly knew you in knee breeches and frock coat; you played that fellow to the life. You do have talent, Áine; but talent is everywhere. If you want to be an actress you will have to work until you drop.'

'I don't care!'

She put her arms around me and held me for a few uncharacteristic moments. 'God bless you anyway and guide you.'

The school play ran for a week, the performance beginning at seven in the evening, and finishing in time for a late bus home.

One night during this period, when I came out of school, I saw a hunched figure on steps a few doors down from the school, half hidden by the Georgian railings and the shadows of night. Even before I saw him my heart started thumping, as though it knew something I did not. There were only a few people about, and the bus stop was just a couple of paces away from where this immobile figure sat. It's only some homeless yobbo, I told myself. You're too jumpy! I glanced back at the school, wondering if I should go back and phone home, look for a lift. But when I looked again the figure was gone.

I walked slowly towards the bus stop. 'He's dead,' I told myself. 'He died in a ditch.' I wanted to run, but my feet were wooden. I wanted to retreat but kept on, like a ship committed to a certain course and too full of pride and momentum to change it. The street echoed with my footsteps.

'Whoever it was, he's gone,' I assured myself. 'You'll have to pull yourself together. You're seeing him everywhere.'

I reached the bus stop and stood there. Behind me came a furtive, shuffling sound, and glancing over my shoulder I saw a hunched figure creeping up the steps of the nearby basement area; he was wearing an old greatcoat, with a hat pulled down. I could not see his face. And then I got a faint, sickly-sweet scent, and I was back on the headland while the sea hungered below.

'Go away,' I said in a small voice. 'Leave me alone . . .'

A car pulled up beside me at the bus stop. A friendly voice said through the window, 'Do you want a lift, Áine?'

It was one of my classmates, Mary Kennedy, sitting behind her parents in their car. She opened the door. I got in, with the jerky movements of an automaton. My breathing was coming in small gulps and I was covered in cold sweat.

'Are you all right, Áine?' Mrs Kennedy asked.

'Yes.'

I looked through the back window and saw the figure on the Georgian steps, in old coat and peaked cap, straighten and stare after us.

'Who was that?' Mrs Kennedy demanded, glancing into her rearview mirror.

'Oh it's just an old tramp who's been hanging around the school for the past few days,' Mary said.

'I'd hate to be homeless in this weather,' her mother said. 'It must be awful!'

The old dread returned. The street lamps outside our house were interspersed with plane trees. I was used to the shadow of a tree on the pavement below my window but now it was sometimes augmented by a motionless addition, a figure that stood beside the trunk. I never let him see I was watching, although once when my mother came into the room after I was supposed to be in bed she exclaimed, turning on the light, 'Áine . . . what on earth are you doing peering behind the curtain?'

'He's out there!' I said. 'He's there nearly every night now.'

Her face became set. She pulled back the curtain and looked out. 'There's no one there, child! What you are seeing, Áine, is the shadow of a tree.'

I stood behind her and looked over her shoulder. What she said was correct.

'Of course there's no one there now, Mummy. He saw you at the window and legged it.'

She made a small, exasperated sound, sat on the end of my

bed and pulled me down beside her. Then she took my face in her hands.

'Oh Áine, my dearest child, when are you going to stop this . . . It is absolutely essential in life that you keep a firm hold on your mind, and your emotions. If you don't you are immensely vulnerable.' She paused and said after a moment in a very controlled voice, 'Believe me, I know what I am talking about.' Then she added, 'Would you like to talk to someone about it, a professional?'

This startled me. I was certain that if the shrinks got me I was finished, and would probably end up in the loony bin.

'No, Mummy! I'm not a nut case.'

My mother murmured something about not saying that I was. I got back into bed. She tucked me in, kissed my forehead, turned off the light and said goodnight. I lay in the dark, anxiously mulling over what she had said. I decided I had better change my story.

After a while it began to rain. I heard the drops pattering on the window and the cry of the rising December wind. This comforted me; nobody would sit out all night in a downpour.

Next morning I told my mother at the breakfast table that I must have been imagining things.

'You're right, Mummy,' I said ruefully. 'I was just applying a bit of creativity to the shadow of the tree. And I was so tired last night . . .'

I saw the relief sweep her face. She smiled. 'You always had a vivid imagination, Áine,' she said. 'When you were small . . .'

'I know. I made up a story about a squirrel.'

She gave a rare chuckle. 'That's right. But you're a big girl now.'

I looked at my mother's face. Nothing was worth her anxiety; nothing was worth the relieved apprehension I saw in her.

'Yes, Mummy.'

When I left the house later that morning I found something wedged inside the front railing. It was a small parcel, wrapped in brown paper, saturated from the rain. I bent down to examine it, but when I prodded it with the toe of my shoe I drew my breath in sharply. The wet paper fell away and a doll lay there, smiling up at me. Its head had been twisted to the back. I picked it up and turned it over. It had a long hatpin through its belly.

As I stood staring at it the front door opened and my mother appeared, waving my dog-eared copy of *The Merchant of Venice*. 'Áine, do you need your play today?'

I jerked and said, 'No, Mummy . . .'

'What's that?'

I could not answer. She came down the steps and took the doll from my hands. I was about to say, 'He left it! Now will you believe me?' but she just turned it over gingerly and said, 'Oh, it's just an old doll someone dumped! I'll put it in the bin!' Then she exclaimed: 'That's a very old hatpin. I haven't seen one like it for years.' She glanced at me and added, 'You'll miss your bus, Áine, if you don't hurry!'

I walked with studied nonchalance to the bus stop. Then I caught the number eleven bus, and arrived at school just as the bell rang. The motions of scholastic life, morning prayers, classes, were carried out automatically; but my mind was feverish. No matter where I looked I could see no solution. I had not detected the slightest concern in my mother as she had examined the doll and I dared not bother her further with the morning's development, nor my father either. The only thing I could do was be as circumspect as possible, careful about where I went, careful not to be alone. I decided to drop the study period during the winter months and always be home before dark. There was one prospect with which I comforted myself. When I finished school I would go to London, to RADA if they would have me, or, if not, to any job that would take me away from Ireland.

That night I checked the pavement outside my window. But there was nothing more sinister than the shadow of the plane tree. The following night the same story obtained, and it was the same every night thereafter that I checked, until I began to think my mother was right and that I had been over-active in the fantasy department.

Simon was now adolescent, sprouting physically, challenging every received parameter aggressively. Occasionally, and with breath-taking impertinence, he berated my mother for having left us, as though he wanted to thrust against filial limits and see if she could be made susceptible to his mastery.

'You're a little shit!' I told him. 'If I ever hear you talking like that to Mummy again I'll break your face!'

'Yeah? What army will you get to help you, you stupid little cow. At least I don't run away from school, fall off cliffs . . .'

And so it went on.

What bothered me was that Mummy had not reprimanded Simon, but had taken his cheek like someone whose lot it was and who deserved no better.

One evening in early March I saw her staring at an article in the *Evening Press*. Seán had a date with some friends and had studied the evening paper to see what films were showing.

When he had gone out my mother picked up the paper, glanced through it and then became oddly riveted. We were together in the kitchen; I was doing the washing up and trying to make conversation, but her responses were monosyllabic.

'What's so interesting in the paper, Mummy?'

'What?' she said, surfacing from her concentration, and looking up at me over the reading glasses she had recently acquired. 'Oh nothing, darling.'

I moved across the room to put the cutlery away and glanced over her shoulder. The paper was open at 'Dubliners' Diary', the page that reported on the social goings on of the preceding evening. She closed the paper, sat with a glazed expression for a moment and then got up and went to fetch her coat.

'I'm going out for a spin,' she called from the hall.

The east wind waited in ambush outside the back door, like an enemy. It thrust icy fingers into the kitchen as my mother let herself into the garden. It was getting dark. My father was in his study reading some papers he had brought from the office. I looked through the kitchen window and saw my mother walk down the back garden path towards the garage. She was well wrapped up in her winter coat, with a warm scarf around her neck. She had it up against her nose to protect her face from the cold, a Black Watch tartan scarf she had bought several years before on a holiday in Scotland, and she was wearing the Italian kid gloves she always favoured.

I stood and watched her. The sight of her walking away from the house was troubling, as though at some subliminal

209

level I knew I should hold her and keep her, prevent her from making this journey. She seemed elegant in her dark blue, belted woollen coat and tartan scarf; in the gloaming her hair seemed more blonde than grey, and for a moment she might have been young and stunning as she once had been, with every young man for miles around at her feet. She opened the garage door. I wanted to rap on the window, but restrained myself; the impulse seemed absurd. She did not turn to look at the house, and a moment later the car headlights lit up the laneway. Still I stood, watching the last of her headlights as they disappeared. I was beset by an inexplicable sense of grief and abandonment, and I stood for a long time looking into the darkening garden. 'She's only gone for a spin,' I told myself, 'so stop your crazy ideas.'

I was supposed to be studying for an English test the next day, but felt I could not take anything in. I saw my mother's reading glasses on the table, and beside them the *Evening Press* lying where she had left it and turned to 'Dubliners' Diary' out of curiosity to see what had so held her interest.

There were several photographs:

Penny O'Dea of Cashel who was at the launch of Revlon's new fragrance, 'Souvenir de Moi' at the Beaufield Mews, Stillorgan.

John and Peggy Dolan of Killiney who celebrated their golden wedding anniversary at the Gresham Hotel.

Lovely Mary Connolly of Ballsbridge, and François Duballe of the Alliance Française, who announced their engagement at a party in the Shelbourne Hotel last night.

I looked at the picture of François Duballe and his fiancée, the lovely Mary Connolly. He was handsome after a fashion – dark, romantic eyes and hair streaked with grey. Pretty *she* certainly was, and bright and vivacious.

The house contained all the inadequately muffled sounds that usually drove me crazy; the twins' music, the television that my father had evidently turned on to get the news, the phone ringing. But despite every assurance I gave myself, I wished with a desperate yearning that I had followed my mother, driven with her wherever she went; I imagined how I would make her laugh, how I would share the evening with her. This desperation became so consuming that I could think of nothing else. A chill paralysis overtook me, mind and body. There was no question of being able to study. After a while I picked up my mother's spectacles, held them in my hand as though they contained some essence of her and brought them upstairs. I lay on my bed and pulled the duvet over me, waiting all the time for the sound of her return.

I jumped when my father knocked on the door. 'Someone on the phone for you, Áine . . .'

'Who is it?'

'Some girl.' He looked at me and frowned. 'Are you all right?'

'Fine,' I said, levering myself out of bed. 'Mummy has gone out.'

I looked at him, certain that he too must feel the dread that was filling me with nausea. 'Oh . . . good,' he said nonchalantly. 'Bit of a spin, I suppose?'

'She didn't say.'

But he was evidently anxious to get down to his TV programme. '*The World at War* will be on in a moment. Do you want to watch it?'

'No thanks.'

I went to my parents' bedroom and picked up the phone. My caller was Deirdre Kavanagh, one of my classmates.

'Áine, I can't stand any more of this stuff. What about a coffee in Mad Moll's?'

'No thanks, Deirdre. I can't study either, but I don't want to go out. I've got the curse and the cramps are murdering me.'

She said, 'You poor oul thing!' and ruminated for a moment as to what might come up in the test tomorrow, and then hung up. But I was almost ill with a certainty too terrible to contemplate, and unable to articulate a word of it. My father had gone back downstairs and changed channels, for I heard the signature music for *The World at War*. I went back to my bed and clutched the pillow. Every time I heard the phone ring I stopped breathing. Once I saw reflected headlights coming down the lane, and I rushed to the window but the car

211

belonged to our neighbours. 'It'll be all right; it'll be all right,' I whispered aloud. 'You're imagining things again.'

The police came sometime later. I remember them well; they are etched into memory, two unhappy members of the Garda Síochána, a young man and woman in navy uniforms. I had heard the doorbell even above the noise from the twins' bedroom, and I crept to the turn of the stairs and looked down as my father answered the door. I saw his shoulders stiffen and then slump, but he straightened and let the two gardai in and they followed him to the sitting room. I willed my legs to carry me downstairs, but they would not, and so I sat on the top step and after a few moments the policeman and woman left, letting themselves out and shaking their heads at each other as though to distance themselves from the horrors of their vocation.

Mummy, I thought, beset with a certainty beyond reasoning and trembling all over. Now you will never know how much I love you.

My father came out of the sitting room and looked around like someone who had lost his bearings and could not remember what he had come out for, or whose house he was in. He glanced up at me and climbed the stairs, his face white and his mouth a thin, forced line. He drew me back to the landing window and together we looked out at the garden and the lights in the houses across the way.

'I have just received some very bad news,' he said softly, putting an arm around my shoulder and holding me tightly against him. 'It's about your mother.'

'She was doing more than a hundred miles per hour,' I heard days later.

She had hit a lamp-post on the Naas Road, just at the approach to the town itself. No one else had been involved.

'Of course there was black ice . . . she was just putting that car of hers through its paces . . .'

The comments came and went like snatches of radio conversation. There had been severe head injuries; she had died by subdural haematoma. And all I could think of was, Why hadn't I knocked on the window, called to her, broken whatever fixation had driven her to take out her car on a freezing night and then drive at one hundred miles per hour down the lonely dual carriageway to Naas?

'Death by misadventure' the coroner would say in due course.

She looked very peaceful in the oak coffin, with her hands joined together on her breast. It made no sense; it made me feel that something potent and secret and terrible lay in wait for us – to see this face, the heart of my world, stilled for ever.

Rupert and Aunt Isabelle came from America for the funeral. My aunt drew me to one side and asked me sotto voce if I was still being bothered by 'that man'. 'Your poor mother told me in her last letter that you thought he was following you . . . and that you had found a peculiar doll . . .'

I was appalled that my mother should have divulged anything of the sort to my aunt, but then Mummy had a blind spot where she was concerned. I was also touched that, despite appearances, my mother had registered my chagrin at the bizarre find I had made by the front railings that wet morning. But to discuss anything of this nature with Aunt Isabelle would be to make myself complicit in her view of the world, and this prospect filled me with dread. I needed understanding, but not the understanding of a neurotic.

'No,' I said. 'No one is following me!'

In Mount Jerome Cemetery I tried to hold back the tears, but they came in a torrent when my father, in the timeless graveside gesture, sprinkled earth into the grave. It made a small rattle on the coffin, an echo, and I felt its reverberations in my soul like hammer blows.

Looking up I saw that Aunt Isabelle seemed frightened and clutched her son. But then I met Rupert's eyes through the sticky flood of my tears and saw there his pity and his love.

'At least the son seems to be all right,' I heard my Great-aunt Margaret exclaim at the lunch my father hosted after the funeral. She was what my mother would have described as 'well oiled' and was talking to a friend of the family who had travelled all the way from London to attend my mother's funeral.

'Poor Isabelle was never right,' she continued in a whisper,

213

'and of course you can pass these things on . . . People can be a bit . . . well, *fragile*, you know. I was always glad that I had no children. We're really quite a nutty family.'

I looked around and saw that my Aunt Isabelle was thankfully out of earshot and deep in conversation with a woman I had never seen. She seemed to be 'well oiled' too and I wondered if alcohol was the lubricant for her imagination, or if there were really some disorder wandering among our genes. But I wanted to shove the old woman's mashed potato down her throat and stifle her for daring to refer to Rupert in such terms.

That night I could not sleep, although my eyes were gritty with exhaustion. I lay awake with the light on; I heard the echo of Great-aunt Margaret's voice, '*At least the son seems to be all right . . .*'

I dared not turn off the light. What if Mummy came, a ghost? Although I longed to see her, I felt she must hate me because I had done nothing on that last evening of her life to stop her going out to die. I had been filled with premonition and yet I had done nothing.

Then I heard the footsteps on the landing, and recognized my aunt's tread. My door was ajar and she put her head in to say goodnight. She had a glass of water in one hand and a bottle of pills in the other.

'Can you sleep, Áine?'

'No.'

'You look very pale. You need to sleep. I thought you could take one of these . . . I've just given one to Rupert.'

She opened the bottle and deposited two tablets on the table beside me. 'They're sleeping pills. I take one every night, but you could take two tonight . . . to make sure you nod off . . .'

I thanked her, but she seemed determined to remain until I swallowed the pills so I put them in my mouth and washed them down with a gulp of water.

But still she did not go, but sat on the side of my bed, staring at me. To get rid of her, I settled down in the bed and said I felt sleepy now. She got up, turned off my light, whispered, 'Goodnight Áine.'

Then she went quietly to the window, pulled back the curtain

214

a fraction, and looked out. She stood very still; I could see her silhouette against the light from the street and wondered what she saw to so rivet her attention. Was he down there again? Did she see him too?

But I could not talk to her about this, could not talk about anything. I dreaded what confidences it might unleash in her. I knew she would take me seriously, but I did not want the only person to take me seriously to be someone of her undoubted instability. So I pretended to be asleep and she eventually left the room.

But sleep evaded me. I felt more awake than ever, a feverish wakefulness that defied the powers of Valium: I dared myself to look out of the window, but stayed where I was. Does it matter if he is there again? I asked myself. Does it matter if every nutter in the country is camping under your window? Mummy is gone. I sobbed convulsively, and then the tears were spent. I sat up in bed and listened, wondering if anyone were still awake, half hoping for the sound of the twins' muted conversation which I often heard at the oddest hours.

But the house was silent; my father had retired early, having drunk a lot of whiskey, out of character for someone so naturally abstemious; the boys, shattered and ashen-faced from several nights without sleep, had gone to bed not long after him. I knew Rupert was sleeping in the study on the sofa. The thought of him made me remember what Great-aunt Margaret had said, '*At least the son seems to be all right . . .*' and I cringed at the memory of it.

When I could stand it no longer I slipped out of bed, donned the woollen dressing-gown that had been bought for me when I was going to boarding school, and stood listening for a while at the open door of my room. The house was completely silent, and filled with the new emptiness that had seized it three nights earlier while I waited for my mother's return, as though it had known even then that nothing would ever be the same. There was no light under any of the bedroom doors. Aunt Isabelle had the spare room, which was directly opposite mine, but I had seen her bottle of sleeping tablets and was confident she would be comatose till morning.

I felt as though my mind were spinning, like the gyroscope

my father kept in the drawer of his desk and sometimes played with to amuse his sons. I resisted the urge to go to the window, saying to myself, 'You told Mummy you had put all that stuff behind you . . .'

There was only one port in this storm. I tiptoed downstairs, and opened the study door. I hardly questioned my action. I was looking for the only comfort I knew, Rupert's undivided presence, and was more than happy at the thought of simply sitting in the same room while he slept, as I had intended to do almost four years earlier in Dunbeg. Or perhaps this is not entirely true. I remembered his presence and comfort in Virginia on my last night. There was a strange excitement in me, a compulsion, like a salmon returning to a particular river because it is home.

Rupert was lying on the couch, his head on a pillow, his bare arm thrown out and both feet sticking out from beneath the duvet. It was strange to see him there, because that couch, before it had been banished from the sitting room, had seen me through many an evening of childhood illness, when, wrapped up in a rug, I had been allowed to get up and watch telly for a few hours. It was also this couch that had cushioned me when, during the insomnia of my childhood, I had come downstairs in the night to listen to music. The desk reading light was on, and the curtains were half drawn. Some empty beer cans stood on the hearth. Clothes were dumped on a chair, and all six feet of my cousin were apparently asleep. I stood and looked down at him, saw that the legs which stuck out from under his covers were hairy, that his mouth was sightly open and his eyes shut. His face had the innocence of childhood, even though his body was a young man's. The sight of him brought a strange peace, a surcease from the numbing bereavement that had made a void of my innards and turned my heart to stone. I switched off the light and sat back against the couch, hearing the rise and fall of his breathing, and positioning my shoulder against his outstretched arm. Little by little the pain in me eased. I rested my head against his hand.

'Oh,' his slurred voice, heavy with sleep, said sometime later, 'Cheryl?'

I thought he had called me 'chérie'; it was only later that I was disabused.

He moved a fraction, and then gave a single snore and resumed his deep breathing. I was cold and climbed in beside him beneath the duvet. He was in his vest and underpants, but I didn't give a damn. He was deeply asleep and after a moment or two the sleep I too so desperately needed began to claim me; the drug I had been fighting kicked in, sending me to merciful oblivion.

The kisses on my face and neck some time later might have been from a dream. Held in a slumber that was slow to release me, I registered the blind hands on my breasts with the knowledge that they were Rupert's hands. The fierce, quickened breathing I heard in my ear seemed to belong to someone I had never met. I was still half torpid, half awake, curious and trusting, yielding in sleepy ecstasy to the moist mouth on mine and the novelty of total communion. But when I felt his weight on me and the attempt at penetration, the pain jerked me into full consciousness.

'Rupert,' I said, my voice sounding flat and frightened. 'It's hurting!'

He suddenly sat up, stared at me, scrambled off the couch and said in a fierce whisper, 'Jesus Christ, get out of here, Áine . . . I didn't realize it was you . . . I thought . . . Oh Jesus, I drank too much last night, and I took one of Mom's goddamn pills . . . I was dreaming . . . Get OUT!'

I obeyed. I got off the couch, slunk out the door and heard his self-directed whisper, 'Oh Jesus . . .'

I crept back upstairs to bed, but as I passed Aunt Isabelle's room I saw with a start that she was standing in the open doorway. It was dim on the landing, and her sudden materialization nearly frightened the life out of me.

'I know where you've been, you little slut!' she said in a voice slurred with sleep. 'Sarah was a slut too . . . which is why William had her killed . . .' Her eyes were wide, the pupils dilated.

'I don't know what you're talking about.'

'Oh yes you do! You're the one who knows everything in this family. You're the real linchpin. Why do you think that creature in Dunbeg made a bee-line for you? He knew what he had. He knew you were kindred . . . another like himself. And that is why he is waiting for you. That is why he is trying to find you. He will always try to find you, Áine. He comes from the past, you see . . .'

I ran into my room, shut the door and pushed the chair against it.

But I heard my aunt hiss through the keyhole, 'Stay away from my son, Áine . . .'

'Oh Mummy,' I cried a moment later into my pillow, 'what is happening? Have I done something terrible?' I listened to the bewilderment of my body, the bruised pride, the sense of having trespassed on an alien landscape that I had mistaken for my own.

Next day I rose when I heard my father's step on the landing, and I went downstairs behind him. In this way I hoped to avoid any confrontation with my aunt. Downstairs, Rupert had already emerged from the study, but his demeanour to me was distant when he met us in the hall, and he did not look at me when he said 'good morning'.

I did not want to look at him either. The cold light of morning put a different complexion on what had taken place the night before. I knew that he had been ready to do with me the thing all of my peers referred to obliquely with bated breath. It was called Sexual Intercourse.

Aunt Isabelle was making breakfast. She seemed perfectly normal, and said a 'good morning' to me that did not seem to harbour a single recollection of the night.

While we had breakfast she asked my father if we intended going to Dunbeg in the summer, and I wondered for a moment if she was thinking of joining us. Then I thought of Johnny Eagles and his warning: '*It is best that you do not go again to that place.*'

I whispered to Seán, 'The Indian whom we met at Gunther's . . . do you remember what he said about Dunbeg?'

Seán was dismissive. 'Oh for God's sake, Áine . . . your imagination is off with you again. If you are going to live your life according to every divination you chance along the way you'll be just a little lost leaf in the wind.'

Seán turned to Rupert and asked him about Harvard. He answered without enthusiasm and his mother said that he was overworked. 'But he always wanted to do medicine . . .'

Simon, for whom the prospect of eventually getting away from home had all the lure of Nirvana, now demanded, 'Do you have your own flat in college?'

'No, freshmen live in halls within Harvard Yard – that is a walled enclosure with buildings from the early eighteenth century, now used as dorms and classrooms, with libraries and dining facilities . . .'

Surreptitiously watching the play of light and shade in his expression, the earnestness, the way his eyes shied away from meeting mine, I wanted to reach out and touch his hand. I knew that he was ashamed, ashamed not only of himself, but also of me.

Later, chancing him on his own as he brought his mother's bag down to the hall, I whispered, 'Rupert, it's all right . . . it was my fault. I was frightened. But if *everything* had happened it would still be all right.'

'It certainly would not,' he hissed. 'You're only thirteen years old, for Chrissake! And you must never, ever, do a thing like that again!'

'I'm nearly fourteen actually,' I said with all the dignity I could muster. 'I just wanted to be . . . near you. Rupert, I love you!'

'You're such an irritating kid, Áine,' he said, 'and that was a disgraceful episode.' He turned and walked away.

I went to my room and locked the door on my sense of rejection and did not come down when my aunt called goodbye. I expected that Rupert would come upstairs and make his farewells in person, but he did not.

It was evening when I emerged again. My aunt and cousin were gone. The house felt like a morgue, a strange abode under a pall of unhappiness, so powerful it was almost palpable. My father looked at my tear-stained face and patted my head.

It must have been about a week later that the phone call came from Sergeant Touhy. I was in my father's study, looking up the word 'mortgage' in the *Oxford Dictionary*. 'A conveyance of property,' it said, 'as security for a debt on condition that it shall be returned on repayment of the debt.'

I jumped when the phone rang beside me. I picked up the receiver. 'Hello.'

'Is that Áine?' the no-nonsense male voice demanded.

'Yes.'

'This is Matt Touhy from Mulvey Garda station.'

'Oh . . .'

'Áine, is your father in?'

'No . . . he's at the office.'

I waited and then the sergeant said. 'I've a bit of news about Aeneas Shaw . . .'

My heart began to canter. 'What news?' I whispered. 'You told us he was dead.'

'Mistaken identity, I'm afraid. The corpse belonged to someone else. But Aeneas has turned up now and been returned to the mental hospital.'

'Where did he turn up?'

'In the cemetery at Askreagh.'

'What do you mean "in the cemetery"?'

'He was found above ground, not under it,' he explained with a curt laugh.

'My grandmother is buried there.' I heard my voice rise. There was a moment's silence.

'So I believe.'

'What was he doing in the cemetery?'

'Eh . . . nothing much. Sure I'll talk to your father about it.' He rang off.

Seán came into the study.

'Who was that on the phone? I'm expecting a call from Arthur.' When I didn't reply he looked at me sharply.

'What's wrong with you? You look pale as death.'

'Nothing's wrong with me! That was Sergeant Touhy on the phone. And for your information Aeneas Shaw is still alive and kicking. He was found in Askreagh cemetery . . . above ground. I don't know what he was doing there and I don't care. But it takes a ghoulish kind of person to hide out in a graveyard.'

'What have they done with him?' Seán said.

'They've put him back where he belongs – in the loony bin.'

220

'Now look what you've done!' His face had a pallor from days of secret weeping, but his ire had not been diluted on the subject of Aeneas Shaw.

'Why am I blamed for this? *I* didn't do anything!'

'It was because of *you* he was put away in the first place. He wouldn't hurt a fly.'

'Is that right? He more or less pushed me off the cliff!' I hissed. 'That's why I fell.'

Seán jerked his head and looked at me closely. 'You didn't say this before.'

'I didn't say it to *you*. What's the point of saying anything to *you*?'

'You're off your head, Áine . . .' my brother said softly after a moment. 'You were always such a bloody nut case. Always a different story. Why would Aeneas do a thing like that?'

I stood up. 'Nobody ever believes me. Mummy might still be alive if you had believed me. I felt things were not right with her and you all thought I was mad. And now she's dead . . . and nothing,' and here in a sudden burst of rage, I threw the dictionary at his head, missing him by inches, 'will ever bring her back!'

Seán turned on his heel. But at the door he paused and said in a cold voice, 'You've become impossible. Everyone in the family is very worried about you. And you had more of a hand in Mummy's death than you realize. It was your shenanigans that drove her off the edge . . . Yes Áine, your shenanigans that drove her to take out her car that night and drive as though she wanted to escape her life. Think about it: there was no one else in the family who gave the kind of trouble you did.'

I covered my ears and screamed, 'Leave me alone, just leave me alone!'

When I looked up I saw my assembled siblings standing at the door of the study and staring at me with a mixture of concern and contempt.

That evening my father phoned Sergeant Touhy. The study door was open and I listened in the hall.

'My daughter tells me you spoke to her on the phone earlier.' There was a pause. 'I see. In Askreagh graveyard? But not so long ago you told me that he was dead.'

He was silent for a few moments, obviously listening.

'Mistaken identity?' he said coldly. 'That's all very well, but here we have a very disturbed individual still at large . . .'

There was another long pause. 'Well I'm glad you people realize it . . .'

I knew by the quality of the silence then that the sergeant was telling him something of moment. I stood still, straining to hear, afraid to move in case I would betray my presence.

'*He was doing what?*' my father asked in a whisper. 'Good God!' Hold on a minute,' he added in a tight voice, 'I'll just shut the door.'

The door clapped to, and I heard no more. I went down to the silent kitchen, sat at the table and stared through the window.

When my father came into the room he seemed pale. 'Well,' he said, 'that episode is over. That fellow is safely locked away. He won't get out this time, Áine.'

'Won't he?' I said dully.

The next morning my father left earlier than usual and when I phoned his office during the day they said he had gone to the west.

The dreams returned. I would wake up, terrified, crying out as we were carried out to sea. In this dream which kept recurring, I was on a raft with Seán and Rupert, and a hand would come from the water and Aeneas would suddenly crawl onto the raft and turn to us, grinning, while the sky turned to blood and an ominous presence filled the air like the harbinger of a storm.

Whom could I talk to now? Rupert, the erstwhile ear for all my woes, was gone, had left my life in apparent disgust, and was back in America. His interpretation of the night-time episode in the study humiliated and appalled me. It had not been preplanned – I was still more or less incapable of overt sexuality – but the gloss I sensed he had put on our minutes together under that duvet revolted me. It reduced it to something seedy, and I hated him for it.

My brothers had reacted violently to Mummy's death. The twins had become taciturn, a small, closed system feeding angrily on itself. Seán and Simon alternated between hostility and silent depression.

'Why did she have to do that to us?' Simon demanded and Seán looked at me as though I had the answers.

After weeks of anguish it came to me that only I myself could determine my destiny. I could either live my life according to my own insights, or I could depend on the endorsement of others until I died. I acknowledged that I was cursed with a sensibility that interfered with the currency of my own life. It had become so acute, that there was now hardly a thought in the family of which I did not hear at least the echo. I knew Seán's manner was based on guilt. I knew my father was bedevilled by doubt and a loss the magnitude of which he had never anticipated and had no idea how to bear. I watched my other brothers begin to give trouble in ways they never had before. The twins looked only to each other for affirmation, challenging everything else. Simon was suspended from school for stealing a cheap little watch, the sort you got with tokens from the cornflakes box, and my father had to grovel to his headmaster.

I thought of Rupert alternately with longing and stubborn anger. He had not written or phoned since his return to the States, and this made me question the validity of my erstwhile belief in him. What I was really questioning was my instinct, which still insisted that we were two sides of the same coin. The doubt that accompanied this soul-searching threatened to destroy my confidence. I asked myself over and over how I could have imagined the kind of mutuality I had experienced with Rupert. And if I had not been imagining it, then why was he silent? I preferred to believe the answer I found one day in school when, during a civics class, Sister Mary-Anne referred to the phenomenon of young girls fainting over pop idols and said it had little to do with the silly and unremarkable young men and everything to do with the creative powers of their fans. She used the word 'projection' to describe the mental processes of the teenage worshippers.

I created you, I told Rupert silently. That's what happened. Now that I know this I can forget you as easily as you can forget me. There was great relief in this thought and it worked well for a while. In Rupert's absence, with no phone call or

223

letter, no funny cards such as he had used to send, I was free to blacken his memory. But when Seán told me casually that Rupert had a girlfriend at Harvard I could not suppress the surge of jealousy.

'How do you know he has a girlfriend?'

'He told me when he was with us for the funeral. He said her name was Cheryl.'

This information came as a body blow: I hated Cheryl. I knew immediately that she had been the person Rupert had mistaken me for that night in the study. I had tasted the kisses he gave her; I had been touched, for a moment, as he touched her, or wanted to touch her; the communion I had known had not been meant for me.

'Go to hell,' I told him within the privacy of my mind. 'Piss off and go to hell!'

But when an envelope came for me, enclosing just a cutting of Rupert Bear and Tigerlily, all the anger left me and dissolved in tears.

The cutting, showing the little bear standing by a gate, watching Tigerlily walk away, provoked in me a mélange of emotions. I felt it was aimed at a child. It made me feel as though I were ten years old again, frightened, insecure, and desperate with hopeless love. The verse was an apology and a farewell.

> Rupert Bear is often hasty
> Often wrong and sometimes testy.
> And, although love comes unbidden,
> Tigerlily should forget him.

For many a morning after this I would wake with a sinking sense of desolation, knowing that he was lost to me and that I didn't really hate him and that I could not eradicate him from my life.

I felt my life was out of my control. Rupert, central to my every breath, had given me the brush off. And the man known as Aeneas Shaw was still alive. Sometimes I thought I saw him from the corner of my eye in the crowded city streets; on the rare occasions when I looked out of my window at night I studied the shadow of any man who passed on the pavement. He's back in the mental hospital, I reminded myself.

But this did not convince me any more.

I began waking with abdominal cramps and when I told my father he insisted that I see our GP. This kind man told me that the cramps were a reaction to my mother's death, and a year of mishap.

'Try not to let things affect you so deeply, Áine. Remember, your will does not and cannot control Fate. You are only one person.'

It was then I made the conscious decision that my survival depended on some rough psychic self-surgery. I would have to stop surfing the emotional highway of existence.

So one day, when I came home from school, I took my courage in my hands and phoned the mental hospital in Ballinaslie. I asked if a Mr Aeneas Shaw from Mulvey Co Mayo, was an inmate.

'Mr Shaw?' the voice said. 'Yes . . . he's here. Are you a relative?'

I hung up. I wanted to cheer. He was definitely locked away. A dead weight was lifted from me.

After that I instructed my subconscious every night at bedtime not to dream about this man, or at least not to have any further nightmares, and this injunction, strangely enough, was obeyed. And when the dreams left me life assumed a brightness it had not had for years. Yes, Mummy was gone. But I ascribed my deliverance to her influence from the hereafter and knew she would not have wanted me to mourn for ever.

And Rupert was gone too, disappeared into the thickets of his adult life. It was his choice, his right, his election. I had my own to make now.

One morning I received an air-mail letter with an American stamp and unfamiliar writing on the envelope. It was from Brigitte to tell me she had heard of my mother's death and to tell me of her sympathy. This was the real start of our friendship, and came fortuitously, just as I was persuading myself I could let Rupert go. I had began the task of effecting change, submerging old terrors, and ending my childhood.

Part Two

Chapter Sixteen

My school reports began to blaze with accolades.

> Wonderful improvement. Keep it up!
> Áine has worked consistently.
> Her maths has come on by leaps and bounds.

As the years went by my teachers said I had become very introverted. 'You're too quiet, Áine. It's as though you're always listening for something,' my maths teacher said, 'but *I've* no problems with that as long as your work continues to improve.'

I had given up any hope of hearing again from Rupert. That small missive with Rupert Bear and Tigerlily, sent after his visit to Ireland for my mother's funeral, was his last. For a while it was as though someone had turned off the oxygen, and I had to survive on gases that did not support life. So I changed, assumed cynicism, breathed the thin air of my double bereavement, and listened for the next footfall of Fate.

Brigitte came to stay with us the summer after my mother's death. We went to Dunbeg because she begged to see it. I remembered Johnny Eagles' warning and dismissed it as just another superstitious rambling. Aeneas Shaw was safely behind institutional walls and we were not troubled by anyone. Various repairs had been carried out to the castle, a new floor laid in one of the bedrooms, and the old laundry was newly buttressed.

The place seemed different bereft of my mother, but I loved it with as much passion as ever and, when the boys had taken Brigitte riding one morning, I walked along the forbidden cliff path to the spot where my troubles had begun. The stones of the ruined cottage lay about where they had been thrown; the sea growled below me as though hungry for the morsel it had not swallowed, and I lay on my stomach in the coarse grass for an hour and watched the tide, thinking of Rupert and that far-off summer. It was while I was there that I remembered what Rupert had said to me in Mount Wexford, about having read something Sarah had written. Where did he say he had read it? Something to do with a Bible.

But I did not bestir myself. I can't be bothered with all that stuff now, I thought.

Brigitte had undergone a metamorphosis. From being a fat, mousey little entity she had blossomed. In one year she had slimmed, was more grown up than I, and light years more worldly wise. Blonde, newly tall, with the added spice of being foreign, she outshone the pretty Gráinne O'Keefe who came around on her bicycle as soon as she heard of our arrival. My brothers were struck dumb by Brigitte. Seán had hardly noticed her in America, but his eyes now followed her wherever she went. She treated him with a carelessness that he seemed to find irresistible. I saw, with a certain satisfaction, the wide-awake look he had when he spoke to her, the desire to please, and thought with some amusement of his comment about her on our return journey from Virginia – that she was a lethal little sausage who would kill anyone she sat on. But Brigitte did not pretend to any stirring of her own heart strings, and was able to kill by just batting her eyelids. She was bubbly and direct, but I noticed how silent and intense she became when we played music in the evening on the portable tape recorder I had brought with us. And I saw how Gráinne, when she came around to visit, looked from Seán to her new rival in quasi-despair. Seán, of course, hardly noticed that the former love of his life was suffering.

'Gráinne was supposed to come riding with us today, but she never turned up,' he said dismissively.

'Do you ever hear from Rupert?' Brigitte asked one day as we sat on the parapet above the rocks, throwing pebbles into the sea.

'We used to be great friends. But he doesn't contact me any more. How long have you known him?'

'Ever since we were small. The first time I met him was at a birthday party some neighbours – the Holdens – threw for their son, Randy, an obnoxious little toad. He was eleven and I was nine. He had a tree house high up in an oak, and to show off I climbed up to see it. But when I turned to get down I froze. The ground seemed far away, and I knew I could never climb down. There was a rope hanging from a branch, which Randy and his friends used for sliding down. I thought I hadn't the strength to lower myself down by it and I couldn't go back the way I had come. I'll never forget the panic. Randy and the other boys were all grinning and gathering around to watch me and the girls were giggling. I couldn't move. Rupert shouted: "Good idea, Brigitte. We'll take turns," and he shinned up the tree to where I was sitting on the plank outside that goddamn tree house and wishing I was dead.

'"You'll just have to grab the rope," he whispered, "and slide. Otherwise they'll know you're chicken. It'll hurt your hands, that's all! Just smile and grab the rope! I'll be watching you!"' She looked at me, half laughing. 'It took the skin off my hands, but I felt I had someone on my side. The boys thought I was great and it wiped the smile off the girls' faces! The point is that everyone, except Rupert, was lined up to have a great laugh at the little fatty stuck in the tree! I told Daddy about it and he said Rupert was a natural gentleman and that there were only a few of them left in the world.'

Then I asked, half ashamed at my own eagerness to stay on this topic, 'Do you know his parents well?'

'No. I've only met them once. He comes to our place to talk to Dad and Johnny Eagles, but we never visit Mount Wexford. His mother doesn't socialize much.'

'I wish you could say the same about her drinking. When I was in Mount Wexford she was always tippling.'

This unkind comment was designed to elicit what Brigitte knew about Rupert's mother, but she shrugged and made no response.

'What did you think of my Uncle Alex?' I ventured.

Brigitte gave me a careful glance. 'I didn't like him very much!'

'Did he try feeling you up?' I asked this in a whisper, fearful of being overheard and fearful of her response.

'Oh God,' she said, 'you too? I didn't dare tell my father

because he would have told the police . . . and I could not do that to Rupert. Poor Mrs Lyall,' she added, 'tied to a man like that . . .'

We wandered around the castle. Dracula no longer haunted the landing; he had long since gone to wherever good bats went, but I pointed out his former lair to Brigitte. We went up the turret stairs and looked across the bay. I remembered the first morning I had stood there with Rupert, and for a moment the taste of being ten years old and ecstatic at a new friendship came back to me.

'I took Rupert up here the first time he came to Dunbeg.'

'When was that?'

'Oh, four years ago. I was ten.'

'Did he like it here?'

'I think so . . . except for something that happened which upset his holiday. It had to do with a crazy old creep who used to hang around on the headland. I used to dream about him for years. I used to think he was following me.'

Brigitte did not seem unduly perturbed by this intelligence, although she looked at me speculatively for a moment. 'And was he?'

'I don't know. I could have been imagining things!'

'Kids are always like that. When Mom was still alive I used to climb into bed between her and Dad every time I had a nightmare. I bet you did that too?'

'No,' I said. 'I don't think I did, at least not after the age of six. But the last night Rupert spent in this house I was so scared I ran into his room and he tucked me up in bed.'

Brigitte laughed.

'Did you ever meet Rupert's girlfriend?' I asked after a moment, in as even a voice as I could muster.

'Nope,' she said. 'I didn't know he had one.'

'Her name is Cheryl, or something stupid. He keeps in contact with Seán and I hear the odd bit of news from him.' The pain of this avowal made my voice stiff.

Brigitte looked at me sideways. 'Is that right? I think it's a nice name! Is she pretty?'

'How do I know? She's probably a raving beauty!'

Brigitte glanced at me sharply and said, 'Áine, are you

carrying a very bright and flaming torch for Rupert or is that just cousinly curiosity I hear in your voice?'

'I used to be mad about him when I was a kid . . .'

She nodded slowly. 'But you're still a kid, at least by some perspectives. And you're still smitten. I can see that.'

'I don't know. I still think about him a lot, or at least I do sometimes. He was my *friend*, you see. And that's what hurts the most – that my *friend* doesn't want to know me any more . . .'

To my consternation my voice wobbled and tears started in my eyes.

Brigitte's hand on mine was unintrusive. I heard her small, compassionate sigh. 'It will pass,' she said gently. 'Everything passes. The pain will go, and when it does you will wonder why you ever let him bother you.'

I shook my head. She didn't understand and there was no way of making her understand, and I didn't want her understanding.

'What are you going to do when you leave school?' she asked after a while.

'Study acting. No need to tell me what you intend to do!'

'Music,' she agreed with a laugh. 'What else is there?' She lowered her voice. 'I'm determined to study piano at the Royal College in London. Do you think I have a hope in hell?'

'Why go to London? There must be fantastic music colleges in the States.'

'Sure. But I want to go to England. I've wanted this ever since I was a kid! I want to suss out my English roots.'

'Practice until you drop,' I said. 'And you'll make it. You have the talent. I've heard you play, remember.' Then I added with a self-conscious laugh, 'I'm going to try for RADA in London. And you never know, if pigs were to fly, we might be together.'

Mrs Maloney made supper that evening, and for a while it was like old times. Gráinne had joined us for the meal, but she became increasingly quiet and excused herself early. She could not compete with Brigitte, for the latter's intensity informed her gestures, her jokes, her body language, so that she seemed on fire with life, and my sardonic brother Seán and my other siblings hung on her every word.

'Pity there's no ghost here,' Brigitte said. 'I'd just love to meet one.'

'I'm sure that can be arranged,' Seán said laconically. 'There's a story about our Great-great-grandmother Sarah who died here . . .'

I shut my ears. But my sibling went on, telling Brigitte the old tale of Sarah's life and death.

'She seems to have got up someone's nose,' Seán explained. 'It had to do with the small matter of an eviction. And this, of course, is not a very good country in which to get up anyone's nose . . .'

'Where is she buried?' Brigitte asked.

'In Askreagh, just a few miles down the road.'

That evening, Seán offered to take us for a drive to Westport. Brigitte accepted with alacrity. En route my brother pointed out the cemetery of Askreagh beside the ruined monastery.

'I'd love to see it,' Brigitte said, and Seán stopped the car, and we walked into the graveyard, stepping over graves in the long grass.

'Where is poor old Sarah planted?' my brother asked, turning to me.

'How do I know?'

I thought of Sergeant Touhy telling me that Aeneas Shaw had turned up in this very cemetery and wondered why he would haunt a graveyard.

Brigitte lost interest, saying the place was spooky, and decamped, with Seán in tow, to the ruins of the monastery, and I walked a few more paces until I found the limestone cross which bore the legend, *Sarah O'Malley, 1830 – 1860. Requiescat in Pace.*

It was a calm and lovely evening with pink streaks on the horizon and the sound of homecoming bees. But as I looked at my ancestor's grave I saw that the grass on her plot was flattened and the clay exposed, as though the earth had been recently disturbed and replaced. I rejoined my friend and my brother in silence.

'Are you all right, Áine?' Brigitte asked, looking at me strangely. 'You're looking very pale.'

'I'm just tired.'

I cannot bear any more, I thought. I cannot endure the speculation as to who, or what, or why. If Aeneas Shaw is responsible for this I don't want to know. Blank it, blank it out. Blank it all out and live!

But suddenly Rupert's words came back to me: 'The Bible is on the bottom shelf by the window . . .'

That night, when we returned from Westport, I slipped into the library. It was forbidding. The curtains were open, the night outside was moonless, and the room itself, with its dark oak panels, swallowed the electric light. I scanned the bottom shelf for the Bible and found it, just as he had said, half-hidden by the curtain. It was a very heavy Bible with faded gold lettering, its black and dark green leather cover nicely tooled. I put it on the table, and opened it. It smelled musty. The first page was redolent of Victorian piety:

The Life, Doctrine, and Sufferings of our Blessed Lord and Saviour Jesus Christ, as recorded by the Four Evangelists, with Moral Reflections, Critical Illustration and Explanatory Notes by the Rev Henry Rutter.

I leafed through it to the end, saw how the inner lining at the back had come away. Putting my finger tentatively inside, I found a folded sheet of paper. I drew it out, closing my mind, thinking I should just put it back in the Bible and forget about it. One side of the yellowing page bore writing in Irish, while the other side was inscribed in English in a sloping hand. I flattened the page out on the table, turned on the table lamp. But before I could read, Simon came into the room.

'What are you doing in here? Everyone is in the drawing room!'

'Go away. I'm busy.'

'What's that?' he demanded, reaching for the page on the table.

I tried to snatch it from his hand but it tore in two.

'Now look what you've done!'

'It's only an old letter, or something,' Simon said, examining the piece left in his hand. 'What do you want it for?'

235

'I'm interested in it. It's probably valuable; I found it in a book, and now you've ruined it!'

'Don't be stupid. All it needs is a bit of sellotape. There's some in the kitchen.'

He left the room, returning in a moment with a small roll of sellotape which I took from his hand.

'I'll do it. You've done enough damage already!'

He flounced out. 'You needn't be so snide. I only wanted to ask you if you'd like to play charades.'

When he was gone, I carefully joined the two split halves of the page together, and when the task was done laid it flat on the table once more and sat down to read it. Almost from the first sentence I was riveted:

This man's wife and three of his five children had died of typhus during the Hunger. He fished and grew a few potatoes. He was a strange fellow, with penetrating eyes, and he seemed to be watching and waiting for me everywhere, besetting me with his dark looks. I was with child and surprised by his looking when I went out to take a walk along the cliff path. When I passed his cottage he would come to the door, nod at me. I suppose, with hindsight, that I should have taken my walks somewhere else, but I like the vista from the headland, and if truth be told, felt a certain fascination for this silent man with his sad and intense eyes.

William sent the agent, O'Mara, to spy on me and, to my astonishment, confronted me with an absurd jealousy. He demanded that I cease walking to the headland, or that I go with my maid. I was angry; I am often lonely, notwithstanding the presence of the children, and a walk is an innocent diversion and good for the constitution, especially in my condition, as I know from experience. I refused. I told William that my walks were the only exercise I had and that I would not live in a straitjacket. But William told my father of his suspicions and my father sent his bailiff to turn the tenant out. I did not see the eviction, nor did I know that it was to take place. But the following day the servants' demeanour told me that it was not pretty. It had rained that night, and Mr Shaw and his son and small daughter who was sickly, were put out into the ditch.

The little girl died the following day and the father took refuge with his son in the workhouse. But he died himself there some weeks later. I do not know what has happened to his son.

Kitty, our housekeeper, would not be drawn about it, but crossed herself when I spoke of it and looked at me strangely.

'It was not my fault, Kitty,' I said. 'I had no hand in his eviction!'

''Troth then, he thought you had, ma'am,' she said.

'How do you know this, Kitty?' said I.

'He said somethin', ma'am, whin he was dyin'.'

'What did he say, Kitty? You can tell me.'

'I don't want to repeat it, ma'am, for the bad luck that's in it.'

'Can you write it?'

And so she wrote it down, and it is on the other side of this page. I never learnt the Irish, but Kitty's father was a hedge schoolmaster and taught her how to write in the old tongue. If that unfortunate man has cursed me I forgive him. We are a deep, black race, we Irish, and I am greatly troubled by this episode.

I turned back to the writing on the back of the page, but realised on closer inspection that it was in the old Irish script and that I couldn't decipher it. I was shaken by what Sarah had written and strangely glad of the excuse to put the page away in my pocket, thinking I would vet it again carefully in due course, perhaps when I was safely back in Dublin and two hundred miles from Dunbeg.

On the morning she left Brigitte sat on the edge of her bed and invited me to come back to America. 'Dad said to tell you how welcome you'd be . . .'

I sat down beside her. 'I can hardly do that. I'd be staying just down the road from Rupert! And quite honestly Brigitte, I don't want to see him any more.'

'What's that got to do with it?' Brigitte put an empathic hand on my shoulder. 'Look, he's obviously hurt you a lot, but pain feeds on itself . . . And it's your world too, Aine. You can see him if you like and not if you don't.'

I imagined how strange it would be, living twelve miles away from Rupert's home, meeting him there as though he were a stranger. I would not be able to cope with that.

'I'll come, but not yet. I'll come when I'm rich and famous.'

And I suddenly imagined, in my innocence, that I would impress him by my fame and wealth, and that he would see, and know me again. Once he had said, 'I know who you are'; the strangest thing that anyone had ever told me.

'I'll miss this old place,' Brigitte said, 'I've never been anywhere so spooky. Makes you wonder, doesn't it, where atmosphere comes from? I could imagine doing extraordinary things here with a grand piano. What would you say to *Rondo alla Turca* with the loud pedal? Wake the place up, wouldn't it? It's probably dying for a bit of life.' She added in an eerie voice, 'But it might wake the ghost of your grandmother . . .' She grinned at me. 'De dum . . . de dum . . .'

I put my hand in my pocket and took out the folded page I had found at the back of the Bible.

'I don't know . . . Would you like a piece of authentic commentary upon which to base your interpretation?'

She took the page from my hands. 'What is it?'

'Sarah's words – in her own hand – and something more. To tell you the truth, it gives me the creeps.'

Brigitte took it from me and I left the room. I would never have to translate the strange writing in Irish now, I thought with a ludicrous sense of triumph. But in this I was wrong.

The years suddenly somersaulted. I had crawled, month by month, through most of my life; now the years took off and, in what seemed a very short space of time, landed me face to face with my eighteenth birthday and the end of my schooling. During this time Seán had gone on to study accountancy, the twins had left school and gone to UCD to study engineering, Simon had continued to give us all hell, and my father's air of bewilderment had changed into acceptance. He spent most of his free time at home, his head in his books, and had become the most indulgent of fathers. Every year, during this period, we went for a few weeks to Dunbeg; small improvements were made to the fabric of the old house, but still it needed more.

Every time we went there I felt my roots in the place go deeper. *It*, at any rate, knew me. I did not re-visit Askreagh graveyard, although my father went there and returned without making any comment on the state of Sarah O'Malley's grave. The sense of belonging cocooned me again, bound me to a past older than memory.

But four years is a long time during the formative period of a life and, as time went by, uneventful except for the milestones of birthdays and exams, I relegated my old fears to the realm of childhood nonsense. Rupert ceased to occupy the frontal lobes of my brain. I had other dreams now, to do with the future and London. After four years I tried not to think of him any more, or Aeneas Shaw either. I just wanted to be free.

'I am thinking of selling Dunbeg,' my father announced one evening to the assembled family. There was stunned silence and then consternation. 'But you can't sell a deadly place like Dunbeg,' Seán expostulated. 'I never heard anything so naive, Dad! Where would we go for the summer?'

'The upkeep, or rather the downkeep' (and here my father wrinkled his nose in appreciation of his little joke) 'is costing a fortune. I can't afford it indefinitely. It needs a great deal of money spent on it, and I'm not sure there's any point in the expenditure!'

'I'll be qualified soon and if you put it in my name I could get a loan,' my brother said.

My father looked at him with amusement. 'Could you, indeed! Well I'm not giving Dunbeg to any one of you. That would not be fair.'

'I'll buy it from you, Dad . . . As soon as they give me a partnership.'

'I won't hold my breath,' my father said with a wry smile. 'But I won't make any decision about its sale for another while. We'll see what happens.'

I said nothing, but I had already made up my mind. Dunbeg was mine. Somehow I would find the means to buy it.

Not long after this Brigitte phoned me, her voice husky with happiness. She had been accepted by the Royal College of Music.

'I was afraid to open the envelope,' she said. 'I walked around with it for half the morning!'

'How is your dad taking it?'

'He's delighted . . . aren't you Daddy?' she called and I heard the deep tones of Gunther's voice in the background.

'We'll have to get her somewhere to live,' he said, his half-German, half-southern drawl coming on the line. 'Áine, do you know any suitable nunneries in London, any places where they chain them to the wall after eight p.m.?'

'I live in Dublin, remember, Gunther, and I don't.' We laughed.

Brigitte came back on the line. 'Don't mind Gunther!' she said. 'Now it's up to you, Áine.' Her voice was full of excitement.

'Don't worry.' I lowered my voice. 'I'm applying to RADA. I haven't asked Dad, but I have filled out the form and I'm rehearsing for my audition in secret. But even if I don't get into RADA I'll get something in London and we can be together.'

It was true that I was rehearsing in secret. When the boys were out and my father in his study, I would lock myself in my room, march up and down in front of the mirror and go through every line of my school plays, and several others that did not feature on the curriculum. I haunted the theatres, worked at weekends for pocket money to indulge my passion.

At least, I told myself, I am alive and I know what I want to do. And that is a great deal.

There was a phone call from Rupert one September evening during my last year at school. It was taken by Seán.

'Oh hi, Rupert. How are you?'

How do you rid yourself of an old grief, when every time a button is pressed it returns with all its original immediacy and freshness? I had not thought of Rupert for some time, but the knowledge that he was on the other end of the phone filled me with turmoil.

Seán and Rupert had remained episodically close, albeit from a distance. I knew that Seán wrote to him at Christmas and on his birthday, but this friendship was a unit from which I was excluded. Now my brother sat down by the phone, delighted to be chatting to his cousin who had gone to the

240

expense of phoning him from America. I quelled the old yearning, and because I could not bear to be in the house while my brother monopolized the object of my first passion, I got up, found my jacket and went out.

'Where did you get to? Rupert wanted to speak to you,' Seán said when I got back.

'Oh just down to Tolka Park for a walk.'

'Why didn't you stay and talk to him?'

'He phoned *you*!'

'He wanted to share his news.' He glanced at me as I hung my jacket up and was about to go upstairs. 'Well, don't you want to hear it?'

I shrugged, paused on the bottom step of the stairs. 'Sure, if it's interesting.'

'It's very interesting. He has just got engaged!'

My heart, so well schooled, so uncaring and free, dropped through the soles of my shoes. I felt like someone who was climbing out of a well only to slip when safety was almost within reach. I knew the cavern waited below to swallow me. But I put a nonchalant face on it; anything else with my brothers had always been dangerous.

'Who's the lucky lady?' I asked sarcastically. 'Is it Cheryl?'

Seán gave a hoot of laughter. 'Cheryl? She's yesterday's news! No, it's a Gloria someone or other. The match has been sanctioned by Aunty Isabelle who is over the moon. I spoke to her for a moment and she's simply delighted.'

Gloria, I thought. The name rang a bell and then, with sudden clarity, I remembered my aunt murmuring: '*Their daughter, Gloria, is sweet on Rupert . . .*'

'Is her surname Penrose, by any chance?'

'Yeah. I think so.'

'It's an arranged marriage,' I whispered. 'Aunty Isabelle's dream. She's wanted this for a long time. Gloria's family is very rich.'

Seán clicked his tongue, tut-tutting with his irritating, elder-brother presumption. 'The things you come out with, Áine! For your information, they only arrange marriages in India and China and places. You must think Rupert is a total wimp.'

'No. But he has a blind sense of obligation. I think he knew

241

this was coming. I think he would do anything to please his mother. He told me once that his future was mortgaged.'

Seán considered me for a moment in silence. 'Anyone would think he had jilted you! I never knew you were gone on him.'

'Oh I'm not gone on him. I just happen to know him quite well.'

'You hardly know him as well as I do. I've been his friend now for years.'

'When is the big day?'

'Plenty of time for them to decide that. After all, he's only pushing twenty-three, and he won't be qualified for another two years . . .'

'That won't matter if she's rich.'

He looked at me in silence. 'What's wrong with her being rich? I'm going to the States in the summer. Why don't you come with me and meet her, wish her and Rupert well?'

'I won't be able to go,' I said. 'I've no money and I've other fish to fry. As soon as the Leaving is over I'm going to London.'

'I thought you wanted to go to college. You filled in the CAO form . . .'

'So what? I don't want a stuffy college. But just watch this space.'

I said this with a confidence I was far from feeling. The Royal Academy of Dramatic Art had called me for audition. This was my secret, hugged to myself as the promise of a new dawn, and shared only with my father. Brigitte was already in London, awaiting the start of her academic year. She was not chained to the wall in what Gunther called a 'nunnery'. She had a flat in South Kensington and had written to tell me about it.

'It's in one of those Regency London houses, in a place called South Kensington. The College itself is a redbrick Victorian building, just opposite the Albert Hall. I can't wait for term to start.'

The RADA audition took place on an October afternoon. Candidates for places had been advised to present a Shakespearean piece suitable for a young person, so I had rehearsed Portia's speech from *The Merchant of Venice*, 'The

242

quality of mercy is not strained . . .' and another piece from Seán O'Casey's *Juno and the Paycock*. My father had allowed me to go to London on the basis that I would stay with his old Aunt Margaret in Chiswick. I wanted to stay with Brigitte at her flat in South Kensington, but this was not permitted.

'What have you got against Brigitte?'

'Nothing whatsoever! I just think you should stay with Aunt Margaret.'

I flew to London, took a taxi to RADA from the airport, as instructed by my father, who had been unable to get away to accompany me. I put my heart into all six minutes of the audition, lost myself in Portia and the quality of mercy, until I felt I *was* the young Venetian woman who had assumed male disguise to save her lover's life. Three inscrutable RADA judges sat and took notes and said I would hear from them. When the audition was over the nerves that I had succeeded in suppressing asserted themselves and I was violently sick in the loo. Then I went to South Kensington and discovered Brigitte's private fastness, a first-floor balcony flat overlooking a private garden.

'This is heaven!'

We were sitting in front of her gas fire and eating buttered toast. 'If I do not get into RADA, Brigitte, I think I will die, or pine into a spectre.'

'Don't do that. You're thin enough as it is.'

'Thank God for this huge, impersonal city,' I said after a moment. 'It breathes indifference to everything except status and money. It makes me feel real!'

'But you are real,' she replied with a laugh.

'I sometimes think, Brigitte, that in Ireland everyone is just a ghost of another time.'

She looked speculative and said, 'We all have chemical and genetic memory. Is there anywhere, Liebling, where they make people straight from the Mint? Everywhere you go possesses the echo of its past.'

Brigitte and I laughed a good deal that day, mostly with the joy of reunion and the prospect of my pending autonomy. I eventually got a taxi to Chiswick where old Aunt Margaret didn't really remember who I was, much less that I was

243

supposed to stay with her, but she made the best of it and I went back to Dublin next day.

The results came the following week. I had passed the audition and was invited for the next one. This time my father was more accommodating and allowed me to stay with Brigitte, and it was in her flat, in the heart of London, that I savoured the first sweet morsels of adult freedom. But I was so nervous setting out for my interview that she sat me down and said, 'Look, if they don't take you it's their loss! You'll find another college. You are a talented actress so get out of your own way and let it happen!'

There were nine judges assessing my performance. On this occasion I also had to sing, and I chose my mother's favourite song from Evita – 'Don't Cry for Me Argentina', and I had to struggle to compose myself at the end, thinking of her in the kitchen at home on the last evening of her life.

I went home, wondering if I had blown it, but the letter came the following week: I was through to the third interview.

This took place in May and involved a day's workshop in which the candidates were introduced to Movement and Voice. We worked on *As You Like It*, with which I was not familiar, and the day ended with some despondency on my part, and a sense that I had not measured up to what was required of me.

Then came the first letter, putting me on the reserve list, which I assumed was a nice way of saying that I had failed. But a second letter from RADA came in July, offering me a place. It contained a further missive from the Registrar, with details of fees. The sense of triumph drove me to playing Beethoven's Fifth very loudly, so that the house resounded, and my brothers came to complain.

I showed the letter to my father when he came home from the office. He had not believed for a moment that I would be accepted, and now groaned at the expense and dithered for a while as to whether he would allow me to go.

'I have to go, Dad. One way or the other . . . I'm almost nineteen. If you feel you cannot pay the fees *I'll* just have to find some way of paying them. I'm of full age!'

'Of full *what*?' he intoned with a laugh. 'Full of dreams, perhaps. But are you sure you really want a hazardous commitment to an uncertain profession?'

For a moment the prospect of losing my miraculous chance of freedom rose before me, and I said through my teeth, 'Dad, I cannot tell you how badly I want this. I would sell my soul for it!'

He looked at me, frowning, disliking intemperate language. 'Well, you won't have to do that, at any rate!' he observed drily. 'Hold on to your soul, whatever else!'

'What are your college choices?' Sister Josephine demanded in my last week at school.

'I'm going to RADA.'

'RADA?' My science mistress sounded doubtful.

'The Royal Academy of Dramatic Art. It's in a place called London.'

'There's no need to be sarcastic, Áine. Does this mean you want to be an actress?'

'Yes!'

'God above! You'd want to be careful of your soul in a profession like that . . . Do you know any people in London . . .?'

'A friend of mine is studying music there.'

'That's better than being an actress,' Sister Josephine said. 'All these actresses are doing nothing but living in sin.'

Living, you mean, you mad old bat, I thought. Living! And I will be living too as soon as I can.

'You'd better talk to Father Moriarty . . . I wonder, have you really thought about why you want to do this? What would your poor mother have said?'

The mention of my mother opened a wound that had never fully healed. I checked the ambushing tears, furious that her name should have been invoked. I didn't want to be told how to pray to Our Lady and how good God was. I didn't want any straightening out. Father Moriarty and the rest of them could take a running jump into the Liffey.

I knew why I wanted to be an actress. It was the only place where I could become someone else, submerge my own identity and its self-hatred and its bloody awful, useless longing. I wanted to be grown up and invulnerable. I wanted to be far away from Ireland and the burden of its moral imperatives; I wanted to be free.

My father insisted on coming to London with me to find me accommodation, and plumped for St Mary's Hostel, run by the French Sisters of Charity in Westminster.

'I don't want to stay in a hostel. I want to stay with Brigitte.'

'You're nineteen. You're staying with the nuns!'

'Until when?'

'Until I say so!'

'Christ, Dad. I've had enough of them!'

'Well, please don't run away again, Áine. I'm paying a fortune for this course as it is.'

Blind obedience was not, to my mind, compatible with freedom. The London girls' hostel chosen by my father seemed a watered-down version of Alcatraz. It reminded me of boarding school and I felt as though I had been shuffled back to Kildruid.

There was a curfew. You had to be back in St Mary's Hostel by eleven p.m., because at that time the door was locked. Sometimes, in the dead of night, a nun checked to see if you were in your bed. If you were not you were thrown out. This enabled me to see my way out of the problem.

Brigitte's flat in South Kensington, in Onslow Gardens, consisted of a big bed sitting-room with a bay window and balcony overlooking a private garden, a kitchen and a small bathroom. The sitting-room had a Regency marble mantelpiece, white and elegant, and she had decorated the walls with various posters of concerts and recitals.

'Why don't you share?' I asked her the first time I visited her abode. 'There is plenty of room here for another bed.'

'I'm waiting until you're available, sweetie!' She looked at me with a questioning grin. 'Oh come on Áine; get out of that dump. There must be some way you can give them the slip.'

I thought for a while. I knew that if I stayed at Brigitte's for a few nights in succession my absence would be noted by the religious Gestapo and I would be turfed out of the hostel. Then Dad would have to agree that I could share with Brigitte.

It was simple, but it worked. I was discovered missing at three o'clock in the morning when I should have been tucked up in my virgin cot. Questioned by the distracted Sister who dealt with erring inmates, I could not satisfy her as to my whereabouts during the night in question, and was told to pack my bags. The inference hanging sulphurously in the air was that I had been up to no good with a member of the opposite sex, and consequently was not at all the kind of girl the Sisters of Charity wanted to shelter under their umbrella.

In fact I was up to nothing at all with members of the opposite sex. Although there were more men than women in my class, I was nervous of them, terminally shy. I loved RADA and adored what I was doing. Acting was not work; as far as I was concerned it was experimentation with life. I often asked myself how anyone could go through the whole of their lifespan being just one boring person. With acting you could change your personality, your identity, almost as often as you washed your hair. With acting you did not have to sit down and confront your small, lonely self. With acting you were not shy, because you were not you.

The flat in South Ken blossomed to accommodate me. The landlord put in another sofa-bed; there was plenty of room in what had once been a Regency drawing room. Sometimes we wondered about the other inhabitants of the house, people we saw traversing the stairs and to whom we said hello. But we never saw anyone going or coming to the flat next to us on the first floor.

'That apartment is empty,' Brigitte said when I questioned her about it.

It was a very happy time. After the first 'induction' day, when we were given a pep talk to prepare us for the hard work ahead, I loved going to college, getting up every morning, getting the tube. It was late September and London was mellow with dying summer, only barely touched by autumn.

I enjoyed what I was doing in RADA, although I was chastened when informed in a phonetics class by our teacher Mr Geoghegan, a middle aged man with a shock of prematurely white hair, 'You'll just have to get rid of your rhotic Rs, Áine! I'm Irish myself and I know how hard that will be, but go they must!'

I loved the lessons in movement skills, the classes in

interpretive expression, the acting exercises, although initially I thought some of them were over the top. On one occasion we were asked to 're-create' our own bedroom for the class, but although I tried to use my room at home in Dublin, it was my chamber at Dunbeg that cried out for expression. I struggled to evade it, and saw my teacher, Mrs Harris, observe me closely.

'Your performance was wooden,' she told me bluntly. 'What were you trying to avoid? You have to be prepared in this profession to let yourself go. Otherwise you're simply wasting your time and ours!'

I bit my lip and nodded.

'Forget yourself!' she went on. 'On stage you are only a vehicle for an art form, and there is no room for private insecurity!'

The following day, when someone in acting class spoke of the importance of cutting yourself out, of being totally 'in the moment', I reacted without thinking, standing up as I had many years before at Dunbeg when my ten-year-old fist had thumped the supper table.

'I am so sick of your bullshit! Where I come from, you don't agonize about whether you are in or out of the frigging moment. You just frigging *act!*'

Afterwards I apologized. But my teacher's eyes contained no censure and I realised she was secretly delighted that my reserve had been punctured.

One night, returning home from South Kensington Underground I thought I was being followed. I came down Onslow Gardens noting the footsteps behind me, ascertaining after an automatic fashion that they were male. I turned left and still they followed; I turned right and they followed on. But when I walked up the front steps of the house they crossed the road and faded down a mews laneway. I stood at the door searching for my keys, turning once to look over my shoulder.

A young man walked up the steps behind me just as I was putting the key in the lock. I jumped; the keys slipped from my fingers and fell to the ground with a small metallic clink.

'I'm so sorry,' a languid voice said, stooping to pick them up. 'Did I startle you?'

'Yes . . .'

There was nothing sinister in this voice, just politeness and fatigue. 'I live here,' he said. 'In fact I've just moved in.'

He indicated the flat above our heads, where there was a balustraded balcony over the door. Something resembling a crocodile's snout thrust itself through the balustrade. I took the keys from his hand.

'Thank you. Is that your crocodile?'

'It's a stuffed gharial actually.'

'What's that?'

'A variety of croc found in India. They eat fish.' He was dressed in a nice bit of herringbone tweed, with a nice pullover and one of those very English expressions of subdued propriety. He was young, maybe twenty-seven, but to me he seemed very mature. His hair was sandy and had started to recede, and there was a certainty around his mouth that I mistook for wisdom. I had so little of my own that I tended to find it everywhere. But his eyes were disconcerting, for they had the quiet hazel gaze I associated with Rupert. He opened the door for me with something of a flourish and I tripped, literally, into the hall, for I lost my balance and fell over the mat.

'You bowled me over on our first meeting!' I would sometimes say to him afterwards. Our conversations initially never went much deeper than badinage. I was still haunted by the memory of an empathy that transcended all the promptings of common sense.

Being away from home I was cut off from any news of Rupert. Sometimes I took out the folder in which my Rupert Bear cuttings lived, pored over them, noting the date pencilled on each one, aware that they reached back to my tenth year, and tried to find evidence of a genuine involvement with me at any level at all. I remembered the words he had whispered to me in the car the night we returned from our first visit to Gunther: '*I love you too, little cousin . . . but they would burn us first . . .*'

When Brigitte surprised me with this scrap book I told her that the cuttings were from Rupert and that I liked to look at them when I felt lonely. It gave me an excuse to talk about him for a while, provided a strange and welcome relief, made my increasingly obsessional perusal of these scraps of paper something that enjoyed the normalcy of a hobby. But when I looked at Brigitte I saw a strange expression on her face: concern, compassion, and the sort of determined look people wear when they are intent on finding the answer to a problem.

If anything, this annoyed me. I could not distance myself from what haunted me – Rupert was now engaged, courting someone else, presumably telling her he loved her, kissing her as he had kissed me that night after Mummy's funeral.

I had heard nothing of him for several weeks now and was beginning to feel that without some word of him nothing mattered. Another part of me, the part that had to do with pride and justice for my own life, derided this fixation.

Sometimes I forgot him, of course, distracted by my work and by the novelty of my existence, determined to succeed. After all I had to make my fortune. I needed it to save Dunbeg.

The owner of the stuffed gharial and our new neighbour, was Nigel Freestone-Hill.

'You sound like the product of a long line of avalanches,' Brigitte told him.

Nigel was sitting on one of the two chintz armchairs in the bay window of our flat. He had been invited in for coffee one Sunday afternoon and he sat with his head thrown back in a semi-studied attitude as he regarded both of us young women with a quizzical urbanity not unmixed with condescension.

'Pardon?' he said.

'Avalanches,' Brigitte repeated politely.

Nigel got it, laughed shortly and said no actually, nothing so exciting. He came from a long line of army types, who had never precipitated themselves into anything exciting, though they enjoyed the odd bit of shooting to kill. There was the slightest hint in the air that, properly speaking, he should not have bothered himself with people like Brigitte and me. One was a Yank, and therefore suspect until her provenance was proven; but I was a Paddy and consequently suspect for ever. We represented something rootless and bohemian, improper in the divine order of the English class system.

'What do you do for a crust?' Brigitte demanded.

'I work in the City.'

'We all work in the goddamn city. Which part?'

'He means the City of London,' I ventured. 'Where the banks are.' I turned to him. 'Are you some kind of financier?'

'I'm with Tiddloe and Greening, Merchant Bankers.'

'Oh, *money*!' Brigitte said. 'Why didn't you say so? I'd have given you a bigger mug!'

We became friends. We made him laugh; he seemed increasingly interested in dropping by. Initially Brigitte orchestrated the relationship.

'Hey, Avalanche,' she would call to him through his keyhole on Sunday mornings, 'would you like some toast?' Brigitte's ebullience was the carapace that protected her complex, contemplative nature, an electrical discharge from the contained passion for her music.

'What do you think of Nigel?' I asked her one day.

'He's stiff as a board, but underneath it he's vulnerable . . . And he's got really cute manners.'

Although she was a stunning beauty, at least to my eyes, Nigel seemed impervious to her charms. For some reason it was me, too quiet, hair untamed, whom he began to follow with his eyes.

'He fancies you,' Brigitte said with obvious satisfaction one morning after he had waved up at me at the kitchen window from the street. 'If he asks you out you should go.'

'But I don't want to go out with him! Anyway why would he ask me out when he could ask you?'

Brigitte pursed her mouth. 'Why don't you go and look at yourself in the goddamn mirror?'

'Compared with you I'm not even interesting . . .'

'No? You only have the magnetism of an electric shock. Everyone stares at you. Yet you creep under stones as soon as you leave that place.'

'Don't refer to RADA as "that place".'

'Oh for God's sake . . . get yourself a life. You come home here every evening as though you were a nun. Stop thinking about Rupert.'

'Nuns have a lot going for them,' I said, forgetting a lot of things. 'And what on earth makes you think I have Rupert on my mind?'

Brigitte sighed. 'Áine, I could be wrong . . . but I see the way your attention is riveted every time I mention his name . . . And you're always looking at that collection of notes and cuttings he sent you . . . It's just not healthy!'

'It's just that I have a long day and I'm tired in the evenings! Looking at my scrap book is something to do. I'm not outgoing like you . . .'

'If you're shy,' Brigitte said, 'act! It's your métier, after all. You don't have to keep it just for the boards, remember. Act and see what happens!'

'I'm happy as I am.'

'Look, do it to please me, just once . . . I promise I'll never nag you again if you do. It just bothers me that you're so much alone.'

I think it was the following evening, when returning home late, that I heard the footsteps behind me again all the way down Onslow Gardens. I tried to dismiss them, but if I slowed they slowed, and if I hurried they hurried after. I stood at a corner and looked back, but only saw a shadow melt into the shadows by the railings. And that night I dreamt of the sea and Dunbeg, a lonely dream where I was by myself, bereft, staring at an unnaturally calm sea. When I turned back to the castle, hoping to see Rupert, I found that the familiar turrets of Dunbeg were gone and that the house was a ruin, flattened like the old cottage on the headland.

This dream left such a taste in my mouth that, next morning, I decided to act on Brigitte's advice.

Yes, I thought, stop being so bugged by a man you cannot have and a place that is five hundred miles away. Find yourself a real life.

Nigel invited me to dinner, and I borrowed a dress from Brigitte because I had nothing glamorous to wear: most of my things were black, and I was tired of being sombre. The dress was green, with a wide belt and a tight waist. I tied my hair back with a black ribbon.

'You look lovely!' Nigel said when he came to collect me at seven-thirty. I was aware how his manner had changed, how it had lost the languid patronizing air with which he had originally favoured me. In its place was a courtesy bordering on deference.

'Bring her back at a reasonable hour,' Brigitte intoned severely, coming out of the kitchen. 'Otherwise Teacher will be cross.'

We went downstairs. He took my hand in his, as though it were a small creature that demanded care, hailed a cab and gave directions to the West End.

We saw Agatha Christie's *Mousetrap*, which I was curious about, having heard about it since my childhood, and later went to supper in a rather posh restaurant called La Vie Dorée with a French menu and horrendous prices. But Nigel seemed unfazed. He was clearly out to impress, which touched me, because I could not understand why he should bother.

I offered to go Dutch, but he seemed almost affronted.

'Certainly not! I invited you, remember.'

Initially we talked about trivial things; then he asked about RADA and what I was studying and I told him about voice training and how I had always wanted to act.

'But you seem such a quiet girl,' he said with a smile at me across the pale pink damask and the solitary candle.

'Yes . . . I come from a family of boys!'

'And that has something to do with it?'

'Probably,' I replied with a laugh. 'They jostle so much for position that it's easiest not to join in!'

Then he asked me where I lived and I told him about Dublin and that my mother was dead and my father was a lawyer, and the boys were doing their studies. And that the only other family I had were an aunt and uncle in Virginia who had a son, my Cousin Rupert.

'You look a bit like him in fact,' I said, 'around the eyes . . .'

Nigel told me that his family lived in the Cotswolds and that he had a younger brother, John, who had followed their father into the army. His family evidently enjoyed a genetic longevity. His parents were still alive and his grandparents were still alive and he had a great-uncle of eighty-five who was doing fine.

'Mad old berk. He has a house on the Norfolk Broads. We used to have our holidays there. Do you holiday with your family?'

'We used to go to the west, to a place called Dunbeg.'

Even the name had a resonance. I said it slowly, letting it

253

echo in my mouth. 'It's by the sea, a Victorian castle.'

'Is it a hotel?' he asked.

'No, it belongs to my father. But it's falling down,' I added hastily, anxious to disabuse him of the notion I saw forming in his eyes. 'It costs a lot to keep it going at all. My father is threatening to sell it, not that he'd get that much for it . . .'

'It's important to you?' he said softly after a moment. 'I can see that.'

For a moment Rupert's eyes looked out at me from this perceptive stranger's face. But I did not want Nigel to know Dunbeg was important to me. He had no way of knowing what its 'importance' really meant; nothing he had ever encountered would enable him to imagine my relationship with Dunbeg; he could not guess at the hold it had on me. He would not understand how I was perpetually drawn to it and perpetually in retreat from it. He could not know that if Dunbeg were to disappear from the planet I would cease to exist.

'You look very pensive,' he said, and then he reached over and took my hand. There was something in the grave set of his face and the grasp of his hand that pleased me, even as another part of me said that this well-meaning young man would never do at all.

We came back to Onslow Gardens and he asked me, almost diffidently, would I like a coffee or a nightcap, and I said no, that I was tired.

'It was a lovely evening, Nigel,' I told him on the landing, looking up at him as he stood uncertainly before the door of the flat as though hoping I would ask him in. Brigitte and I had an arrangement. The flat was our space; we could invite people by mutual consent, but not otherwise. And we certainly would not intrude on each other by returning with someone in tow when the other was already in bed.

I put my finger on my lips. 'Brigitte is probably asleep by now.'

He nodded, said, 'I really enjoyed this evening. Do you think you could bear to do it again? Have dinner with me, I mean.'

'Of course I would love to have dinner with you again! Thank you, Nigel . . .'

He bent down and kissed my lips, a peck, quite proper and

254

unintrusive, and would have prolonged this contact, but I put my hand against his face and then put the key in the door.

I let myself into the darkened flat. There was a faint scent of incense, something that Brigitte had taken to burning when she was listening to music on her headphones. But the curtains were still open and she was not at home. I kicked off my shoes and sat in an armchair in the dark, glad somehow to be back in the flat and alone, away from the earnest young man who had given me such a sumptuous dinner. I saw the tree outside the window bending towards me, and the eyes of a cat that hid in the hedge and caught the beam from a passing headlight.

Listening to the stillness, throwing back my head and closing my eyes, I let myself become one with the night and its muted sounds. For a second it reminded me of the sea, and, after a moment of surfing this imaginary flood, I felt as though I were not in London any more; my head was spinning and it seemed to me that I belonged to the hidden matrix of the cosmos, something without form or substance, like a piece of plankton on the tide. Frightened by the sense of dissolution I sat up and opened my eyes. The net curtains shimmied in the bay window and abruptly the shadows on the balcony parted. In the half light a man's face stared in at me with a sneer that I remembered from long ago. I started and cried out. All I could think of was that if he had found me here I could not run from him. I looked around for some weapon with which to defend myself. But when I looked back the face had disappeared and there was only the light from the street.

'Don't be absurd!' Brigitte said when I told her next day that I was convinced some kind of doom was following me. 'Don't be so damn Celtic! You have an imagination so vivid in its ramblings that you let it convince your brain. You were tired. That's all!'

'Oh, I know now it wasn't real, if that's what you mean, Brigitte. I'm not a nut case. But why did it happen at all? I honestly don't believe I'm susceptible to hallucinations.'

'What you need is a good love affair to take your mind off all this nonsense. How did your date with Nigel go?'

'Grand. We saw the *Mousetrap* and had dinner in some posh place and Nigel paid a fortune and was a perfect gentleman and didn't make any passes, except one half-hearted attempt on my virtue at the door of the flat.'

'Good,' Brigitte said. 'I was afraid that he might be scared of you.'

I stared at her in consternation. 'Why should he be scared of me?'

She looked back at me laconically. 'Your silence, honey, can be very disconcerting. Oh, not to me; I love it and I make enough noise for two. It's why I asked you to share with me! But to others it is frightening because you cannot be read.'

'Fiddlesticks,' I muttered under my breath.

Brigitte was going to a recital that evening and said she would be home late. I got back from RADA reasonably timely that evening, and watched out of the kitchen window for Nigel. During the day I had thought of Brigitte's advice: what I needed was a good love affair.

I saw Nigel – suit, briefcase, umbrella – turn the corner of Onslow Gardens and come up the front steps. I opened the door of the flat, went back to the kitchen and commenced making supper. I couldn't cook, but I knew how to operate a tin opener.

In a moment there was a knock and his head appeared round the door. 'Hello . . . anyone at home? Ah, there you are, Áine . . .'

'Would you like some beans on toast?'

Nigel's face did not register any great transport, so I added, searching for the Sharwoods curry powder, 'Well, *curried* beans? All the way from the golden Orient . . .'

'Mm . . . what a wonderful idea. Just let me get rid of my stuff.'

He was back in a moment, in slacks and jumper, with a bottle of wine by the neck.

'Would you be interested in coming to see *Macbeth* at RADA?' I demanded.

'Are you in it?'

'No. But I'm an usher.'

His face lit up. 'I'd be delighted . . .'

'Next Saturday?'

'Great!'

That night I slept in Nigel's bed. I had drunk too much wine, and ended up there almost by accident. It's no use saying that I did not know what I did. The wine had released a grief in me that I needed to quench. I knew as soon as Nigel touched me that he was no sexual neophyte, but he was not arrogant or greedy either, just anxious to please. There were no great transports; it hurt a lot, but I hid the pain. In the morning he got up and made me breakfast, and this touched me, soothed the reproachful discourse I was conducting with myself. This discourse reminded me that I loved someone else, and that my body was not really mine to give away. If you mean I should keep myself for that fellow in America, that *engaged* fellow in America, I told my reproachful self, you've another think coming . . .

Nigel put the breakfast tray on my knees and said he had to go to work. He kissed me gently.

'You should have told me you were a virgin, love,' he murmured, his eyes full of tenderness. 'I've never been with a virgin before.'

'Where I come from,' I said tartly, 'no one would dream of mentioning such a thing . . . We don't have sex in Ireland.'

Nigel looked puzzled. 'Really?' he said.

For a moment, borne up by a private sense of the absurd, I almost loved him. I felt warm again, and almost at peace, as though the night before had been something I could sanction and not just a reaction to pressures I was trying to free myself from at any price.

When I returned to the flat, Brigitte was dressed and about to leave. She gave me a wry smile. 'Have you gone to the dogs, or what?'

I shrugged. 'I've been bedded, if that's what you mean! I decided to take your advice.'

She seemed taken aback, and then said shortly, 'That wasn't my advice. I hope you took precautions?'

'I'm not two years old, Brigitte! Nigel had the necessaries all ready. I suspect, somehow, that he's done it before.'

Brigitte gave a snort. 'Of course he's done it before! But . . . I didn't realize you were in love with him.'

'In love with him? What's love got to do with it? Can't I go to bed with someone without being in love with him?'

She looked at me for a moment. 'No,' she said, 'I don't think *you* can!' Then she added with a half laugh, 'And for that matter, I don't think I can either.'

I worked like a demon all that day. But when the momentum eased, when concentration flagged, I found myself thinking of Rupert. Why the hell is he in your mind at all? I asked myself. Why can't you exorcize him? Just because you made love with someone else you feel as though you have betrayed him. What did he ever do for you except sweet-talk you and engage himself to marry someone else? He's probably screwing her every single night and never gives you a thought.

And then, all of a sudden, I thought of the footsteps that had followed me in the street.

Whose footsteps were they? A chance pedestrian, who just happened to favour the same side of the street as I did? A potential opportunist who followed a lone woman? Or someone else? So why did I feel I knew that footfall?

In acting class one day, one of the group became very emotional and excused himself. Mrs Harris said, 'Acting is frequently a catharsis in which people work through their own traumas, and this is fine so long as trauma is not a substitute for talent! Now, for tomorrow I want you to bring in some item that is really personal to you and tell the class about it.'

Later that evening I said to Brigitte, 'Do you still have that piece of paper I gave you in Dunbeg . . . you remember . . . with Sarah's writing?'

She nodded. 'Sure. Do you want it?'

'Yeah . . . I'd like to read it again. I might use it for something in class tomorrow.'

She searched through her filing system, and eventually brought it to me without a word. Then she whispered, 'I didn't give it back to you because I thought you would be better off without it.'

'Brigitte,' I said, 'I keep telling you. I am not a child any more.'

I put the old sellotaped page into an envelope and put it into my bag.

The following day, I produced it at acting class, spread it

out, and allowed the class and the teacher to inspect the soot ink writing, explaining how I had found it in the family Bible. I read out Sarah's account to a hushed audience.

'What an extraordinary find,' my teacher observed. 'But what is the writing on the back?'

'It's in Irish,' I said. 'But it's in the old script and I can't decipher it!'

'Would Mr Geoghegan know what it means? He's Irish.'

'I don't know. It depends on how familiar he is with the script. They changed it, you see, to make it compatible with modern type . . .'

'You have him next class. Why don't you ask him?'

I put the page back in its envelope, suddenly fearful of having the mysterious writing translated, sorry that the topic had been raised at all.

When Mr Geoghegan appeared, Mrs Harris, who was on her way out of the door, accosted him and said in her no-nonsense voice, 'Are you any good at Gaelic?'

'Tolerably,' he replied. 'I spent a year in an Irish-speaking boarding school when I was twelve. But I've probably forgotten most of it. Why do you ask?'

'Áine here has a strange missive with which you might be able to help her . . .'

My phonetics teacher looked at me with raised eyebrows. 'What is it, Áine?'

Reluctantly, I put the envelope into his hands. He took out the dog-eared page, read Sarah's testimony, and then glanced at the back.

'Ah,' he said. 'It's the old script, isn't it? This was already out of fashion in my time.'

He spread it out on the desk, opened a note pad and took a pen from his pocket. 'You see,' he said, pointing, 'how the Rs and Fs and Ss are all very similar?' He glanced at me. 'I'll write it out for you in modern Irish, Áine, and you can translate it for yourself.'

In a couple of minutes he tore the sheet from the note pad and handed it to me.

'There you are. Bit cryptic, you'll agree. Sounds like a lover's vow!'

I read the two lines, whispered them aloud.

'Tiocfaidh mé thar nais duit, Sarah Uí Mháighille! Cinnte gur tiocfaidh mé.'

'What does it mean?' Mrs Harris asked.

'I'll come back for you, Sarah O'Malley,' I whispered slowly. 'It's certain that I'll come.'

Chapter Seventeen

'Is this a dagger which I see before me, The handle toward my hand?'

Macbeth, excitable, suggestible, moved towards his hallucination. Out there in the dark were the audience, possessing the judgemental powers of God. I was a cog in the machine, invisible, my job to usher the audience to their seats. I thought of Nigel sitting among the silent watchers of the drama and wondered what he thought of the production.

At the weekend he had taken me home to meet his family, a visit for Sunday lunch.

'How do you do, Áine. We've heard so much about you!'

'How do you do.'

I suppressed as much of my brogue as I thought might displease in this world. To my unprogrammed eye they seemed like characters in a play, composed of certain words and rituals rather than flesh and blood. Nigel's father had a military stance; his mother was tall and thin, and both were evidently bemused by the young woman their son had brought to meet them. I did not meet his brother on this occasion; he was in Sandhurst.

The house, ivy-covered red brick, stood in its own acres at the end of an avenue, about four miles from the picturesque Cotswold village of Shepton. The house was called Session House and its architecture dated from the end of the eighteenth century; it had tall chimneys, and a lawn bordered by chestnut trees, now yellow and amber with dying leaves. The drawing room was a medley of cream and old gold, with a gilt overmantel and a Bergère suite with heavy velvet cushions. Everything was perfectly polished, from the Victorian brass fender to the silver-framed photographs on the mantelpiece.

Nigel took me out for a walk and I registered how lovely this place was, even while I realized how its limits were set and contained. It was Olde England, and every person I met was charming, as though they belonged to Olde England too; but I sensed their alertness at a level beyond ordinary deliberation, as though each of them were a sentry patrolling forever the boundaries of their world. Their perspective seemed to say their world contained the only true human beings, although they recognized that, outside of it, there were other classes of persons, principally servants and foreigners. I, pending evaluation, fell somewhere in between. I fell into no immediate category, being Irish and *ipso facto* dubious, being young and innocent yet an aspiring actress, belonging to neither of the two recognized categories of Irish person – neither a bricklayer nor a poet. I saw my own eccentricity in their eyes.

'Áine's family have a castle in the west of Ireland,' Nigel said at one point during the lunch. I registered dismay, but realized immediately how this intelligence brought me within a tacit pale, for the atmosphere at the table subtly altered. I knew that I was now entitled to eccentricity; eccentricity blessed by a castle was acceptable.

I didn't even argue or disclaim. Dunbeg was not explicable. To tell them it was falling down was pointless, because, whole or broken, it was, for me, fundamental, essential, irreplaceable.

'He seems very smitten,' I heard Nigel's aunt tell her sister when she thought I was out of earshot. 'And she's quite a lovely gel . . . But of course . . .'

His mother said, 'You mean that business over Valerie?'

Their voices dropped, they moved away and my curiosity was frustrated.

On the way home Nigel was in fine form. 'You're my pride and joy,' he said at one point, pulling into a layby and leaning over to embrace me. 'They all adored you . . .'

'Don't be silly. They certainly did not . . . They danced around me with a kindly interest that was really a discreet concern for you.'

I knew he wanted to make love, but I was not going to make love in any layby, nor did I want to make love with him or anyone else again. This thought process had little to do with him; it was not his fault. Sex was useless, painful, demanding;

above all I felt I was dishonoured because I had not engaged in it out of any kind of passion.

In truth I was a little appalled by myself, by the sense of unease at trying to swim in unfamiliar waters where my toes kept scraping off the rocks; by the unsuccessful attempt to force my life into a mould and a milieu that would take me away from myself, force on me some kind of rebirth or oblivion. But then again, I argued privately, you must try. Give it time. Rupert is gone; stop thinking about him. The world is full of diversity and you must acknowledge and delight in it. Give it time and see what happens.

We went back to Onslow Gardens that autumn evening in virtual silence. When Nigel glanced at me I smiled; when he asked me what I thought of his family I said truthfully that they were very nice. When he pressed me I said, 'Are they rich, Nigel, or is that an illusion? If they are they won't want me. Money always seeks money.'

He gave a short mirthless laugh, the one he used as comment on the ways of the world. 'I believe my father is solvent,' he replied. 'My mother has a certain competence of her own also. The golden fish in our pond is my Great-uncle Toby. And if they continue to want me, they will have to want you.'

I had the feeling, as I regarded the sudden intensity in his face with a great deal of misgiving, that things were spiralling out of control, and that he was talking one language while I was trying to make myself understood in another.

When we got back to Onslow Gardens he invited me in for tea, and tea we had, a pot of it by his gas fire, with a packet of chocolate biscuits. His flat, which was painted white, was pristine, with something of the antiseptic aura of a surgery, although a few vivid prints and a nice Indian rug saved it from complete sterility. That and the stuffed reptile. I saw it through the French window, on the balustraded balcony above the front steps, the hideous stuffed gharial, and I hated it and its long, toothy snout.

'What do you want that thing for?'

'It was a present,' he said, 'from Valerie – my ex-girlfriend. She brought it back from India.' He glanced at me uncertainly. 'I'll get rid of it if you like.'

263

'No . . . It's grand.'

When we had finished our tea Nigel knelt beside me, and tried to embrace me. His fingers stroked my forearm, pushing back the sweater. I tried to decipher my body's response, and realized that it was saying nothing at all, and that I wasn't even feeling anything except a mild curiosity.

'Oh God,' he groaned, reaching up to embrace me. 'Come here. I've been thinking about this all day.' He pulled me by the hand towards his neat bedroom, where the bed had been made with military precision. Perhaps it was this military bed that galvanized me. I pulled back, reaching for the age-old excuse.

'I have a headache, Nigel. And, to tell you the truth, despite last week, I don't go around making love . . .'

'I know,' he said, moving back and looking at me quizzically. 'But you should have told me that you were a virgin. I felt a bit of a heel afterwards, wondering if I had hurt you.'

Suddenly, looking at him perched on the edge of his beautifully made bed, I wanted to be sick. It seemed crude in the extreme that he should refer to my virginity or the lack of it. It was as though it mattered more than me, and I felt in him a covert self-congratulation that he had been the instrument of my defloration. But this moment passed, and I saw the gentlemanly way he accepted my refusal, and I remembered that *he* had made the tea and that he would also wash the cups without any of the macho fandangos I was used to at home. This warmed me.

'I'm sorry, Nigel. I'm very tired. And I have to be up early.'

'Of course. You must be bushed. I'm looking forward to the play tomorrow . . . Off you go.' He came with me to the door, kissed my lips gently. 'Don't ever let me do anything you don't want,' he said softly. 'I would hate that.'

'I can really only make love with someone I'm committed to,' I said. 'Perhaps I should have realized it in time . . . It's conditioning, I suppose . . .'

'That's all right.'

His eyes looked at me quizzically. Rupert's eyes; disconcerting, preventing my self re-invention, reminding me.

Always reminding me.

The play ended. Macbeth was dead; his mad lady was gone; Malcolm and Donalbain had taken up the reins of power. The lights came on. The principal actors received an ovation; the witches received an ovation; the whole cast received an ovation by this kind audience composed mostly of parents and friends and relations, and Friends of RADA, inveterate members of the theatre-going public interested in new, upcoming talent.

I searched the theatre with my eyes, looking for Nigel. I did not find him. People were leaving and as I studied them I saw a face in profile that I knew very well. I followed it as its owner turned and moved down the centre aisle. For a moment I doubted and then I was certain. With an abrupt sensation of disbelief I was certain that I had just been looking at Rupert. I watched his back as he moved towards the exit, saw him turn and speak to a young woman who took his arm.

Nigel said to me afterwards, 'The play was very good. But the ushering!' He raised his eyes to invoke Heaven as witness. 'My dear, never have I experienced such ushering!'

I laughed at his antics.

'But, darling,' he said then, 'when am I going to see you on stage?'

'You'll have to wait. We rookies don't get near it. My public will have to contain their impatience until the end of next year.'

'Will you come out for supper? I've booked a table.'

'That would be lovely . . .'

I was glad to go out, glad to be with Nigel, glad to be desired and wined and dined, glad to do anything that would distance me from the picture in my mind of Rupert turning to his fiancée as she took his arm.

'Is something wrong?' Nigel asked softly. 'You're looking a bit grim.'

'No. Nothing's wrong. It's just that I'm almost certain I saw a long-lost cousin of mine . . . He lives in America and I didn't know he was in England. He was at the back of the stalls and he slipped out as soon as the play was over. I think his fiancée was with him!'

'Good,' Nigel said. 'Now I'll get to meet one of your family.'

'I don't even know where he's staying.'

I wondered at my own reluctance, at the warning cymbals

that clashed in my skull. Had I not felt my heart leap at the sight of him? Was I not sick with the hunger the mere glimpse of him awoke in me?

'Presumably they'll get in touch with you themselves, love,' Nigel said, tweaking a few strands of my hair.

I drank plenty of wine over dinner and laughed a good deal, the determined laughter of someone out to enjoy her evening. But the mood did not last. The lurking malaise overtook me on the way home. Nigel glanced at me from time to time and eventually said, 'You've gone very quiet. A minute ago you were positively garrulous.'

'I don't know why you bother with me at all,' I told him. 'When you think about it I'm really rather odd.'

He laughed. 'How are you odd?'

'I'm embattled in some way; I'm never at peace. And the world is full of fabulous women you could have . . .'

'Oh I've met them,' he said tonelessly, 'the fabulous women.' When he did not go on I looked at him, but could not read his face.

'Or was it one in particular?' I suggested gently. 'One fabulous woman?'

'Yes.' He smiled as though at my perceptiveness. 'It didn't work out . . . She met a millionaire.'

'I'm sorry.'

'I'm not. At least not any more. But it has left me with a need of the ingenuous, and an allergy to deceit.' He glanced at me. 'But I shouldn't rattle on like this . . .'

Then he added, taking my hand, 'I know you're embattled, Áine. I don't know why; maybe sometime you will tell me. But there's nothing wrong with turmoil. At least it is passion-driven and authentic; it is entirely natural to an intense nature still unsure of its own identity. It has life.'

I made no answer to this assessment, which seemed profound and out of character for this very civilized Englishman. It made me address my own presumption, question the extent to which I had underestimated him.

He did not drive straight home as I expected, but took me down to the river and parked the car near Tower Bridge where we could see the night-time majesty of the Thames.

'Áine,' he said, turning to me in the half dark, his voice husky, his hand reaching out to stroke my face, 'there is something important I want to ask you. I meant to wait for another while, but I must ask you now.'

Afterwards I would remember every nuance, the vulnerability in his face, the gentleness of his hands, the kisses he pressed into my palm, the tenderness with which he leant towards me, as though he wanted to cosset and protect me for ever.

'I want to ask you if you will do me the honour of becoming my wife.'

I was unprepared, but even as I stared at him I knew I must treat this seriously, must answer carefully. I knew this man would be my port in every storm, my haven, my loyal and trusting friend. I also knew that if I rejected him he would not ask again.

I loved him in that moment. I say this with my hand on my heart, despite everything that came later. I needed the haven he represented, the possibility of peace. I needed his love and was ready and willing to give him everything I could of mine. Did I not already know that certain other doors were closed to me for ever? Was it not absolutely essential that I should love someone else? Was not Nigel good and tender and trustworthy? Could I not adore him as he deserved, given time and space?

'Will you, Áine?'

I smiled, put my hand against his face and whispered, 'I'm very flattered, Nigel. May I sleep on it?'

'Of course.'

On the way home, he said, almost conversationally, 'Sometime I hope you will tell me what *is* driving you . . . why you are so strange and intense.'

'I am being stalked.'

He laughed out loud. 'What a funny little thing you are.'

I smiled back at him hastily to indicate my appreciation of his humour and my own.

Brigitte was in bed when I got home and seemed to be asleep. I did not disturb her, tip-toeing softly into the flat, shutting and locking the door gently. But my hands were unsteady and, in the kitchen, I dropped a glass while getting a drink of water. It shattered on the tiles and I found the dustpan and swept up the pieces.

When I got into bed Brigitte surfaced and said, 'Áine, Seán telephoned.'

'What did he want?'

'Just a chat. He said to tell you that Rupert is in London.'

'I know.' I kept my voice even. 'I think I saw him in the Vanbrugh Theatre tonight, when the lights came up.'

Brigitte turned in bed. 'He's doing a year's stint in one of the hospitals. I got a letter from Dad today.' She reached into the drawer of the table by her bed and extracted an air-mail missive. 'Here, read it for yourself.'

I picked up the letter, glanced through it, skipped the father-daughter stuff. Halfway down the page I read:

Rupert has gone to London, where he will be working for a year in University College Hospital. His fiancée has gone with him for a short stay.

I looked up from the letter and Brigitte raised her eyebrows. 'Are you sure you saw him tonight?' she asked.

'Almost sure. Gloria was with him.'

'Well,' she said caustically, 'why not ask them around for some of your flatulent beans? There's nothing like your old love farting to make you see him in a different light.'

She paused and looked at me keenly. 'You're not still tender as regards Rupert, are you Áine? Not now . . .?'

'Don't be stupid, Brigitte! As a matter of fact I have something important to tell you . . .'

She sat up abruptly in bed and turned on the light. 'You're not pregnant?'

'No, I'm not pregnant! I just wanted to tell you that Nigel has asked me to marry him.'

She was shocked. 'What a dark little filly you are! You never pretended that this was coming.'

'I didn't know.'

'Really? Did you think he brought you home just so you could admire the silver?' Then she added, 'But you're much

268

too young to be engaged. And you haven't even known him that long. Have you accepted?'

'I told him I would sleep on it.'

Sleep took me only to an alien landscape, a windswept heath, with mountains dark and sullen with the approach of night. The figure in the distance saw me across an expanse that seemed to serve infinity, for he raised his hand in recognition. I could not see his face, but I knew it was Rupert, as I would know him even if he stood at the end of eternity. I saw him run towards me and I raced towards him, but caught my foot in the heather. The ground underneath was marshy and sucked at me greedily. I looked desperately towards my cousin; my ears were filled with the wind as it prowled across the bleakness. Rupert, in the distance, was making little progress in the storm. And then came the white wolf, raising his muzzle at the rising moon. It had come from the mountains, and I saw the red retinas of its eyes fixed first on Rupert and then on me.

I woke, startled by my own cries.

Brigitte's voice was saying, 'Áine . . . Áine, it's all right. It's only a dream.' She got up, brought me a drink of water and herbal palliatives that she used when she could not sleep.

'Getting engaged is supposed to agree with people,' she said, 'not the other way around.'

'I drank too much wine,' I whispered, grateful for the light from the kitchen and the sight of her face. 'It always gives me nightmares.'

The following evening as I was leaving Gower Street I was stopped in reception and informed that a young man had been inquiring for me.

'What did he look like?' I assumed it was Nigel, and looked around to see if he were still there.

'He was tall, brown hair . . .' the receptionist said with a smile.

'Did he leave a name?'

'No. He said he'd be back.'

I knew you'd come, Rupert, I thought. But you shouldn't have. It's too late!

He was waiting for me when I left the building, standing in the shadows.

'Áine . . . ?'

His voice, its timbre, its accent, opened the past, like the scent of another time. I had not seen him for more than four years, and time had wrought a sea-change. The youth I had left behind in Virginia was now a young man; his body was fuller and taller, and the uncertain innocence that had graced his eyes was gone.

'Rupert?'

'My God . . .' he said, drawing his breath in sharply. 'I can hardly believe it . . . You look . . . so different.' He took my arm. The contact was assured, gentle, the touch of a man who knows the territory without effort or exploration. He looked down at me appraisingly. I did not smile at him.

'You've grown up!'

'It happens. So have you.'

He smiled. 'Aren't you glad to see me?'

We stood there in the London street, in a cocoon, a space private to us, in a silent intimacy that was not of our creation. I didn't answer the question. It was rhetorical. I don't know how I found myself in his arms, or how long we stood there on the pavement, wrapped around each other in complete silence, insensible to the city sounds and the passersby.

Later, in a nearby bistro, he said, staring fixedly at me across the tables, 'Why didn't you tell me when you were a child that you would look like this?'

'Like what?'

'Like . . . a woman.'

'Would it have made that much difference?'

'No.'

'You'd still have gone off and engaged yourself to Gloria Penrose, daughter of the man who owns the world?'

His eyes flickered and he looked at me warily. 'I went to the theatre in your college last night,' he said, ignoring the question, 'in the hopes of seeing you . . . I thought they might have given you the part of one of the witches.'

I didn't respond to this badinage, but said, 'I was an usher. I saw you, as you were leaving . . . with Gloria.'

'Yes. She enjoyed the production.'

'Does she like London?'

'Yes . . .'

'How are your parents?'

'Mom is not the best. She wanders at night . . . Áine, there are things I need to talk to you about . . .'

He leaned across the table. He had a startled look to him, a man who had left a childhood relationship behind him and now met it in another guise, but in a place and time where he was no longer in control of it. The avid fixity of his stare, the famished dilation of his pupils as he looked at me, told me that all the fantasies I had had were not just self-deception.

I waited. Let him say it now, I thought. Let him say what he wants, what he needs, what, if anything, he is capable of doing about it. Let him be a man and say it.

But he composed his face to normal urbanity and said conversationally, 'Áine . . . Do you ever think of Dunbeg?'

Deflated, I nodded and looked away. Outside the rain was beating against the window and the pavement was a mushroom field of umbrellas.

'I can't rid my mind of the damn place. Mom keeps saying, "Don't go back, promise me you won't go back." But it's stuck in my head as you once said it would. And you're there too . . . It's as though you're the missing piece of some jigsaw . . .'

His eyes never left me. They said something his lips did not articulate. I felt the surge of my disappointment and angry contempt. Had he come to London to deliver himself of this? Was this the man for whom I had knotted myself?

'No I'm not, Rupert. You've got it wrong! I'm not a piece in anyone's damn jigsaw! And you've become a stranger.'

'That isn't possible!'

I looked into his startled eyes. And for a moment I was ten years old, desperate for love, and Aeneas Shaw was lurking downstairs, and Rupert was the only buffer between me and nightmare.

'I had to stay away . . . we couldn't go on like that, Áine . . .'

'Why?'

'You were growing up. It was a very odd relationship, too intense . . . even abnormal, Áine, if you think about it. It would have been . . . an interference with your development . . . I almost wronged you the last time we were together . . .'

This reduction of my life's passion to something that could be dismissed as 'abnormal' edged me towards tears. I found anger instead. 'Christ! There's no "almost" about it! You did "wrong" me, as you so quaintly put it, but not by trying to shag me. You wronged me by debasing it, by planting guilt and shame in me. I've spent years trying to forgive myself for that night! You made me feel like a precocious slut who had tried to seduce you. And to someone who is thirteen and in love, Rupert, that is doing a great deal of mischief.'

Rupert looked stunned. And for a moment I wondered if I were wrong, if the fierce knowledge I felt of this man were only delusion, unshared, despised. But his eyes never lost their focus and his mouth softened. 'Oh no . . .' he whispered, shaking his head with a half laugh, 'you've got it all wrong.'

'Maybe. You left me to construe the silence, after all. But you are here now, and the hunger staring out of your eyes gives the lie to everything you did. You dumped me, closed off your friendship; you chose pragmatism, you have the good marriage lined up. Oh, I've no doubt your mother pushed it at you! And maybe you're right to go along without a whimper.'

Rupert's mouth tightened and his eyes became cold. But before he could tell me where I could put myself and my tirade I continued, 'Maybe the kind of relationship we had *has* no value. But I don't believe it! And I don't believe in the icons known as Duty or Common Sense either. Gloria may be possessed of both, but she will never know you as I do. I thank God I will become an actress, and never have to live in your nice, hidebound little world. You'll never have a moment's wild joy in it, Rupert, or real peace!'

I stood up, half appalled at myself. 'I have to go now. I'm meeting my fiancé.'

I got him with that one. He looked winded and his eyes gave him away.

'Áine . . .'

'Goodbye, Rupert.'

I shut my ears, shrugged on my coat, picked up my bag, and headed for the street.

You're a wimp, Rupert Lyall, I told myself as I hailed a taxi, a wimp, a wimp, a bloody wimp.

And then came the memory of his eyes, the hurt in them, the shocked expression as though a bomb had gone off in his vicinity, and the unspoken self-righteousness of a man who is already committed and who will abide by his troth notwithstanding any lunacy that may be thrown at him. And through it all I had felt the magnetism, pulling me away from everything that was sane. For the first time in all my thoughts of Rupert, I felt fear.

Somehow or other, I thought eventually, sitting in the back of the cab and stifling the rage and grief, I will have to break your hold on me, get you out of my system. I am afraid of you and the power you have over me.

The taxi splashed its way through the wet, congested streets, bringing me to my date with Nigel. I had intended to ask him for a bit more time, but now I knew how I must answer.

Chapter Eighteen

That night Nigel produced a solitaire diamond ring from a small black leather box. Because of my unexpected meeting with Rupert I had been late for our date and had given a lame excuse. I felt like a traitor as I looked at the shining gem that evinced one man's genuine love and hope, while my body still resonated from a charged emotional exchange with another.

But it had been much more than an embrace, that convulsive clasping with Rupert on the Gower Street pavement. It had been more like a meeting of some driven reality at the core of each of us, like a recognition from some shared primal clay.

Frightened by what I had subsequently said to him, ashamed of the way I had behaved like the bad fairy, troubled by the ferocity of my emotions, I decided I could not see Rupert again unless I was already anchored by a commitment that weighed more than anything else, or, at least, that weighed as much as the one he had already made to another woman. And I needed someone to whom I could legitimately vent the power of my feelings, now that the real object of them was lost to me. I did not ponder the selfishness of this; I believed that my will would determine the future.

'Well,' Nigel whispered, his voice husky, 'do you like it? Will you marry me?'

I kissed his lips, and he slipped the ring on my finger.

'Say you love me . . .' he said in a low voice. 'I need to hear it.'

'Do you need to ask? Of course I love you.' But there are many kinds of love.

Later I said to Nigel, 'I think we should get married without waiting around.'

'Get married soon? In the New Year, you mean?'

'Yes. I don't want a fuss, church service, white veil, tons of flowers, relatives. What about a quiet register office thing?'

He laughed. 'Áine,' he said with the patience of one addressing a child, 'you're only nineteen! And I haven't met your father yet. I should speak to him.'

'So? Come to Dublin for Christmas. Dad will love you. You're his kind of bloke . . .'

Oh, just marry me, I thought. Marry me before I see Rupert Lyall again, before he opens a can of worms that you cannot even imagine. Marry me and make both of us safe.

'Well,' he said slyly, 'if we're getting married that soon – you could even move in, I suppose?'

I mulled this over. The reaction in my gut said, 'Don't!' But the voice of embattled pride and fear decided me. I smiled at Nigel. 'I suppose . . .'

When I got home Brigitte was reading in bed and looked up expectantly. I showed her the ring.

'It's a beauty,' she said whistling. 'About a million carats! Are you happy?'

'Of course. Look, if Rupert phones tomorrow, tell him I've gone away.'

My friend stared at me. 'But why . . . I thought you were over him . . .'

'Of course I'm over him. But he came around to RADA this evening – and I wasn't very nice to him.'

'Well, you don't have to see him if you don't want.'

You don't understand, I thought. I *do* have to see him. I have no choice in this. The only thing I have a choice in is whether I am committed to someone else and saved by that commitment from making a fool of myself, or whether I make a mistake that will destroy me.

Funnily enough, I believed all of this. I believed I could rationalize my way out of it, set up parameters that would be politely observed on all sides like the rules for a game of golf. But I had, as yet, only glimpsed the obdurate forces moving life.

'Nigel and I are not waiting around, Brigitte. We're getting married in the New Year.'

My friend's face betrayed consternation. 'Why so soon?

Have you considered the fall out . . . your father . . . Nigel's family . . .'

'They won't mind. They'll come around!' I said, parroting Nigel. 'I happen to believe it's the right thing.'

'You're sure you're not running away from something, are you? I suppose your meeting with Rupert has nothing to do with this.'

Sometimes Brigitte, with her penetrating pragmatism, reminded me of my mother. I denied the truth. I was an old and practised liar, after all. But I was also half-blinded, my vision tainted by anger and desperation, and the need to escape a force I felt in the air, like waiting Nemesis. I wonder now how I could have believed that a few words and signatures on a page would act like a spell.

I moved into Nigel's flat. He had given the horrible, stuffed gharial to Oxfam and I thought that, in the summer, I would replace it on the balcony with something more suitable, potted plants perhaps, geraniums or something of that order. I had some notion that I would become domesticated, be a dab hand with flowers, and whisk up delicious suppers in a twinkling. Already my books – poetry, Shakespeare, dog-eared plays by the dozen, were lending a lived-in ambience to Nigel's pristine surroundings, making it feel more tolerable as a home.

Nigel tried to make up for my lack of culinary expertise. On the evening I moved in I came back to the flat to find that he had made a chicken curry, and had an incongruous bottle of Veuve Clicquot on ice. We dined sitting on cushions in front of the fire.

'Here's to the next Mrs Freestone-Hill,' he said gravely, raising his glass.

'That may be, sir, when I am Mrs Freestone-Hill,' I said, paraphrasing Shakespeare's Juliet, and suppressing the chagrin I felt immediately at the prospect of being owned.

'Could I interest you in a mattress, Madame?' Nigel inquired when we had finished the champagne and he was interfering with the zipper of my dress.

I went with him to his single bed. It was the second time we had made love.

Nigel was tender and very gentle, and whispered afterwards in my ear, 'I am so happy, my darling.' He raised himself on an elbow to look into my face, and added half anxiously, 'What about you?'

I smiled up at him, and he raised a long tress of my hair and kissed it.

Then he began to discuss how we would break the news to our families. 'Will we phone them now or wait until tomorrow?'

'Wait until tomorrow,' I replied. 'It's nearly eleven. And we need some sleep.' I was aware of the exhaustion, more of the spirit than the body.

'We'll have to get a double bed.'

'Why? I like it like this.'

'But what happens if one of us gets fat?'

He went to sleep before I did, suddenly spent. As I drifted off myself I told myself I was relieved at my bespoken state, relieved that the world was renewable and full of chapters. I had turned an important page now. So long as a certain hazard was kept at bay, the wild woman locked up in the attic, so to speak, all would be well.

But when I went to sleep I did not dream of married bliss. I dreamt I was running as hard as I could and that whatever was on my tail had found me.

Next morning I phoned my father and broke the news of my engagement. He was stunned and reproving.

'Dad!' I was suddenly stricken. 'I'm sorry to dump this on you like this . . .'

'Is there some reason for this precipitous action, Áine?'

He was wearing his old juridical voice, the one calculated to inspire terror in the heart of the world's chancers. But it did not disguise his anxiety for his unpredictable daughter.

'No reason, except that we love each other.' This avowal, for some reason, did not seem to wring his withers as much as I had expected.

'Who is this young man?' he demanded on an even sterner note. 'What does he do?'

'He's a merchant banker . . . or will be in due course.'

'Sounds like history repeating itself,' my father said on a bitter note.

'Oh come on, Dad, you'll love Nigel! It isn't a bit like Aunt Isabelle getting married in Gretna Green. This is all kosher and above board. Nice bloke, good family. I'll bring him home for Christmas and you'll be able to vet him for yourself!'

'But why . . . ?'

'Did we get engaged so soon . . . ? Simple, we want to be married. And no Dad, although you wouldn't ask it, I'm not in the family way.'

There was a reproving intake of breath on the other end of the line. I didn't tell him I was sleeping with Nigel. That would have provoked an explosion.

'And when do you propose to get married?'

'In the New Year, Dad.'

'Áine, this is much too precipitous. I'll go to London immediately.'

'Don't, Dad. I'm bringing him home for Christmas . . .'

'Who are his people?'

'Oh, you'll meet them in due course. Top drawer, as they say in these parts . . .'

Before he rang off my father asked: 'Have you met Rupert? He's in London. He was looking for your number a short while ago.'

'I saw him the other day. He dropped by RADA . . . He's grand.'

I said I had to go, and he murmured, in a voice stricken by parental consternation, as though aware for the first time he had lost the role of leading man in his daughter's life, 'You'll be married from home, of course. Will I speak to Father D'Arcy?'

'Dad, I don't want fuss. I want to get married in a register office.'

'You'll do nothing of the kind! Is this Nigel's idea?'

'No. It is mine. Look, Dad, I have to go now. But we'll see you on the twenty-third and we'll make no final decision until then.'

There was silence, the hush of defeat. Then he said, his voice very strained and low, 'I'm always here, you know, my darling . . . if something is wrong . . .'

'Oh Dad,' I said, 'Of course I know that.'

279

Nigel came home later with the news that his mother had invited us down to Session House for the weekend.

'Everyone assumed you were preggers. But I told them that you were just lusting after my body and couldn't wait.'

'They must think I'm awful,' I muttered, but inside I was cheering. A new world was opening its doors, forced to accept me. I would not fail it. I was strong now, armed against silly, childhood crushes, buttressed against life's shifting sands.

The days went by. Nigel liked to remind me constantly of our engaged state, spoke constantly of our marriage, as though he needed to remind me of it, as though, at some subliminal level, he was afraid I would fly away. He wanted to make love all the time we were together. Part of me knew perfectly well that he was trying to imprint and hold me, without knowing that he was doing so, without any conscious knowledge of his insecurity. But I wished he were anything else, dominating, selfish, arrogant, anything that would compel me to engage with him as a force.

We discussed the date of our wedding. I was getting my way, my heart was leaden and no matter how much I told it I was delighted to be engaged I could not lighten it.

Brigitte did not look for a replacement for me, and it became a joke that we were still living cheek by jowl.

'It's almost like a ménage à trois!' Ralph Garnard said when he called in for a drink one evening. He was a friend of Nigel's who had taken to calling. I saw the way he eyed Brigitte and wondered if she was the reason for his visit. But she did not seem to return his glances, or notice his existence.

'Didn't you like Ralph?' I asked her after he was gone. 'He certainly seemed to like you.'

She laughed. 'Is the old engaged woman becoming a match-maker?'

Brigitte took Rupert's call when he phoned some days later. It was the second time he had phoned since our chance meeting.

'He thought you were joking when you told him you were engaged,' she confided. 'But I told him there was no mistake, and that you had moved next door to live with Nigel. Then he said he and Gloria want to take all of us out to dinner. Do you think you could talk to him the next time he rings?'

'Sure.'

All very proper and friendly. Just the way I liked my life. But although I was newly engaged and living in a married state, although my husband-to-be talked to me every night of his love and of our future, something inside me waited for Rupert's next phone call with longing and dread.

I had a lovely weekend in Session House, where people seemed more relaxed than formerly, as though making the best of what had occurred, and relieved that at least I was white and presentable. There was a dinner party for the extended family, at which the elderly Great-uncle Toby, who was seated beside me, became quite misty-eyed.

'You're still a child,' he whispered. 'Quite a romance, what! Gretna Green, was it?' And when he was disabused of this notion and informed that Gretna Green was no longer in the elopement business and that we were not yet married, he turned on Nigel and said he was a cradle snatcher. Later he asked, 'What did you say your father did?'

'He's a solicitor.'

'When are we going to meet him?'

'Soon,' Nigel's mother said diplomatically.

Uncle Toby winked at me and whispered in my ear, 'He's one of my heirs, you know.' And then he winked again.

Nigel's brother, John, watched me from the other side of the table. I knew he was vetting me, but he seemed eventually satisfied as to my bonafides, for his eyes lost their suspicion. But he could not contain his curiosity.

'So how long have you and old Nigel known each other?'

'Months and months,' Nigel said in a straight voice.

'Only *months*?' He turned to his brother. 'Not like *you* to be swept away, old boy! You've been living like a monk since Val upped and married that chappie from Yorkshire . . .'

His mother gave him a murderous look and suggested that we might like to take coffee in the drawing room. Over petit fours she asked what our plans were, did we intend moving to a flat with more room.

'You only took that small place as a stop-gap, Nigel.'

He smiled at me and took my hand. 'Good thing too,

281

otherwise I would never have met Áine.'

'I think we'll stay there for the time being,' I said, thinking of Brigitte. 'There's no hurry. And it's quite a nice flat really.' I turned to him. 'Isn't it?'

He nodded. 'I've ordered the double bed, though,' he whispered in my ear, making me flush, because I thought his mother could hear. But she only looked at me with the smiling, penetrating gaze of the adult examining the child.

'Will you be coming for Christmas?' his mother asked then, and Nigel said that we were going to Ireland.

When Nigel excused himself and went upstairs John sat beside me with a photograph album and showed me pictures of Nigel in his baby bath. He laughed and said, 'He always liked water . . . used to think he'd make a sailor. He was quite keen on the idea of the Navy before he met Val . . .'

I nodded politely. John glanced around. The older generation were talking among themselves.

'Like to come out for a stroll before the light goes?' he asked.

I stood up and followed him to the garden.

A pair of white-painted cast-iron planters ornamented either side of the patio. Growing out of them was some kind of greenery that I couldn't identify. Here and there on the grass were small drifts of dead, russet leaves. A mist had risen and rubbed itself through the branches of the trees.

'This is a very pretty place,' I said. 'You must miss it when you are in Sandhurst?'

'Well, it's home, I suppose. But we all have to move on, don't we?'

He turned to me. 'Áine,' he said suddenly, 'I can see you are fond of Nigel?'

It was a question, not a statement.

'Of course I am "fond" of him!' I replied with some indignation. 'Why do you think I am getting married to him?'

'You're very young to be married . . . almost nine years his junior . . .'

'So what?'

'Thing is – if you changed your mind or anything . . . well, what I mean to say is that he would be very cut up . . .'

I looked at him, frowning, trying to read between his words. 'If I changed my mind . . . ? I don't understand.'

'He was engaged before, you know – to Valerie, but she dumped him. So don't mess him around, Áine, will you? He's been hurt already and he's vulnerable.'

An indignant reply was on the tip of my tongue, but Nigel's cheery voice behind us said: 'So this is where you two have got to . . .'

'Just showing Áine the garden!' John said.

'I suspect she's about as good at horticulture as she is at cooking,' Nigel said with a straight face.

'I'm better at horticulture,' I said. 'I can identify at least three varieties of plants!'

When we returned to London Brigitte said, 'Rupert phoned again while you were away. He wants to take us all out before Gloria goes home. He suggested next Friday. I gave him Nigel's number.' She looked at me keenly. 'I hope that was all right?'

'Of course.'

'Your American cousin and his fiancée?' Nigel said, sounding pleased. 'Jolly nice of him. I'm looking forward to meeting them.'

At about ten that night the phone rang. I let it ring for a moment although it was beside me.

Nigel glanced at me and said, 'Aren't you going to answer that thing?'

'Hello?'

His voice came through, strong and teasing, as though we had not parted in turmoil only a couple of weeks earlier. And against my will, something flowed from me into his voice, as though he were the earth and I the rain.

'Hello Áine . . .' He paused as he spoke, just long enough for me to have heard the strain in him. 'Just wanted to confirm you and your fiancé can make it for dinner on Friday. Gloria is going back to the States on Saturday, and is sure looking forward to meeting you.'

Nigel, who was sitting beside me, raised his eyebrows when he heard the male voice. I kept mine level and conversational.

'Thanks, Rupert, that would be lovely. Nigel is looking

forward to meeting both of you. He's here beside me right now.'

When next he spoke, Rupert's voice was very low, almost a whisper. 'Why did you rush off and get engaged?'

'Why not?'

'I hope you'll be very happy.'

He gave me the name of the restaurant where we were to dine, in the Hyatt Regency in Cadogan Square.

'Seven p.m. Don't be late.'

'Is Brigitte invited too?'

'Of course! I've asked her already!'

And there you were, Rupert, in the Hyatt Regency, well dressed in a grey suit with a waistcoat and a red silk tie. It was a very cold evening in December and you and your fiancée were drinking Martinis when we arrived. I shook hands with Gloria. She was what my mother would have called 'handsome', which is to say she had regular features, and was well made, but she did not possess the alchemy that transforms flesh into beauty. She was too perfect somehow, too groomed; there was nothing about her of individual quirkiness. But she stood up with a welcoming smile and extended her hand. She had very white, even teeth and a pleasant face. I liked her. And yet the desolation tore at me when she turned to you, Rupert, and called you 'honey' and put her hand lightly on your arm in that timeless gesture of intimacy and possession.

The table overlooked the square and even as we sat down the first snowflakes had begun their dance, swirling on the other side of the glass and filling the square with magic.

I can't remember what everyone had to eat. The wine was good; its scent is still in my nostrils, its fumes in my brain. The reflection in the window showed the candle flame, the faces, mixed with the waltzing snow. I saw Gloria turning to you, and I saw myself, quiet, observant, in my black velvet dress.

But mostly I remember your eyes, Rupert, bright in the candlelight, deliberately meeting mine whenever I looked at you, angry, haunted eyes.

'Are you staying here?' Nigel asked.

'For the moment,' Gloria said with a laugh. 'Until tomorrow

when I go home. Rupert has a little apartment in St John's Wood.'

I excused myself and went to the ladies' room and when I came out you were waiting.

'You shouldn't have done it; it's not fair to him,' you said, and you hesitated and stared at me and went into the men's room.

'*You* should talk!'

But your hand touched mine in passing, a gesture of need, perhaps, or was it acceptance?

When the meal was over we said our goodbyes, Gloria saying how glad she was to have met us.

'Look after him for me, Áine,' she said as she shook my hand in parting. 'I won't worry so much about leaving him behind now, knowing he has family here.'

'You must come and dine with us soon, Rupert,' Nigel said. 'Áine here is dying to try out her new cook book.'

'What one is that?' I demanded, knowing that among all the stuff I possessed there was not as much as a pamphlet on how to scramble eggs.

'The one you're getting for Christmas!' There was general laughter.

'Better still,' I quipped with assumed gaiety, 'come to Dublin with us for the holiday. Brigitte is coming.' Somehow the thought of this, the thought of my father, and my warring siblings, was normal and restored my equilibrium.

'We're not going to your castle for Christmas, then?' Nigel asked. 'I'd like to see it.'

I knew immediately that I could not bear the thought of showing Nigel Dunbeg. I did not know why; it had something to do with the level at which he had pitched his expectations of the place; he would not, in a million years, see it and feel it as I did. He would say that it was 'interesting'; he would say it had 'potential'. He would calculate the sums required for its complete restoration. He would put all its fury and wildness, all its esoteric magic, into a box labelled 'Potential Irish assets' and close the lid.

'It's not *my* castle!'

'Well, it might be some day,' he said cryptically. 'I mean,

you're so fond of it . . .'

'Rupert's coming back home for Christmas,' Gloria said stiffly, sounding a bit miffed and territorial, although she smiled as she spoke. But I saw her mettle and knew that she was indeed the daughter of Theodore Penrose II who owned the world.

Rupert nodded, and said he would be glad to dine with us as soon as he came back in January.

'Well, I suppose we'd better get going,' Nigel said. 'I have to get these ladies home.'

Rupert came around to the passenger door to see me into the car. My small evening bag chose that moment to fall, and opened to disgorge lipstick, comb and hair clips onto the ground. Rupert helped me retrieve them and returning the bag to me said, almost without moving his lips, in a voice so low and intense it might have been the sussuration of the wind, 'You've got your revenge.'

I glanced at his impassive face, jumped into the car. He shut the door and in a moment we were waving goodbye.

Nigel sighed happily as we drove away and said it had been a lovely evening and that Rupert and Gloria were charming people.

'I couldn't help wondering if she is related to Theodore Penrose,' he said in a musing voice after a moment, 'but I didn't like to ask.'

'Why? Do you know him?'

'Not personally of course. But I hear his name mentioned in financial circles.'

'He's her father.'

He reached for my hand, held it for a while before releasing it. Brigitte in the back was silent. It had stopped snowing, but London was covered in a thin dusting of white, like icing sugar, and all I could think of was that it would soon be Christmas and I would be going home.

As I was putting my things away that night I opened the black velvet purse to empty it and found there a small, tightly folded piece of paper that had not been there before. On it were two short verses in Rupert's writing. I heard Nigel coming and I slipped it into the small space between the bathroom cabinet and the wall. But later, when he was asleep, I got out of bed and went to the bathroom. There I opened the note again and read the scrawled lines:

> Even now the fragrance of your hair
> Has brushed my cheek and once in passing by
> Your hand upon my hand lay tranquilly;
> What things unspoken trembled in the air.
>
> Ah might it be that just by touch of hand
> Or speaking silence, shall the barrier fall;
> And you will come with no more words at all.
> Come into my arms and understand.

Underneath these lines an address was scrawled: 'Flat 3, 42 Norton Road, St John's Wood. Tomorrow 2 p.m. Please!'

Chapter Nineteen

That night I dreamed of Dunbeg. In the dream I was in the castle forecourt. It was dark and the sea was troubled, throwing spray onto the rocks and up against the walls of the house. I tasted the salt; it was like the taste of blood. The house was in darkness, but I knew there was something waiting there, for I felt its presence. I had trouble breathing; the wind had knocked the breath from me, and fear was everywhere. And then I saw Rupert on the edge of the sea where the tide was thumping the rocks, but he was gone before I could call out to him.

I woke. Nigel was murmuring, 'What's the matter . . . Did you have a dream?'

It was cramped in bed. His presence seemed incongruous, as though he came from another time, from a future *I* had not yet accessed.

If I could go back and cure it all, make it right I thought, without quite knowing what I wanted to rectify. Nigel, as though telepathic, put his arm around me.

Next morning I got up early, and looked through the window at the thin shim of snow on the rooftops. I went to the bathroom, took the folded paper of the night before from its hiding place behind the cabinet. I re-read the verses and the address in St John's Wood. I folded and replaced the page, ran a bath and lay back in the tub. Nigel came in and sat down on the edge of the tub.

'Have you been up long?' he asked, playfully pulling a few strands of my hair. 'You didn't sleep well last night. Was it a very bad dream?'

'I've been up about half an hour,' I said. I didn't want to talk about the dream.

'Come back to bed.'

'No, Nigel.'

'Is something wrong?'

I shook my head. But I wanted to say, please give me space. Let me think. Why am I still caught up in these dreams? What is the connection between Rupert and Dunbeg? Why does he want to see me? What do his verses mean? A declaration of love? A promise for the future? Or just an acceptance and a farewell? But I said none of these things.

Nigel looked at me with uncertain desire, and playfully tried to put bath foam on my nipples.

'Please, Nigel!'

'Sorry.'

He left the bathroom and closed the door.

It's not too late, I told myself. Is that what Rupert is saying? Or is he inviting my understanding and complicity? Maybe what he really means is: 'I must marry someone else, but I love you, and would have you for a lover'. Is that what he thinks he can line up for me – the marriage prop, the exploited corner of the eternal triangle? You're at it again, I reminded myself. You should become a novelist and to hell with acting.

Nigel put in his head around the door. He was dressed.

'I'm just popping out for a while!'

'Where are you going?'

'Christmas shopping,' he said in a mysterious tone. 'Your present, actually. And a few things to bring to Dublin.'

The phone rang and he went to pick it up.

'Hello?'

I heard him replace the receiver. He returned to the bathroom door, shrugged. 'Caller hung up. Must be your lover! Ha ha.'

Ha, indeed! I said to myself. Some lover . . .

He came into the bathroom in his coat and scarf, kissed the crown of my head. 'Have a nice soak. I'll be back around one. I thought we could have lunch at the Oriel?'

'Can I take a rain check on that? I'm going to do my own bit of shopping.'

'OK. See you later then.'

As he shut the door of the flat, I thought of how much I

cared for him, how safe he made me feel, and then came the memory of Rupert's eyes the night before, the electricity of our brief contact in the hotel corridor, the sense of excitement and incipient peril. I took out the wonderful verses and read them again.

'*Come into my arms and understand*' I whispered aloud. But I want an honourable life, Rupert! I don't want to be the prop for your convenient marriage. I cannot betray Nigel to suit you. What are you saying to me?

'He's had years to contact you!' a cold and angry voice inside me said. 'You'd be a fool to bother with him now. He's got his life sewn up with someone else. It was his choice and he can stay with it!'

The bath water was getting cold. I got out, towelled myself, saw in the mirror that my eyes were bright.

'I can't visit him on my own,' I told my reflection, but then I added, desperately needing justification, 'But I would just like to see where he lives. What harm is there in that?'

I knew he was due to see Gloria off at Heathrow at eleven. If I went to St John's Wood *now* I could see the place where he lived. He wouldn't be there, and I would have done something to assuage the blind and powerful prompting that said Rupert was the key to everything, that caution was petty and should be thrown to the winds.

Rupert's flat was in a white stuccoed Victorian house, with a front door reached by three stone steps. It had begun to drizzle and the remainder of last night's snow was lying in icy patches at the inner edges of pavements and turning to slush in the gutters. I read the names; opposite the button for flat No. 3 it said 'Rupert Lyall'. Here, in this London street, lived my cryptic correspondent through so many years, the boy I had lain beside on a cliff one far-off summer's day, the youth who had afforded me a refuge on that terrible night in Dunbeg, the young man who had held me in Mount Wexford, and whose body I had come so near to knowing on the night of my mother's funeral. But he was much more than all of this. He was the past incarnate – Dunbeg, my childhood, the interrupted momentum of my adolescence, the only person that the core of me could speak to and know it would be heard. He had been present at my making, after a fashion, and knew me as no one else ever could. Or was I imagining all this?

'Men know nothing,' my aunt had said to me once. 'All the things you might feel they cannot even guess at. So never imagine for a moment that one of them can ever feel or share your reality!' The counsel of a cynical and disappointed woman? Or the advice of someone who knew the score? My heart said the former; my mind insisted on the latter. Suddenly I saw myself, a ridiculous figure hanging around outside a young man's lodgings, while at home I had a loving and loyal fiancé and a future that promised prosperity and life.

Go home, Áine, my common sense said. You are engaged to be married.

I turned suddenly from the door and walked rapidly down the street. I did not heed the footsteps that hurried behind me, until a hand was placed on my arm.

'Áine,' Rupert's voice said in my ear, 'Áine, thank you for coming!'

His flat was spacious and warm, too warm perhaps for someone used to a North Atlantic climate. There was a bookshelf overflowing with medical textbooks, and a music centre with a stack of discs beside it. He touched a button and I heard the strains of Beethoven's Pastoral Symphony, but so low that it was barely audible. The curtains were chintz, and a few bright, modern prints adorned the walls. The settee had a bright throw on it, and a faded oriental rug of dubious provenance covered the space before the hearth. A table lamp with a gold shade threw muted light over the room.

He took my coat, hung it up in the small lobby and said, glancing back at me, as I stood uncertainly by the gas fire and shivered in the heat, 'You're wearing black again. Is that a comment?'

'Don't flatter yourself, Rupert! I always wear it.'

'It's armour, of course,' he said.

'If you're getting psycho-analytical, you're on the wrong tack. I don't need protection any more.'

'Good!' he laughed, like someone venting private tension. 'I'm so glad you came . . . You can sit down if you like!'

I sat on the settee and he went into the kitchen. I heard the clatter of cups.

'Tea or coffee?'

'Tea for me.'

He came in with a tray, deposited it beside the table lamp which he pushed out of the way. He handed me a mug of tea and offered a plate of scones.

'I got them in the corner shop, in case you came. I remember how you used to like them in Dunbeg.'

I took one and picked at a raisin. There was an awkwardness between us: the memory of our meeting in Gower Street, the knowledge of the verses he had left in my evening bag the night before. Perhaps he had been half drunk, I thought, and now regretted it. The music lulled the silence; the gas fire hissed. But the room filled with an intimacy, powerful and unspoken. When I looked up I saw that his eyes were fixed on me, with intense and almost melancholy avidity.

'You sit there, a beautiful young woman!' he said after a moment. 'But in your eyes I see the ghost of the little girl I knew!'

'Really?' I replied tartly, disturbed by the intensity. 'That makes two of us! You are your own ghost too, you know, in case you think you have a monopoly on reality.'

Rupert relaxed suddenly and regarded me with his old, slightly lop-sided, teasing smile.

'But reality is uncertain; it has no fixed abode. Quantum Mechanics – which is all about sub-atomic particles – proves the normalcy of inconsistency or the inconsistency of normality!'

'Does it, indeed? Well I don't know anything about physics. What did you want to see me about, Rupert, or are you going to be inconsistent and prove the theory?' He seemed to wince.

'Áine, I know you are angry with me, but I need to understand something, and you are the only person who can tell me. Everything in my life changed after I went to Dunbeg . . .'

'Is that why you asked me to come here?' I whispered. 'I don't want to talk about Dunbeg. Leave it alone now. I went back there with Brigitte and it was tranquil. I prefer to think of it like that.' I put my mug down and looked around for my coat. I knew I had to leave this room, find the cold street outside and go back to South Ken.

'But can you explain why my mother has an obsession with that place?' he went on. 'She's increasingly disturbed by something she saw there. She says you saw it too. I would like to take her back there . . . prove to her that there's nothing in the old pile but a lot of stones and mortar . . . It's the only way she will be able to let it go. But she won't hear of it.'

He sighed, leaned back and added, 'It would be so wonderful to see her well again, see her happy! What did she tell you she had seen, Áine? She won't discuss it. Was it Sarah's ghost?'

'Yes,' I replied earnestly. 'I thought I saw her too, as I told you once. But lots of old places are haunted, but probably only because the place itself has absorbed the force of some awful trauma. At least, that's what I think now. The only real problem with Dunbeg was . . .'

'Aeneas Shaw?' He said this quietly, more as a statement than a question. My breath stuck in my chest. To hear *his* name spoken, to remember his shadow outside my window, to recall his face in the light of his fire, to smell the woodsmoke as he thrust the burning faggot at me, to have it all come back here in this London flat when I thought I had escaped it . . . To be suddenly certain, even while Rupert sat there looking at me with his strained smile, with his voice so deliberately laconic, that the story was not over, that the denouement was yet to come, that some nameless horror waited. And I also realised that Rupert had not asked me here for any reason to do with Dunbeg. His eyes were hungry and, unguarded, were full of something like desperation. When he turned his head to one side I saw the old vulnerability in him and my heart turned over with an old passion, a sudden, overwhelming longing for his touch, and a curious desire to comfort him. But the thought of Nigel on his way out to buy my present intruded, and I stood up abruptly. 'Thanks for the tea . . . I really have to go . . .'

Rupert, with a sudden movement, caught me to him, and crushed my head against his heart.

I smelt the heathery scent of his jumper and the strands of wool against my lips. Then his mouth came down on mine.

'I love you!' he said after a moment, releasing me and looking down at me with a dazed expression. 'I always have. I do not understand it or even want to understand it. But I am powerless against it!'

The yearning to lose myself in him was fierce; the prospect of a couple of hours in his arms had the lure of an enchantment. But I reminded myself that I was promised elsewhere and was not some treat at the end of a string, to be hauled in, the moment Gloria had gone home.

'I am engaged to Nigel, Rupert,' I said quietly, 'and you are promised to Gloria. You seem to have forgotten.'

'Oh no, I haven't. But I am like a man who has woken in a country he thought he had left a long time ago, and now finds it is the only place where he belongs. I realized last night that if I have to live away from you, I will live in exile! Do you feel like this too?'

'What are you trying to say, Rupert?' I said shakily. 'Are you expecting me to love you as I once did, after all this time? Are you suggesting that we make a stand for each other, even now, before it is too late!'

'I wish to God I could . . .' he whispered, looking me in the eye as though challenging me to insist on the impossible. For a moment I felt as though he were reproving me for selfishness, as much as if to say we could have each other without disturbing the projected pattern of our lives, or the lives of others. 'We could still be together . . . sometimes,' he went on. 'Couldn't we? Áine, we can't simply lose what is between us.'

Anger curdled my stomach. I wanted to be sick. I shook my head.

'But anything else is hopeless, Áine, much as I would want it. I'm in the middle of it all,' he went on, 'and so much depends on me . . . The business at home . . . my mother . . . my father . . . the Penroses who have given Daddy a loan . . . Gloria . . .'

'Oh, just fuck off Rupert,' I interjected angrily. 'All of it is something you have accepted; in effect, something you have chosen. What do you want of me? Am I to be the sweetener for the luxurious pill you intend to swallow, the expedient palliative for the dose, available, perhaps, whenever you decide you can get away? Am I to betray my husband for the privilege of being shagged by you occasionally? What makes you so certain of your own centrality? What makes you think my life is of no account compared to yours?'

He started as though I had struck him, and into the stunned silence I added sarcastically, 'Who was the poet? It obviously wasn't you!'

'It was Ernest Dowson!' he said, looking at me with unhappy eyes. 'I'm only competent with Rupert Bear.'

'Right you are!' I said. 'But you should remember one thing. Rupert Bear is a cartoon character, and he's two-dimensional! And if you cannot stand up for your own life, if you are not man enough for that, you also are only two-dimensional. That's what the term means after all: a lack of depth or substance, a surface show to fool an audience. And no man answering that description is man enough for me.'

I grabbed my coat from its peg in the lobby and went to the door.

'Áine!'

'Oh, just go to hell and leave me alone,' I hissed at him, holding back the tears and shaking his hand off my arm. 'I have no time to be used and tormented. I have a life to live.'

On the tube, I coined a miserable ditty in my head:

> Rupert Bear, Oh Rupert Bear,
> Once I thought you were as fine
> As love and truth and happiness;
> But I was wrong . . .

I carried a sick heart back to South Kensington. Nigel was not at home. I had a dreadful headache and thought of going to bed. Instead I took some aspirin and went out. Anything was better than being alone to think. I nursed the sense of outrage, was even glad of it. Had Rupert really thought I would play lovers with him? I demanded of myself in a white-hot rage as I walked down Oxford Street. Was this what he had lined up for us, while he married his Gloria and I gave Nigel nothing but lies? I was so much better off without a creature like that! But eventually the anger faded and only the love was left, like a consummate survivor who knew where to hide.

* * *

Christmas was the time of year when I had always felt most cocooned, and its magic returned on Christmas Eve when Nigel and I got the eight o'clock flight from Heathrow, and eventually touched down in Dublin in the winter night, bumping gently on wet tarmac. For some reason I wanted to weep when I saw my city's name in Irish on the side of the main airport building: *Áth Cliath* – the Ford of Cliath. I felt the raw belonging at the back of the throat for this esoteric patch of earth, where my people had lived and died for five thousand years, this place that was more kin than country.

Nigel had never been to Ireland, and he whispered as the plane taxied to the landing bay, 'But it's such a *little* airport!'

'If you mean it's not as big as Heathrow,' I said crisply, 'that's all to the good.'

'But is it even one tenth the size?' he said indulgently, as though he were to be personally congratulated for having one of the biggest airports in the world.

'I don't give a damn if it's one hundredth the size of Heathrow, or anywhere else. The smaller the better. *We* didn't go around grabbing everything on the planet!'

He looked at me sharply, but his voice was gentle. 'Áine, what is biting you lately?'

'Nothing,' I said. But I was beset again by the sense of my foolishness, even deceit, in going to see Rupert, and I longed for absolution. I touched Nigel's hand in apology and he grasped mine and held it until the plane stopped and we stood up to disembark. I smiled back at Brigitte who had the seat behind us and saw how bright her eyes were, and wondered at her obvious pleasure in coming back to Ireland.

Seán was there to meet us. He shook hands genially, commented on the cold, picked up Brigitte's bag. But as soon as I saw the covert glance he gave her, and the one she gave him when he was not looking, I began to understand the subtle excitement I had sensed in her, began to understand why she had shown so little interest in anyone else in London.

Don't let him know, I mentally warned her, remembering Gráinne and others who had fallen for my brother's acerbic charm. If you let him see it he'll be gone. Keep him on the

297

chase! Never put him out of his misery, at least not until you have him in the bag. This made me want to laugh, the thought of Seán 'in the bag', like one of his own wily mullet.

Seán had a new car, a red Toyota, of which he was inordinately proud. We congratulated him on it, and he seemed gratified and said he'd had a salary hike. We slid out of the airport onto the dual carriageway. Brigitte sat in front with our driver, and when we stopped at the Whitehall lights, I saw again the sly movement of his head as he turned to glance at her.

'How does Rupert like London?' He asked this out of the blue.

I stiffened despite myself, but Nigel replied, 'He's gone back to the States for Christmas. We'll be seeing him in the New Year. He and his fiancée took us out to dinner . . .'

We were in Upper Drumcondra Road in a moment. There, across the street, was our house in its Victorian terrace; there, to the left, the Archbishop's Palace; there were the trees I had heard swishing through many a summer night; and there the lamp post that threw strange shadows on the night-time pavement. Everything looked so normal; the torment of my adolescence here had left no trace.

Seán turned into Alphonsus Road in order to access the laneway to the garage. The laneway was unlit, but the headlights probed it down to its end.

It was empty, but when we got out of the car and I looked back down its length, I saw something move in the darkness. I started, and Nigel said, 'What is it?'

'There's something there!' I whispered.

He called out, 'Hello . . . ?' and the shadow leaped over a wall and disappeared.

'It's a cat!' he said. 'What a jumpy little thing you are.'

'Squirrel was always like that!' Seán said in a tone of voice that held its own commentary on my peculiarities.

My father came down the garden to greet us. He held me for a moment, shook hands with Brigitte and with Nigel, and I saw, even in the dim light of the garden, the penetrating inquiry of his stance, as though he would like to vet every atom of this stranger who had arrived as fiancé to his only daughter.

'How do you do, sir!' Nigel said, straightening his back as

298

though under military inspection. This was followed by a moment's pregnant silence.

'Come in,' my father said then. 'It's very cold.' No sooner were we indoors in the basement hallway than we heard the thunder on the stairs, my other siblings descending with enough clatter for a herd of elephants.

'Hi, Brigitte!' they called and fell over each other to embrace her.

They looked suspiciously at Nigel.

'Hi . . .'

'This is Nigel!' I said.

'Are you really getting married to Áine?' Simon demanded. 'Or is there some conspiracy afoot of which we have not been appraised?'

I thought Nigel would be fazed by this, but he didn't bat an eyelid. 'Of course I'm getting married to your sister, old boy,' he said. 'Who wouldn't be, given the chance?'

Later, in the sitting room he regaled them with an account of how we had met. 'And there she was, standing on the steps, looking back at me as though I were Jack the Ripper.'

Seán shook his head. 'God, Áine, it's a wonder they didn't deport you for the illegal importation of imaginings.'

The twins laughed in unison. 'I mean they can get you for all sorts of hallucinogens,' Martin said reasonably, 'but *they're* only trotting behind what Áine can do without any assistance!'

'They haven't made it a crime yet,' Nigel said, 'to have a vivid imagination. And how else do you think she is going to become a famous actress? I only wish I had the same facility.'

He winked at me across the room, evidently already at home in this noisy family, where every spare moment was spent sharpening your wits.

'No you don't,' Jack said, putting his oar in. 'It makes you do weird things! She ran away from school once. She had some notion or other and ended up in Dunbeg . . .'

There was a sudden silence, as though this comment touched something near the family quick. Nigel looked at me with a half frown, as though to say, 'You never mentioned that?'

'I was all of thirteen,' I said evenly. 'And there has to be a Statute of Limitations. We never hear about the childhood

299

peccadillos of these smart Alec brothers of mine, Nigel, and, believe me, *they* are legion!'

'Well said,' Brigitte responded. 'I don't know how you survive at all with this bunch. I think I'd murder the lot of them!'

'Can I be first?' the twins clamoured almost together, and threw themselves with a thud to the floor at her feet. 'To be murdered by the divine Brigitte . . .' Nigel gave a loud hoot of laughter, and Seán addressed a secret smile into his beer.

My father, who had taken a phone call, now came into the room, and I saw the sharp, assessing glance he threw in Nigel's direction, like an arrow loosed by an bowman. 'One look at him should be enough,' he had once said about a prospective interviewee for the post of assistant solicitor, and I wondered if my prospective husband had now passed muster.

He asked Nigel about his work in the City and Nigel, not without embarrassment, began to speak of his prospects, as though he deemed it the proper thing to do. This was the signal for everyone else to leave the room.

My father nodded from time to time and then relaxed a little and mentioned the name of some financial guru whom he knew. I switched off, wondering whether Rupert was in Mount Wexford, reunited with Gloria and his parents for Christmas. It would be around four p.m. over there now, I estimated, given the time differential. What was he doing? What kind of a man was he, to say the things he had said and to be so powerless? But I had already projected myself into his shoes, felt the weight of his parents' expectations, and the inertia of the situation, the momentum as the time shortened and his in-laws prepared his nuptials. I was his advocate against myself.

He's a sacrificial lamb! came the thought. Used, offered up to the powers of other people's dreams. All very well, another thought said, but he's complicit in it. He's bound to be dazzled. Think of what a billion dollars would do for the future of a struggling young medic!

But no matter what I told myself I could not sustain the bitterness. It always blew away like a storm in the night and everything re-emerged when it was over. I could try hypnosis, I thought. That might rid me of him. Nigel, at least, deserves a wife who is free of fixation on another man.

I came out of my reverie to find my father and Nigel evidently getting along very well; their conversation was flowing.

'Remarkable old cove . . .' Nigel was saying. 'I met him last year . . . He's done wonders for that fund since he took charge . . .'

'Are you two going to talk about boring money all night?' I demanded. 'It's responsible for more trouble in the world than anything else except religion!'

My father paused, gathered his brows together and lowered his voice: 'No, Áine. In fact it's a good time for us to discuss your . . . present situation.'

He got up, shut the door and resumed his seat, looked at my fiancé with stern, unblinking eyes. 'Nigel, you seem a decent young man. But I gather you expect to marry my daughter in a register office?'

'That's right,' I interrupted, raising and waving my hand. 'Hello, Dad? I'm here. Ask me . . . I told you already.'

My father ignored me. Nigel was nodding. 'That's right, sir, it's what Áine wants . . .'

'Áine is nineteen years old,' my father said in the same stern voice. 'She is a Catholic and should be married in church. Are you agreeable to this?'

'Of course . . .'

The open alacrity of this reply mollified my father, who seemed to relax a bit, for when he spoke again his voice had lost its edge.

He looked at me. 'Áine, I presume you want to do things properly?'

I stood up. 'I won't be press-ganged, Dad! I won't go through any church ceremony until I'm good and ready. If I get married in a register office I'll be legally married and that's good enough for me.'

'It's not good *enough*, Áine! Your aunt did this kind of thing, remember? A hasty civil marriage, without the blessing of the Church . . . And you saw yourself how that turned out . . .'

For a moment I wanted to scream at him, 'And I know how *your* marriage turned out, Dad, although it had all the benefit of Bell, Book and Candle. Do you think I don't know why my mother died?' But I could say none of this. I was, for all my

301

private bravado, pathetically glad to be home. I saw my father's grey hairs, and knew he could not change. What is more, I saw his mortality for the first time and a new compassion for him filled me, and a desire to please. I thought, Do what he wants. Nigel and I can embark on our life together under full sail and with my father's blessing and put the past and its silly horrors and mistakes behind me. And perhaps I also assumed a church ceremony would deliver me from thoughts of Rupert.

'All right, Dad,' I said after a moment. 'If that's what you want, I'll do it to please you.' I glanced at Nigel, who smiled.

My father gave a short, relieved laugh. 'I knew you'd be sensible! There are a few bottles of champagne in the fridge,' he added, as though we were good children who deserved a treat. He rose to his feet. 'Will you get out the flutes, Áine?'

When he was gone I looked at Nigel and bit my lip.

'Whew!' he said, making mock movements of someone mopping his brow.

From downstairs I heard the boys and Brigitte laughing in the kitchen.

'Let's go down and join them,' Nigel said.

'No. They'll be up in a minute to demolish the champagne. Let's enjoy the little bit of peace we have.'

We drew closer to the fire. He leant over to take my hand and whispered, 'I do want this, you know, Áine! I want to do the whole thing absolutely kosher. The parents will be glad, too, and are looking forward to meeting your father!'

The troops came up from below decks, the champagne was drunk with toasts and laughter, the firelight glowed, the family photographs, my mother's face, smiled from the sideboard and the mantelpiece. Seán teased Brigitte, making her laugh as I had never heard her, a surprised giggle that rippled into mirth.

I willed and willed and willed that everything inside me would honour the whole thing too, and would never betray it again.

It is purely a matter of commitment, I told myself on a sudden surge of confidence, glancing at Nigel's happy face.

That night I shared my old room with my friend, while Nigel slept in the guest room.

Brigitte said, 'Poor old Nigel, in his lonely cot! I don't mind if you want to swap beds . . .'

'Oh no, darlin' dear . . . Not in this house. My father's ears are out on stalks.'

Brigitte laughed. We talked for a while after we turned out the light.

'Reminds me of old times,' she said into the darkness. But it wasn't like old times. She was much quieter than formerly, like a girl who has things to mull over in the privacy of her mind.

Eventually I went to sleep.

Chapter Twenty

Not since my mother's death had the house been so lively at Christmas. A Christmas tree, something we had never bothered with in the years succeeding her death, had been erected in the hall, and its resinous scent filled the air with festive nostalgia. Simon had decorated it, a job he had taken to himself as a child, and it sported the well known angels and tiny candle lights and a few birds with red plumage and silver eyes, all dug out of the old cardboard box in the attic. Fairy lights in the shape of Cinderella's coach and various twists of tinsel completed the adornment. Underneath the tree the presents had been placed, a nice mound of them, well wrapped, with small bright labels.

'That's a nice tree,' Brigitte said.

'I did it all myself to please you, Madame,' Simon intoned, with a flourish.

'I don't think you're the only member of this family who's going to end up in RADA,' Brigitte said to me.

Christmas morning was sunny with the bright, crisp daylight so typical of winter. The radio was on, and Christmas carols filled the house from the kitchen. They brought back my childhood, and I thought of my mother on Christmas mornings, sipping a glass of sherry while she did the cooking.

Mrs Flynn, who lived in one of the cottages behind Drumcondra Road, and who had helped out since my mother's death, came in to give directions about the dinner, but Brigitte said with a straight face that she need not worry, that Áine was a great cook.

Mrs Flynn eyed me for a while, and made no comment, except to say, 'Well sure let's see yez do it so, before I go.'

The bird had been prepared and stuffed and left in the fridge and all we had to do was put it in the roasting tin. The ham had been left soaking overnight, and was put into the big pot to boil. The vegetables – Brussels sprouts, celery and cauliflower, potatoes for roasting and boiling, were all peeled and ready. Cranberry jelly was procured from a pre-stocked Christmas cupboard, and mustard was made up from the yellow tin of Colman's.

'Will ye be all right now?' Mrs Flynn inquired. 'Sure there's nothin' to do except fire those vegetables into boiling water and haul them out as soon as yez can smell them. The potatoes take longer, mind . . . And yez know how to make the gravy and prepare the melons . . . and the plum duff. Use plenty of brandy butter and yez are grand.'

We said we *were* grand. She got her Christmas box and went home to cook for her own family, and Brigitte and I were alone in the kitchen. My father and brothers had gone to Mass; Nigel had gone out for a walk. The garden outside the window was tired and resting, although a few of my mother's Christmas roses bloomed by the south-facing wall.

Brigitte said, 'Will I set the table upstairs?'

'I'll do it,' I said.

I went to look for the antique lace cloth my mother had always used for state occasions, and found it in the camphor chest on the landing.

I said to Brigitte when I returned to the kitchen, 'Did you ever notice how men always vanish as soon as there's work?'

The basement doorbell rang. I went to open the door and found Nigel on the step, looking sheepish. 'I forgot to bring a key.'

Outside, Upper Drumcondra Road was empty, the only day of the year when it was almost without traffic.

'I was just thinking of your cousin Rupert,' Nigel said, as he came into the kitchen, 'wondering what Christmas is like in Virginia. I suppose we'll see him when he returns to London.'

Being reminded of him filled me with misery. I muttered something about that being likely, and then forbade myself to think of him, or remember the recent afternoon I had torn myself from his arms. I wished with all my heart that I hadn't gone to St John's Wood, and wondered if my forthcoming church wedding would make amends to Nigel in some way. And even as I pondered all of this the longing for Rupert that lived within me like some kind of virus sent a rush of yearning through my heart.

'Right now,' Brigitte said, glancing at the clock, 'it's six o'clock in the morning in Mount Wexford. The day has yet to dawn.'

I thought of the house and the trees and the harsh birdsong and the humidity that smothered everything. I thought of the training track and the stables and my aunt swaying on her cane swing on the verandah, sipping, sipping, while my Uncle Alex disappeared into the trees to the black woman with the long gold nails.

'Can I do anything to help?' Nigel asked.

'Plenty,' Brigitte said. And proceeded to give him orders. 'And when you've done that you can bring a few bales of briquettes upstairs for the fires.'

I went upstairs and set the dining room to rights, pulling out the table to the middle of the floor and setting it with the lace cloth and the silver and my mother's crystal. Then I went out to the garden, cut the Christmas roses that were fit to be seen, and put them in a small bowl in the middle of the table. Two Georgian silver candlesticks that had belonged to my grandparents were invested with red candles and positioned. Nigel brought up two bales of peat briquettes and set the fires in both sitting room and dining room, opening back the dividing doors.

When my father and brothers returned from Mass the house was filled with the scent of cooking, and cheery with two blazing fires.

'Ah me, what a woman's touch can do,' Seán exclaimed to Brigitte.

She replied with a laugh, '*Two* women actually!'

'And what about the *man*?' Nigel demanded, panting with mock exhaustion. 'That's what I want to know.'

'What about him?' I said teasingly. He put his arm around me, drew me to one side and whispered into my ear, 'You're looking very sumptuous, Ms O'Malley.'

'None of that now,' the twins said almost in unison. 'This is a respectable house.'

My father came into the room and beamed at the laughter. 'Would everyone like to open their presents?' he asked almost diffidently, and there was something in the set of his grey head and the sudden vulnerability in his face – the lonely patriarch glad of his family – that was touching and new.

We went upstairs, and the presents were handed around. We opened them in the sitting room, and there were the usual exclamations of delight as jumpers and books were revealed to the light of day.

I saw Brigitte exclaim at the small, gold ring in a box.

'Look what Seán's given me.' She held it up to the light. 'Two hands holding a heart!'

'It's a Claddagh ring,' my brother said, not without embarrassment. 'Sure you can't visit Ireland and not own a Claddagh ring.'

But Brigitte was reading the gold-edged slip of paper that had come with the ring. 'The legend is,' she said, 'that if the ring is worn on the right hand, with the crown turned inwards the heart is free; turned outwards a love is being considered . . .'

Simon took the slip and finished for her, 'But if worn on the left hand, crown turned outwards, two loves have become inseparable.' He looked at her with a grin. 'Which hand are you going to wear it on?'

'That is for her to decide and you to find out,' I said. 'You should mind your own business!' But privately I was thinking, Oh, lucky oul loves.

My father handed around envelopes to everyone, each containing a small Christmas card and a cheque.

'Thank you, Dad,' the boys said.

'Thank you very much, Mr O'Malley,' Brigitte said.

I looked at the cheque, registered its four noughts, then went over to him and put my arms around his neck, tears in my eyes.

'Thank you, Daddy.'

'It's your wedding present,' he whispered. 'I thought you might do with a little plenteousness.'

My present to Nigel was an Aran sweater, and he put it on immediately and asked if it made him look desirable. But I was slow in opening his present to me.

'Don't you want to see what's in it?' Nigel asked eventually.

I took off the paper with care and found a serious, flattish, square box in dark blue leather. Inside, nestling on satin silk, shimmered a double row of pearls. I took them out, looked at the fine diamond clasp, and whispered to the fiancé who was eagerly watching my face. 'Oh Nigel, they're unutterably divine, but they must have cost the absolute earth.'

'*My* wedding present!' he whispered in my ear. 'And for *my* wife, the earth is not enough.' He put them around my neck.

I looked around at the happy, smiling faces of my friend and family, at the trusting face of my fiancé, and for some reason words intruded that my mother had spoken on a long-ago day in the garden: 'I am corralled by love . . .'

I barely remember the Christmas lunch, the wine, the laughter, my father sitting at the head of the table, Seán glancing constantly at Brigitte as though she contained the answer to some immortal riddle. She wore the Claddagh ring on her right hand, with the crown turned outwards, and when Seán was not looking I saw her eyes riveted on him with a gentleness I had never seen in her except when she was listening to music.

After the meal Nigel and my brothers began the task of clearing everything away; my father went downstairs to his study, saying there was something he had to do and he'd be with us shortly, and Brigitte and I sat by the sitting-room fire.

'So you're going ahead with the church wedding?' she asked softly.

'I suppose so,' I said ruefully. 'There will be no peace for me unless I do.'

'Nigel's family will come?'

'Of course! Nigel phoned them this morning and they're just waiting for confirmation of the date.'

The doorbell rang, and Seán ushered Father D'Arcy into the room.

'Áine,' he exclaimed, 'the last time I saw you you were just a child!'

'You saw me last June, Father,' I said. 'Would you like a drink?'

'June, was it? Yes, whiskey, thank you, just a little water. Well, you young people grow up so rapidly nowadays . . .' He

309

dropped his voice and spoke gravely, 'Now what's this I hear about you getting married in a *register office*?'

I put the drink into his hand. 'Yes . . . My fiancé is here. In fact he's washing up downstairs,' I said languidly, noting the effect this intelligence had. 'I'll introduce you in a minute.'

'So what day will suit you for the wedding?'

Well done, Dad, I said to myself. You don't lose any time. 'Oh we'll have to think about it. I suppose it's just a question of suiting everyone, making sure the English contingent can come.'

Father D'Arcy looked at Seán and Brigitte and said, 'I'd like a quiet word with Áine . . .'

They disappeared downstairs.

'Áine,' the priest said in a low voice, 'what about the children? Will your fiancé agree to bring them up as Catholics?'

'He probably doesn't care,' I said. 'But as I don't care either I can't see that the matter is other than academic.'

I heard the phone ring. It rang in the hall and it rang downstairs. It rang upstairs too in my father's room. I don't know why I was so acutely aware of it, or why it seemed to speak, why I wondered who was phoning in this house where Bell's invention never stopped its clamour. After a little while, during which I noticed the clatter of dishes from the kitchen and the settling of the fire and made small talk with Father D'Arcy, I heard my father's voice in the kitchen, followed by absolute silence. Then I heard his step on the basement stairs.

'Ah, there you are Noel,' Father D'Arcy said, rising from his armchair. 'A Happy Christmas to you . . .'

But my father's face was grave. He returned the seasonal greeting automatically, took a deep breath, cleared his throat and said, 'I'm afraid there's some very bad news from the States.'

'Not Rupert?' I whispered.

'No,' my father said slowly. 'I've just spoken to him. It seems there's been a tragic accident . . . Alex has been killed.'

That night Brigitte and I talked for a long time, whispering in the dark. It had been the stallion that had attacked Alex: Rupert had seen it happen. There had been head injuries.

'Stallions are very dangerous,' Brigitte said. 'Poor Rupert.'

'He never got on with his father,' I said. 'But it must be a terrible shock all the same. I suppose there'll be an inquest. And what will Aunt Isabelle do now?'

'Stay in the house, I guess. It's the only world she knows.'

We slept eventually, but in my case not for long. When I awoke some time later Brigitte seemed to be soundly asleep, for I heard the rise and fall of her breathing. I do not know why I got out of bed and went to the window. I pulled back the curtain and pressed my face to the glass, as though I already knew what I would find. I saw the figure standing beneath the street lamp in an old black coat. He was wearing a scarf against his chin and some kind of hat with a brim. His face was in darkness, but it was raised to my window. I stood and looked at him without moving and he stood and looked at me, patient and immobile, surreal in his absolute stillness. Something passed between us in silence: an acknowledgement perhaps, on my part and, on his, the triumph of a man who knew that the time of his waiting was over.

I did not sleep for the rest of that night. In the morning I was up before the household awoke, went downstairs to my father's study and rang St Fintan's Hospital.

'I'm phoning about an inmate – Aeneas Shaw,' I said when I was put through to his ward. 'Can you tell me if you have let him out for Christmas?'

There was a moment's uncomprehending silence at the other end of the line.

'If this is a joke, it's in poor taste,' the voice at the other end said, and would have hung up had I not shouted, 'No. Please! I need to know. I'm . . . connected with him!'

'Mr Aeneas Shaw died in his sleep last night,' the doctor said. 'We didn't realize he had relatives. His funeral will be tomorrow . . .'

I put down the receiver, noting after a detached fashion that my hand was shaking.

Am I free of you now, I wondered? Or will I ever be free of you?

Chapter Twenty-One

I found the Nuptial Mass in my father's old missal next to the Churching of Woman. The Blessing was addressed exclusively to the groom and summed up the various benefits he might expect from the married state. I saw, with rueful interest, that I was to be a 'fruitful vine' around the sides of *his* house and my children to be 'as olive plants' around *his* table.

I came downstairs and said to Nigel, "It looks like I'm going into compulsory grape production.'

He looked a little bit lost, suspecting perhaps that this was another Irish crack which his British propriety dreaded like the plague. So he fell back on being languid and unflappable.

'Is that one of your esoteric witticisms, darling, or are you merely off your head?'

I retreated upstairs and brought down the black-bound missal, and showed him chapter and verse.

'Well, I say . . . they seem to have got things right.' He read aloud, 'And mayest thou see the good things of Jerusalem all the days of thy life and mayest thou see thy children's children . . .'

'If that's what you want you'll have to buy an incubator.'

'They'll all be good little Catholics,' he said, ignoring this comment. 'I've agreed . . . Father D'Arcy took me to one side . . .'

'Oh Nigel . . . You let him bully you!'

'Not really. I don't care much about the religion thing . . . I just want us to be . . . proper.'

You want us to be nailed down, I thought. You feel the space in me you cannot touch because someone else lives there. And you do not deserve this.

'Nigel,' I said, 'I would like to be a good wife to you. But I

313

am a bit haunted . . . in fact last night . . .'

But Nigel did not want to listen. He kissed me. 'I know you are haunted, my darling. It doesn't matter because time will heal it. And you will be the best of wives.' And he whispered with a conspiratorial laugh, 'And soon all our nights will be ours together . . .'

No, I thought, without knowing why. Nothing will heal it now!

It was all arranged; we were to be married in February. Father D'Arcy would perform the ceremony in the local church in St Alphonsus Road. Nigel's family would come over. My father would give us a wedding breakfast in the hotel of my choice. But meanwhile he was going to Virginia for Uncle Alex's funeral.

'I'll be back in plenty of time to give you away, Áine.'

'Dad, I'm not a bloody box of Turkish delight!'

He laughed. 'No. You give far too much trouble for that.'

'Are you going to bring Aunty Isabelle home?'

'To what? To live here? She can't do that. To inhabit some nursing home far from her son? No. She wouldn't want it.' He glanced at me. 'It's all up to Rupert now. He'll make the decisions.'

'Will he be going back to London to complete his year?'

My father raised his shoulders. 'I suppose so. Isabelle will have a companion now, it seems, and there's no reason why he should not.'

'And what will happen to Mount Wexford?'

'I don't know. You'll have to ask him.'

It was St Stephen's Day, which the English call Boxing Day. My father had left for the flight that would take him to Washington. Simon went out with his friend Fergal. The twins had one of their friends in, David O'Neill, and they sat in the kitchen making turkey sandwiches. They were deciding what they would do with the day. Meanwhile they scoffed all the mince pies. We, the elders, looked at each other.

'Let's go to the Fairyhouse races,' Seán said. 'Brigitte would like that.'

Brigitte looked up and laughed. 'Would I?'

'Of course you would. Racing's in the blood!'

314

'Is it?'

'Sure is. Haven't you a drop of Irish blood?'

'I'm three-quarters German.'

'None of us is perfect,' he said, evading the cushion she aimed at him. 'But it's the other quarter that counts.'

'The other quarter is English.'

Seán recovered quickly. 'Well you're wearing a Claddagh ring and that makes you Irish. Now do you want to go to the races or don't you?'

'The crown is turned outwards,' Simon said slyly, 'so a love is being considered.'

Brigitte said she would thump him, but we all agreed that go to Fairyhouse we would.

Before we left the phone rang. I was on the landing and went into my father's bedroom to take the call, sure that it would be for one of the boys.

'I was hoping it would be you,' Rupert's voice said on a strained note after a long-distance pause. 'Oh Áine, you were right! I tried to tell my father . . . But I want you to know that whatever happens you are my one and only love . . .'

'Rupert? I'm very sorry about—'

The line went dead.

It was a bright day with a bitter wind. I was glad of the fur-lined boots that had once belonged to my mother and that I had found in the cupboard under the basement stairs. I watched the horses thundering around the race track and thought of the stallion that had killed Uncle Alex. I thought of Rupert's words on the phone just a few hours earlier. I nursed them to me in secret: *You are my one and only love . . .*

Brigitte won a few pounds on a hunch of her own and Seán said admiringly that she had a nose for the Sport of Kings and should become a professional. Nigel, who had been very taciturn since we had left the house now said suddenly, 'But we're all professional gamblers. Isn't that what life is about . . . risk and hope?' He was wrapped up in his sheepskin jacket, and his new Aran sweater, but his face was pinched.

Seán looked at him in surprise.

'What's the matter?' I whispered.

'Just savaged by an attack of philosophy,' he said with his short laugh. But there was a new doubt in his eyes when he looked at me. I tried to understand it, wondered if I had said or done something to hurt him. I put my hand in his but he did not return the pressure and when I glanced up at him I saw the query and the pain in his eyes.

When we got back that evening there was no sign of the twins or Simon. Seán said what bliss it was having the house to ourselves, until he discovered that my father's car was missing. 'Dad'll do his nut,' he said, 'if he finds out.'

Nigel went upstairs, complaining of a headache.

I followed him. He was sitting on the double bed of the guest room, but when I sat beside him he did not reach out to hold me or draw me towards him.

'Nigel,' I whispered, 'what is it?'

'Áine . . . you are my fiancée . . . we are shortly going to solemnize our marriage . . .'

'Yes?'

'But I do not think I have ever heard you say, off your own bat, that you loved me.' His unhappiness filled the room, dimmed the desultory traffic noise from the road below, caught for a moment in his throat.

'Why is this bothering you now?'

'I always assumed it. Surely you would not marry someone you did not love.'

'It depends what you call love, Nigel. I care for you a great deal . . .'

He sat up and stared at me angrily. 'I don't want you to "care for me a great deal". I am consumed with you! I want you to feel the same for me. I thought I was the happiest man in the world, meeting your family, looking forward to our wedding . . . Everything was going so well and then . . .'

'Then what?'

The tone of his voice changed, became crisp and cold. 'Then this morning, Áine, I picked up the phone in the hall and heard your cousin's voice . . .'

'I see.'

The silence filled with all the things I could say to deflect this moment. I could say that Rupert was my childhood friend.

316

This was true. I could say that he was merely seeking comfort on his father's death, which was probably also true. I could tell Nigel he was overreacting to a trifle, that he should be more mature than to take offence at emotive words from a bereaved man. And indeed, sensing his self-doubt and knowing his generosity of spirit I knew this would probably work. But his instinct was correct. And I could not lie to him again.

'Rupert and I love each other,' I said. And in the very act of talking about it I saw with a clarity that had always been denied me. I understood at last that I would never be free.

'I see . . .'

'No, you don't see. It is an accident of our shared history. We did not create it or want it. It happened. We don't have an option on it; we cannot escape it. If we live for ever it will be there for ever. I wish it were otherwise. Life would be simple . . .'

'But he is marrying someone else . . .'

'He is doing what is expected of him.'

'*What is expected of him*?' he echoed. 'Don't kid yourself. He is marrying money, a princely future . . .'

'It won't be so princely. It is never princely to be owned.'

'And you two live on different continents . . . and you have *this* between you!'

'We could live at opposite ends of the galaxy and it would make no difference.'

'Why don't you get together, get married, stop messing other people around?'

I winced. I remembered his brother's words, 'Don't mess him around, Áine. He's been hurt already.'

'I am very sorry if I have hurt you. I really care . . . and I am really confused . . .'

I burst into tears, got up to leave the room. But as I reached the door he said in the same cold voice, 'Áine . . . there is one thing more.'

'Yes?'

'Have you and Rupert ever . . . made love?'

Somewhere downstairs the television was belting out Christmas carols. The doorbell rang, and I heard Simon's voice in the hall and the voices of yet more of his friends. This house

317

is like a railway station, I thought, echoing an old complaint of my mother's. Have they no homes to go to?

'Will you answer me, Áine? The truth, please.'

'The answer is yes and no.'

He put his hand to his head. 'What does that mean, for God's sake!'

'It means that he has held me in his arms and told me he loved me. It does not mean that I ever slept with him, or at least not since I was ten.'

'When did he tell you he loved you? Was it before we met?'

'No. It was in London,' I said. 'The day after he took us out to dinner. I went . . . to his flat in St John's Wood . . .'

Nigel pulled down his suitcase from the top of the wardrobe, and methodically began to pack. He did not look at me; I might as well not have been in the room. I said, 'Please Nigel . . . I did not mean . . . I am very sorry about it. I made up my mind that it would never happen again.'

'No,' he said in the same toneless voice, 'it certainly won't.'

He turned to me with burning eyes. 'What kind of a woman are you? You get engaged to me and carry on with your own cousin! God knows what else is going to happen, what kind of dance you would lead me.'

The zipper on his suitcase was closed with a sound like tearing silk.

I stood at the top of the stairs and watched him go. I saw his face, stiff and angry, and wanted to run after him and beg him to remain. I saw the chasm he would leave behind in my life yawning before me.

Brigitte and Seán were standing in the hall when I came down, looking at the front door that had just closed behind Nigel.

'What happened?' Brigitte whispered. 'Did you two have a row?'

I sat on the second last step of the stairs.

Brigitte put a sympathetic hand on my shoulder. 'Don't worry,' she comforted. 'It'll blow over. These things always do.'

I went back upstairs and lay on my bed. Nigel would be at the airport shortly, waiting for the next flight to London. I had lost him, and in losing him I had forfeited a friend, a grounding, pragmatic presence in my life, a lover and husband. This loss seemed incalculable. I had lost all of this for a shibboleth; for a man who fooled around, for a man who couldn't stand up for what he really wanted.

Was the situation irredeemable? And who was I? A young woman looking forward to her imminent wedding, or a creature possessed? What if I were to go downstairs and tell Seán and Brigitte that Aeneas Shaw was dead, but that he had stared up at me from the pavement the night before? What would they think of me then?

I thought of Rupert's abruptly terminated call that morning, of his words whispered hoarsely. It was something that had come and gone all day, not just the words but the quality of them, the strange intensity as though the speaker were under incalculable stress.

Something was wrong with him. It wasn't just his father's death.

I went into my father's room, found his dog-eared book of phone numbers, and sitting on his bed, telephoned Mount Wexford. Milly answered the phone. Her voice awakened the sense and scent of Virginia.

'This is Áine,' I said, 'Rupert's cousin. Do you remember me?'

'Sure I remember you, honey.'

There was a hiss on the line and I raised my voice. 'May I speak to him?'

'But he's not here, sweetheart chile,' she said. 'He's gone to collect your daddy in Washington.'

'How's Aunty Isabelle?'

'Sleeping, chile. Havin' her nap . . .'

'Is she all right?'

'As right as can be expected . . .'

The lovely lilt of her voice reached me across the wind-torn Atlantic. For a moment I saw the wires on the ocean bed carrying the sense of her and Mount Wexford under the schools of fish and the drowsy creatures of the deep.

'Will you tell her I called, Milly. I was sorry to hear about Uncle Alex . . .'

'Well he's sure dead, chile! They're doin' an autopsy today.

319

Have you a message for your daddy?'

'No. Just tell him everyone is fine here.'

No point in bothering him with the latest developments, I told myself.

I put down the receiver and returned to my room, wondering why I felt the way I did – dread creeping up on me, like a mud-slide about to engulf a settlement. I reminded myself that everything was patently normal in Mount Wexford, or as normal as one could expect given the circumstances. And as for my own life, it would soon be sorted out. Nigel would come back. He would forgive me and come back. Nothing had happened that was unforgivable. I tried to promise myself resolution and forgiveness, anything to shift the malaise that filled me with such nausea.

Brigitte knocked, came in and sat beside me in silence.

'Nigel's gone back to London,' I said to pre-empt her question. 'I'll phone him later.'

'Áine,' she said after a moment, 'give him a little while to cool down. He's such a good person and he's besotted with you . . . But *what* had him so uptight – if you don't mind me asking?'

'He asked me about Rupert and I told him the truth.'

'The trouble with the truth,' Brigitte said after a moment, 'is its potential for destruction. But didn't you also point out that Rupert is outside your real life . . . he lives in America . . . he's getting married . . . you're just friends . . . Nigel can't be jealous over something like that.'

I shook my head.

The phone rang. Someone picked it up downstairs. After a moment I heard Seán yelling, 'Áine . . . Dad is on the phone.' Then he raced upstairs and put his head around the door. 'Will you take the call, for God's sake, before it costs the earth. And Rupert wants to speak to you too.'

'Did you tell Dad . . . about my row with Nigel?'

'Do you think I'm half-witted?'

I went into my father's room and picked up the receiver. My father's voice came down the line, surprisingly strong.

'Well, I've just arrived. Tired, but in one piece. Rupert met me in Washington. He and Isabelle are bearing up well. The funeral will be the day after tomorrow.'

'What was the cause of death?' I whispered. 'Was it really a stallion?'

'Yes. Poor Rupert saw it happen. There were extensive head injuries. They found traces of iron in the skull . . .'

'From the hooves?'

'Yes . . . from the shoes. Oh . . . here's Rupert now.'

I held my breath.

'Hi, Áine,' the cool voice said.

'Rupert!'

'It's nice to hear you.'

I drew a deep breath. This was not the same Rupert as the one who had phoned me that morning. 'Rupert, I'm sorry about what happened to your father.'

'Thank you. It's been a terrible time, but these awful accidents happen . . . I warned my father about that animal more than once . . .'

I don't remember the rest of the conversation. I just know that it was calm, that his voice was slow and sensible, but I heard the strain in it. He sent his best to Nigel and Brigitte and to the rest of the family. When Brigitte went downstairs I opened the drawer where, in the cardboard folder which I brought with me everywhere, the little bear and Tigerlily danced on a myriad scraps of paper.

You must escape this, a voice inside me said. You must grasp the life you have made and not let it slip from you. You are being sucked into something very like madness, where nothing has its feet on the earth.

'Nigel has his two feet planted on the earth,' I whispered aloud.

When Brigitte came upstairs I said, 'I'm going back to London. I have to see Nigel.'

'I think you should.'

'Are you coming?'

Brigitte did not reply for a moment. Then she said: 'Would you mind if I stayed for another couple of days?'

It was the first time I had ever seen her blush.

Chapter Twenty-Two

I looked at my watch. Seven p.m. Nigel would surely be in the flat by now. I had taken the tube from Heathrow and now walked briskly around Onslow Gardens and up the familiar steps. I looked up at the windows of the apartment with the balustraded balcony over the porch, but there was no sign of life. The curtains were drawn and I could not make out if any light burned behind them. I put my key in the door of the flat and walked in tentatively. The place was dark and empty. I switched on the light. Everything was as we had left it, but as I went from one room to another one thing became abundantly clear. Except for his computer, all Nigel's things were gone. His note lay on the kitchen table:

> Áine,
> As you can see I've moved out. The flat is yours until the lease expires in April. I'll drop by some time to collect my PC.
> I'm sorry about everything.
> Nigel.

I struggled with the sense of abandonment, with the sense of being in the wrong, with the sense of having let down someone who genuinely cared about me. I thought of Rupert's changed voice on the phone, and in that moment I hated the fascination he had for me.

Your presumption is horrible, I told him in silence. You have mucked up my life!

I thought of phoning Nigel's office, but it was still closed for the holiday. I called Session House, but was informed that he was not at home.

I waited in the following morning, sure that he would call me, or that I would see from the window his familiar stride crossing the road. But the hours passed. I spent most of the time looking out at people moving on the street, like the shadowy Lady of Shalott looking down on Camelot. I pondered the way I had lived the last nine years, beset with abnormal terrors, like a head case.

'It has to change!' I whispered, eventually. 'And I am the only person who can change it. But how do I go about it? Is there some spell that will rid me of it, some potion I should drink that will free me?'

When the telephone finally rang I let it ring twice before picking up the receiver. But it was not Nigel. It was my eldest brother.

'Oh, Seán . . .'

His voice had a strangely diffident quality, as though he dreaded the import of what he had to say.

'Áine, there's been a development . . . Have you seen Rupert?'

'How could I?' I demanded. 'I'm in bloody London. He's in America and even *my* long-range vision isn't that good.'

I was quite pleased at this piece of brilliance. But my brother remained subdued.

'He's not, you know. He left yesterday without telling anyone. He left before his father's funeral. The police have ascertained that he took a flight to Heathrow. It got in before they could alert the British police that he was on it . . . and now it seems he's disappeared. Well, he's not at his flat . . . and the hospital don't know where he is . . .' His voice was very grave, half apologetic, half cautionary. 'We thought he might be with you . . .'

'With *me*?'

My stomach began to churn. Something was patently very wrong. It wasn't so much what Seán was saying as what he left to be conjectured from the unnaturally cautious tenor of his voice, and his unspoken pity.

'What is it, Seán?'

'They want to interview him in the States . . .'

'What for?'

'Look, Squirrel . . . that story he told about the stallion . . . and his father's death . . .'

'What about it?'

'It can't be true.'

The silence lasted a long time.

'Are you still there, Áine?'

'Yes,' I whispered.

'It seems the stallion wasn't wearing his plates,' my brother went on, his voice uncharacteristically gentle. 'Turner is certain about this. He had taken them off because Magister was giving trouble. The animal had no shoes, Áine. So the rust particles they found in Uncle Alex's skull came from something else. It looks like Uncle Alex was murdered!' In the ensuing silence Seán added, 'Hold on, here's Brigitte.'

'Is this true?' I whispered, when she came on the line, and her voice was very low and tentative as she answered.

'Yes. The problem is, Áine, that Rupert quarrelled with his father the night before his death . . .'

'But . . . they don't think . . . ?'

'I'm sure they just want to eliminate him as a suspect,' she said soothingly. 'But he has compounded things by leaving so unexpectedly. Is Nigel with you?'

'No. He's left me a note. It's over, Brigitte. He's broken it off . . .'

'He'll be back, Áine. He loves you.'

'Do you really think so?' I said, suddenly longing for any confirmation that I was loved, and that the world was not as cold a place as it seemed at that moment. 'But Brigitte, if I can contact Rupert I'll warn him to lie low.'

'He can't lie low, Áine! Don't you understand?'

When Brigitte rang off I searched frantically for the piece of paper with Rupert's number in St John's Wood, and found it eventually in the zip pocket of my shoulder bag, where I had placed it the day I went to see him.

But the number rang until it was guillotined. As Seán had already ascertained, Rupert was evidently not at his flat. But where was he? I sat on the couch, gnawed at my nails, going over in my mind the content of the phone call from Dublin and all that it portended.

How could Rupert, reliable, responsible Rupert, be a suspect in his father's death?

Then I thought, if the police were looking for him they would probably come looking for me too as someone who might know his whereabouts. Seán and Brigitte could not be the only people to assume I might know something. But I knew nothing. All I could think of was my cousin's voice on the phone two days before, the overwrought voice of the morning, and the cool, strained voice of the evening, and Seán's voice telling me that Rupert's story had not been true.

'You didn't do it, Rupert?' I whispered. 'You couldn't, could you? Not your own father!'

He was the kind-hearted boy at Dunbeg that long ago summer, the iron-willed aspiring doctor, the responsible son, the pragmatist who would not allow love to stand in the way of what he regarded as his duty. Nothing would ever convince me that he was capable of murder.

But then I thought of the weals I had seen across his body that last night in Dunbeg, and I thought of Milly's voice, 'He beat that pore lil chile, honey, till he was black an' blue . . .'

This prompted me to ask myself, How well did any of us know anyone? What depths were there in Rupert that I had never seen? What repressed rage festered in him that had never found an outlet? And what might his father not have done in that last quarrel that might have precipitated a blind reaction?

But where was he? If the American police were correctly informed, he had come to Heathrow. Where had he gone from there? He wasn't in his flat. Where could he go where he would not be easily traced? Where could he go from London without a passport? There was one place. He could go to Ireland!

'I know where you are, Rupert,' I said aloud. 'I know where you have gone.'

I looked through the window, saw the watery winter sunlight, the pedestrians in warm coats, the black railings stretching around the garden across the street. For some reason it brought to mind Drumcondra Road, the small parcel I had found one morning on the wet grass.

'But Dunbeg is not a safe place for you,' I whispered aloud, beset suddenly by the unreasoning certainty that had dogged my life. Almost for the first time I had no pleasure at all in the thought of the castellated house by the sea. 'You would be better off anywhere else. But you need a friend. And who will help you now, except me?'

I put my engagement ring in an envelope with a note and put it on the table.

Dear Nigel,
You are the nicest and kindest man. I'm very sorry I hurt you. I did not mean to do so and was so sure everything would work out for us.

What you do not know, Nigel, is that when I was a child something happened to me that I cannot understand. It is connected with the west of Ireland and an old shibboleth. You would dismiss it out of hand. I have tried to do the same, but it has dogged me and I do not know if I will ever be free of it.

I must go away for a while. But when I come back I will see someone and try and get my brains reorganized.

You are much better off without me. I do understand. Find someone else and forget me.
Love
Áine.

As I was halfway down the stairs the phone began to ring. I ran back to take the call, but the caller was gone. There was no message on the answerphone.

In the Underground I was so caught up in my frantic reverie that I hardly registered the presence of others around me, but sat without seeing or hearing. The stations en route to Heathrow came and went. But when I got the sweetish smell of decay I looked up and saw, directly in front of me, the reflection in the window of a tramp with a dark hat pulled low over his face, sitting beside me in perfect immobility. I started and drew my breath in so sharply that another passenger stared at me strangely, but, although I flinched and turned my head to confront my familiar, the seat beside me was empty.

So you're still following me, I thought. You don't give up. But do your worst, Aeneas Shaw! You are suffering from one major drawback, even if you don't know it! You are powerless now. You are powerless because you are dead.

That night I came to the big iron gates, slipped in past the dark gate lodge and up the avenue as silently as a ghost. I measured each footfall, careful that it made no sound. The avenue was in total blackness, except for the merest suggestion of night sky through the bare branches. There was no moon. I was glad of this, aware that any evidence of my presence might alert anyone who was about.

The tide was out. I came from beneath the tree canopy to see the long stretch of wet sand, the inlet dark with inky pools. I could see the island, a shadow in the darkness, with its stark pre-historic ruin. Every sound, the roar of the retreating sea, the occasional rustle in the undergrowth, was magnified. I heard the thud of my own heart.

The castle rose before me as I came up the last turn of the avenue, a haughty presence in stone. The windows were dark and seemed to watch me, as though alerted by the grating of forecourt stones beneath my feet. The cold sea wind swept in a sudden stinging rain, and I tasted it on my lips with a sense of déjà-vu.

Was I a fool to have returned here after everything that had happened? What if he wasn't here and I was simply repeating the old, foolish exercise that had once almost killed me?

I walked around the house, glancing at the bay window of the drawing room where Aeneas Shaw had, long ago, pressed his face against the glass. It was shuttered as was the library window which I passed en route to the garden.

The small gate in the stone archway leading to the garden was open and I went through it and across the wet grass to the terrace where Sarah had met her death. I tried the French windows to the library, but they were locked, and the thick old curtain was drawn across them on the inside. The kitchen window was uncurtained, but the room was in darkness and its door was locked. Then I went to the pantry window, put out my hand to test it, and saw that it was broken. 'Rupert,' I called, keeping my voice low. But there was no response and I climbed up onto the windowsill and after a bit of manoeuvring was standing in the kitchen staring out at the night.

The air inside the house was stale. No one had lived in it for months. It smelled musty, and had the refrigerated cold of a tomb. I left the kitchen, crossed the dark back hall, glancing down towards the library door which I could not see in the darkness. I had forgotten the sprung board and it creaked suddenly under my foot. I opened the door to the main entrance hall. There was a dim light here, cast from the glass canopy overhead in the landing. I could make out the shadow of the dusty moose looking down at me. I was about to call Rupert's name aloud, when a thought occurred: what guarantee did I have that it was Rupert who had broken the pantry window? How did I know the identity of the intruder who might now be in the house? I stood back against the wall in the niche where a grandfather clock had once kept the hours.

There was a sound above me, coming I thought from somewhere on the landing, a very soft, low sound, as though something crept above me. I backed against the wall, afraid to speak or move, imagining for a moment that Aeneas Shaw's silhouette would suddenly loom at me over the banister. You cannot hurt me, I thought, repeating the mantra I had coined for myself in the Tube. *You are powerless because you are dead!* In that moment there was a step behind me and something touched my arm.

'Áine,' Rupert said a few moments later as he patted and comforted me, 'I didn't mean to frighten you like that!'

Surfacing to find his young face looking at me tenderly my heart resumed its beat.

'I thought you were . . .'

'A ghost? But you'd hardly worry about a friendly spectre, would you, Áine?' he asked with his old, wry grin, and for a moment I felt as though I were ten years old again and my new-found American cousin was introducing me to a new vision of the world.

'There was something moving upstairs. I'm sure of it!'

'There was a cat upstairs, little cousin. A big black and white tom who has now decamped into the kitchen and out the pantry window. And I have been all over the place and the only living things in this house are you and me and a family of mice and possibly a bat or two in the landing.' He laughed. 'Your old pal Dracula's descendants!'

We were sitting on the big old couch in the library. In the grate was a turf fire. There was a loaf of sliced bread on the table and a carton of milk. The room was shuttered and full of shadows, but the area around the hearth had warmth and light. An aluminium kettle that I recognized sang on a makeshift stand above the fire. Rupert was unshaven, very pale, had a livid bruise on his face, and a healing cut under his eye.

'Funny,' he said. 'I knew you'd come.'

Listening to his words, sensible, reassuring, it all felt like a bad dream from which we would awaken any moment.

'What happened, Rupert?' I whispered. 'Are the police really looking for you?'

'I guess.'

'Did you kill your father?'

'What do you think?'

I saw his pallor, his unkempt air, a different Rupert to the one I had always known. My teeth began to chatter.

'I am *so* cold!'

Rupert threw a few tea bags into the singing kettle, removed it from the fire, and placed some more sods among the embers. He poured the brew from the kettle into cups and added milk, handing me one.

When I had finished it he took my head between his hands and whispered, enunciating each word evenly, 'I did not kill him.'

I drew back and looked at him in relief. 'So it *was* an accident?'

'No.'

'So someone else killed him?'

When he didn't reply I pressed on, 'But *you* had a row with him?'

'Yes.'

'Why?'

'I told him the truth. I said I was not going to marry Gloria. I said that she deserved better than a lie, and that I did too. I said that I had told her this and that the engagement was off.'

'When was this?'

330

'On Christmas Eve, the night before he died. He blew his lid, wanted to know if I had met someone else.'

'And had you?'

'Oh yes,' he whispered, drawing me to him, 'a long time ago! It was only when I met her again in London that I realized the full impossibility of what was expected of me. It was a strange awakening; even sitting across the table from her, surrounded by other people, I knew an intimacy, an empathy, beyond sense or reason. And then she came to my apartment and read me the riot act! But my father was not amused.'

I laid my head against his arm and took his hand. 'What did he say?'

'Initially something to the effect that the girl was my cousin, and I could never have her anyway and where was the point in letting everyone down. And then he became . . . kinda rough.'

'How do you mean – rough?'

'Violence had always served him, Áine! He broke one of my teeth!'

He pushed up his lip and I saw the ragged, broken canine.

'Are you in pain?'

'I'm taking pain killers.' He fished a packet of tablets out of his pocket. 'I can't blame him,' Rupert continued with an attempted laugh. 'You have to see it from his perspective. He would have given his eye teeth for an heiress! And now, because of me, all his plans had gone up in smoke . . .'

'What did you do?' I whispered.

'I hit him back. I'd been longing to belt him one for years.' Rupert put his head in his hands. 'I think I broke his goddamn nose.'

I gasped.

'But all I felt, Áine, was elation! He went berserk when he saw the blood, wrestled me to the floor. Oh, there was a ghastly row, me knocking over chairs, his roaring that he wished I'd never been born, that he'd had a *real* son.

'Milly and my mother came rushing in, and I got off the floor and fended off another blow. Mom was shrieking, "Stop! Stop! Stop!" Dad's face was scarlet and he could hardly breathe. I thought he was going to have a coronary. I backed off, told him to cool it; I was more terrified for Mom than anything else; she had begun to shake. But he just stood there panting for a moment, and then he pushed her out of the way and stormed out.' Rupert looked at me, hunched his shoulders.

'Did you follow him?'

'No way! You should have seen him. Mom was in an awful state, but I said I was fine and went to the sink to wash off the blood. She stood staring at me, in one of those fierce silences of hers. Her eyes had that awful glitter they get. I told her everything was OK, and to take one of her pills and go to bed. Milly found her pills, but she wouldn't take any. I took her to her room. She went in quietly enough, but she must have been up half the night; I heard her pacing while I was packing my things. It must have been nearly dawn when I heard her go downstairs. When she came back it was to tell me that he was dead.'

'But . . . you told the police you saw Magister attack your father?'

'I told them the first damn thing that came into my head. But because I'd been in England I didn't know the animal wasn't shod.'

'But . . . if the stallion didn't kill him . . . who did? Was it Turner?'

Rupert shook his head. 'Turner has no violence in him. Áine, do you know what a Stilson is?'

'It's a monkey wrench. Dad has one.'

He nodded. 'My mother killed him with it early on Christmas morning.'

Ah, Rupert, I saw it all then. She had waited for Alex, swung the heavy wrench at him. And then she had come to tell you, trembling, but coherent, as though she were imparting a dramatic change in the racing calendar. 'Your father has met with an accident.'

'I hid the weapon,' Rupert went on, 'but they will have found it by now. I wiped it, then made sure my own prints were all over it. And after your father had arrived, I left. It's more convincing, isn't it, to get the hell out if one is trying to give the impression of being a fugitive from justice?' He gave a half laugh, put bread on a fork, held it to the fire for a moment and offered it to me.

I took it, but I could not eat. 'Your mother will never allow you to take the rap for her.'

'She lives in confusion, Áine, and doesn't remember what happened. She thinks the stallion killed him because that's what I told her.' He paused. 'But at least I can ensure that she will never know the inside of a State institution.'

'I'll tell them the truth,' I cried.

'Do you think they will believe you? It's a heavy weapon, remember, and my prints are decorating it, the prints of a son who, only the night before, had a bitter row with his father!'

The tears rolled down my face. 'What will they do to you?'

He seemed to shrink and when he spoke again his voice was shaking. 'Thirty years, perhaps worse . . . Virginia still has the death penalty.' He raised his eyebrows and looked at me with an attempted half smile, but he just looked young and very frightened, 'unless, of course, you are under some delusion that I can hole up here.'

'You need a good lawyer . . . he'd get you off!'

'I haven't the money for lawyers. Mount Wexford is mortgaged to the hilt!'

'But Gloria's family . . .'

He looked at me pityingly.

'But Rupert, the police are not fools. You can't even tell them precisely when your father died. Once they start questioning you, they'll *know* you didn't do it.'

'And where would that leave my mother? In an asylum? Like that crazy who used to scare you around here years ago?'

'Stay in Dunbeg,' I whispered. 'They'll never find you here!' But even I knew this was untrue.

'I'll go to the police tomorrow, Áine. Anyone passing near the house, anyone passing along the shore will smell the turf smoke. Anyway, I'm a credible runaway now . . . wouldn't you agree?'

My mouth was dry, my tongue sticking to my palate. Eventually he said, shakily as though his courage had finally left him, 'I am very tired. You can have this couch and I will take the armchair . . .'

'We'll stay here together,' I said. 'It's too cold to be apart any more.'

We lay, wrapped in the tatty old rug, crushed together.

After a while I whispered, 'Were you really going to give up Gloria . . . because of me?'

'Not just because of you! I'm a bit too old to be a pawn!'

'Does that mean that you really . . . love me?' My voice was very small.

He laughed softly, shifted a little. 'Oh Áine, I have already told you. But come here . . .' His hands traced the lines of my face, cupped my cheek. 'How does one define love?'

For a moment I felt cold, with a sinking sense of let-down, like the silly pursuer of a spectre.

'Is it love to think of someone most of every day?' Rupert continued after a moment. 'To wonder what she is doing, what she is wearing, whether she is asleep, what she dreams of? Is it love to miss her so much that your bones ache? Is it love to remember her as a frightened waif, shivering in her room at the dead of night – the room just above us now, as it happens. And what about the recurring memory of her face when she eventually slept beside you, warm and at peace? What about the sight of her three years later, a girl on the verge of womanhood? Why did her presence in Virginia bring my home alive, so that I discovered for the first time the colours and the sounds and the scents of a place I had known all my life? And how would you describe meeting her on the London pavement, and finding a young woman in your arms, whom you had never known and had always known?' He paused. 'I don't know what love is, Áine. I only know that it never leaves me and that I have no choice in it!'

I was no longer cold. After a while I cradled his head between my breasts; I felt him stir, felt the flicker of his eyelashes against my skin, then his lips, his warm, hungry mouth. We were silent explorers; we did not need words any more. Time let us be, closed away from everything in this room where we had first touched. It had never known lovers before, and it muffled the cry that eventually slanted away into the night.

Rupert covered us with the rug, and we went to sleep. I woke sometime in the night. Something had disturbed me, but although I listened attentively, all I could hear was the wind. It was cold and pitch dark except for the small embers still glowing in the ash-filled grate. Rupert was breathing with shallow breaths.

I was aware of the great house over our heads, the creaking in the timbers, the bluster in the chimney, the rattle of the shuttered windows, the Stygian darkness of the room beyond the hearth, the shadowy bookshelves where thousands of characters might slip any moment from their pages. It was as though it were a sentient thing, this great melancholy pile, and that, from its loneliness, it blessed us. But a thought intruded, incongruous, perhaps, in this context: was it Rupert who had broken the pantry window? I had forgotten to ask him.

The wind and the rain eased towards morning; the dawn came creeping through the faded velvet curtains. Gradually the book-lined walls assumed a sober reality. I saw the familiar works of Dickens, and the Rupert Bear books that had inspired a transatlantic correspondence. I slipped from Rupert's side, looked ruefully at the clothes scattered on the floor, donned my jeans and sweater. He was deeply asleep now, his breathing rhythmic. I raked the ashes in the grate, added some more sods, watched the smoke curl up the chimney. The creel was almost empty, and I thought I would bring it outside to the turf shed to fill it. I put on my shoes as quietly as possible. But first I went to the French window and took a peek into the garden.

It was wet, the rhododendrons dark green and dripping. The red tiles of the terrace were damp, their surface scuffed and pitted with small patches of moss. I returned to the hearth, took up the creel and made for the library door. Rupert stirred, put out his hand and said in a voice thick with sleep and apprehension, 'I don't want you to go . . .'

I put the creel down, whispered in his ear, 'I'm only going for some turf!'

He opened his eyes, stared at me without focusing. 'I've been dreaming . . . the most god awful dream . . .'

'Shh, go back to sleep!'

My heart was full of hope, warm after the heated eternity of the night. I felt sure that even if Rupert went ahead with his insane purpose and confessed, they would have to advert to the possibility that he was shielding his mother. Or even if they believed him, a good lawyer would be able to show the years of brutality he had suffered at the hands of his father. And by being here we had at least a little time to consider all the ramifications; I had time to work on him and get him to tell the truth. I had time to phone Dublin, get the updated news.

I took the creel through the kitchen and fought with the rusting bolts on the back door. They gave with a screech, and I opened the door and brought the creel outside to the turf shed.

Normally I would have enjoyed the coarse, hairy texture of the peat under my hands, the knowledge that it represented thousands of years of vegetation that had lived and died nearby. But my mind was too concentrated on what I should do next, and I jumped when the creel was full and I turned to find the shadow of a man behind me on the grass.

'Áine!' Teddy O'Keefe said. 'You gave me a right fright! I didn't know who was here. I saw smoke from the chimney . . .'

'Teddy,' I gasped, 'I meant to tell you I was coming. I needed to get away for a while.'

Teddy regarded me doubtfully. 'Are you here on your own?'

'Yes.'

He turned away, but then stopped and looked back at me.

'Áine, the pantry window is broken. Do you know anything about it?'

He would report it as a break-in if I denied it, so I said, 'I was desperate to get in. It was late and raining and I didn't want to wake you up for the key. The catch was wonky, anyway.'

'Ah . . . well I'll get someone to fix it later on.'

'No, Teddy. Leave it for a while. I just need some time here alone. I'll let you know when I'm leaving.'

Teddy nodded, but he was looking at me with the same narrowed gaze I had first seen on his face when he had come to see me in hospital, and I remembered the comment I had overheard him make to Gráinne: '*There's a lunatic in every generation of that family.*'

'Your brother phoned me earlier,' he said then. 'He asked me to check if your Cousin Rupert was here.'

I looked into Teddy's eyes. 'Oh no, there's no one here, except me.'

336

'I see.' He regarded me dubiously for another moment. As he was moving away I called after him, 'Was there some message from Seán?'

He stood and looked back at me. 'A strange class of a message. He wanted me to tell Rupert, if he was here, that the police know the true story. He said to tell him that he's no longer under suspicion and to go home at once, that his mother needs him. So if he comes, will you tell him?'

He turned and walked away, and I dropped the creel, and ran back to the library.

'Did anyone ever tell you you're a lazy sod?' I asked on a surge of euphoria as I entered, but I stopped in mid-sentence. Rupert was not in the room. I looked around, went into the hall and called his name, but there was no reply.

I thought he was playing some kind of game, and when he was not to be found in the dining room or the drawing room I mounted the staircase. I looked up at the landing canopy, remembering Dracula, and the nights of my childhood. I thought of my mother and Aunt Isabelle and that long-ago summer.

I went from bedroom to bedroom, but there was no sign of my cousin. Then I thought of the turret stairs, where I had first brought him to view the bay, crossed the room that had belonged to the twins, opened the door to the old stone steps and called again, 'Rupert . . . ?' and I thought I heard his voice coming back to me faintly from the roof.

For some reason I remembered how the twins' feet used to smell, and how Seán used to slag them. In my nose now was a faint sickly-sweet scent. For a moment I thought of dry rot and sprouting fungi and all that another outbreak of it would portend for Dunbeg. But I knew it was not dry rot, but another scent altogether and I ran up the circular stone stairs to the roof. Rupert was standing on the parapet where I had once proudly shown him the world I loved. The wind was cold, boisterous from the storm of the night before; it stung my eyes and ears. Away to the west was the wild panorama of the bay and the drenched blue of Clare Island. I smelt the sea, saw it throw itself against the rocks. The tide was turning, racing past Inishdrum.

Rupert said something. I caught a few words – 'Do you remember . . . ?' – and then the wind carried his voice away.

'Be careful,' I shouted behind him. 'You're too near the edge!' I raised my voice to drown the wind. 'Rupert, I've just got some news . . .'

He turned his head, his eyebrows raised, his eyes frowning, but his focus instantly darted from me to the stairs behind me. His mouth opened; his pupils dilated. I turned my head. I saw nothing, but the sweet smell had followed me up the stairs and was now cloying my nostrils. There was a sudden gust of wind that drove the breath from me.

I barely heard Rupert's cry.

When I got down to the forecourt he was lying on the gravel, as still as that first night I had crept into his room. But I knew as soon as I saw him that he would not wake and speak my name. I held his head in my lap; the blood seeped into my jeans. I told him all about this demon known as love, but my voice was drowned by the careless, relentless song of the tide.

Out on the island something distracted my eye; a dark figure was silhouetted beside the ruin of the Bronze Age fortress, immobile, watching. I wiped the tears to get a better look, but when I looked again it was gone.

Sergeant Touhy had not forgotten me.

'We always seem to meet in difficult circumstances,' he said, shaking his head and trying to comfort me. 'I am very sorry about your cousin! Such a dreadful tragedy! But what on earth possessed him to come here? That police inquiry in the States was just routine stuff . . . An employee of your uncle, a man called Turner, was able to tell the whole story.'

'What did *he* have to say about it?' I asked. I was on Valium, distanced from everything. Most of me was with Rupert's cold body in the hospital morgue.

'He was a witness to what really happened! He says he saw poor Rupert's mother . . .'

'Isn't it interesting,' I asked after a moment, and heard the slur in my voice with detached indifference, 'that the only witness to a murder is someone whose wife was consistently rogered by the deceased?'

'What are you saying, Áine?'

'Do you think this witness would be above planting a certain suggestion in a certain unstable mind?'

The sergeant looked aghast. 'I don't think there's any evidence of that, now! But your aunt'll be all right. You needn't worry about her. They'll put her away somewhere. From what I hear she's not fit to stand trial.' He glanced at me with a sudden expression of surprised admiration, as though he had just noticed I was no longer a child.

'God Almighty, Áine, but you've grown up to be the grand-looking girl! But will you ever forget that daft Shaw fellow you used to be scared of?'

'No . . .'

'Funny the fixation he had on you . . . I didn't believe it until he told me he'd dug up that grave in Askreagh. Your great-grandmother's grave. He said he was looking for your bones! Can you credit that?' He grunted in wry commentary and shook his head, but an old, familiar shiver began in the small of my back.

'Sure don't be minding what I'm saying. Don't look like that. Wasn't the poor oul eejit mad as a brush! Anyway, it hardly matters now, does it? He's gone, poor craythur. And how often will you return here, after this, especially now I hear that your father is putting the place on the market?'

'Who told you that?'

'Seán told me.'

Seán and Brigitte took me back to Dublin. My brother glanced at me in the rearview mirror from time to time, and Brigitte turned and smiled encouragingly and occasionally tried to make conversation.

But my mind was tracking every second of the last twenty-four hours, fixing them for ever. In my nostrils was Rupert's scent. Against my skin was the feel of his body. In my ears was the echo of his voice, and its tenderness: '*I don't know what love is, Áine . . .*' The last nine years, all the years of life, it seemed, made a strange kind of sense. I had been privileged in some strange way; I had known a singular kind of love.

'Seán,' I said as we passed by the Spa Hotel in Lucan, 'is it true that Dad is going to sell Dunbeg?'

Seán started and glanced at Brigitte. 'Who told you that?'

'Sergeant Touhy.'

'That's what Dad said when I broke the news to him. He's just devastated. He said the place is a liability. But he'll be home from the States tonight. When he's feeling a bit better, I'll try to persuade him against selling, Áine. You should too. Think of the future, of what could be done with it. It would be a shame to just let it go.'

'*Let* it go,' I said.

I felt Brigitte's surprised relief. She looked at my brother who frowned and gave his head an almost imperceptible shake as though in warning.

'I was glad your father sold the place,' Brigitte confided to me in London months later. 'I knew Seán was keen on him holding onto it, but it has to be the most unlucky place on earth.'

'It's not the place . . .'

'It *is* the place, Áine. Think about it. Your accident, Rupert's death . . . that nut case who frightened you. What else was there . . . waiting?'

'Well that's all academic now!'

'But have *you* managed to get it out of your system?'

I shrugged. There were some things Brigitte did not need to know, especially now that she and Seán were an item and she wore his Claddagh ring on her left hand with the crown turned outwards.

A year passed; life began to reassert itself, as though it would not be bounded by an obsession that had no future. This reassertion came in small, unbidden spurts, when the numbness would leave me temporarily and life would assume colours I thought had died. I found myself lonely for Nigel. I wanted to talk to him, try to explain. He had represented normalcy, pragmatism, and a love and admiration I had taken for granted, and now I missed him more than I liked to pretend. When I made another attempt to contact him, I learned he had gone to his bank's branch in New York and would be working there for the foreseeable future. I was strangely shocked by this, by his failure to re-establish any form of communication; he evidently had returned to the flat shortly after I had returned to Ireland, for his PC was gone, and he had presumably found my letter and the ring. I had expected some message from him, and had not believed him capable of such sternness and inflexibility. I sent the necklace he had given me for Christmas, in its nice box, well-wrapped and sellotaped, by courier to Session House, but there was no acknowledgement. I stayed in the flat until April, when the lease was up and then I moved back in with Brigitte. I buried myself in work, even found a sponsor – a wealthy woman who thinks I have real talent and is prepared to back me.

I knew it was the end of a chapter. It was up to me to open a new one and make the future.

'See a bloody quack!' Brigitte said, when I woke her one night with a nightmare. 'I've exams to do and I need some sleep! You'll have to let go of that goddamn place.'

She apologized in the morning. But I knew she was right.

I went to see a psychotherapist, a kind, middle-aged woman, Katherine Fenwick, who encouraged me to call her Kate. She listened impassively to my story. But she wanted me to relive it, to face my pain and fear, and in facing it to integrate it. When I asked her what 'integrate' meant she said it was to become aware of it as an aspect of myself, which I should own and accept.

'Perhaps you should go back,' she suggested, 'realize that it is only an old house, and that there is nothing there to frighten you any more.'

'It's sold.'

'Nonetheless . . .'

'I do not think it would be a good idea. It's not just a pile of stones and mortar.'

'We experience the past and the future in the present, Áine,' she said patiently. 'The present is our only reality. The origins of this problem may be far off, but it's a question of how it affects you *now* . . . You see, it had no other power but yours.'

I thought of Rupert on the parapet and the look on his face minutes before his death.

'It *wasn't* just me. Rupert was focusing on something

341

behind me seconds before he fell.'

'Which means . . . ?'

'He saw something . . .'

'Don't you think this could be projection, Áine? He had troubles and agendas of his own, remember . . .'

I was silent. I could not deny the truth of this.

'*You* empowered it,' my therapist went on. 'It only grew in the first place because a highly imaginative child had no secure place in which to share her terror . . .'

'There was one place . . .' I told her, 'one person . . .'

'Your cousin? I know. But he is gone. You must move on.'

'But I have! I have moved on.'

'Good,' she said, nodding, but she did not seem convinced. 'Do you ever dream of him now?'

'I dreamed of him every night after he died . . . for months and months. The last time . . . we were on a quayside . . . There was a ship . . . an ocean liner . . .'

My therapist smiled at me sympathetically. 'And he was boarding it . . . ?'

I shook my head. 'No. *I* was boarding the ship and he was saying goodbye. I was crying. I did not want to leave him. I did not know where I was going, but I had to go.'

'None of us knows where we're going,' she said gently. 'And what about the house? Do you still dream of it?'

I hated to admit that nightmares of Dunbeg still came, albeit infrequently, lurid with colour and terror. 'Sometimes.'

How could I tell her that sometimes in the night I am in the castle by the shore, and the dark figure is on the island, waiting. Always waiting.

Yesterday evening Nigel phoned. It was strange to hear his voice after all this time. He sounded tentative. How was I? Would I come out for a bite? He said he had recently returned from New York where he had been working for the past year.

'I know. I tried to contact you.'

'Did you? You should have left a message . . . I'm very sorry about Rupert, Áine. I've only just heard . . .' His voice was mellow with a new maturity. I said yes, I would love to go out for a bite.

I met him at our old restaurant and we sat across from each other with initial awkwardness, and then a rueful humour in the surprised delight each of us had in the sight of the other. He had changed, acquired a relaxed confidence, lost the suppliant demeanour he had once had towards me, become somehow formidable. But his eyes, gentle, considering, hardly left my face.

'You look wonderful,' he whispered suddenly, adding as he looked around, 'This brings me back!'

'Me too.'

He took my hand abruptly and held it. I liked the comfort of it, the unbidden sense of knowing him, even of belonging.

'I'm sorry about everything, Áine,' he said after a moment in a low voice. 'I know I acted precipitously. Can we put it behind us? Is there someone new in your life . . . are you still free?'

I smiled, touched to the point of tears. 'Sure who'd have me?'

We talked of our families; Seán and Brigitte were getting engaged in June. His Uncle Toby had died.

'He left me quite a bit of money,' Nigel said.

'What did you do with it?'

He laughed a little self-consciously. 'Turned it into more on the US market.'

'Good for you!'

'I've decided to invest it in property. With the present strength of sterling, Irish properties look like good value! In fact I've been to look at one that I find quite fascinating.'

He said this almost coyly, took out his wallet and removed a newspaper cutting, handed it across the table to me. 'What do you think of this, newly returned to the market? I'm thinking of putting a deposit on it!' I took the piece of paper. The words leapt from the print:

'Castellated Victorian house, built c.1850, in need of modernization, commanding a panoramic view of Clew Bay . . .'

I drew my breath in sharply. What is this? I wondered,

momentarily panicked. A dogged and sinister progression, or an innocent coincidence?

But there were no ominous portents as I held the piece of paper, no strange scents of the grave. I heard the discreet restaurant sounds, the clink of plates and cutlery, voices at nearby tables, the everyday topics of conversation, sensed the ordinary preoccupations around me. In the quiet candle-lit corner across the room a man was whispering to his woman friend; there was a sudden laugh from the table beside us and one of the diners said, 'But I *did* suggest it, old boy, but who do you think got the raise . . . ?'

Or could this be a chance for something else, I wondered, a chance for resolution, a new beginning?

Kate's words returned to me as I sat in silence, holding the fragile cutting in my hand: '*It had no other power but yours . . .*'

It occurred to me suddenly that the level at which I pitched my life was a matter of my own volition, that nothing was pre-ordained. I looked up, met Nigel's eyes – smiling, gently interrogative, felt the renewed, quiet pressure of his hand. And, after a moment or two I allowed in the hope and freedom that began to fill me.

'I'll go ahead with it then,' he said softly, 'since it has your blessing. And to tell the truth, I can't wait to see it with you!'

But during the night I woke from a dream where a white wolf ran along the headland and turned to look at me, and for the first time I heard him baying, a long and lonely dirge above the call of the tide.